ALICIA KEYS

GIRL ON FIRE

COWRITTEN AND CREATED BY
ANDREW WEINER

An Imprint of HarperCollinsPublishers

HarperAlley is an imprint of HarperCollins Publishers.

Girl on Fire
 For information address HarperCollins
Children's Books, a division of HarperCollins
Publishers, 195 Broadway, New York, NY 10007.
www.harperalley.com

ISBN 978-0-06-302956-9 (trade)
ISBN 978-0-06-315776-7 (special edition)
ISBN 978-0-06-321075-2 (ANZ edition)

21 22 23 24 25 PC/WOR 10 9 8 7 6 5 4 3 2 1

First Edition

THIS IS DEDICATED
TO EVERYBODY
DISCOVERING THEIR
SUPERPOWER.
NEVER HOLD BACK!

—AK & AW

FOR MY PARENTS,
JAMES AND TERESA
WILLIAMS, WHO
ENDLESSLY SUPPORT
ME AS A CREATIVE.

—BW

CONTENTS

CHAPTER 1

PERFECT WAY TO DIE

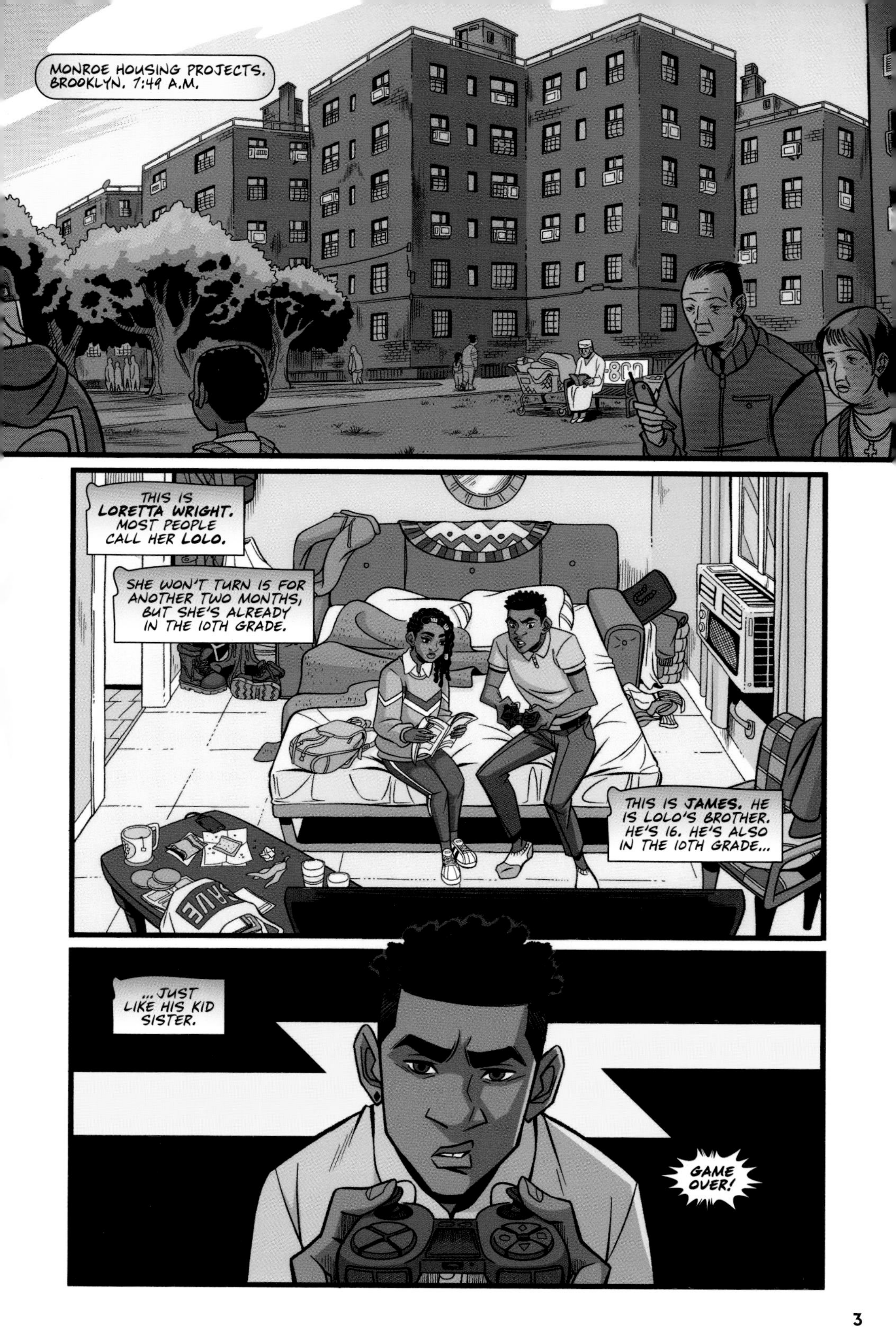
MONROE HOUSING PROJECTS. BROOKLYN. 7:49 A.M.
THIS IS LORETTA WRIGHT. MOST PEOPLE CALL HER LOLO.
SHE WON'T TURN 15 FOR ANOTHER TWO MONTHS, BUT SHE'S ALREADY IN THE 10TH GRADE.
THIS IS JAMES. HE IS LOLO'S BROTHER. HE'S 16. HE'S ALSO IN THE 10TH GRADE...
... JUST LIKE HIS KID SISTER.
GAME OVER!

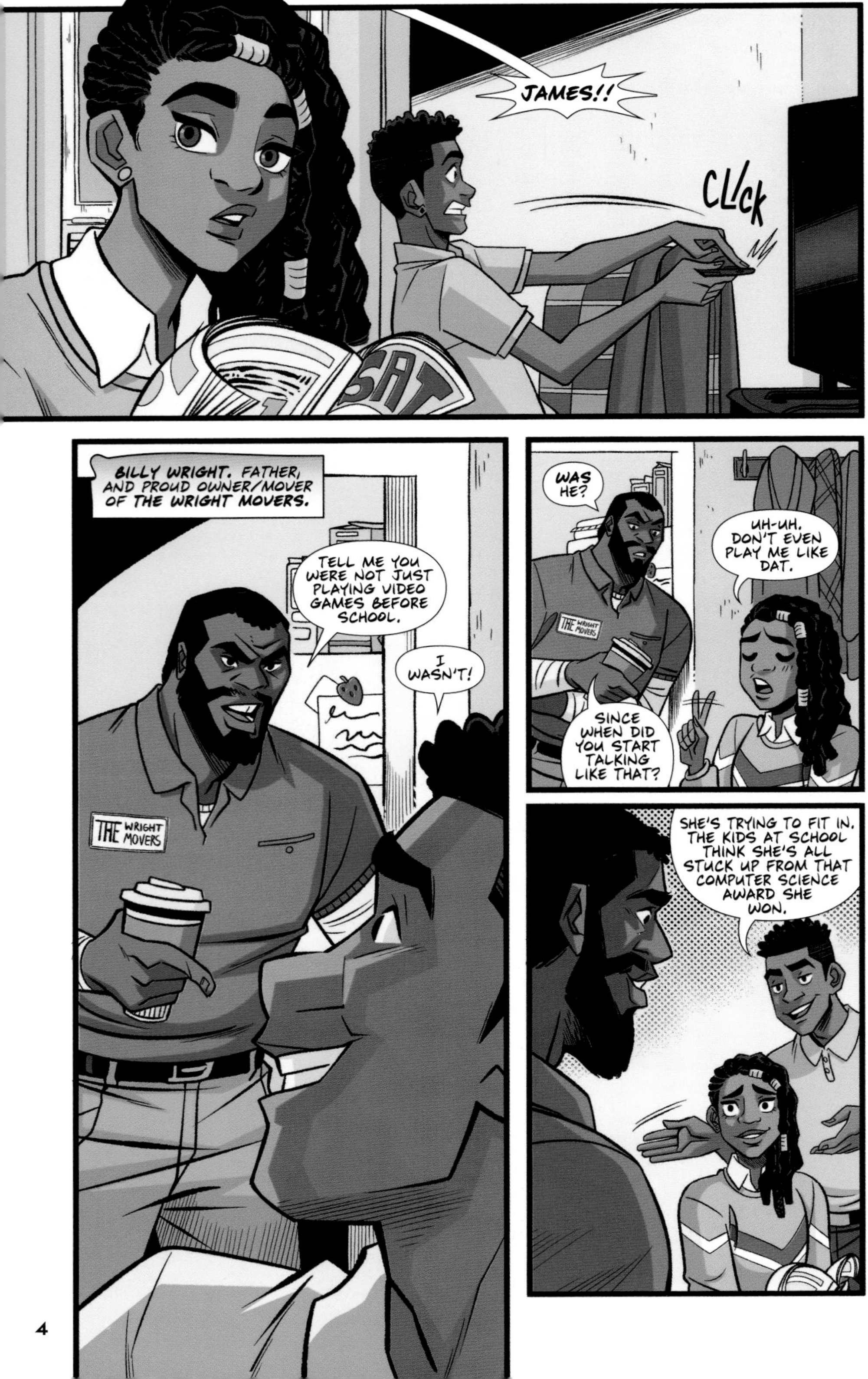
JAMES!!
CLICK
SAT
BILLY WRIGHT. FATHER, AND PROUD OWNER/MOVER OF THE WRIGHT MOVERS.
TELL ME YOU WERE NOT JUST PLAYING VIDEO GAMES BEFORE SCHOOL.
I WASN'T!
THE WRIGHT MOVERS
WAS HE?
UH-UH. DON'T EVEN PLAY ME LIKE DAT.
SINCE WHEN DID YOU START TALKING LIKE THAT?
SHE'S TRYING TO FIT IN. THE KIDS AT SCHOOL THINK SHE'S ALL STUCK UP FROM THAT COMPUTER SCIENCE AWARD SHE WON.

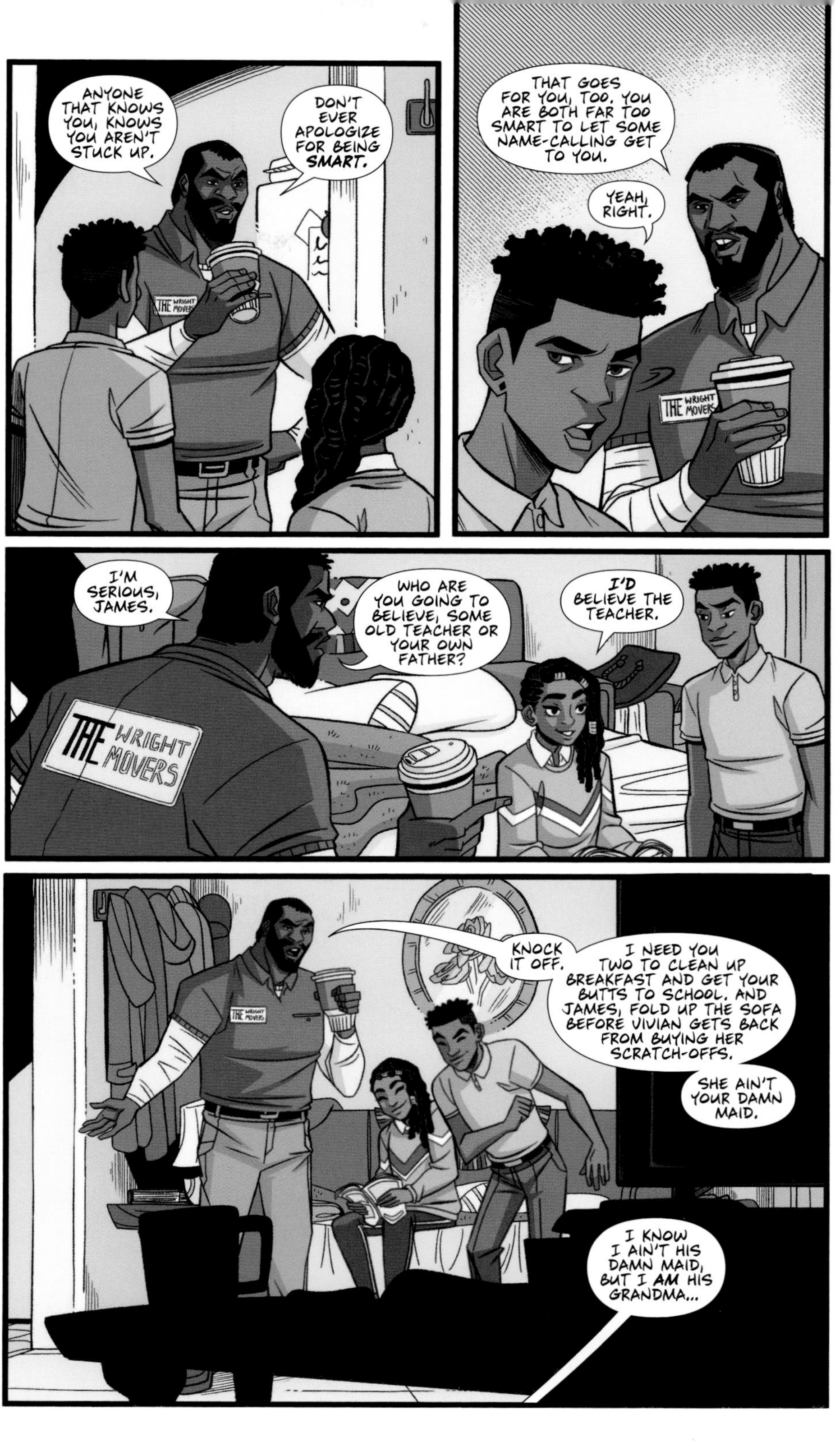
ANYONE THAT KNOWS YOU, KNOWS YOU AREN'T STUCK UP.
DON'T EVER APOLOGIZE FOR BEING SMART.
THE WRIGHT MOVERS
THAT GOES FOR YOU, TOO. YOU ARE BOTH FAR TOO SMART TO LET SOME NAME-CALLING GET TO YOU.
YEAH, RIGHT.
THE WRIGHT MOVERS
I'M SERIOUS, JAMES.
WHO ARE YOU GOING TO BELIEVE, SOME OLD TEACHER OR YOUR OWN FATHER?
I'D BELIEVE THE TEACHER.
THE WRIGHT MOVERS
KNOCK IT OFF.
I NEED YOU TWO TO CLEAN UP BREAKFAST AND GET YOUR BUTTS TO SCHOOL. AND JAMES, FOLD UP THE SOFA BEFORE VIVIAN GETS BACK FROM BUYING HER SCRATCH-OFFS.
SHE AIN'T YOUR DAMN MAID.
THE WRIGHT MOVERS
I KNOW I AIN'T HIS DAMN MAID, BUT I AM HIS GRANDMA...

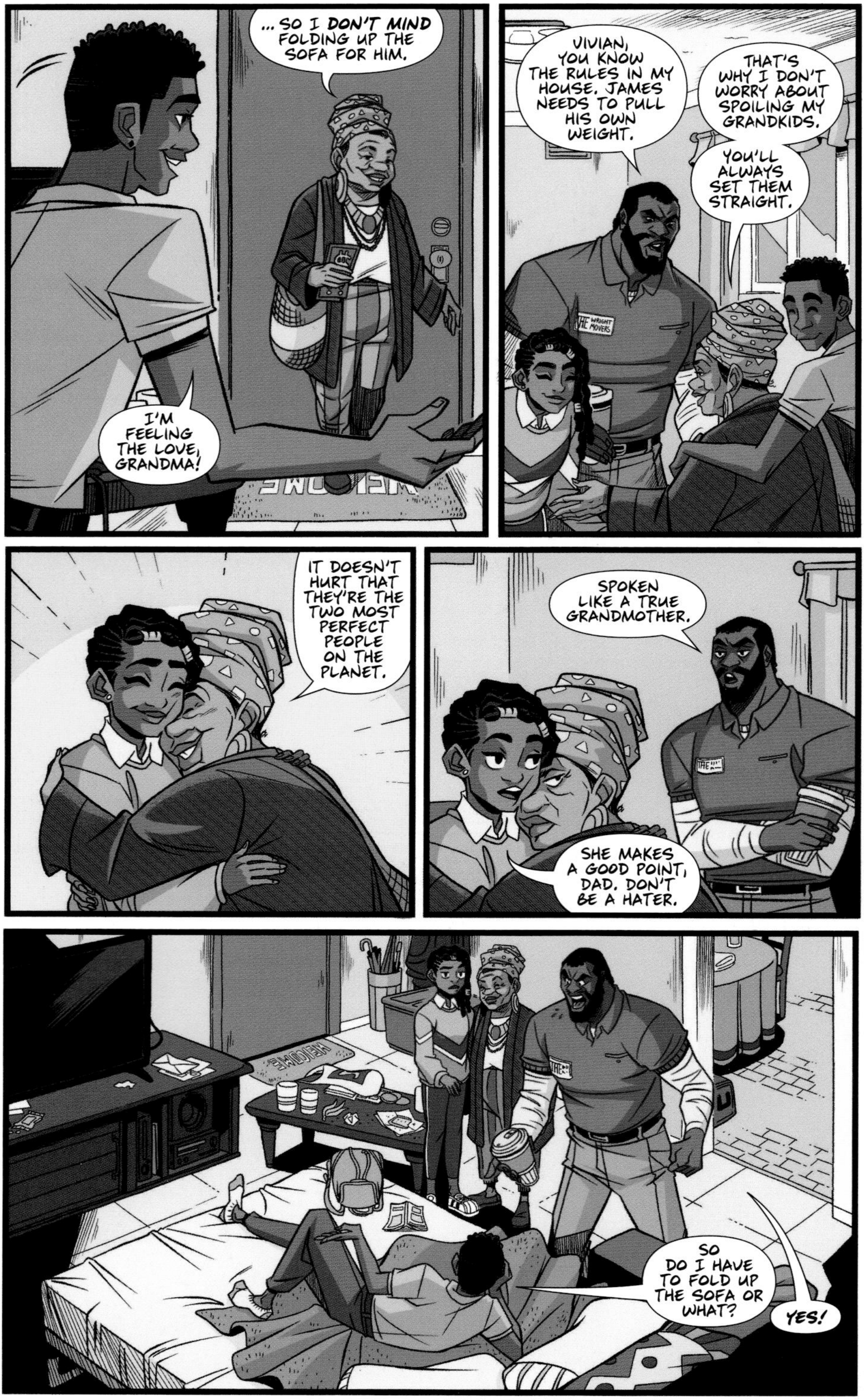
...SO I **DON'T MIND** FOLDING UP THE SOFA FOR HIM.
I'M FEELING THE LOVE, GRANDMA!
VIVIAN, YOU KNOW THE RULES IN MY HOUSE. JAMES NEEDS TO PULL HIS OWN WEIGHT.
THE WRIGHT MOVERS
THAT'S WHY I DON'T WORRY ABOUT SPOILING MY GRANDKIDS.
YOU'LL ALWAYS SET THEM STRAIGHT.
IT DOESN'T HURT THAT THEY'RE THE TWO MOST PERFECT PEOPLE ON THE PLANET.
SPOKEN LIKE A TRUE GRANDMOTHER.
SHE MAKES A GOOD POINT, DAD. DON'T BE A HATER.
SO DO I HAVE TO FOLD UP THE SOFA OR WHAT?
YES!

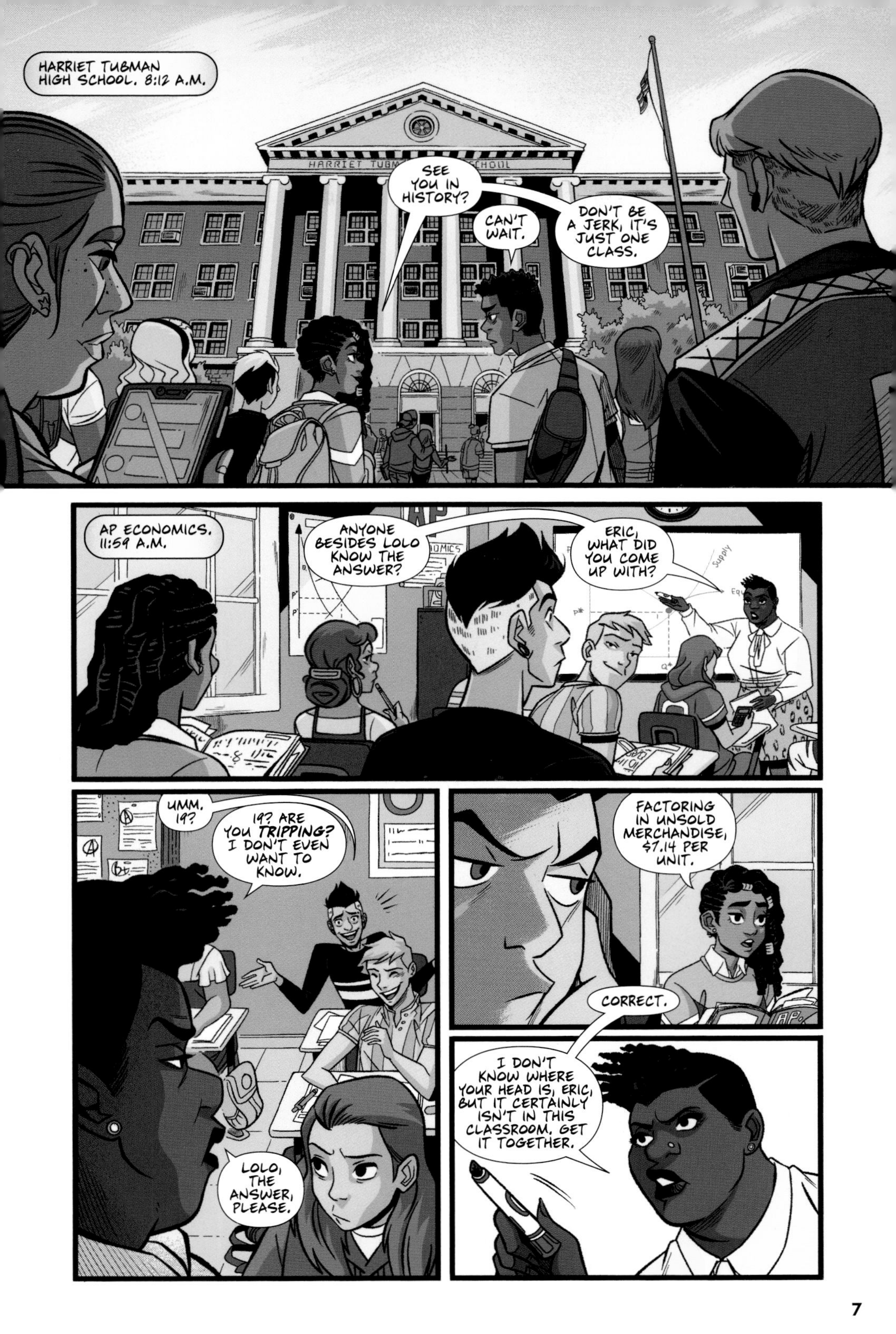
HARRIET TUBMAN HIGH SCHOOL. 8:12 A.M.
SEE YOU IN HISTORY?
CAN'T WAIT.
DON'T BE A JERK, IT'S JUST ONE CLASS.
AP ECONOMICS. 11:59 A.M.
ANYONE BESIDES LOLO KNOW THE ANSWER?
ERIC, WHAT DID YOU COME UP WITH?
UMM. 19?
19? ARE YOU *TRIPPING?* I DON'T EVEN WANT TO KNOW.
LOLO, THE ANSWER, PLEASE.
FACTORING IN UNSOLD MERCHANDISE, $7.14 PER UNIT.
CORRECT.
I DON'T KNOW WHERE YOUR HEAD IS, ERIC, BUT IT CERTAINLY ISN'T IN THIS CLASSROOM. GET IT TOGETHER.

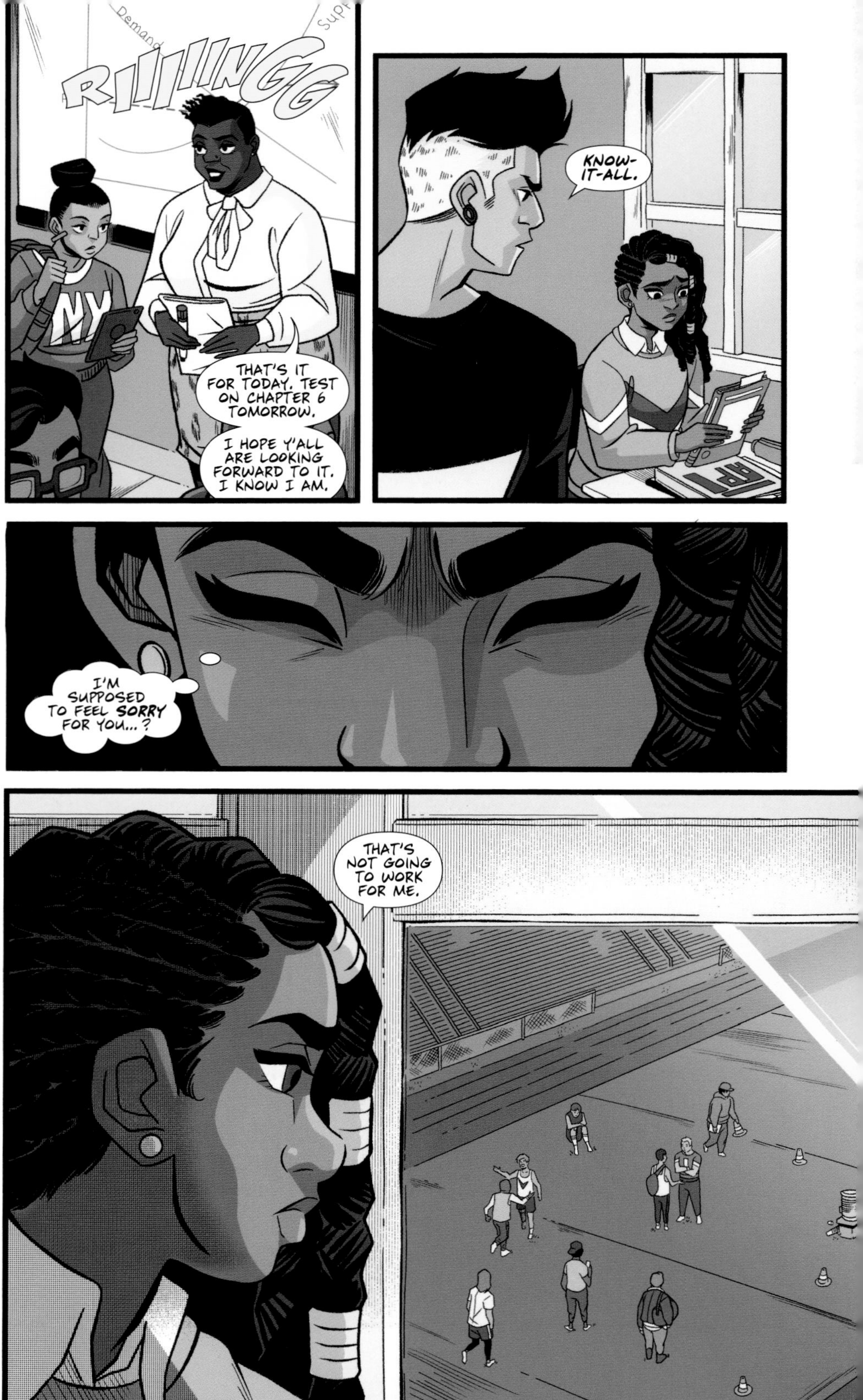
Demand
Supp
RIIIINGG
THAT'S IT FOR TODAY. TEST ON CHAPTER 6 TOMORROW.
I HOPE Y'ALL ARE LOOKING FORWARD TO IT. I KNOW I AM.
KNOW-IT-ALL.
I'M SUPPOSED TO FEEL SORRY FOR YOU...?
THAT'S NOT GOING TO WORK FOR ME.

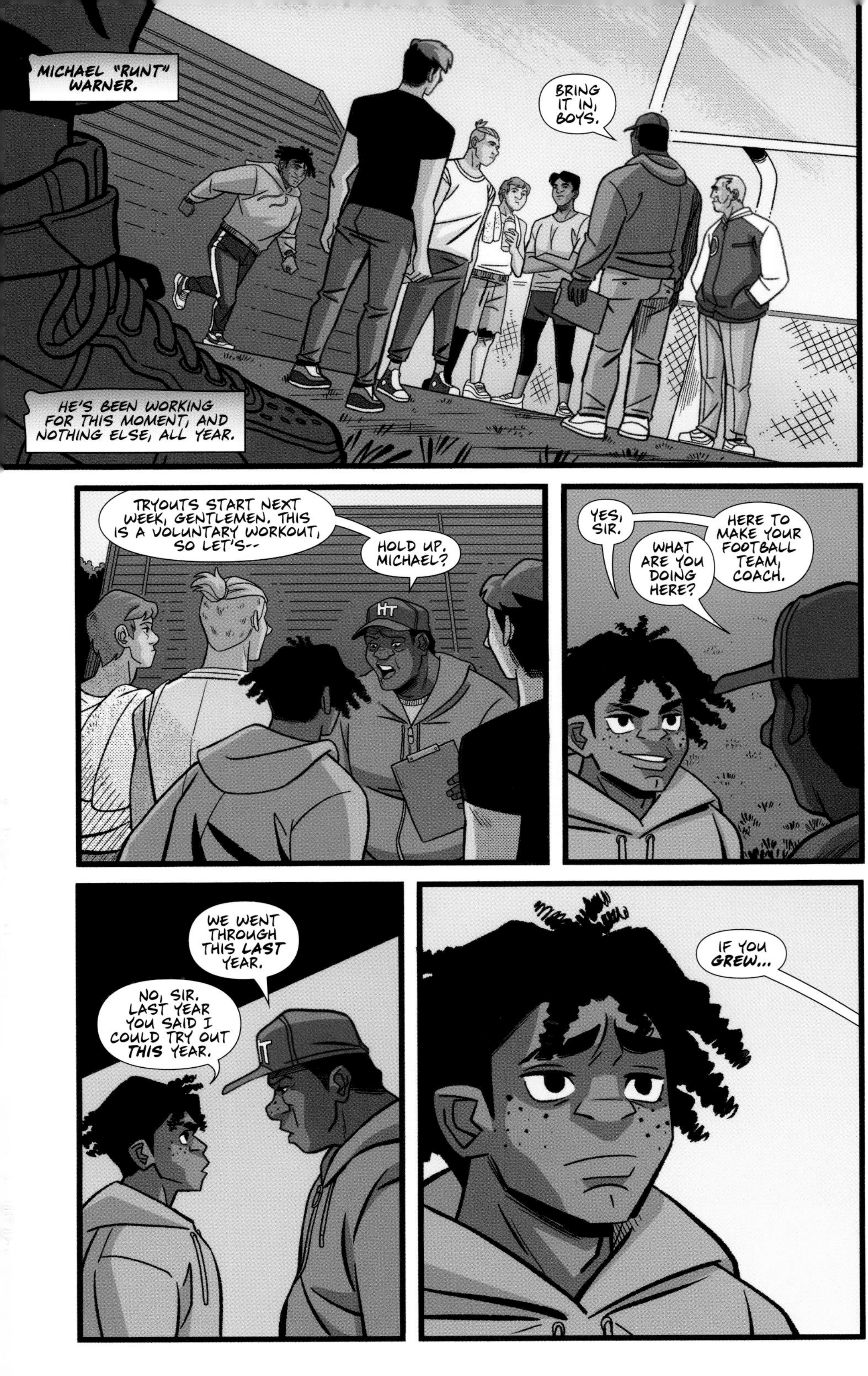
MICHAEL "RUNT" WARNER.
BRING IT IN, BOYS.
HE'S BEEN WORKING FOR THIS MOMENT, AND NOTHING ELSE, ALL YEAR.
TRYOUTS START NEXT WEEK, GENTLEMEN. THIS IS A VOLUNTARY WORKOUT, SO LET'S--
HOLD UP. MICHAEL?
WHAT ARE YOU DOING HERE?
YES, SIR.
HERE TO MAKE YOUR FOOTBALL TEAM, COACH.
WE WENT THROUGH THIS LAST YEAR.
NO, SIR. LAST YEAR YOU SAID I COULD TRY OUT THIS YEAR.
IF YOU GREW...

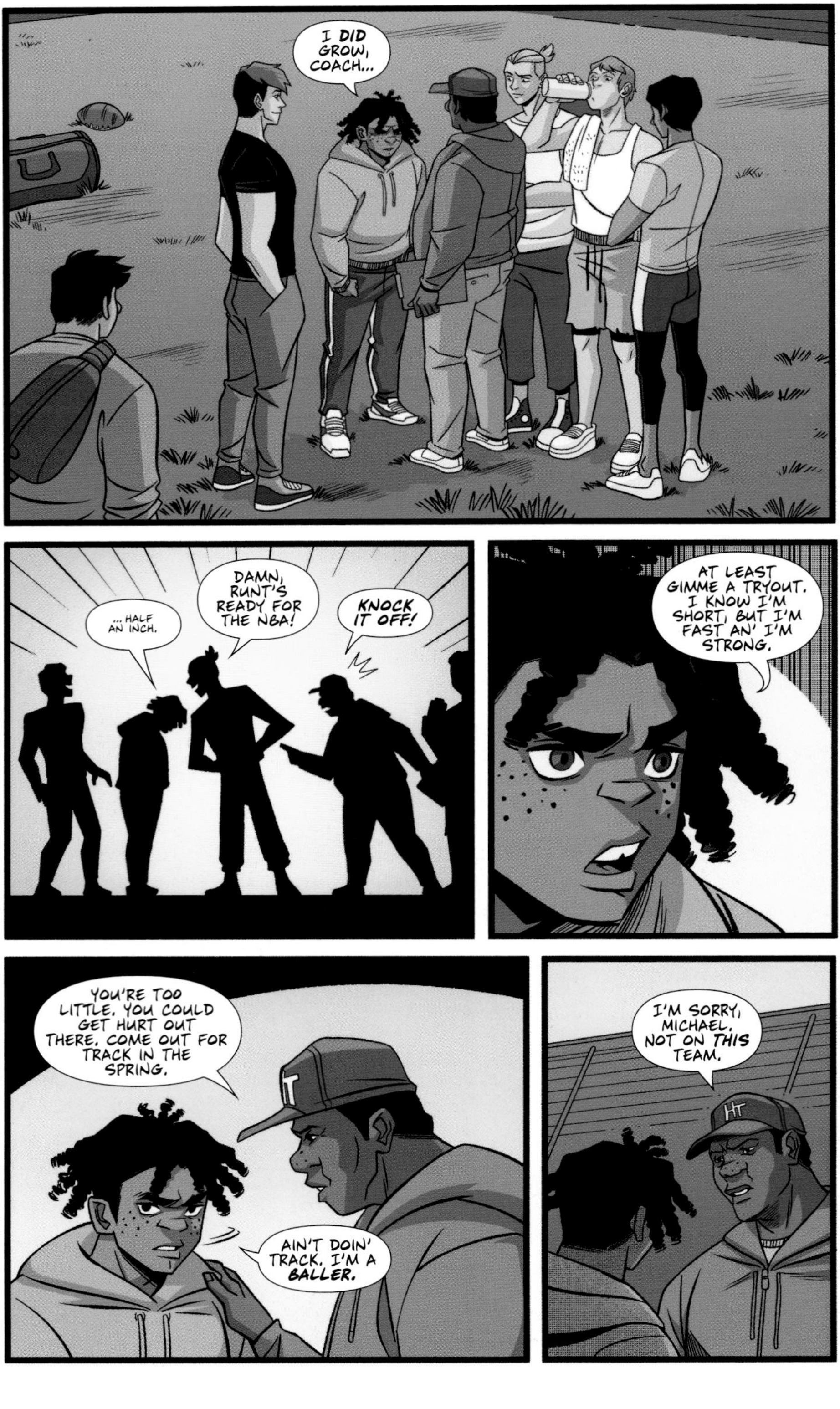
I DID GROW, COACH...
...HALF AN INCH.
DAMN, RUNT'S READY FOR THE NBA!
KNOCK IT OFF!
AT LEAST GIMME A TRYOUT. I KNOW I'M SHORT, BUT I'M FAST AN' I'M STRONG.
YOU'RE TOO LITTLE. YOU COULD GET HURT OUT THERE. COME OUT FOR TRACK IN THE SPRING.
AIN'T DOIN' TRACK. I'M A BALLER.
I'M SORRY, MICHAEL. NOT ON THIS TEAM.

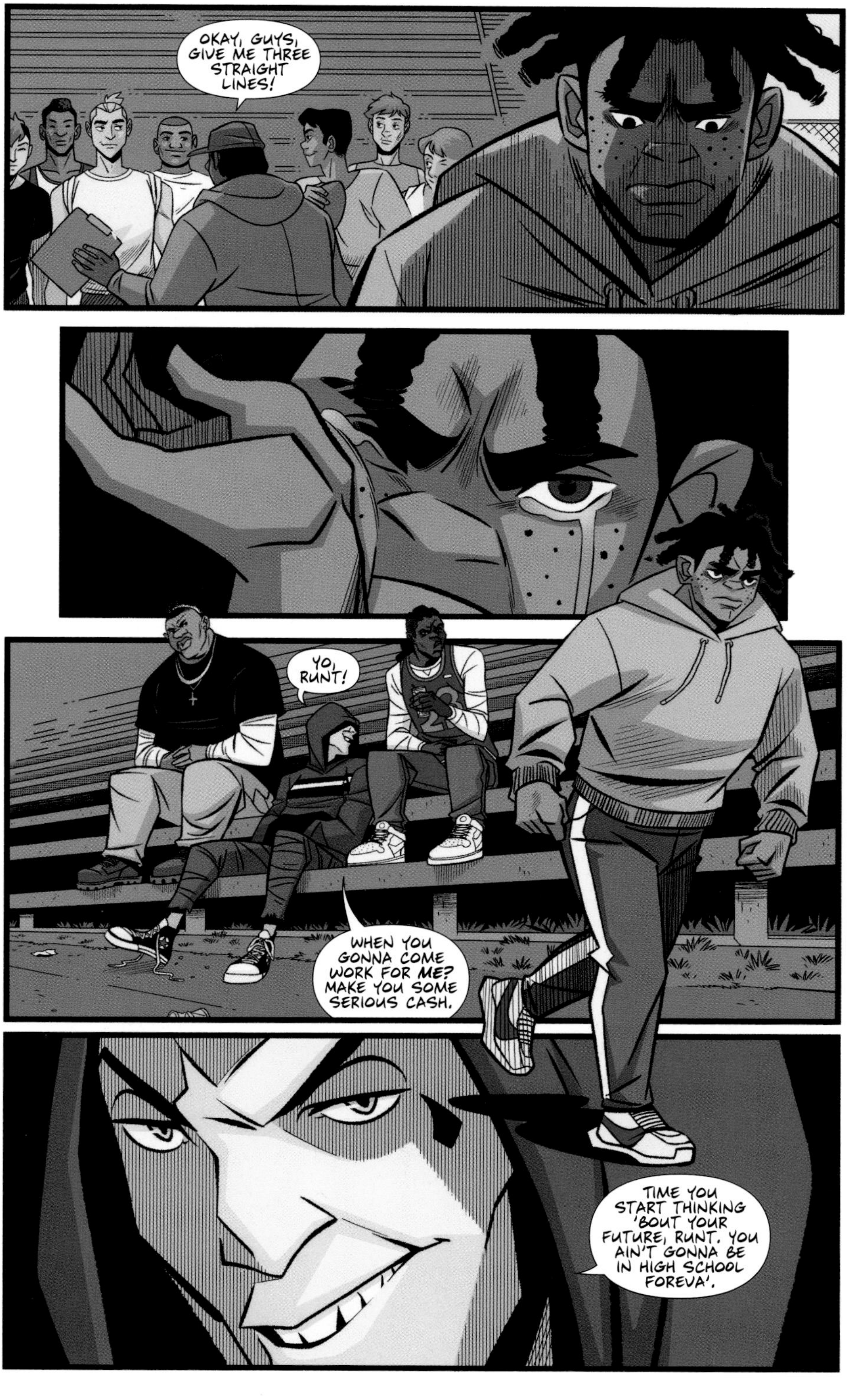
OKAY, GUYS, GIVE ME THREE STRAIGHT LINES!
YO, RUNT!
WHEN YOU GONNA COME WORK FOR ME? MAKE YOU SOME SERIOUS CASH.
TIME YOU START THINKING 'BOUT YOUR FUTURE, RUNT. YOU AIN'T GONNA BE IN HIGH SCHOOL FOREVA'.

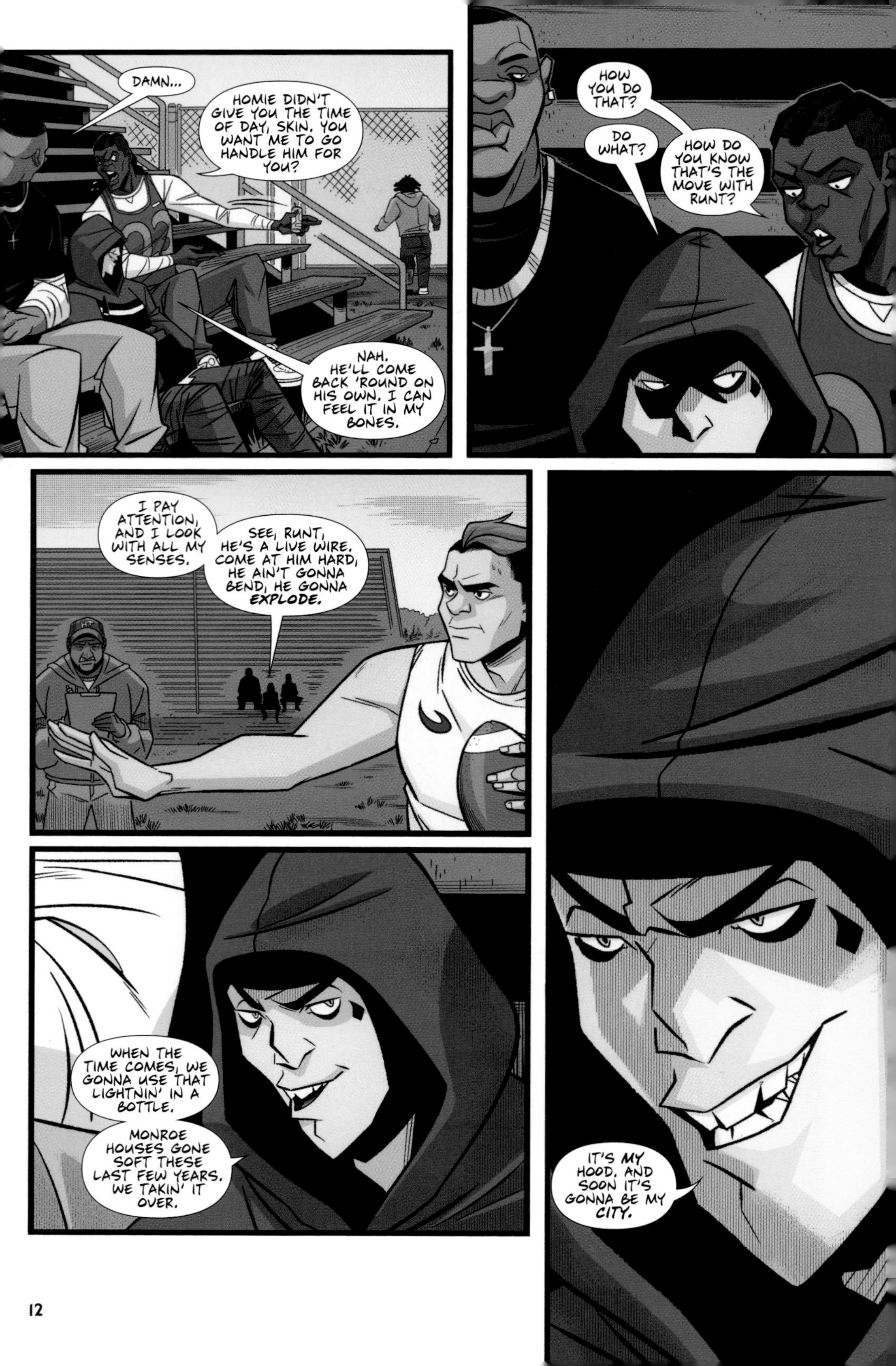
DAMN...
HOMIE DIDN'T GIVE YOU THE TIME OF DAY, SKIN. YOU WANT ME TO GO HANDLE HIM FOR YOU?
NAH. HE'LL COME BACK 'ROUND ON HIS OWN. I CAN FEEL IT IN MY BONES.
HOW YOU DO THAT?
DO WHAT?
HOW DO YOU KNOW THAT'S THE MOVE WITH RUNT?
I PAY ATTENTION, AND I LOOK WITH ALL MY SENSES.
SEE, RUNT, HE'S A LIVE WIRE. COME AT HIM HARD, HE AIN'T GONNA BEND, HE GONNA EXPLODE.
WHEN THE TIME COMES, WE GONNA USE THAT LIGHTNIN' IN A BOTTLE.
MONROE HOUSES GONE SOFT THESE LAST FEW YEARS. WE TAKIN' IT OVER.
IT'S MY HOOD. AND SOON IT'S GONNA BE MY CITY.

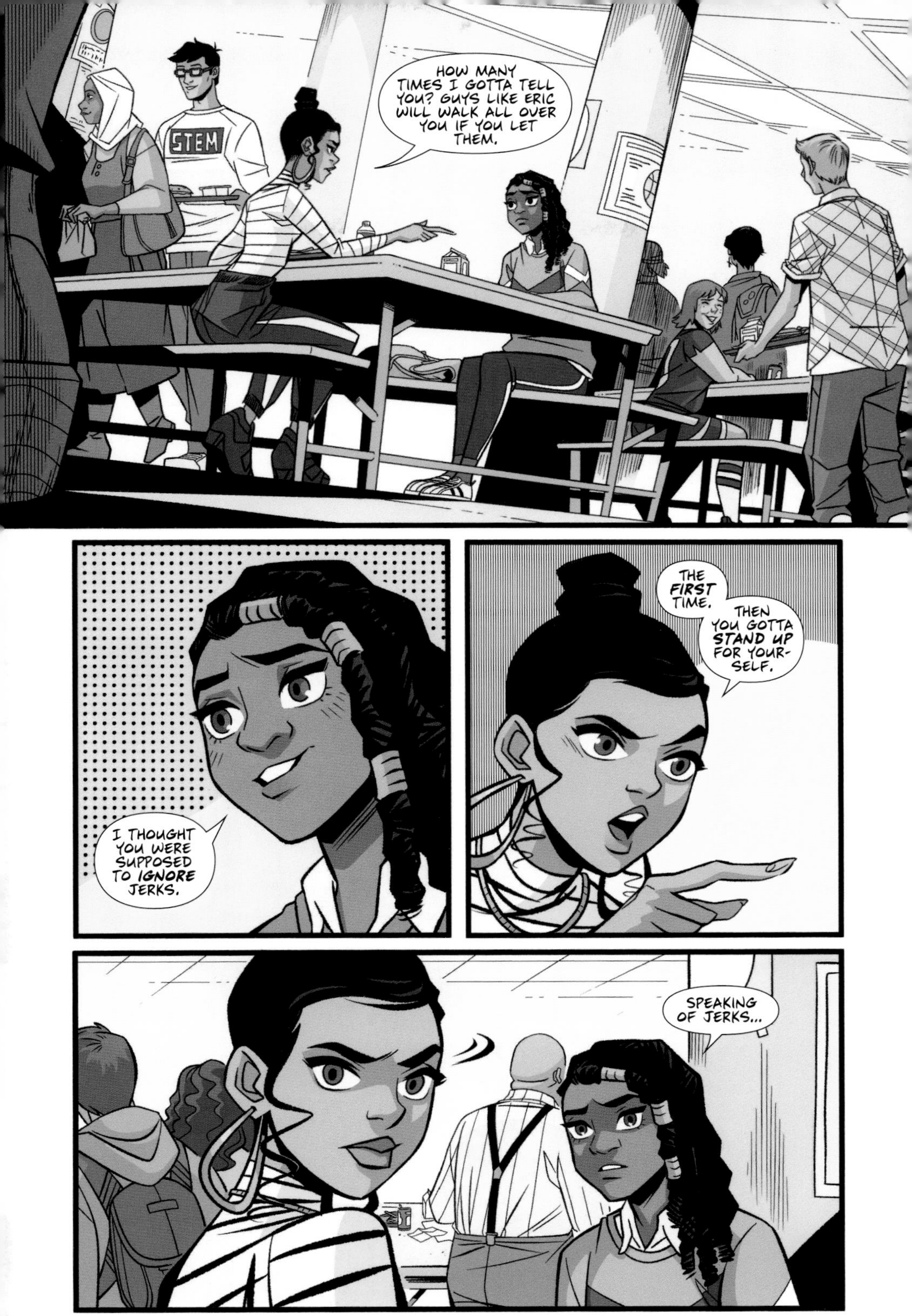
HOW MANY TIMES I GOTTA TELL YOU? GUYS LIKE ERIC WILL WALK ALL OVER YOU IF YOU LET THEM.
STEM
I THOUGHT YOU WERE SUPPOSED TO IGNORE JERKS.
THE FIRST TIME.
THEN YOU GOTTA STAND UP FOR YOUR-SELF.
SPEAKING OF JERKS...

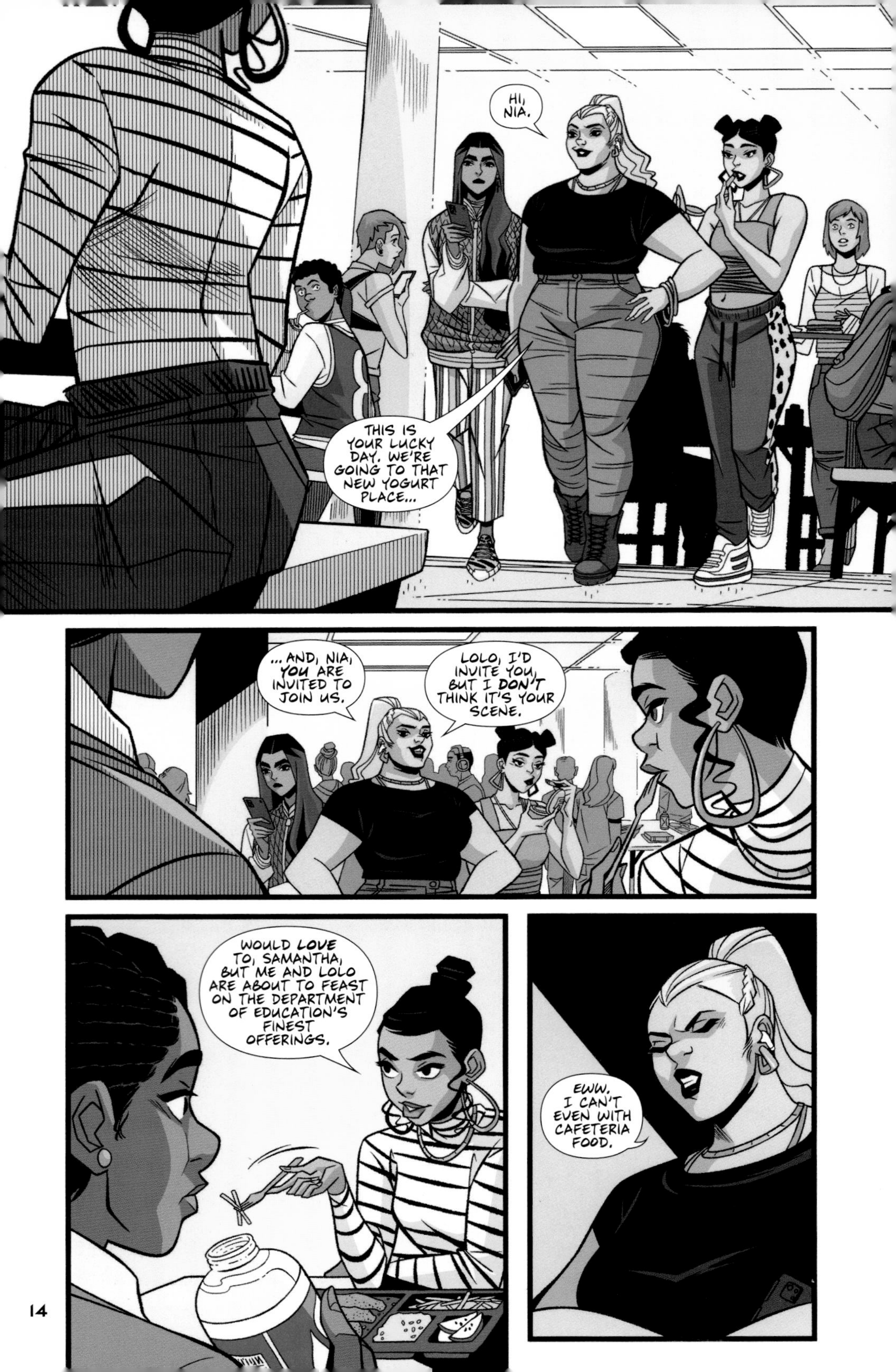
HI, NIA.
THIS IS YOUR LUCKY DAY. WE'RE GOING TO THAT NEW YOGURT PLACE...
...AND, NIA, YOU ARE INVITED TO JOIN US.
LOLO, I'D INVITE YOU, BUT I DON'T THINK IT'S YOUR SCENE.
WOULD LOVE TO, SAMANTHA, BUT ME AND LOLO ARE ABOUT TO FEAST ON THE DEPARTMENT OF EDUCATION'S FINEST OFFERINGS.
EWW. I CAN'T EVEN WITH CAFETERIA FOOD.

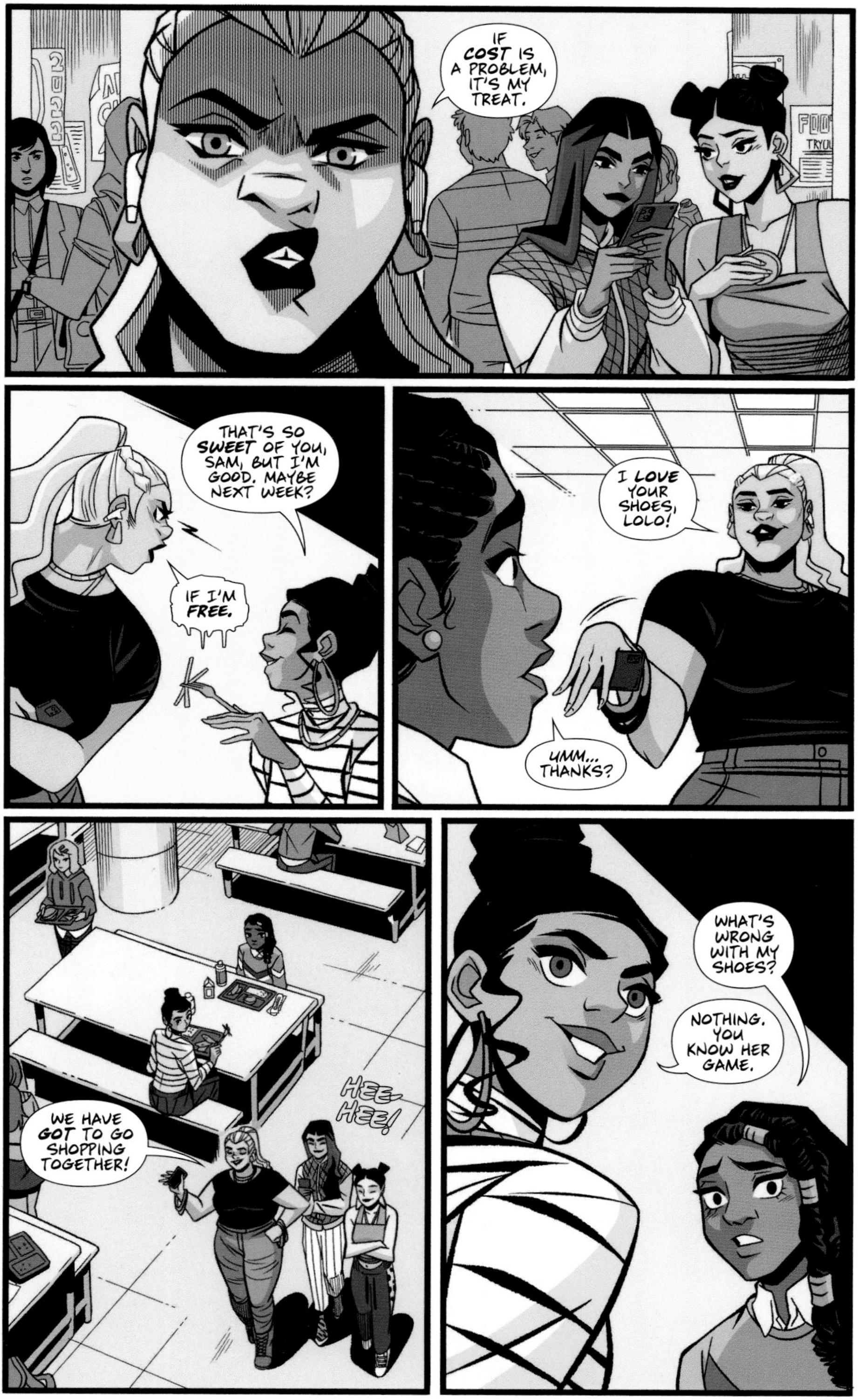
IF COST IS A PROBLEM, IT'S MY TREAT.
THAT'S SO SWEET OF YOU, SAM, BUT I'M GOOD. MAYBE NEXT WEEK?
IF I'M FREE.
I LOVE YOUR SHOES, LOLO!
UMM... THANKS?
WE HAVE GOT TO GO SHOPPING TOGETHER!
HEE-HEE!
WHAT'S WRONG WITH MY SHOES?
NOTHING. YOU KNOW HER GAME.

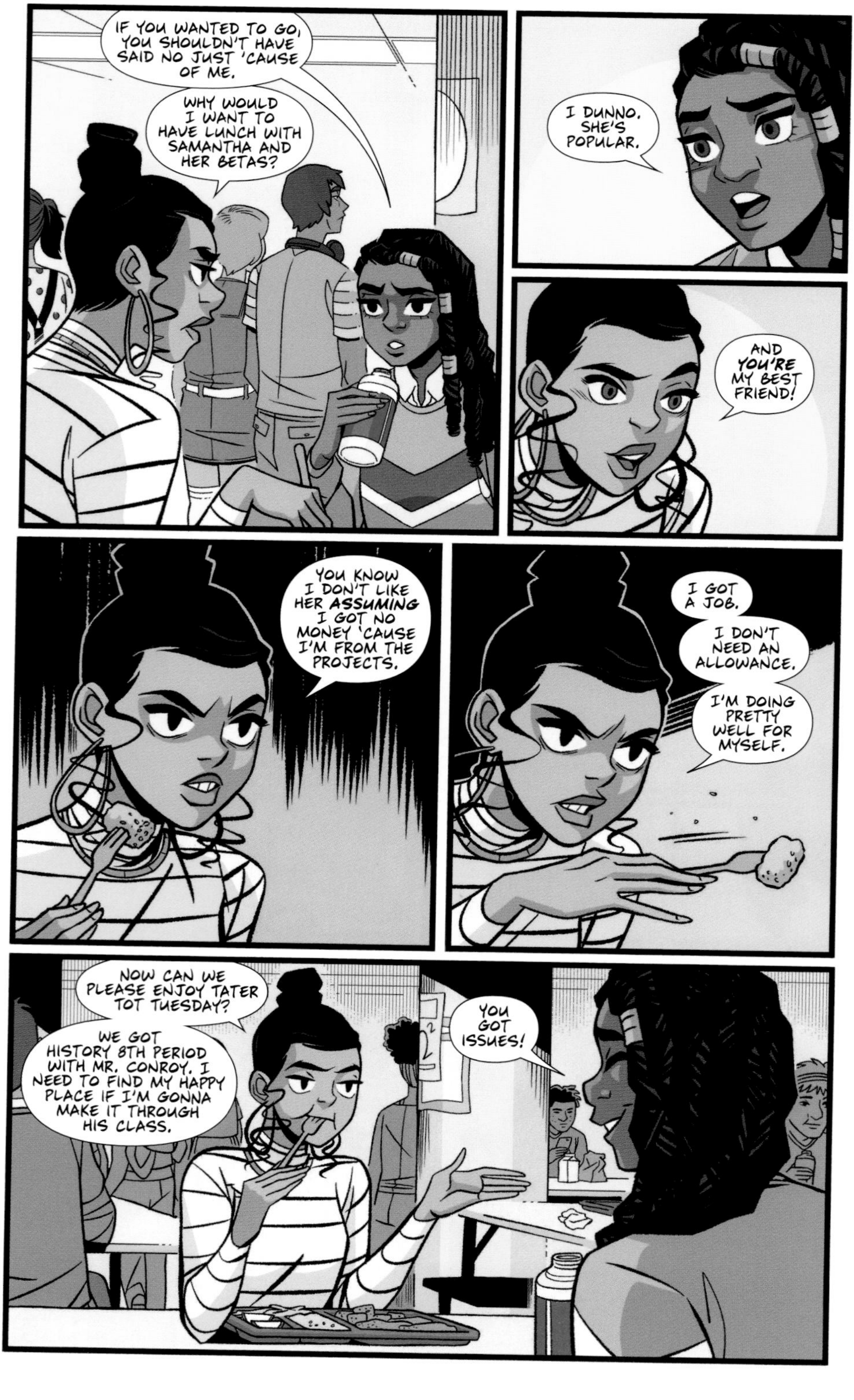
IF YOU WANTED TO GO, YOU SHOULDN'T HAVE SAID NO JUST 'CAUSE OF ME.
WHY WOULD I WANT TO HAVE LUNCH WITH SAMANTHA AND HER BETAS?
I DUNNO. SHE'S POPULAR.
AND **YOU'RE** MY BEST FRIEND!
YOU KNOW I DON'T LIKE HER **ASSUMING** I GOT NO MONEY 'CAUSE I'M FROM THE PROJECTS.
I GOT A JOB.
I DON'T NEED AN ALLOWANCE.
I'M DOING PRETTY WELL FOR MYSELF.
NOW CAN WE PLEASE ENJOY TATER TOT TUESDAY?
WE GOT HISTORY 8TH PERIOD WITH MR. CONROY. I NEED TO FIND MY HAPPY PLACE IF I'M GONNA MAKE IT THROUGH HIS CLASS.
YOU GOT ISSUES!

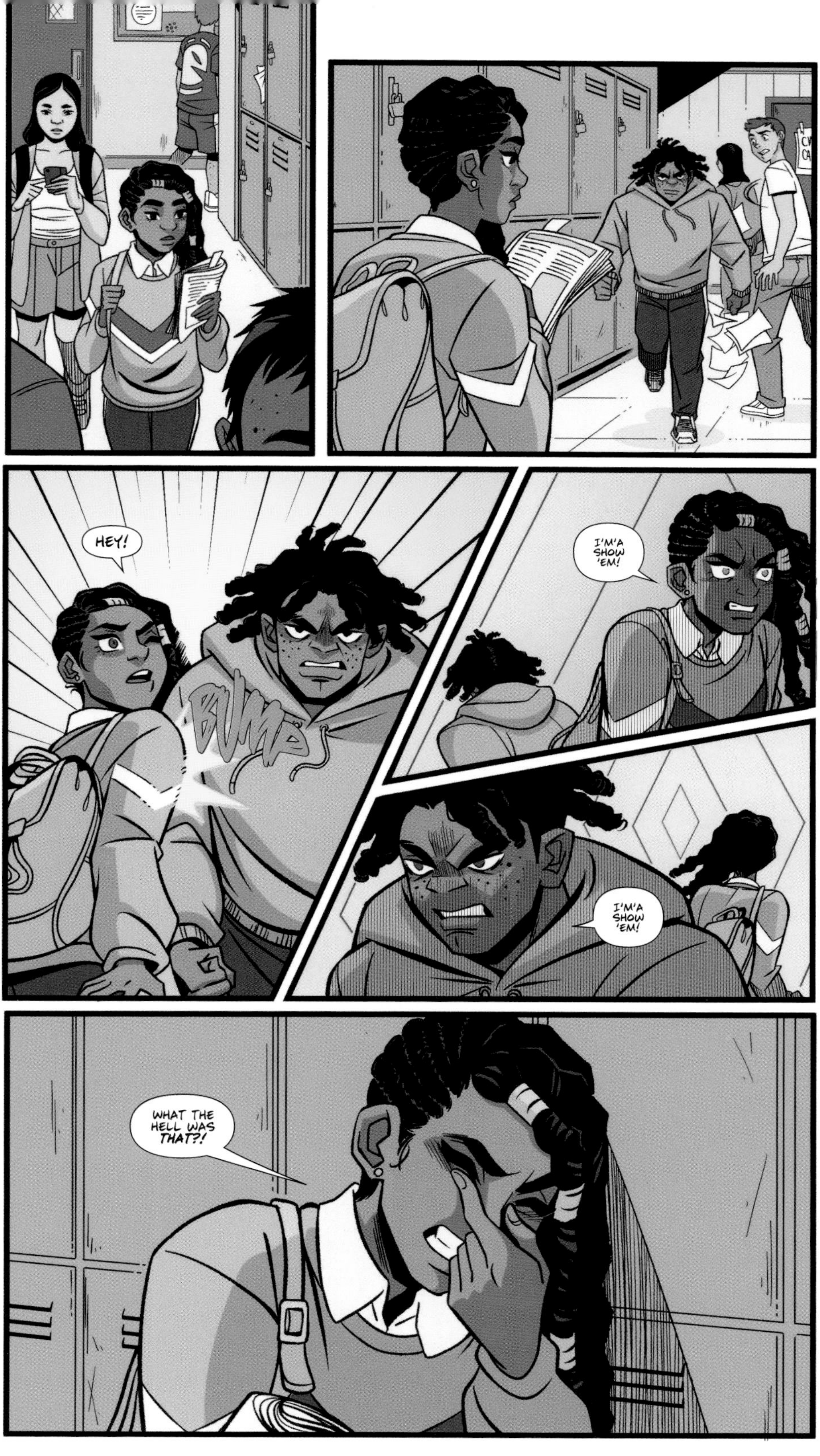
HEY!
BUMP
I'M'A SHOW 'EM!
I'M'A SHOW 'EM!
WHAT THE HELL WAS *THAT?!*

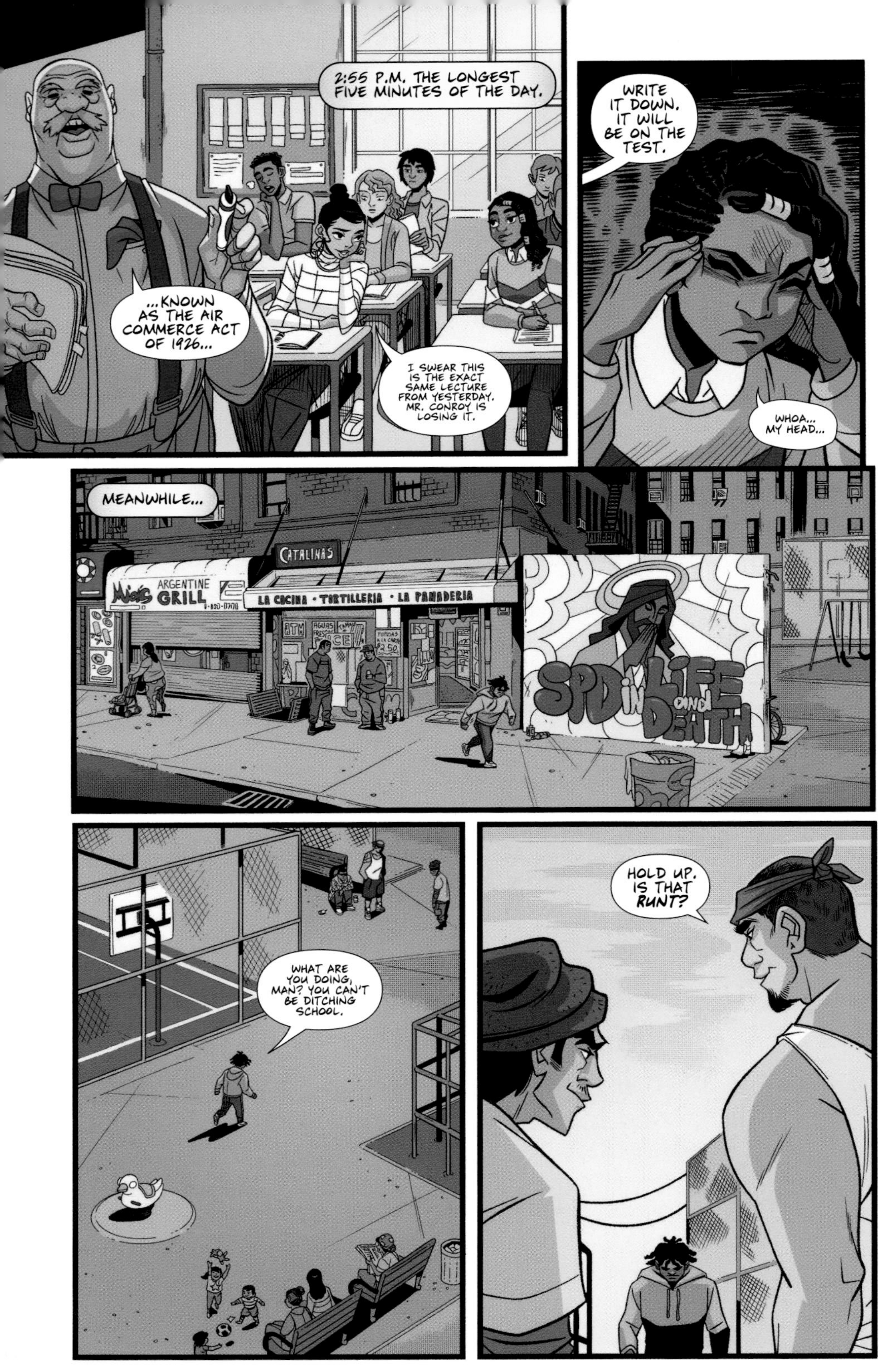
2:55 P.M. THE LONGEST FIVE MINUTES OF THE DAY.
...KNOWN AS THE AIR COMMERCE ACT OF 1926...
I SWEAR THIS IS THE EXACT SAME LECTURE FROM YESTERDAY. MR. CONROY IS LOSING IT.
WRITE IT DOWN. IT WILL BE ON THE TEST.
WHOA... MY HEAD...
MEANWHILE...
ARGENTINE GRILL
CATALINAS
LA COCINA · TORTILLERIA · LA PANADERIA
ATM
SPD in LIFE and DEATH
WHAT ARE YOU DOING, MAN? YOU CAN'T BE DITCHING SCHOOL.
HOLD UP. IS THAT *RUNT*?

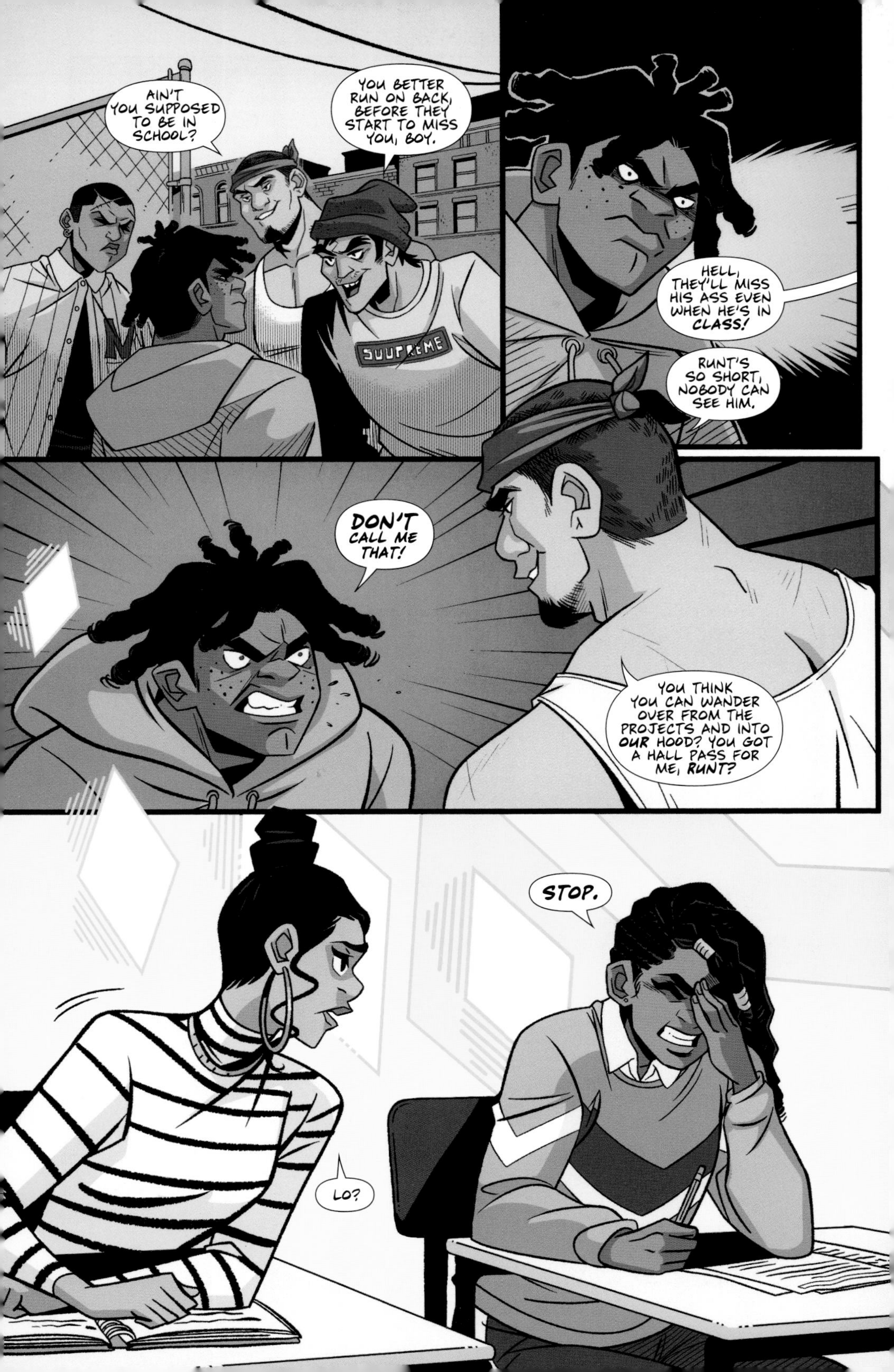
AIN'T YOU SUPPOSED TO BE IN SCHOOL?
YOU BETTER RUN ON BACK, BEFORE THEY START TO MISS YOU, BOY.
SUUPREME
HELL, THEY'LL MISS HIS ASS EVEN WHEN HE'S IN *CLASS!*
RUNT'S SO SHORT, NOBODY CAN SEE HIM.
DON'T CALL ME THAT!
YOU THINK YOU CAN WANDER OVER FROM THE PROJECTS AND INTO **OUR** HOOD? YOU GOT A HALL PASS FOR ME, **RUNT?**
STOP.
LO?

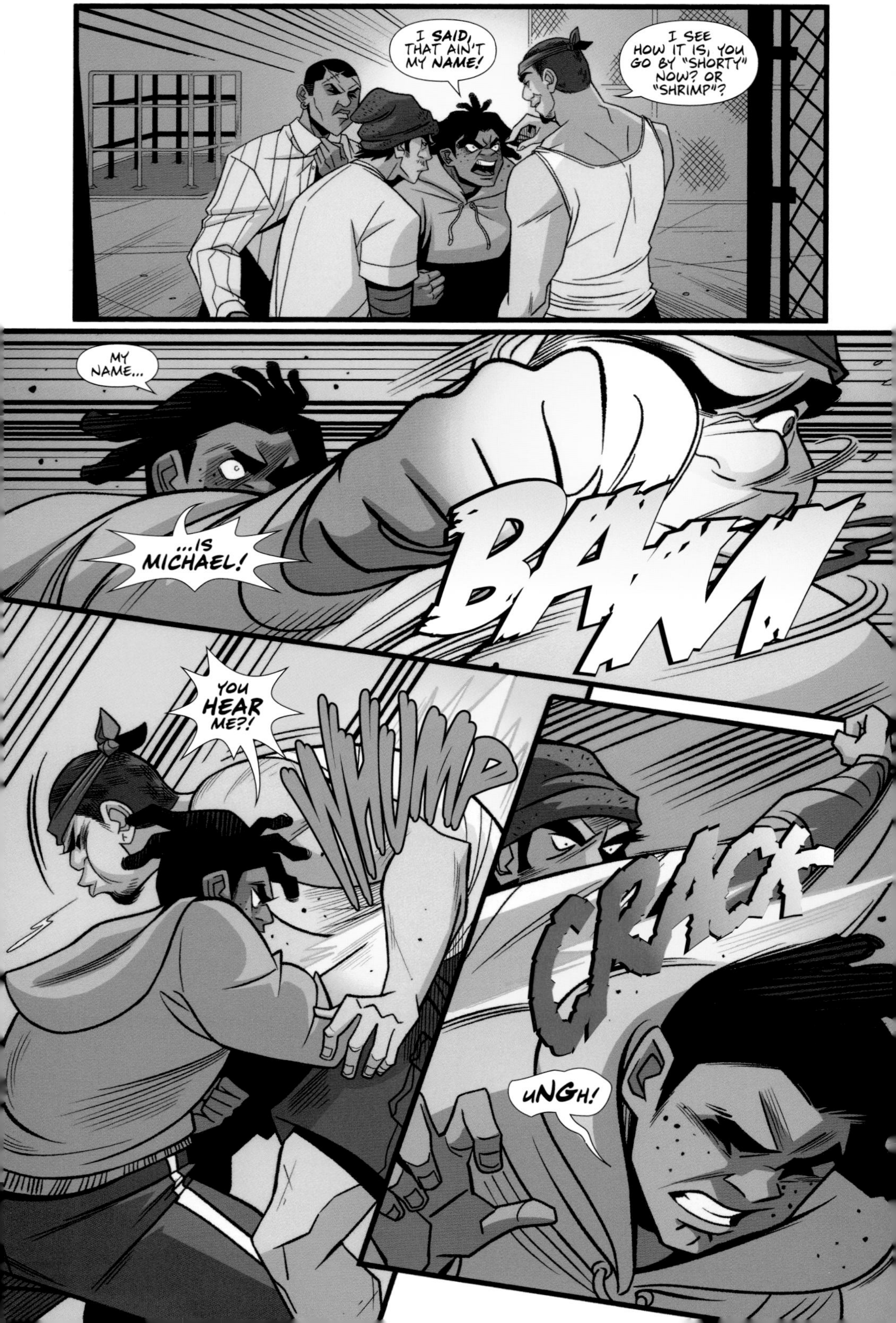
I SAID, THAT AIN'T MY NAME!
I SEE HOW IT IS, YOU GO BY "SHORTY" NOW? OR "SHRIMP"?
MY NAME...
...IS MICHAEL!
BAM
YOU HEAR ME?!
WHUMP
CRACK
uNGh!

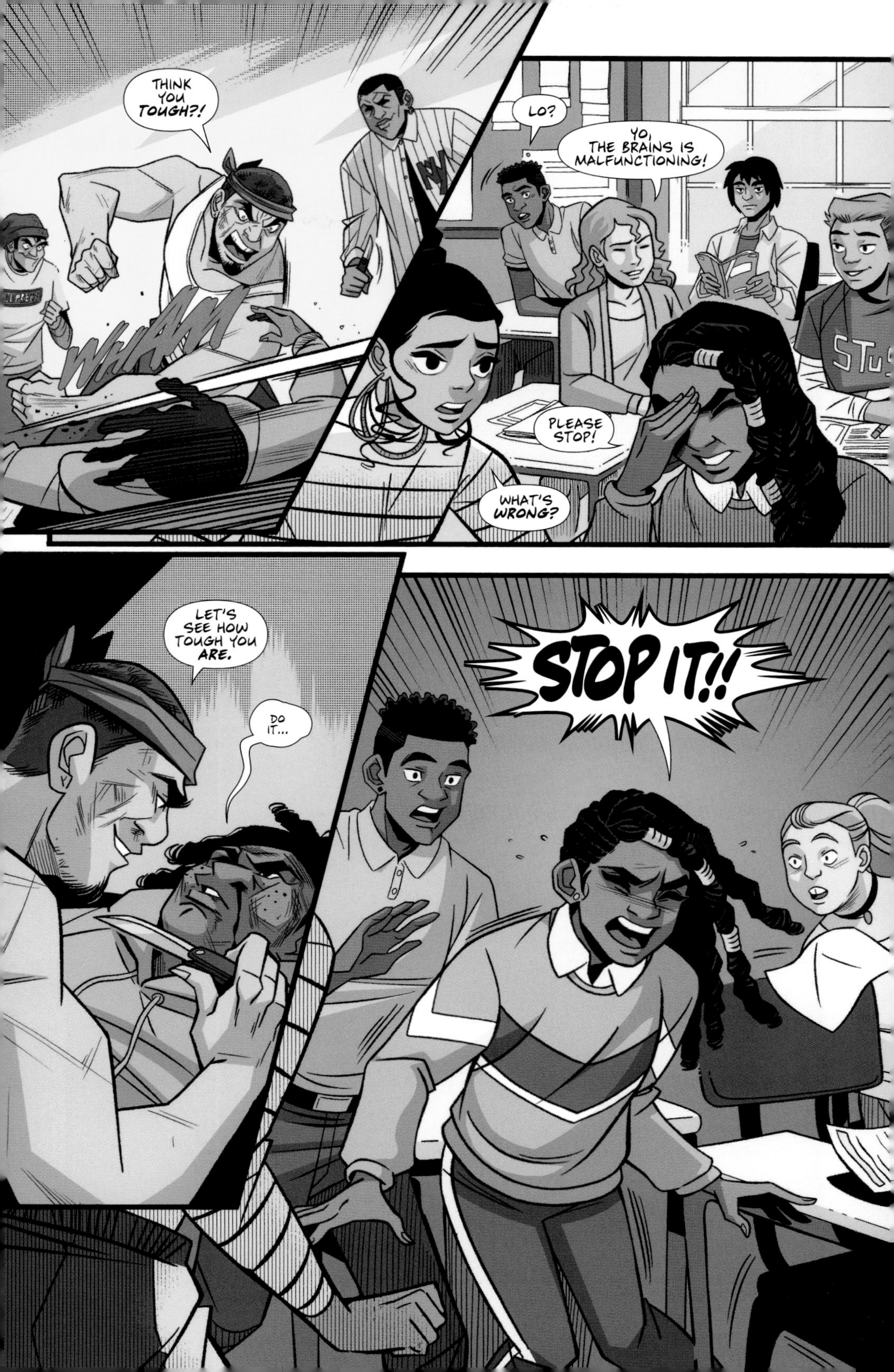
THINK YOU TOUGH?!
WHAM
LO?
YO, THE BRAINS IS MALFUNCTIONING!
PLEASE STOP!
WHAT'S WRONG?
LET'S SEE HOW TOUGH YOU ARE.
DO IT...
STOP IT!!

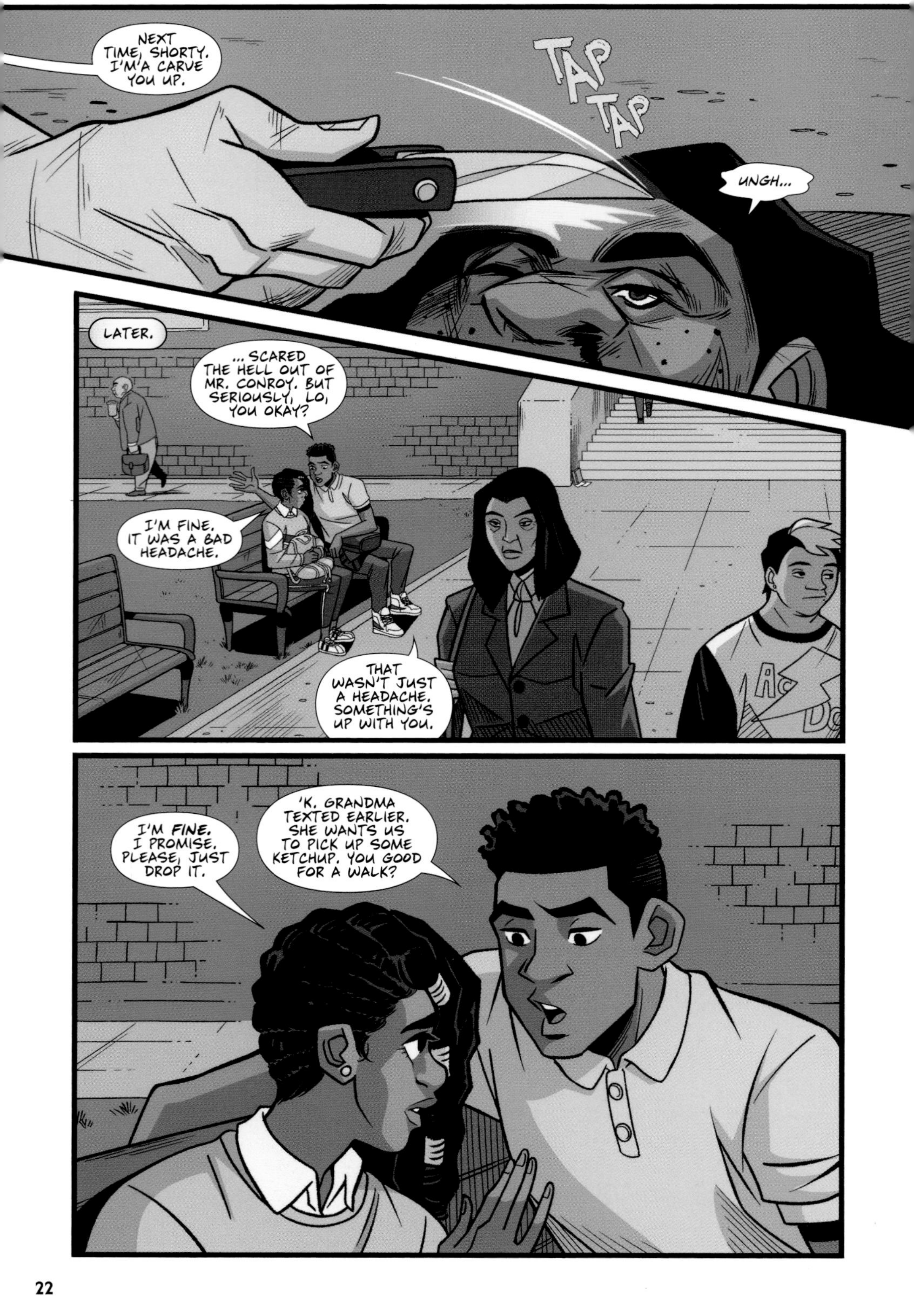
NEXT TIME, SHORTY. I'M'A CARVE YOU UP.
TAP TAP
UNGH...
LATER.
... SCARED THE HELL OUT OF MR. CONROY. BUT SERIOUSLY, LO, YOU OKAY?
I'M FINE. IT WAS A BAD HEADACHE.
THAT WASN'T JUST A HEADACHE. SOMETHING'S UP WITH YOU.
I'M FINE. I PROMISE. PLEASE, JUST DROP IT.
'K. GRANDMA TEXTED EARLIER. SHE WANTS US TO PICK UP SOME KETCHUP. YOU GOOD FOR A WALK?

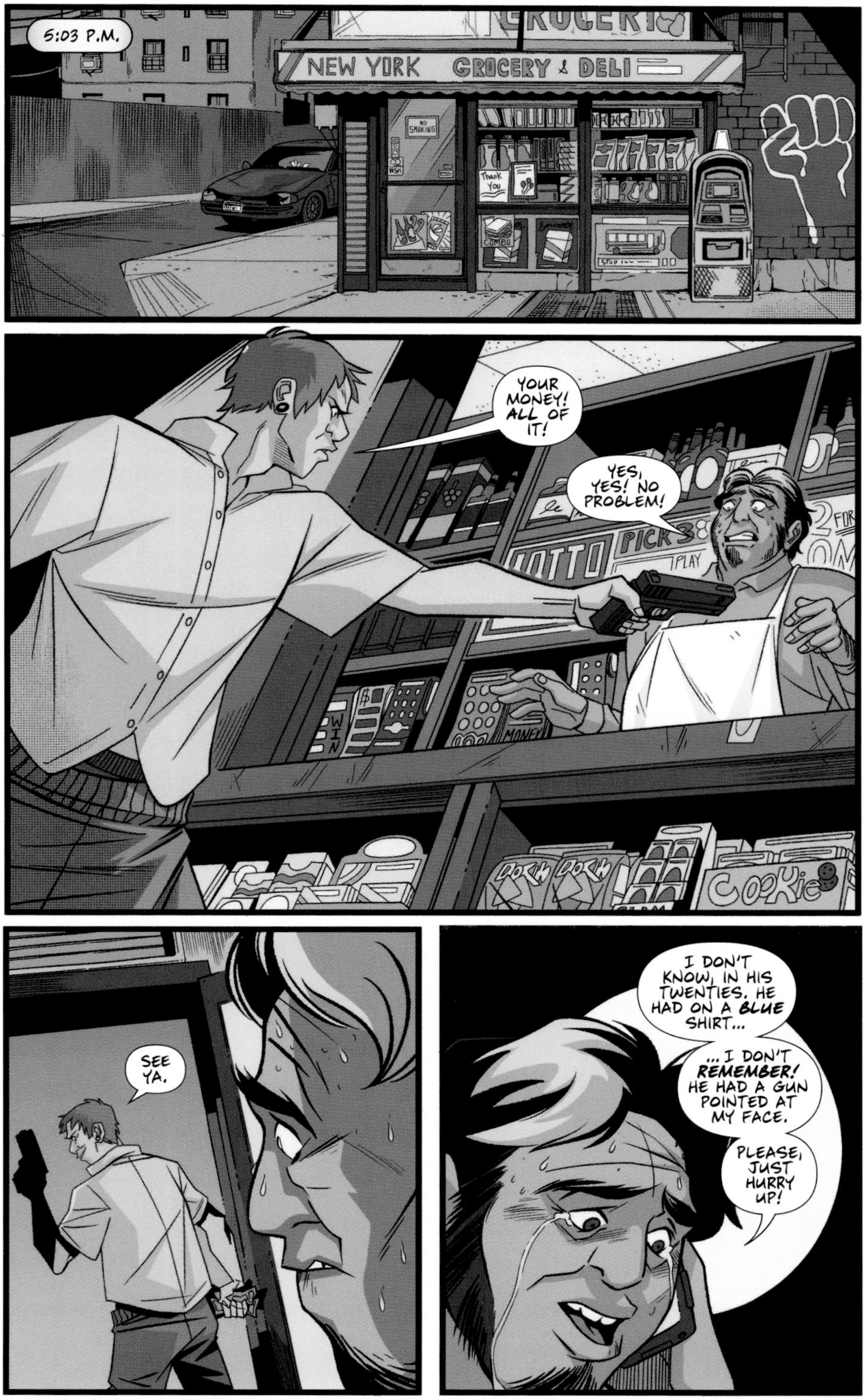
5:03 P.M.
NEW YORK GROCERY & DELI
NO SMOKING
Thank You
YOUR MONEY! ALL OF IT!
YES, YES! NO PROBLEM!
LOTTO
PICK 3
PLAY
WIN
MONEY
Cookie
SEE YA.
I DON'T KNOW, IN HIS TWENTIES. HE HAD ON A BLUE SHIRT...
... I DON'T REMEMBER! HE HAD A GUN POINTED AT MY FACE.
PLEASE, JUST HURRY UP!

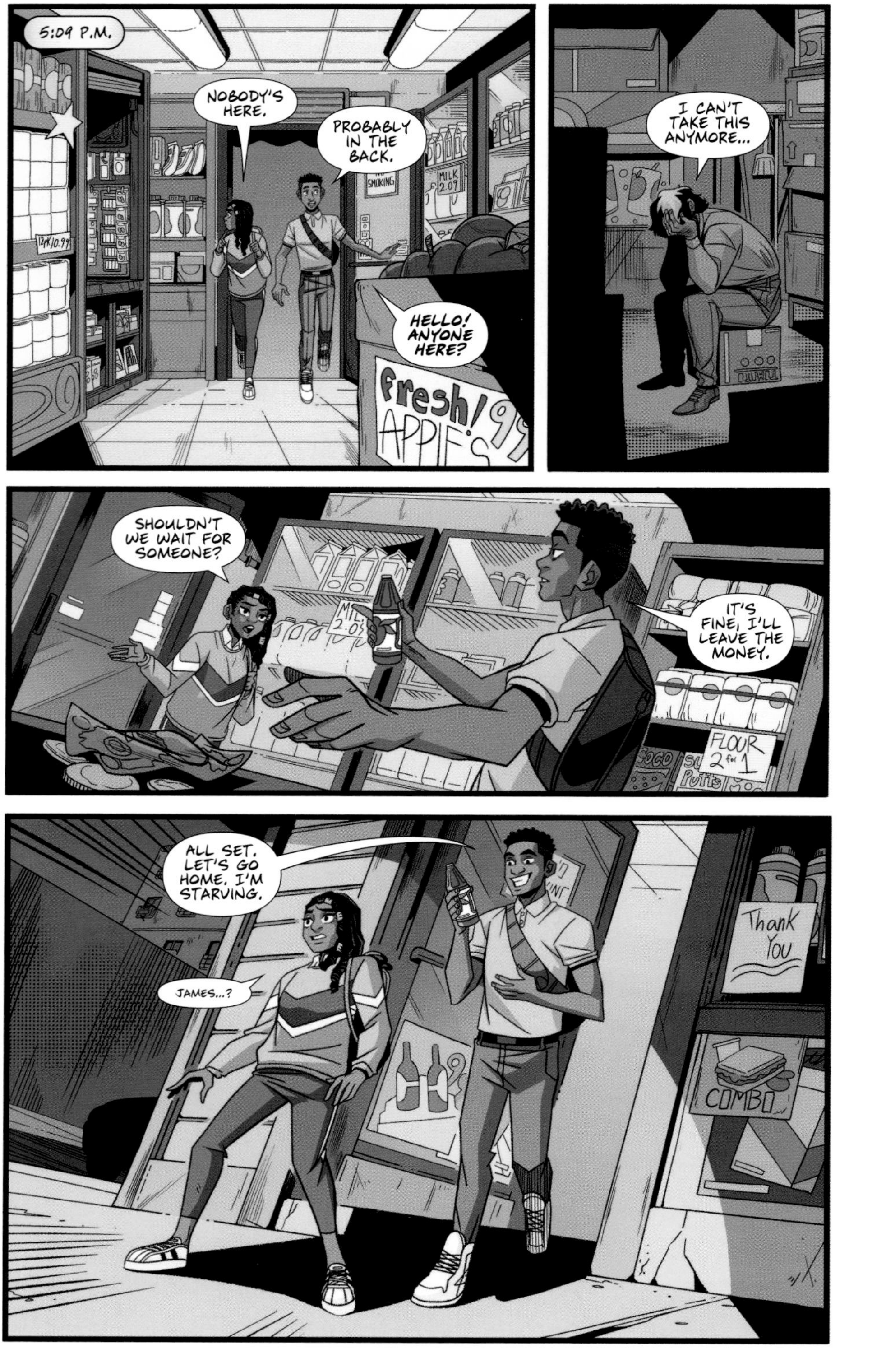
5:09 P.M.
NOBODY'S HERE.
PROBABLY IN THE BACK.
NO SMOKING
MILK 2.09
12PK 10.99
HELLO! ANYONE HERE?
Fresh! APPLES 99
I CAN'T TAKE THIS ANYMORE...
SHOULDN'T WE WAIT FOR SOMEONE?
IT'S FINE, I'LL LEAVE THE MONEY.
FLOUR 2 for 1
ALL SET. LET'S GO HOME. I'M STARVING.
JAMES...?
Thank You
COMBO

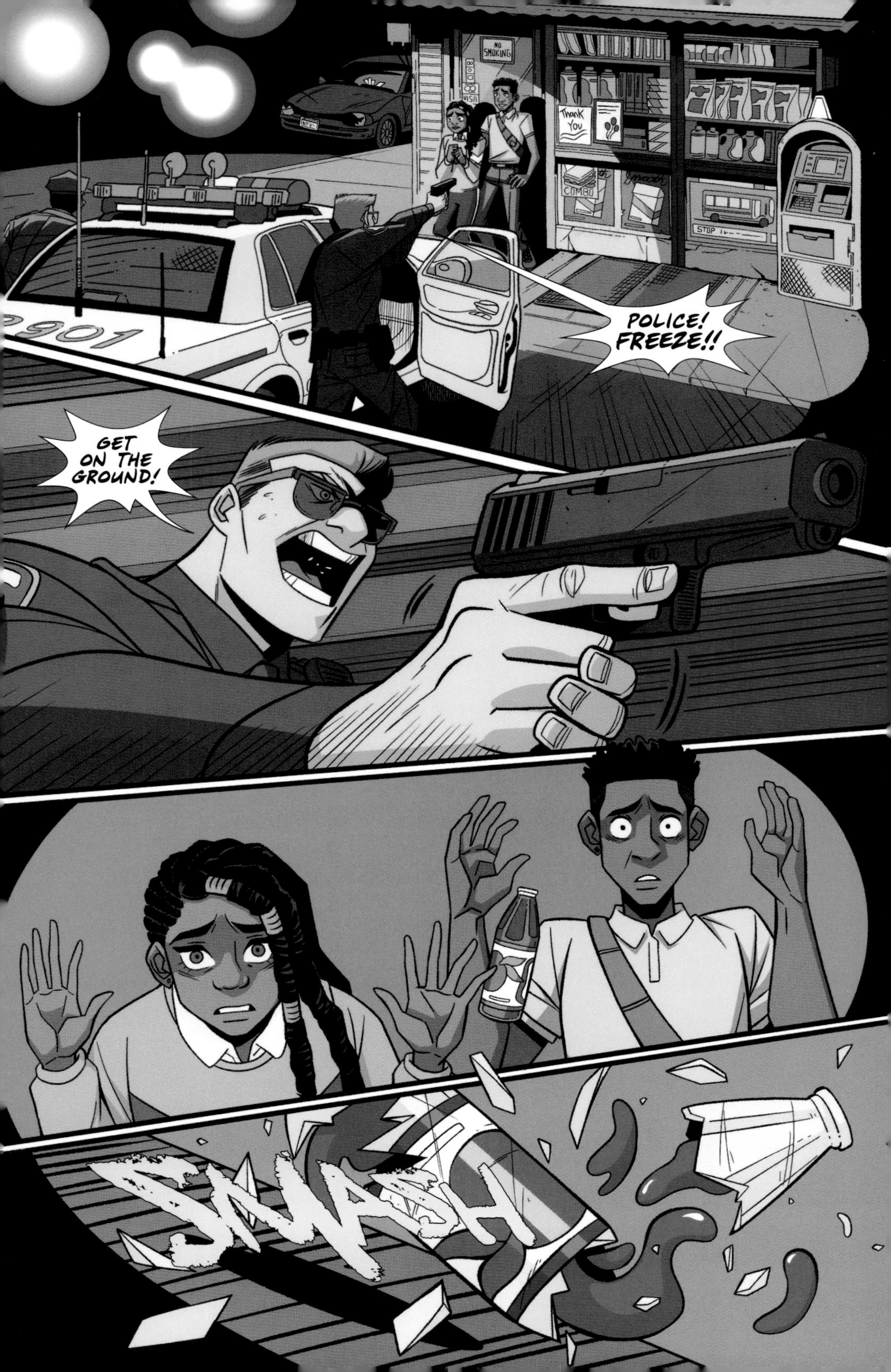

NO SMOKING
Thank You
COMBO
POLICE! FREEZE!!
GET ON THE GROUND!
SMASH

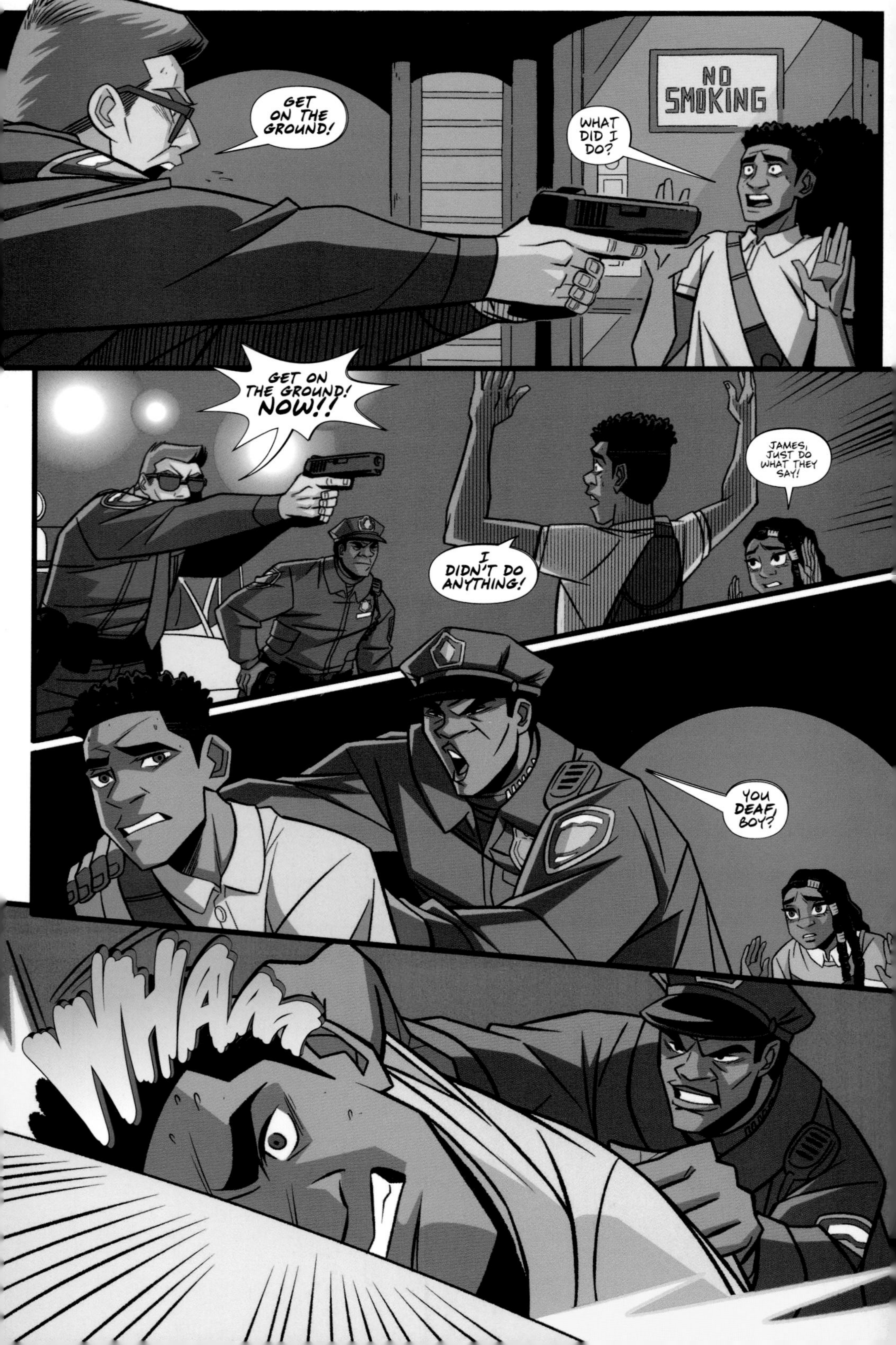

GET ON THE GROUND!
NO SMOKING
WHAT DID I DO?
GET ON THE GROUND! NOW!!
JAMES, JUST DO WHAT THEY SAY!
I DIDN'T DO ANYTHING!
YOU DEAF, BOY?

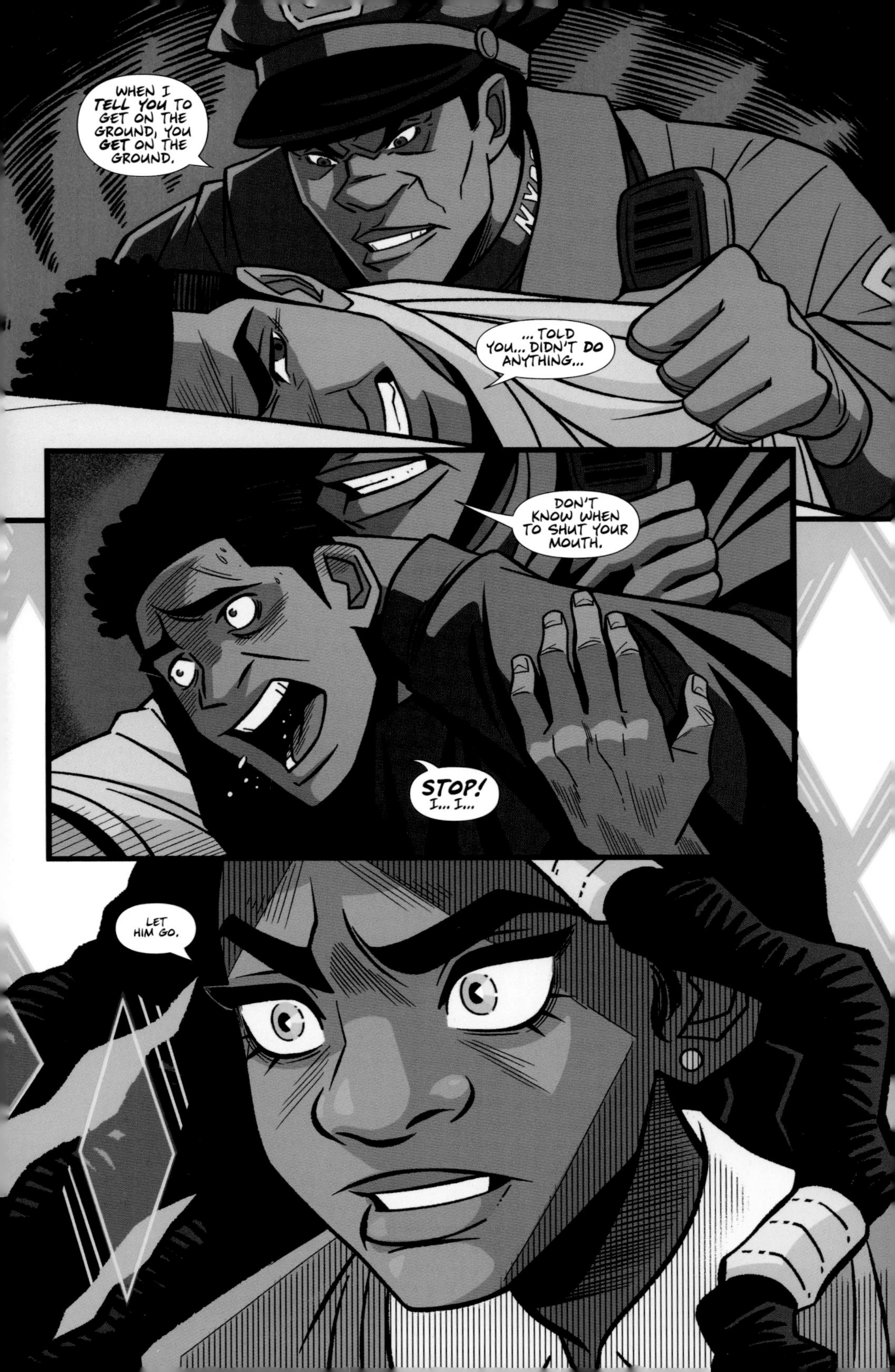
WHEN I TELL YOU TO GET ON THE GROUND, YOU GET ON THE GROUND.
...TOLD YOU... DIDN'T DO ANYTHING...
DON'T KNOW WHEN TO SHUT YOUR MOUTH.
STOP! I... I...
LET HIM GO.

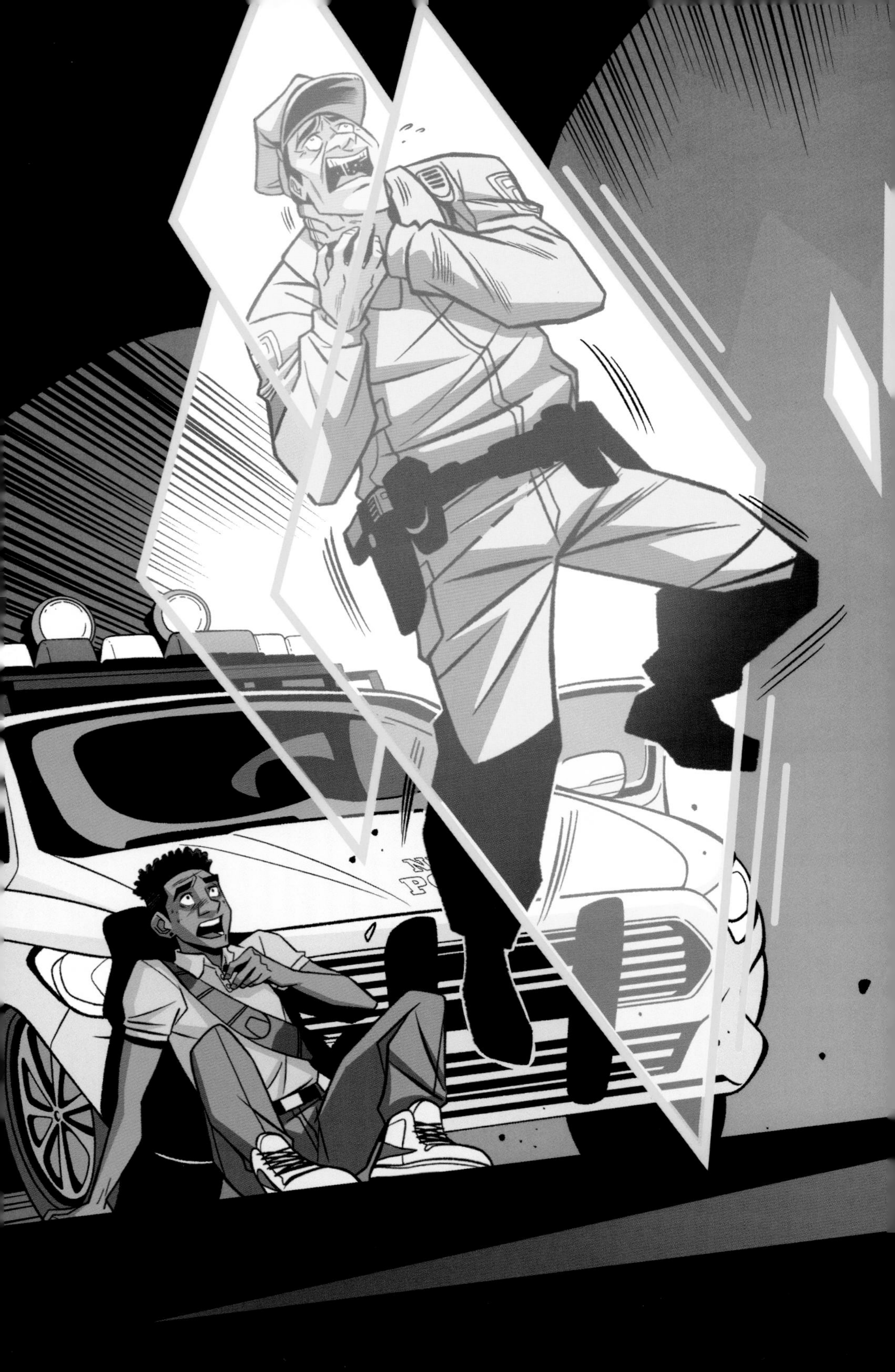

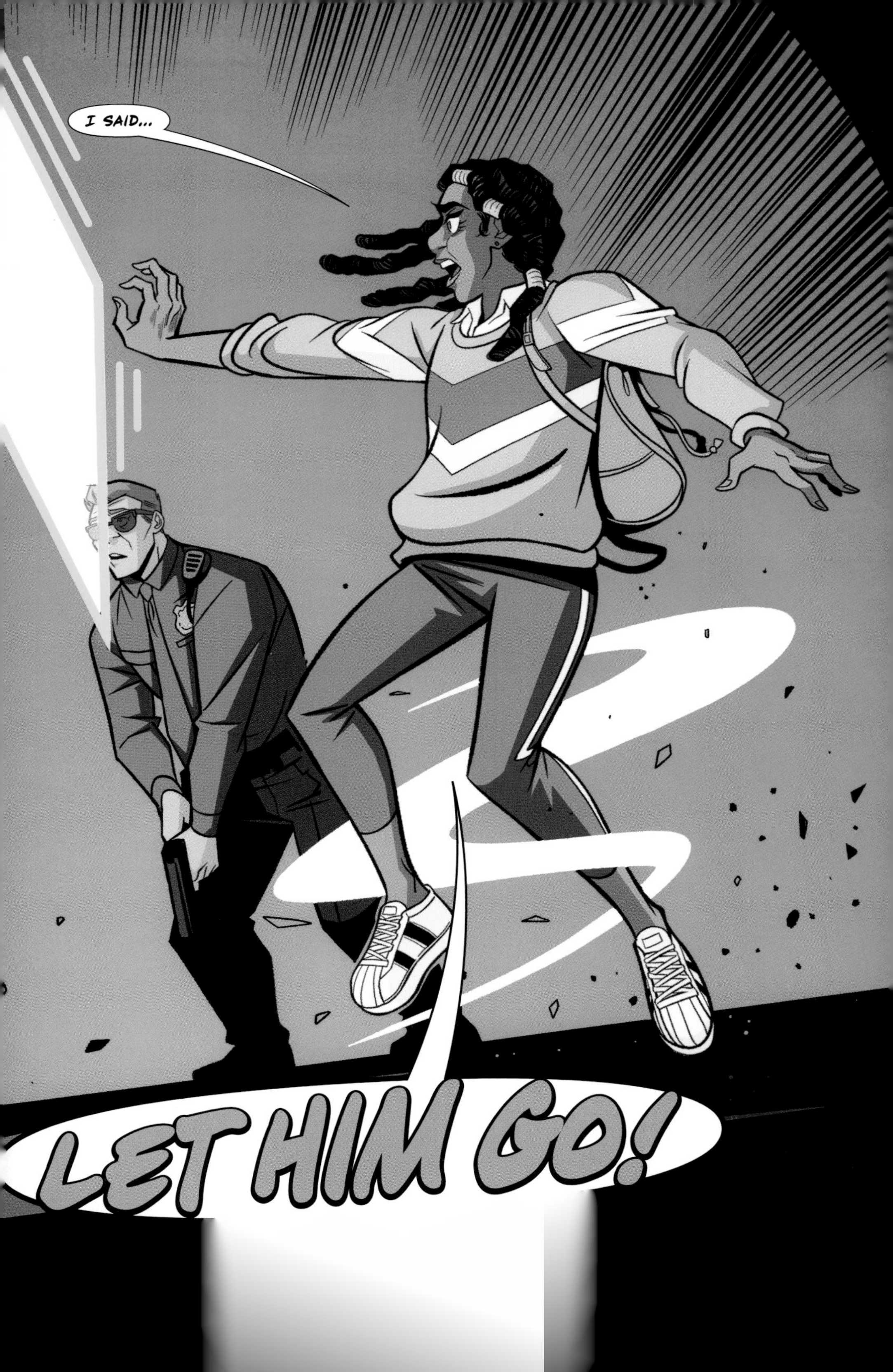
I SAID...
LET HIM GO!

CHAPTER 2

WHEN A GIRL CAN'T BE HERSELF NO MORE

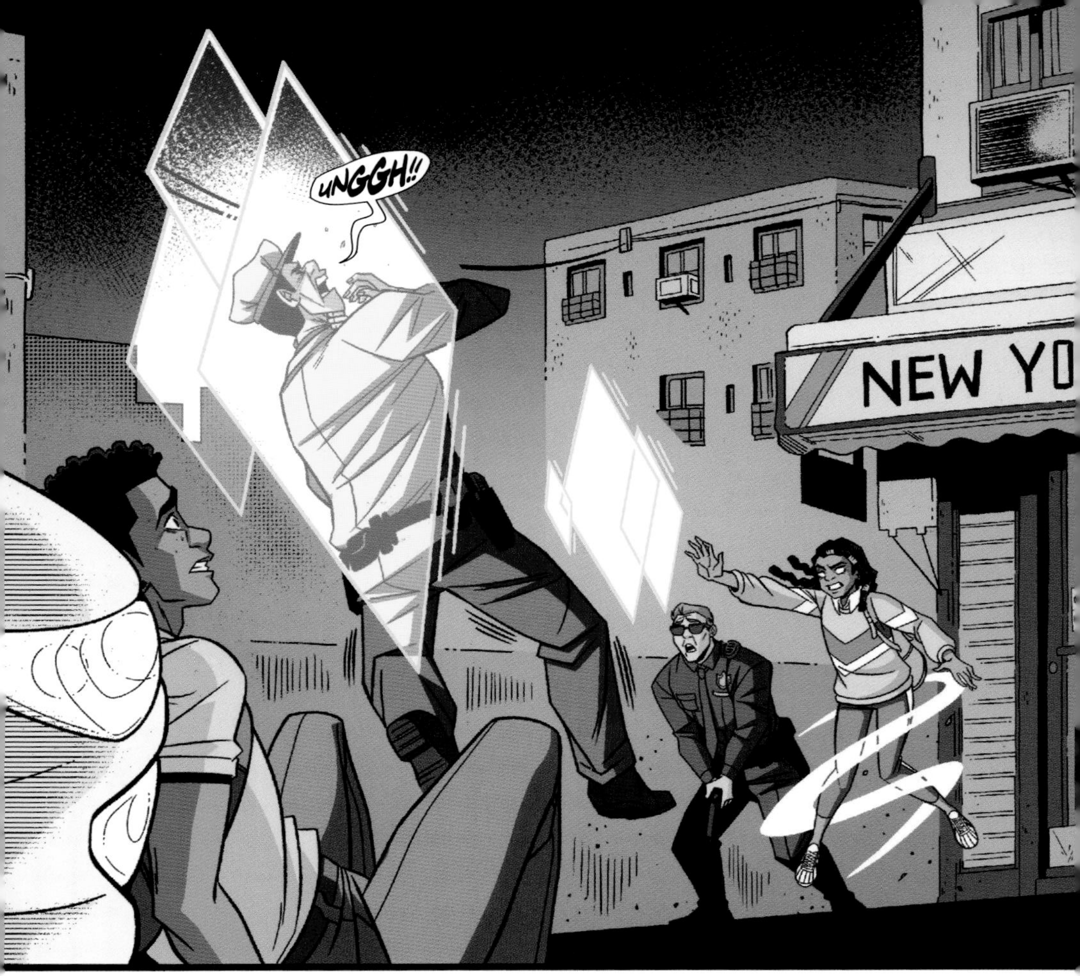
UNGGH!!
NEW YO

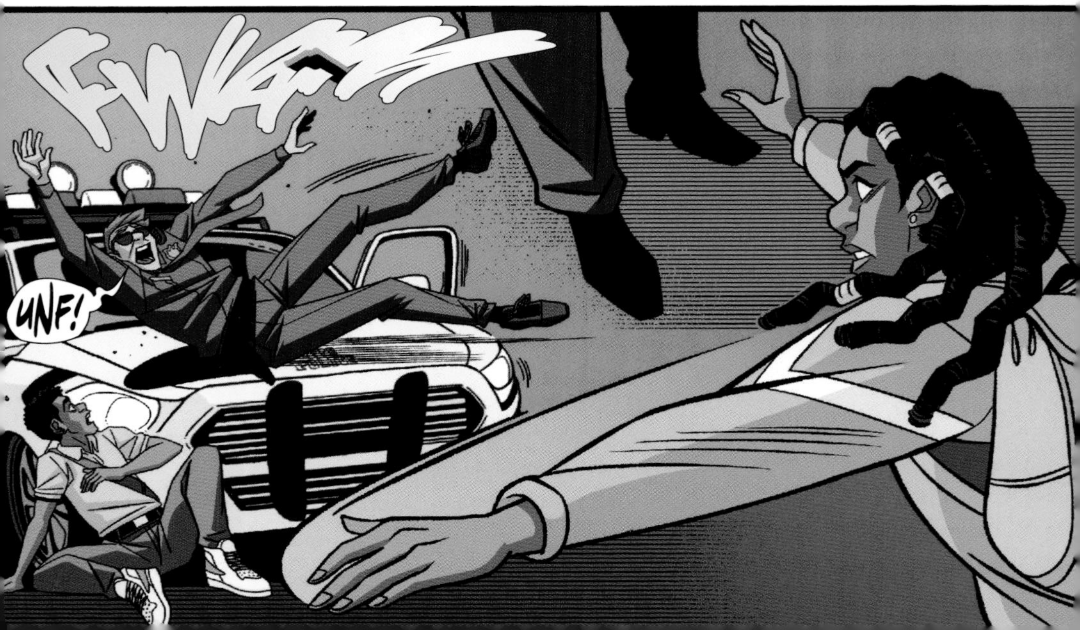
FWAP
UNF!

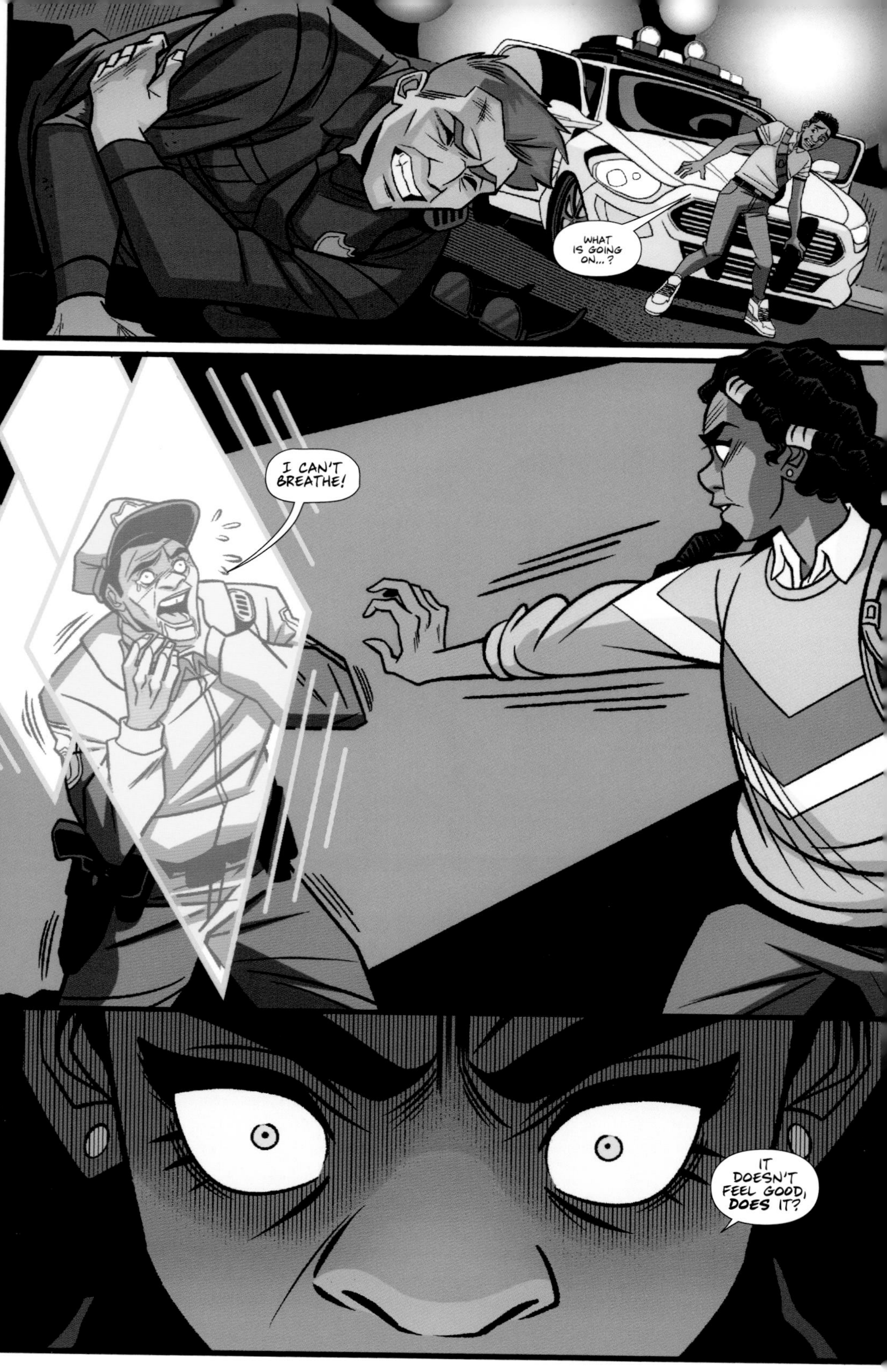
WHAT IS GOING ON...?
I CAN'T BREATHE!
IT DOESN'T FEEL GOOD, DOES IT?

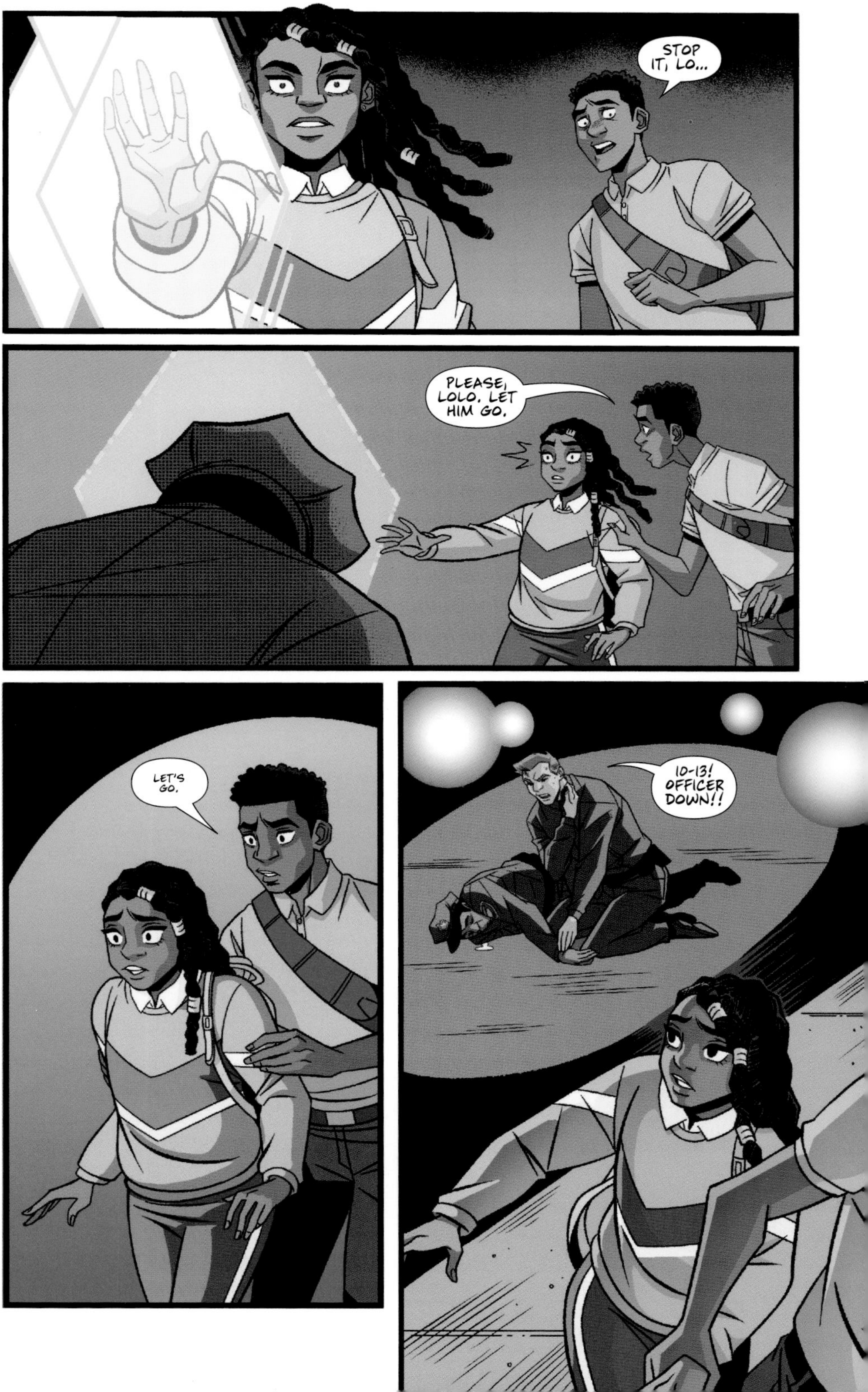
STOP IT, LO...
PLEASE, LOLO. LET HIM GO.
LET'S GO.
10-13! OFFICER DOWN!!

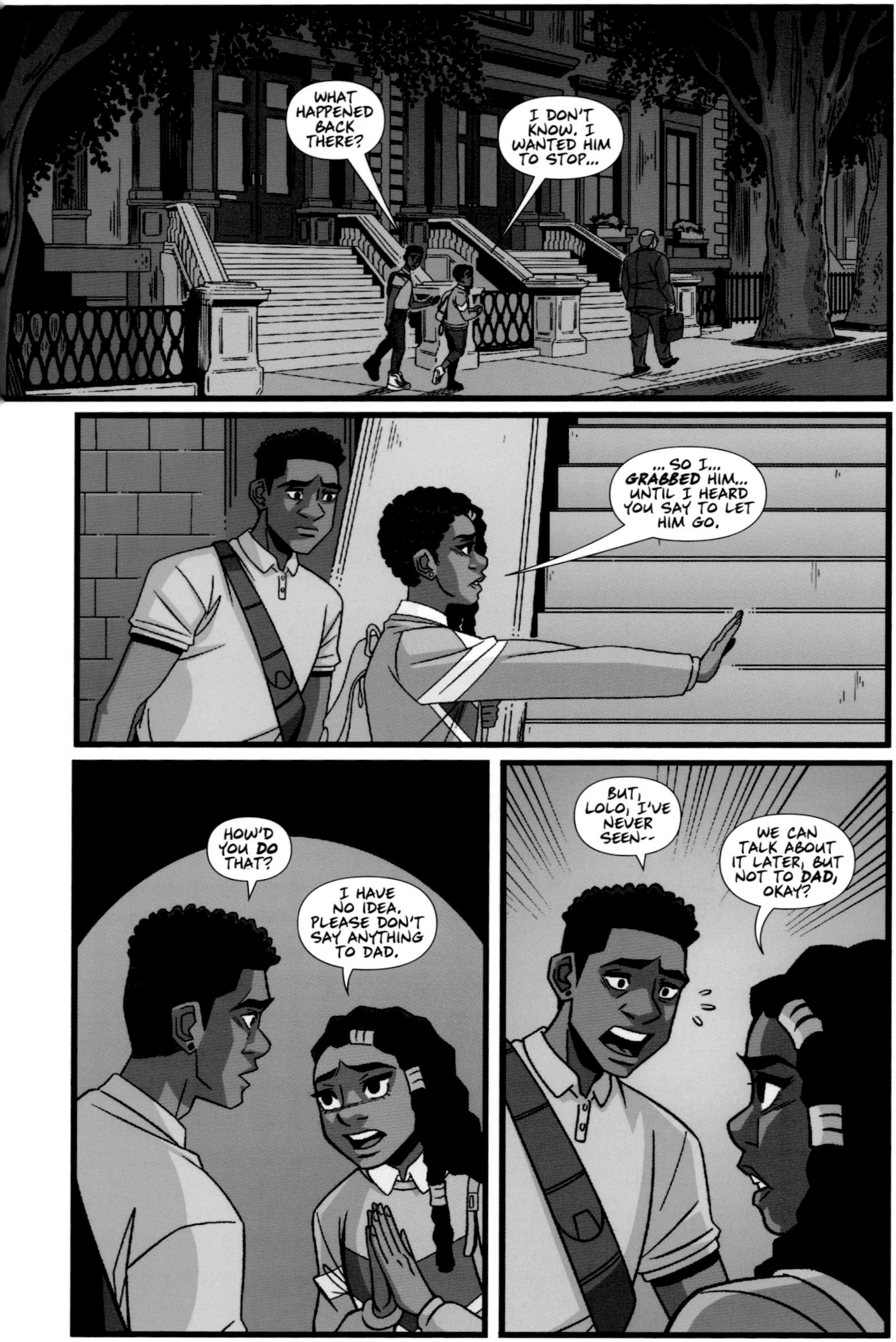
WHAT HAPPENED BACK THERE?
I DON'T KNOW. I WANTED HIM TO STOP...
...SO I... GRABBED HIM... UNTIL I HEARD YOU SAY TO LET HIM GO.
HOW'D YOU DO THAT?
I HAVE NO IDEA. PLEASE DON'T SAY ANYTHING TO DAD.
BUT, LOLO, I'VE NEVER SEEN--
WE CAN TALK ABOUT IT LATER, BUT NOT TO DAD, OKAY?

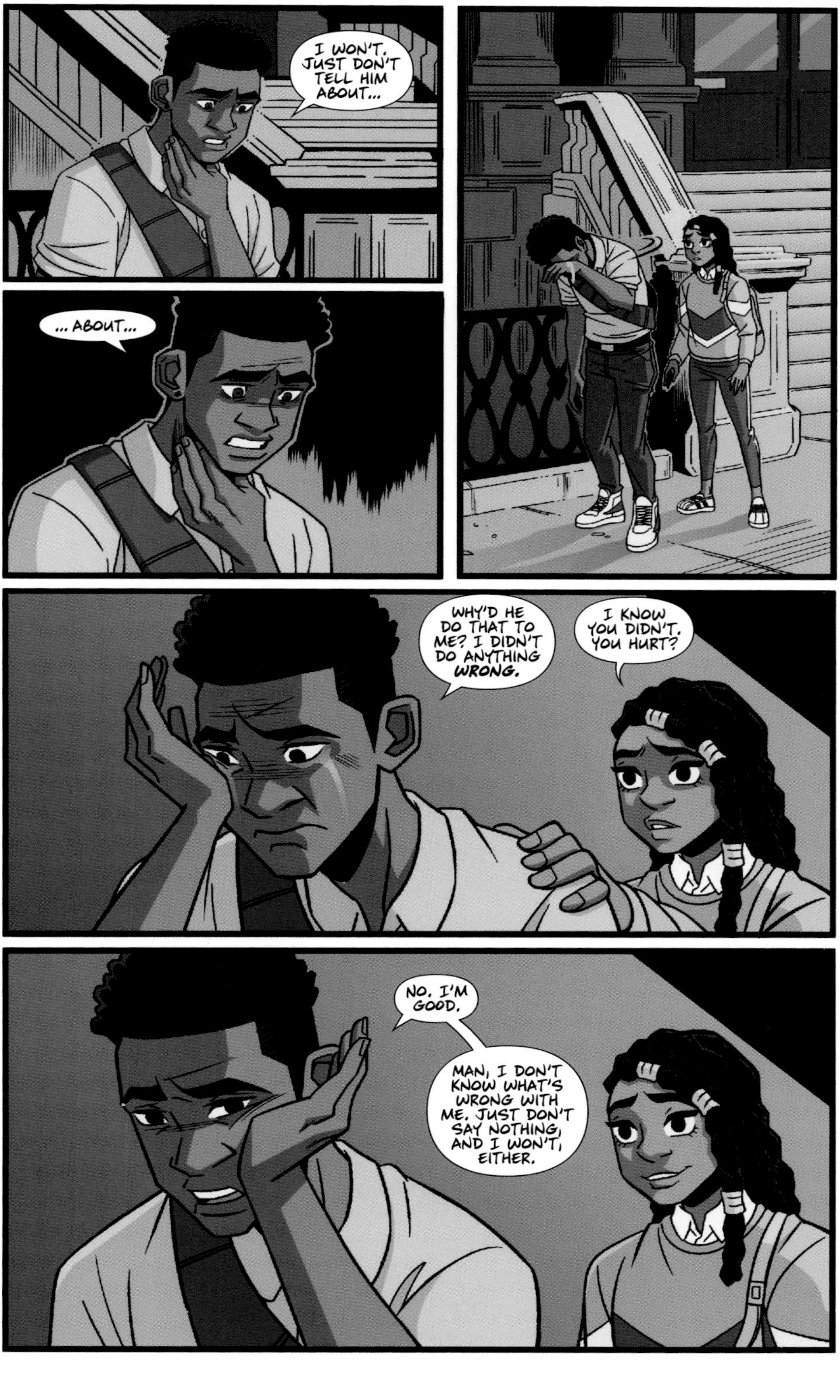
I WON'T. JUST DON'T TELL HIM ABOUT...
... ABOUT...
WHY'D HE DO THAT TO ME? I DIDN'T DO ANYTHING WRONG.
I KNOW YOU DIDN'T. YOU HURT?
NO. I'M GOOD.
MAN, I DON'T KNOW WHAT'S WRONG WITH ME. JUST DON'T SAY NOTHING, AND I WON'T, EITHER.

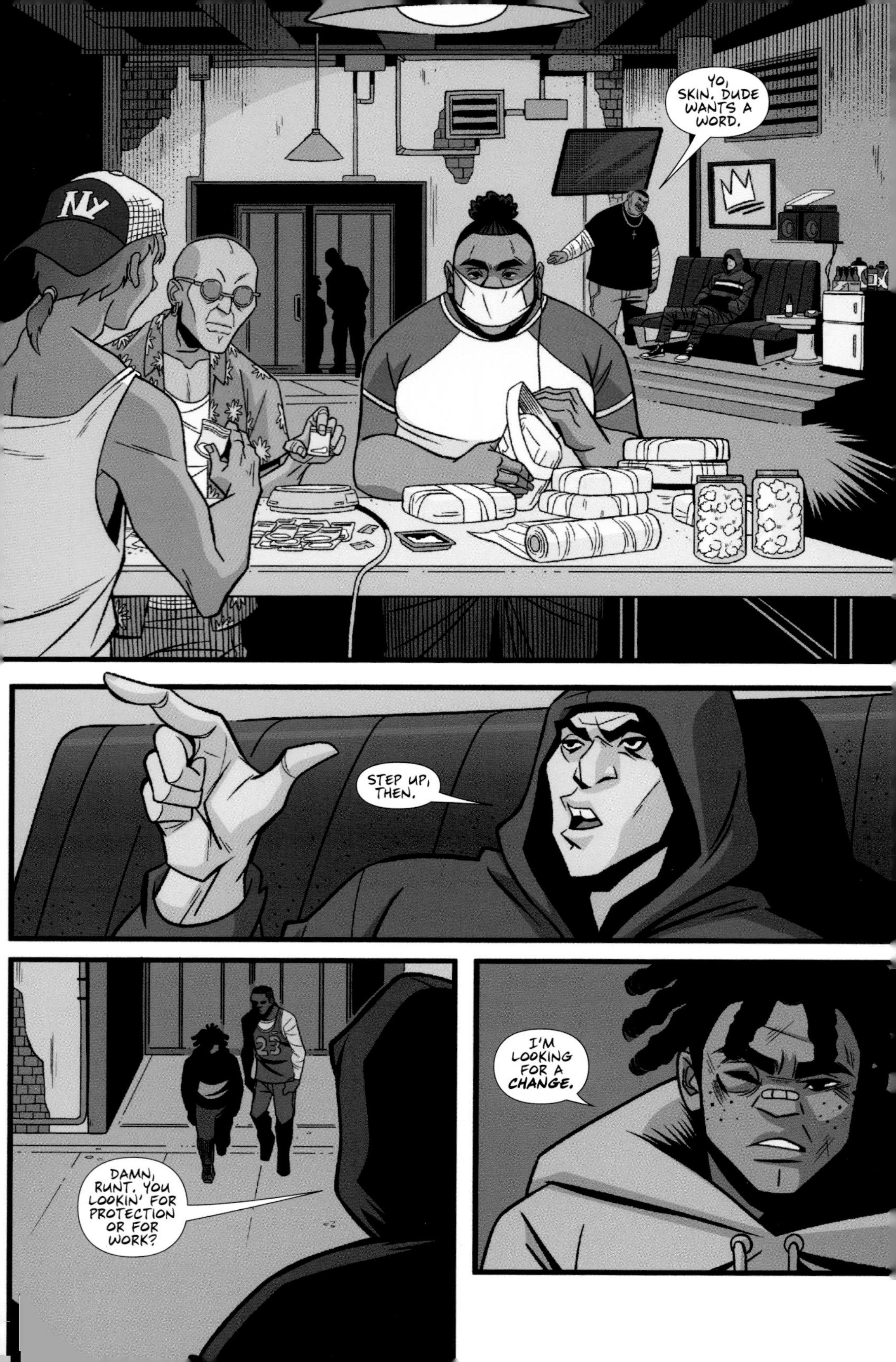

YO, SKIN. DUDE WANTS A WORD.
STEP UP, THEN.
DAMN, RUNT. YOU LOOKIN' FOR PROTECTION OR FOR WORK?
I'M LOOKING FOR A CHANGE.

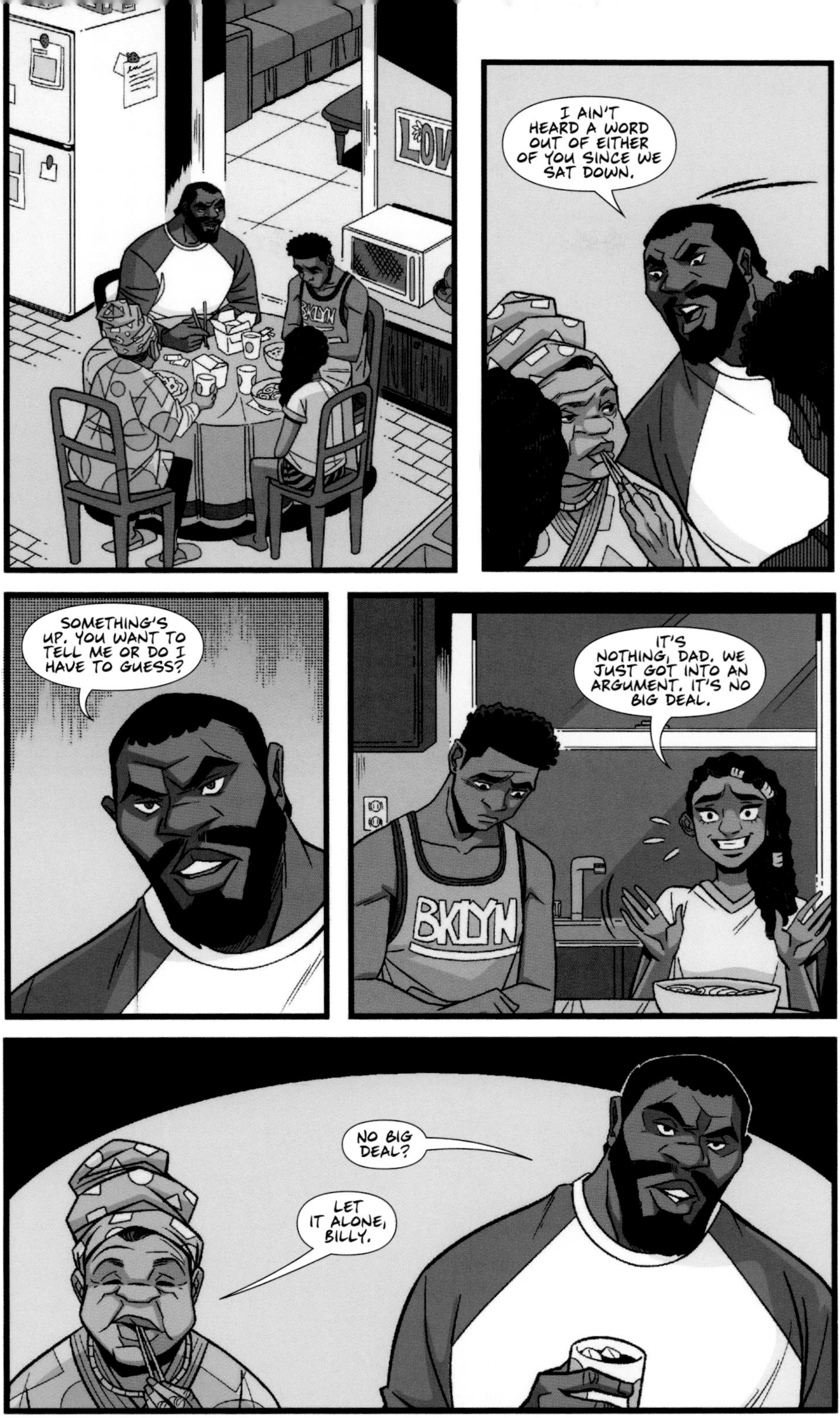
I AIN'T HEARD A WORD OUT OF EITHER OF YOU SINCE WE SAT DOWN.
SOMETHING'S UP. YOU WANT TO TELL ME OR DO I HAVE TO GUESS?
IT'S NOTHING, DAD. WE JUST GOT INTO AN ARGUMENT. IT'S NO BIG DEAL.
BKLYN
NO BIG DEAL?
LET IT ALONE, BILLY.

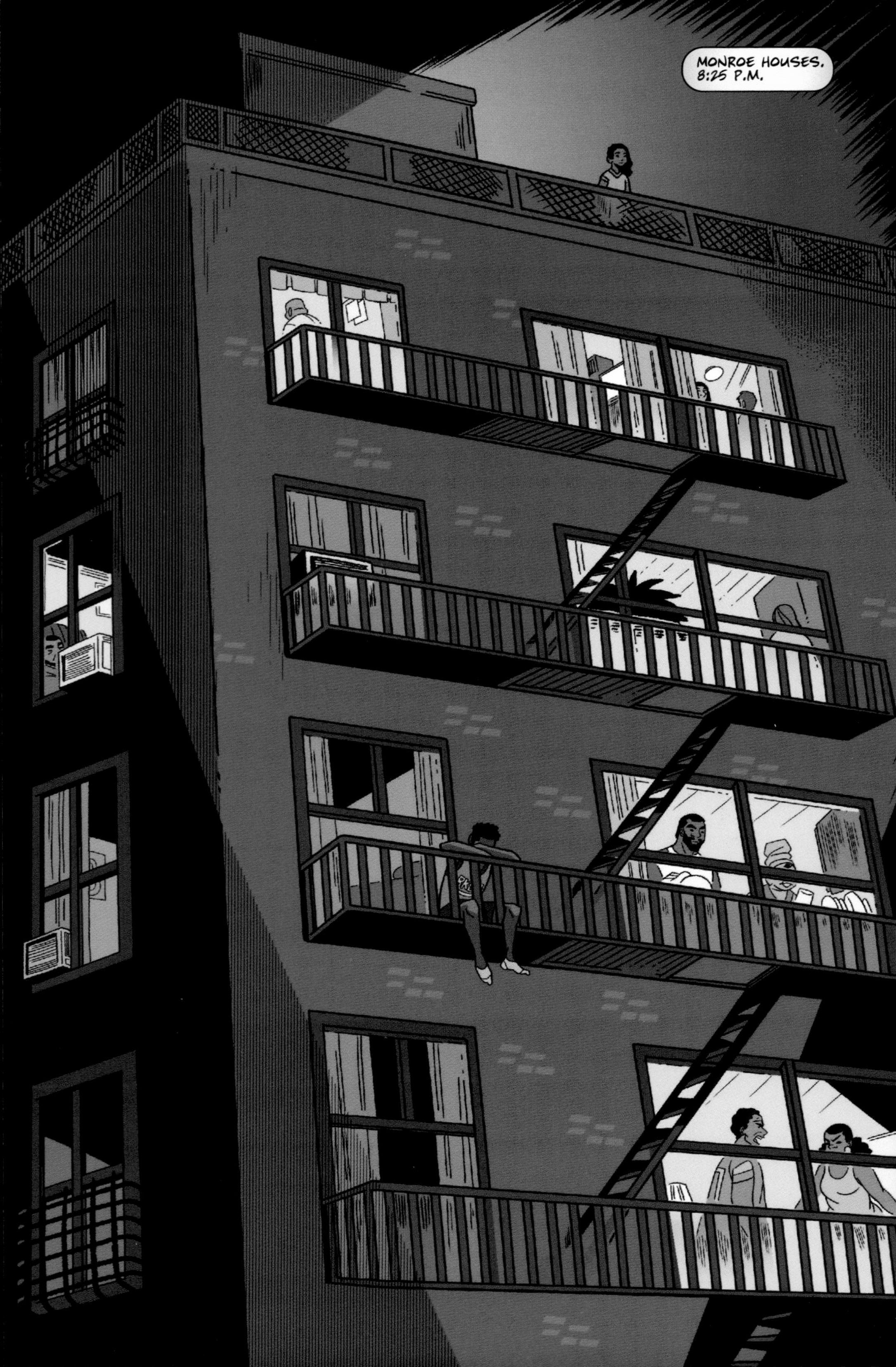
MONROE HOUSES.
8:25 P.M.

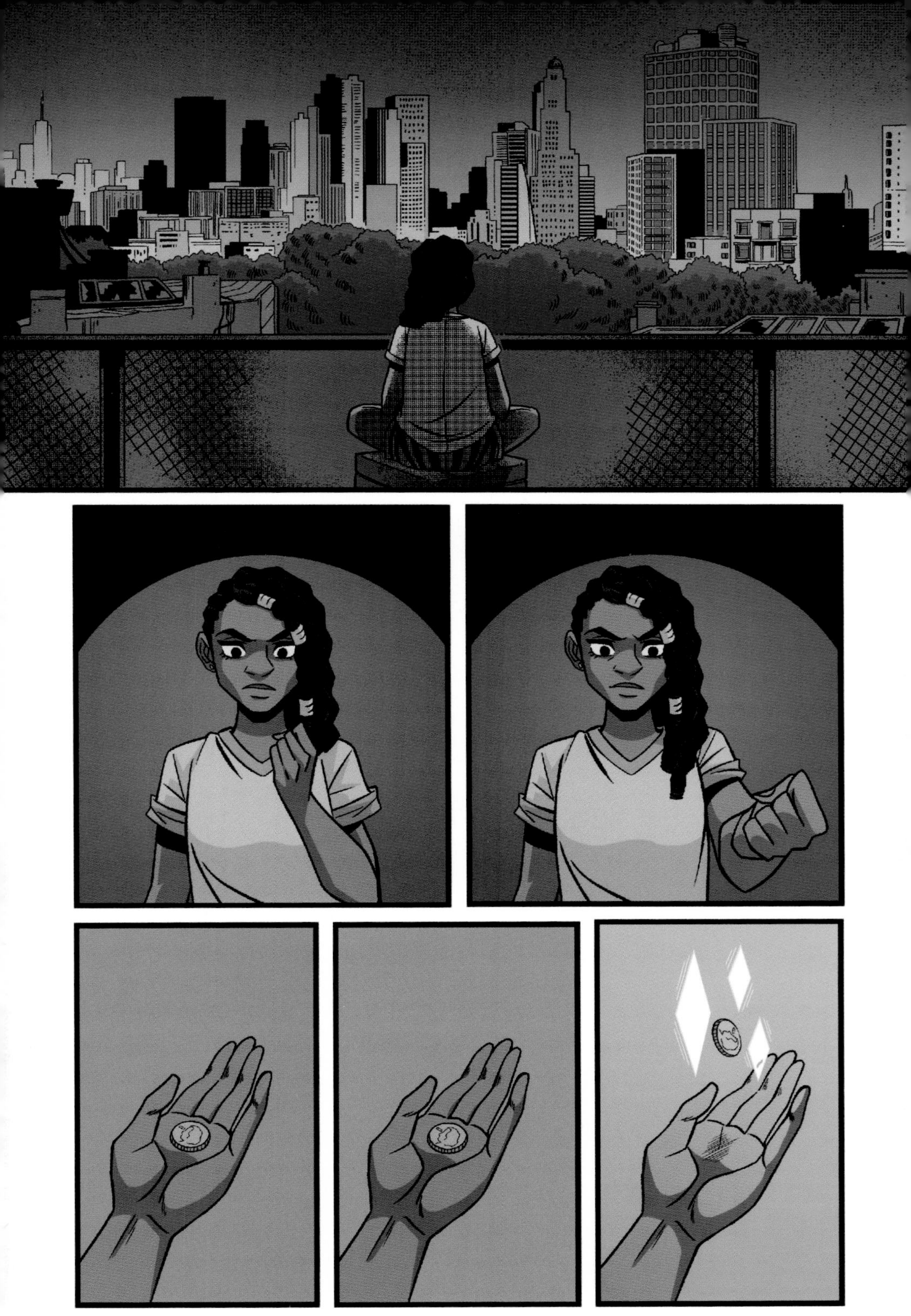

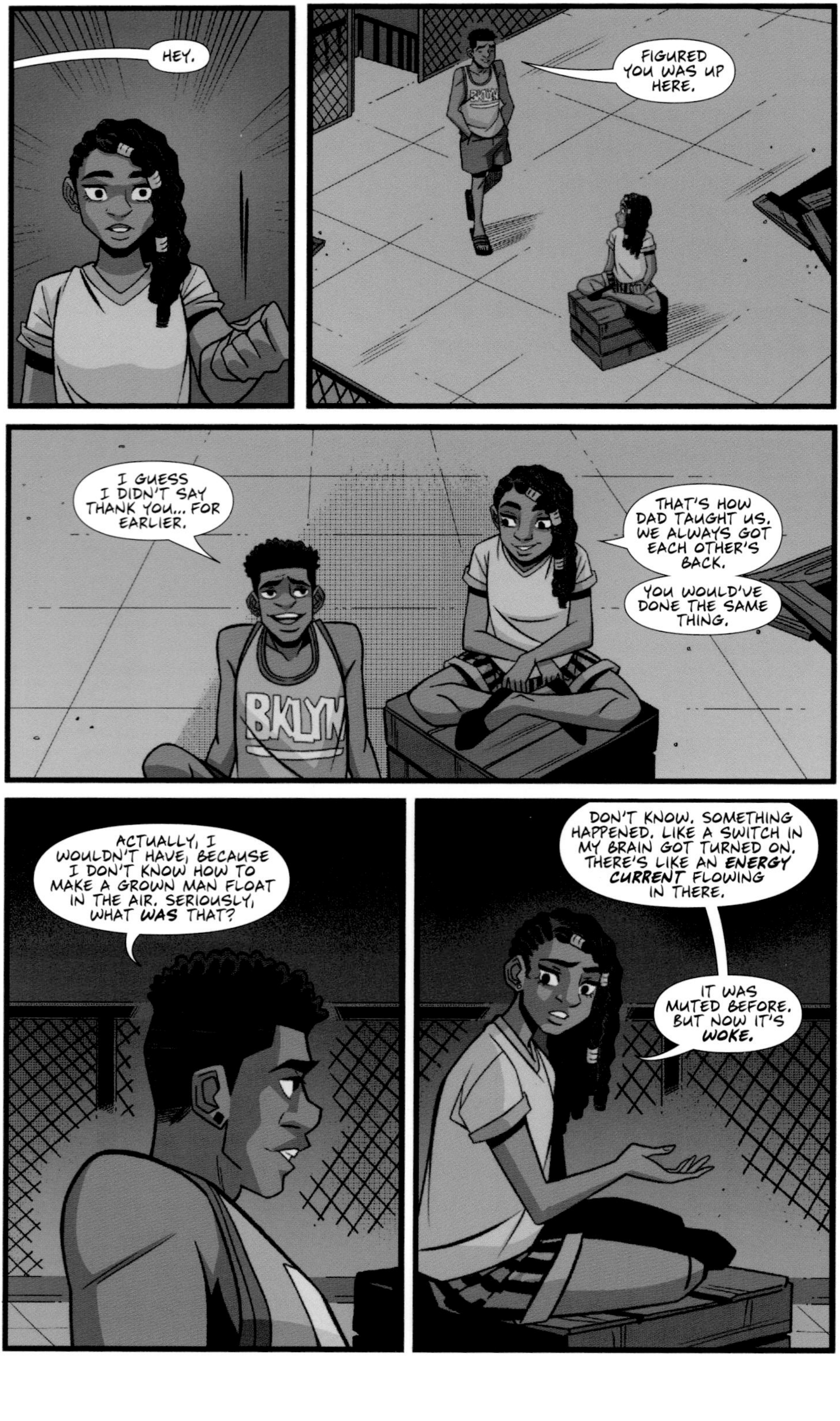
HEY.
FIGURED YOU WAS UP HERE.
I GUESS I DIDN'T SAY THANK YOU... FOR EARLIER.
THAT'S HOW DAD TAUGHT US. WE ALWAYS GOT EACH OTHER'S BACK.
YOU WOULD'VE DONE THE SAME THING.
ACTUALLY, I WOULDN'T HAVE, BECAUSE I DON'T KNOW HOW TO MAKE A GROWN MAN FLOAT IN THE AIR. SERIOUSLY, WHAT WAS THAT?
DON'T KNOW. SOMETHING HAPPENED. LIKE A SWITCH IN MY BRAIN GOT TURNED ON. THERE'S LIKE AN ENERGY CURRENT FLOWING IN THERE.
IT WAS MUTED BEFORE. BUT NOW IT'S WOKE.

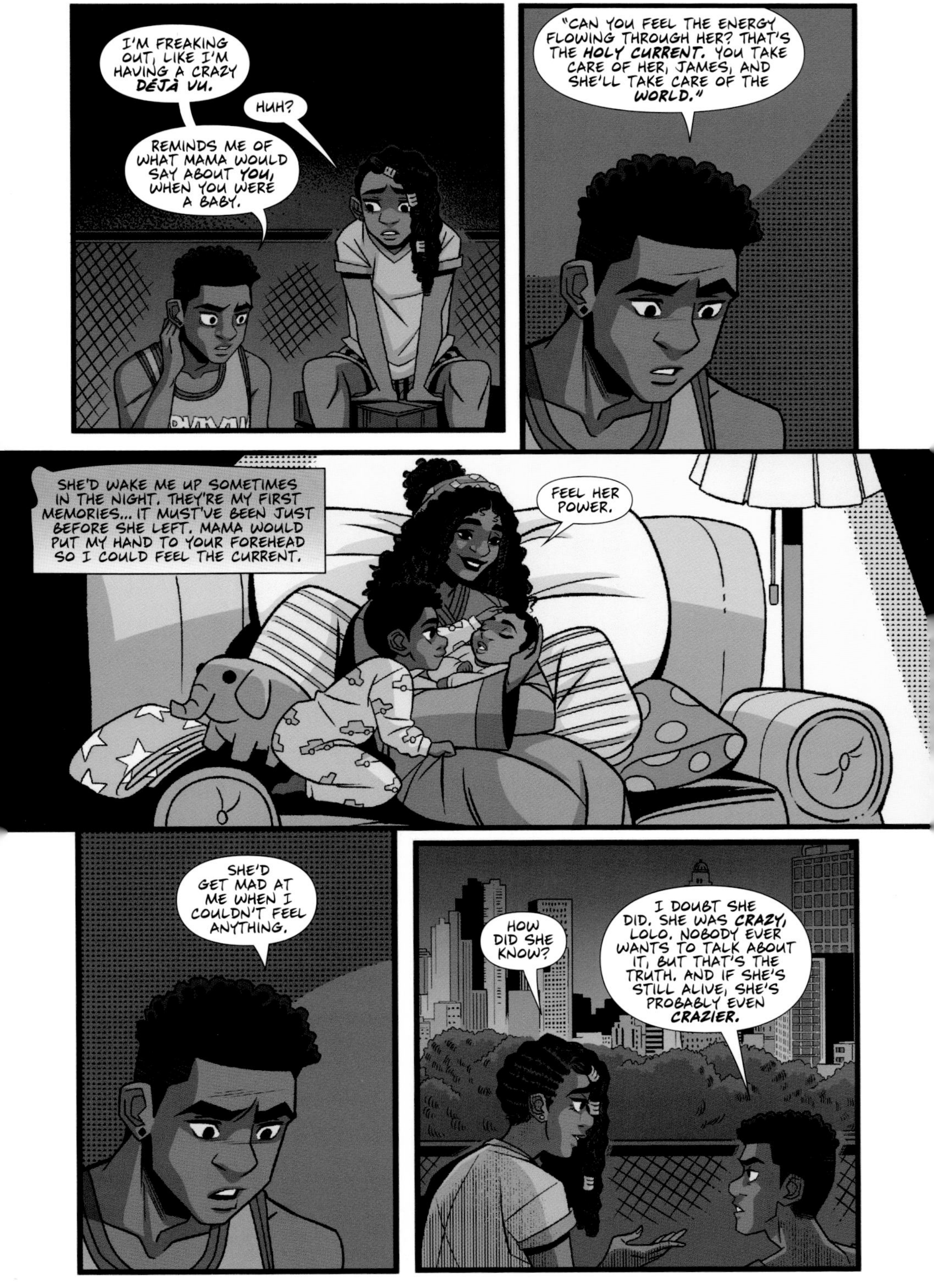
I'M FREAKING OUT, LIKE I'M HAVING A CRAZY DÉJÀ VU.
HUH?
REMINDS ME OF WHAT MAMA WOULD SAY ABOUT YOU, WHEN YOU WERE A BABY.
"CAN YOU FEEL THE ENERGY FLOWING THROUGH HER? THAT'S THE HOLY CURRENT. YOU TAKE CARE OF HER, JAMES, AND SHE'LL TAKE CARE OF THE WORLD."
SHE'D WAKE ME UP SOMETIMES IN THE NIGHT. THEY'RE MY FIRST MEMORIES... IT MUST'VE BEEN JUST BEFORE SHE LEFT. MAMA WOULD PUT MY HAND TO YOUR FOREHEAD SO I COULD FEEL THE CURRENT.
FEEL HER POWER.
SHE'D GET MAD AT ME WHEN I COULDN'T FEEL ANYTHING.
HOW DID SHE KNOW?
I DOUBT SHE DID. SHE WAS CRAZY, LOLO. NOBODY EVER WANTS TO TALK ABOUT IT, BUT THAT'S THE TRUTH. AND IF SHE'S STILL ALIVE, SHE'S PROBABLY EVEN CRAZIER.

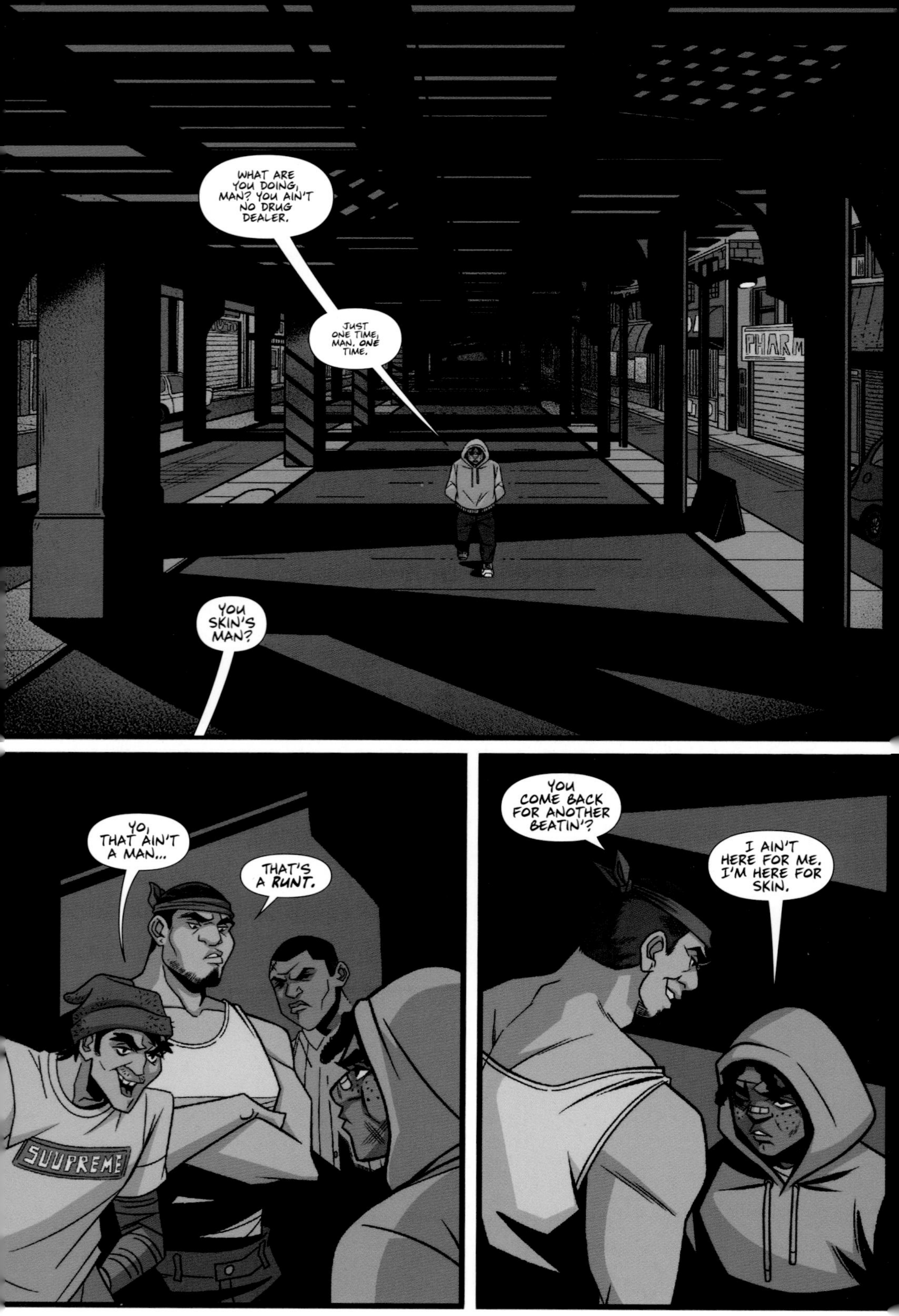
WHAT ARE YOU DOING, MAN? YOU AIN'T NO DRUG DEALER.
JUST ONE TIME, MAN. ONE TIME.
PHAR
YOU SKIN'S MAN?
YO, THAT AIN'T A MAN...
THAT'S A RUNT.
SUUPREME
YOU COME BACK FOR ANOTHER BEATIN'?
I AIN'T HERE FOR ME. I'M HERE FOR SKIN.

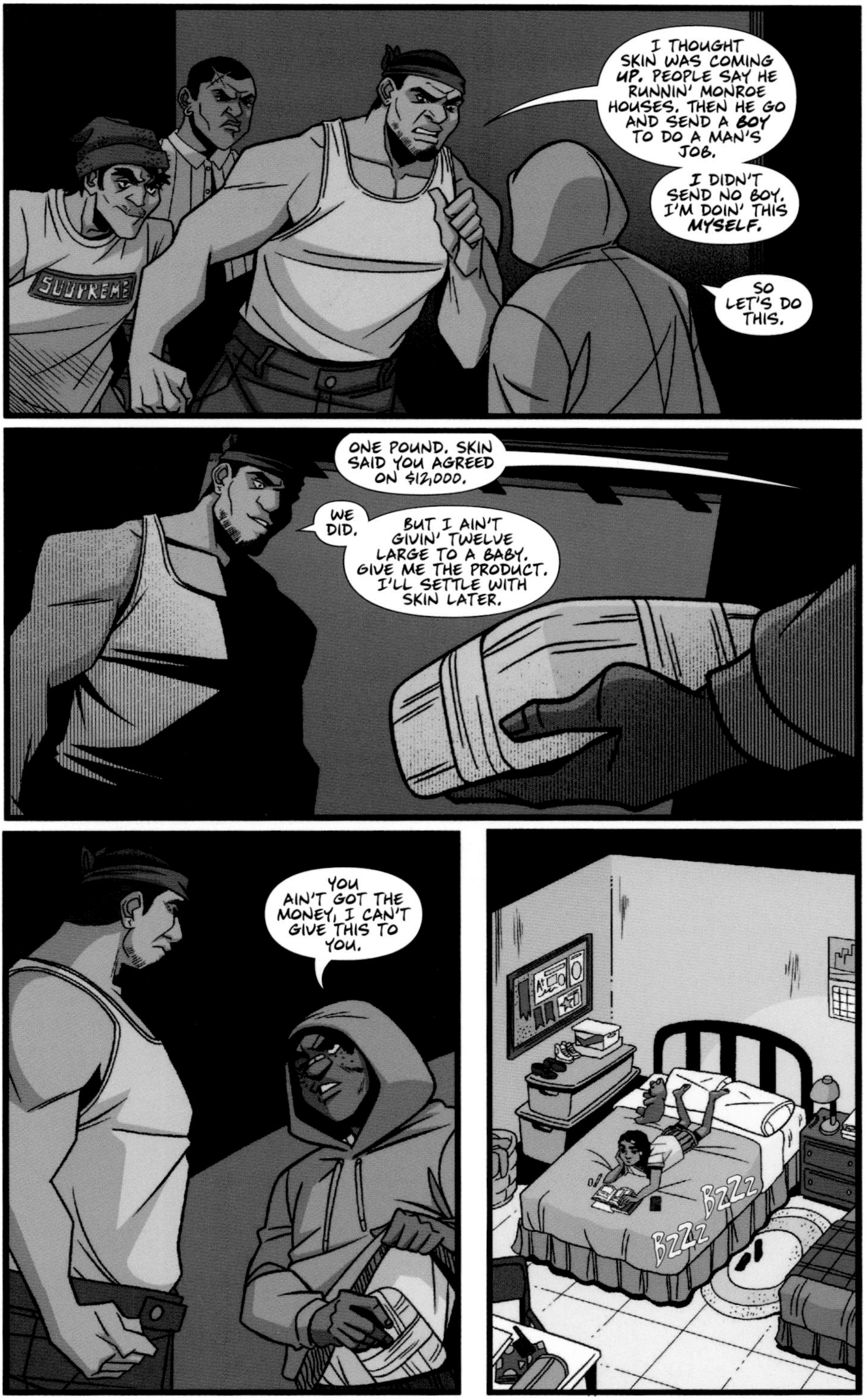
I THOUGHT SKIN WAS COMING UP. PEOPLE SAY HE RUNNIN' MONROE HOUSES. THEN HE GO AND SEND A BOY TO DO A MAN'S JOB.
I DIDN'T SEND NO BOY. I'M DOIN' THIS MYSELF.
SO LET'S DO THIS.
ONE POUND. SKIN SAID YOU AGREED ON $12,000.
WE DID.
BUT I AIN'T GIVIN' TWELVE LARGE TO A BABY. GIVE ME THE PRODUCT. I'LL SETTLE WITH SKIN LATER.
YOU AIN'T GOT THE MONEY, I CAN'T GIVE THIS TO YOU.
BZZZ
BZZZ

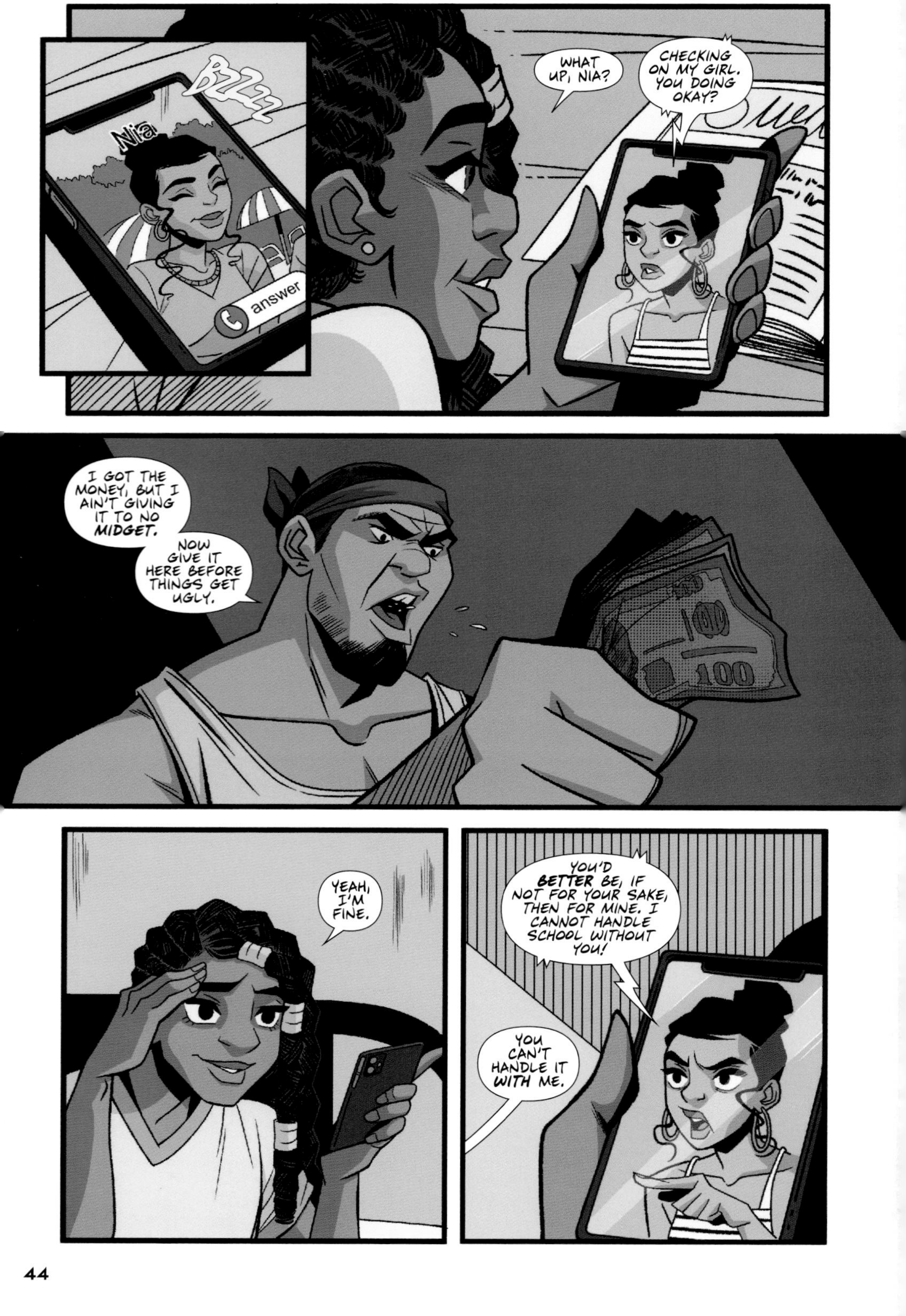
BZZZZ
Nia
answer
WHAT UP, NIA?
CHECKING ON MY GIRL. YOU DOING OKAY?
I GOT THE MONEY, BUT I AIN'T GIVING IT TO NO MIDGET.
NOW GIVE IT HERE BEFORE THINGS GET UGLY.
100
YEAH, I'M FINE.
YOU'D BETTER BE, IF NOT FOR YOUR SAKE, THEN FOR MINE. I CANNOT HANDLE SCHOOL WITHOUT YOU!
YOU CAN'T HANDLE IT WITH ME.

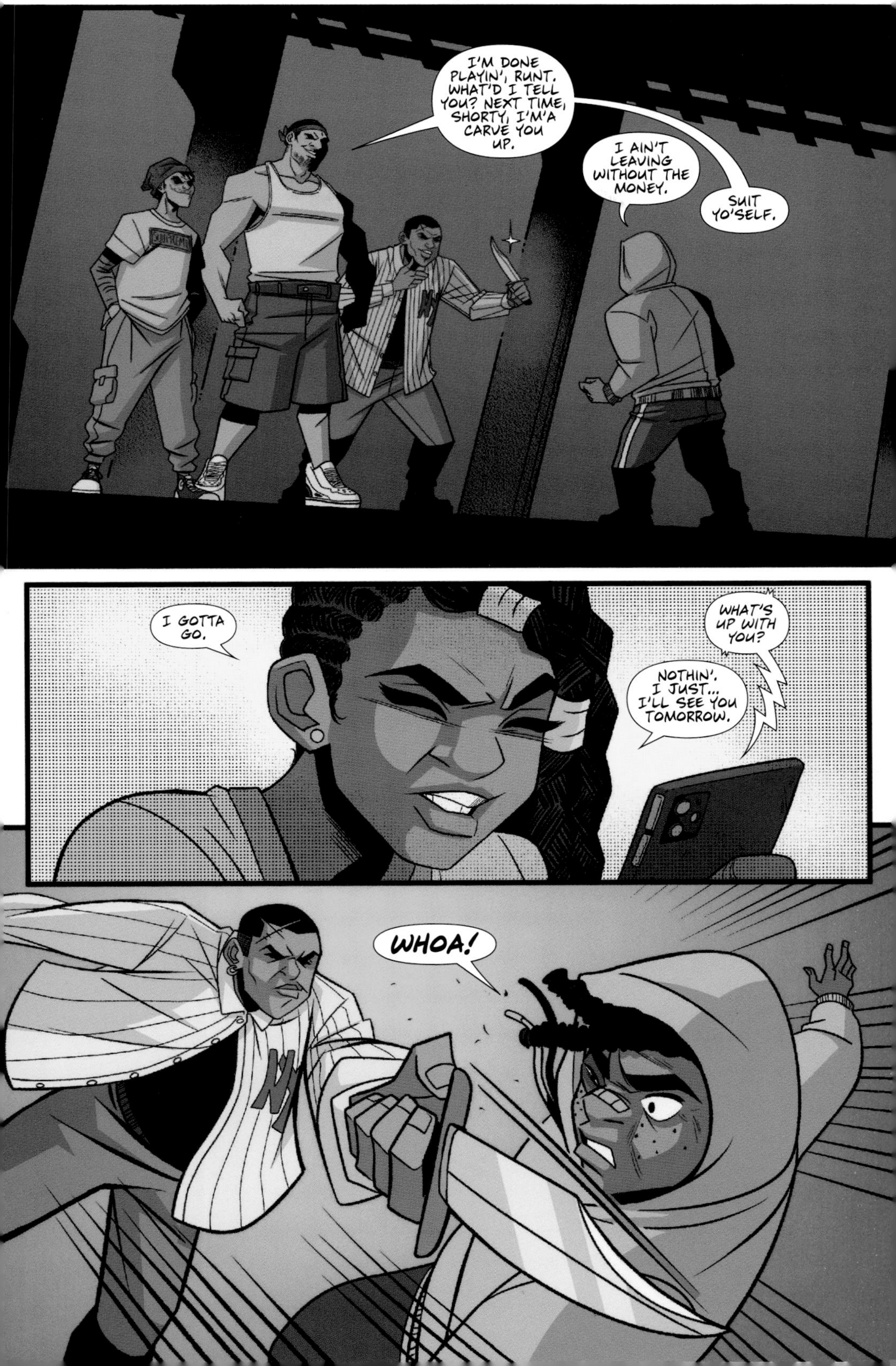
I'M DONE PLAYIN', RUNT. WHAT'D I TELL YOU? NEXT TIME, SHORTY, I'M'A CARVE YOU UP.
I AIN'T LEAVING WITHOUT THE MONEY.
SUIT YO'SELF.
I GOTTA GO.
WHAT'S UP WITH YOU?
NOTHIN'. I JUST... I'LL SEE YOU TOMORROW.
WHOA!

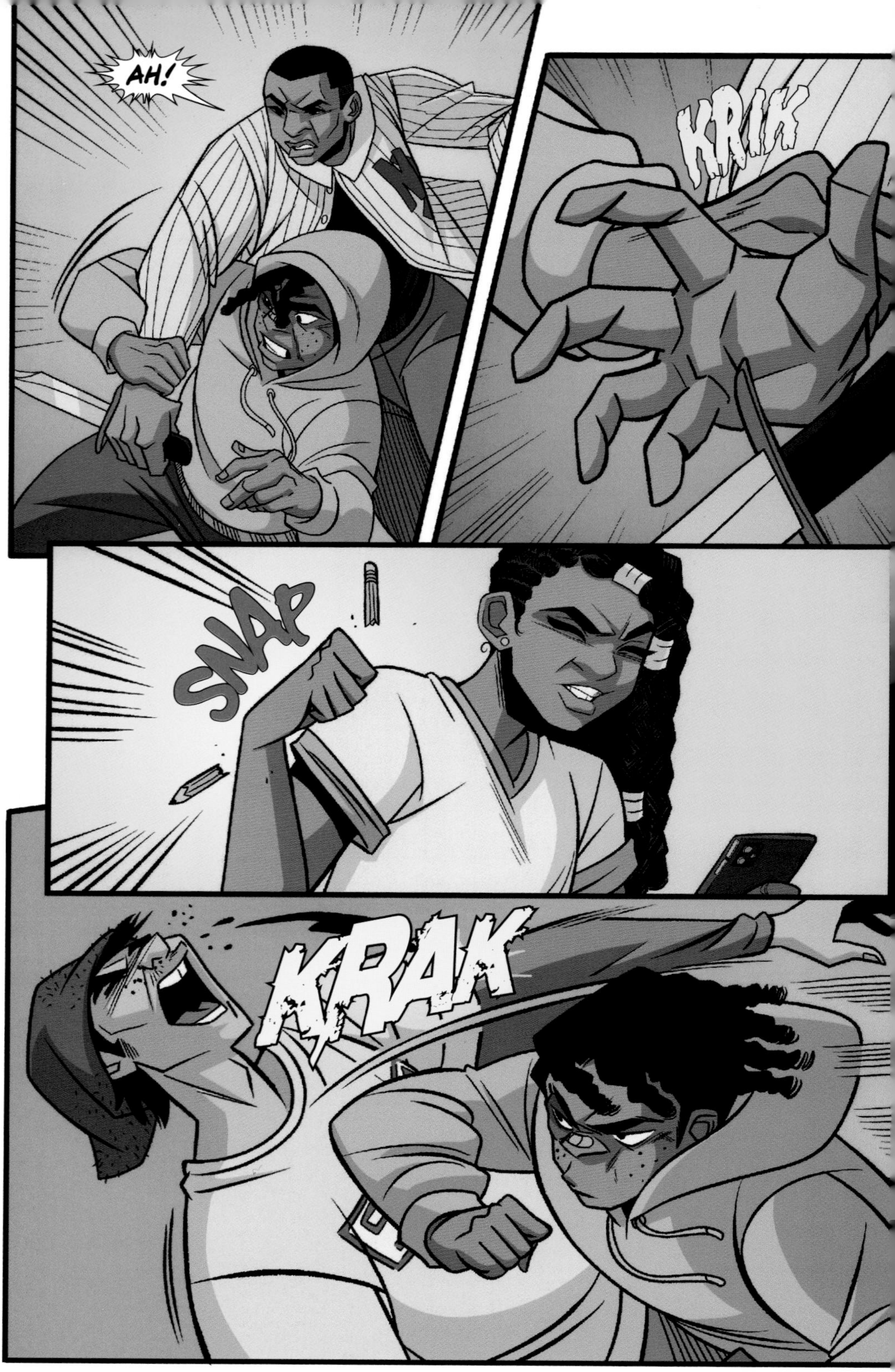
AH!
KRIK
SNAP
KRAK

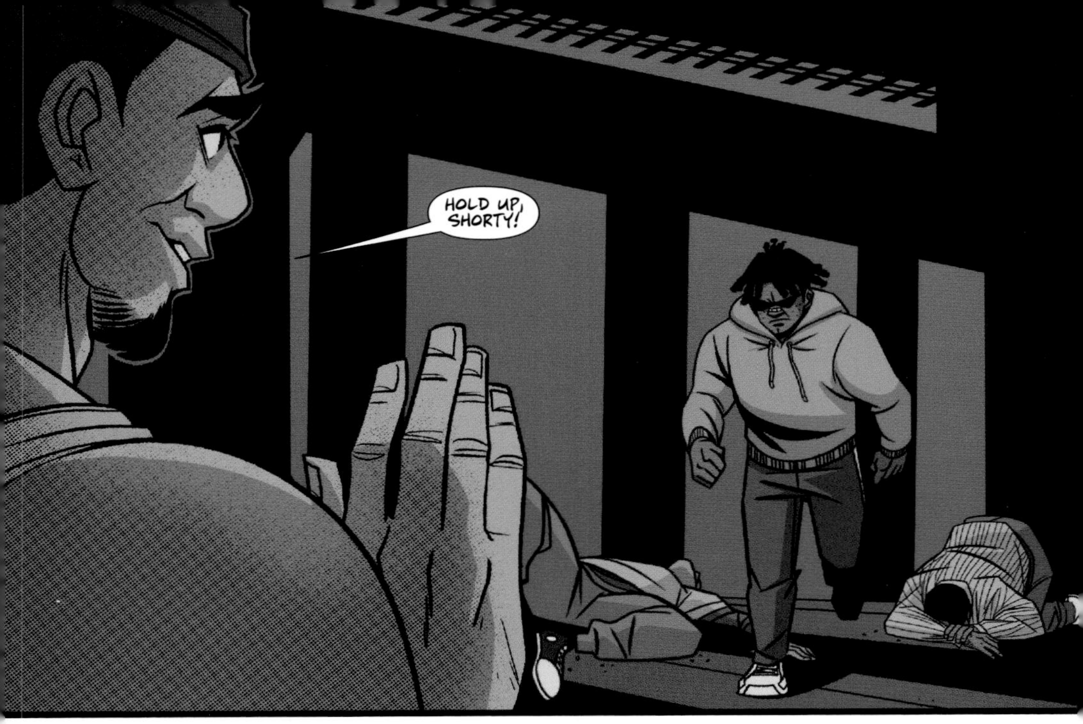
HOLD UP, SHORTY!

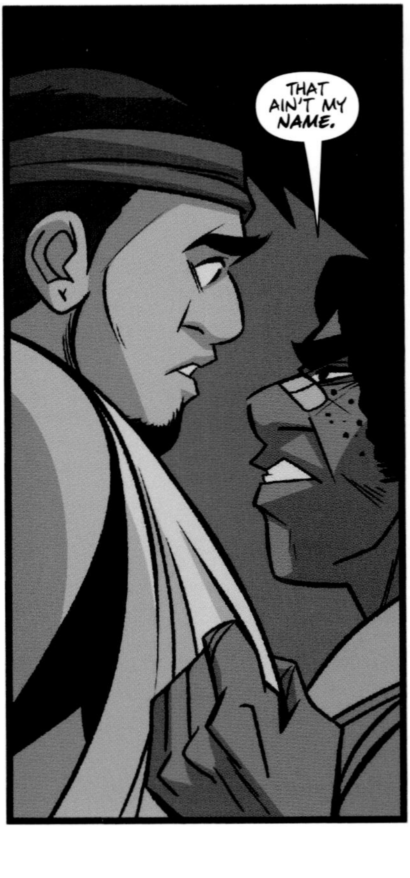
THAT AIN'T MY NAME.

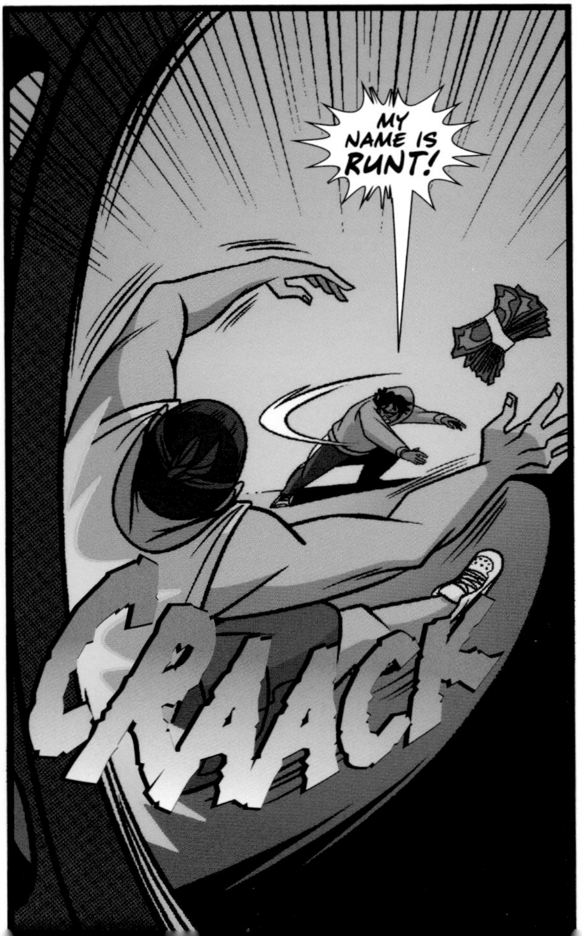
MY NAME IS RUNT!
CRAACK

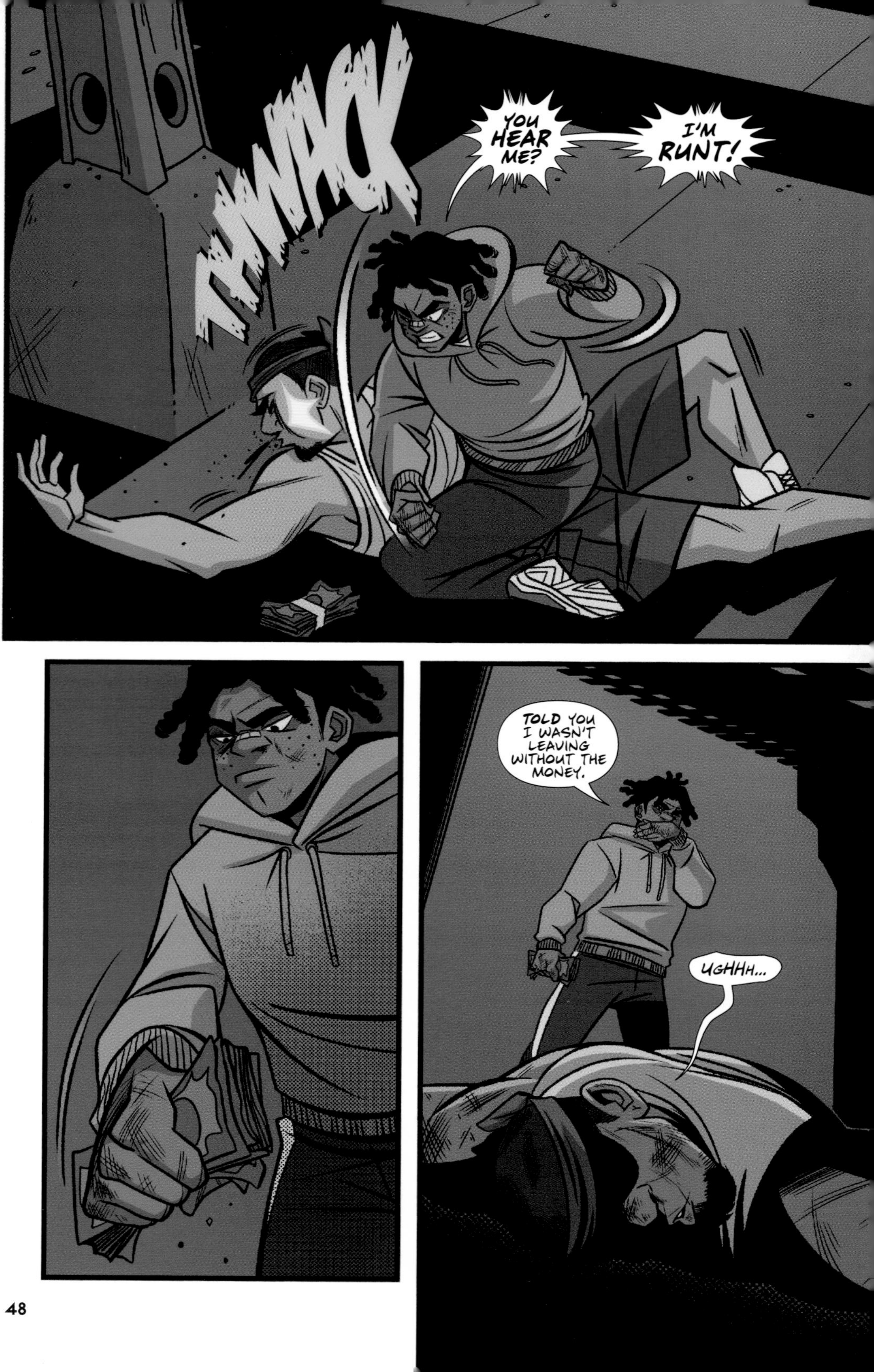
THWACK
YOU HEAR ME?
I'M RUNT!
TOLD YOU I WASN'T LEAVING WITHOUT THE MONEY.
UGHHH...

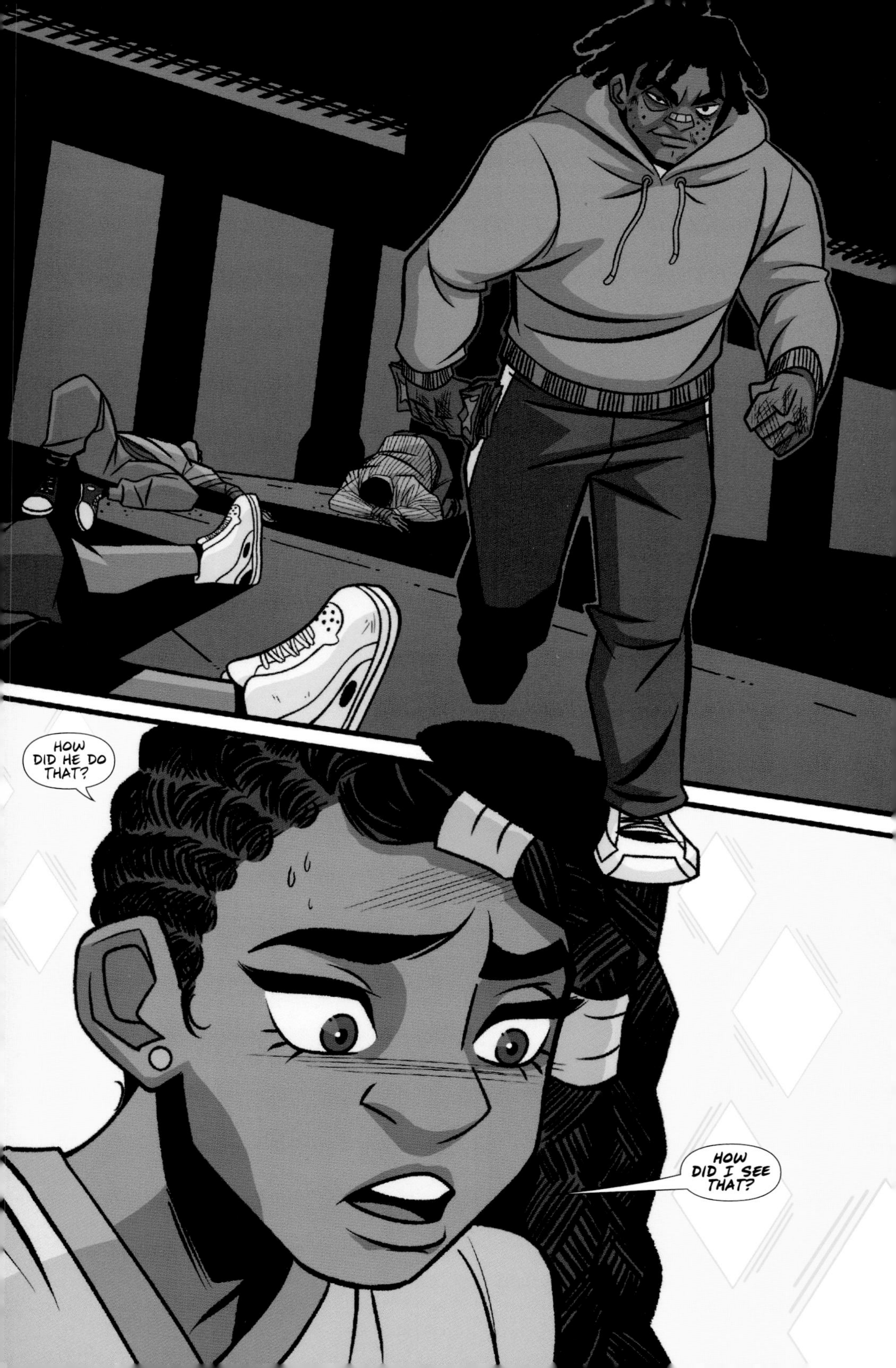
HOW DID HE DO THAT?
HOW DID I SEE THAT?

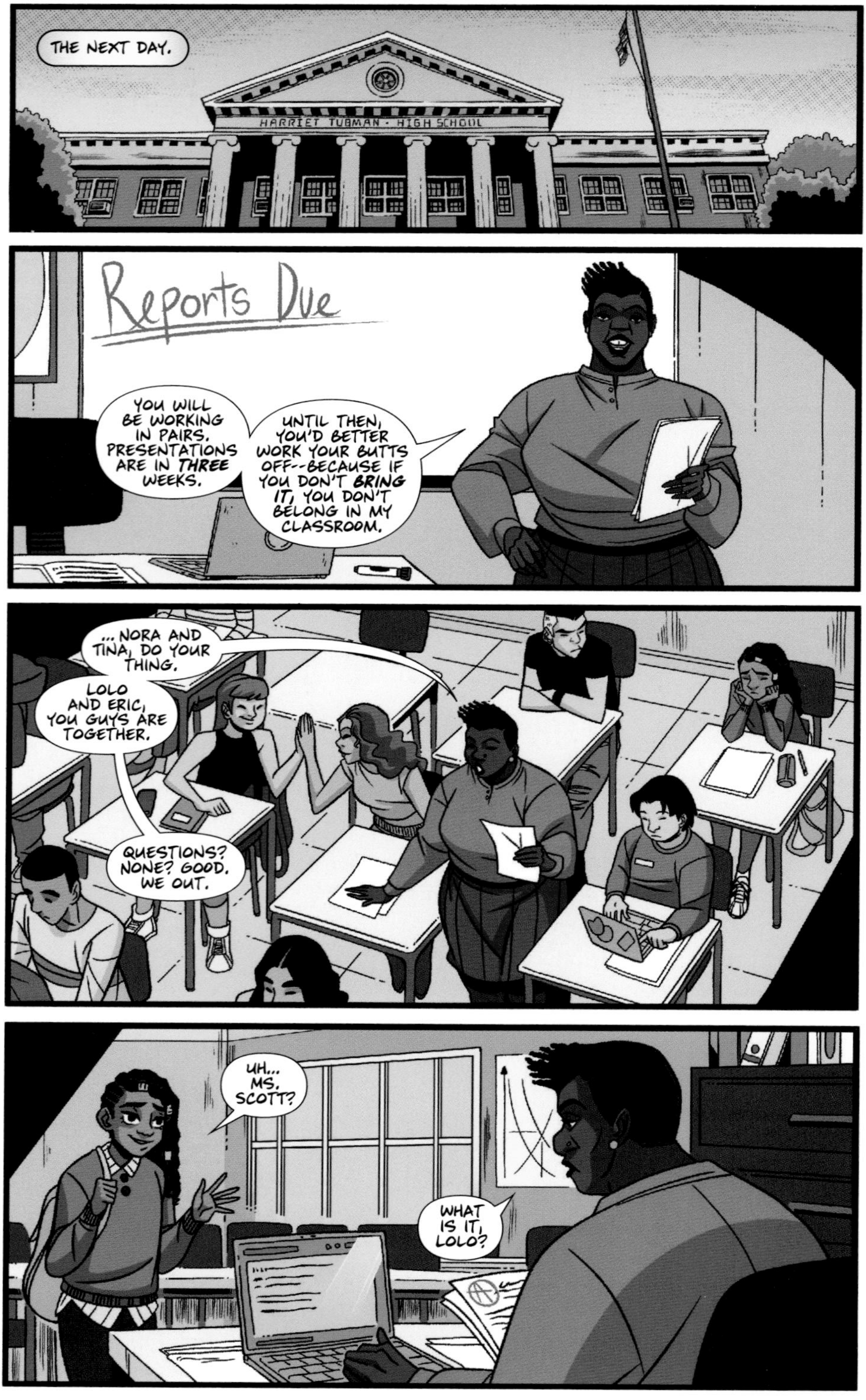
THE NEXT DAY.
HARRIET TUBMAN · HIGH SCHOOL
Reports Due
YOU WILL BE WORKING IN PAIRS. PRESENTATIONS ARE IN *THREE* WEEKS.
UNTIL THEN, YOU'D BETTER WORK YOUR BUTTS OFF--BECAUSE IF YOU DON'T *BRING IT,* YOU DON'T BELONG IN MY CLASSROOM.
...NORA AND TINA, DO YOUR THING.
LOLO AND ERIC, YOU GUYS ARE TOGETHER.
QUESTIONS? NONE? GOOD. WE OUT.
UH... MS. SCOTT?
WHAT IS IT, LOLO?

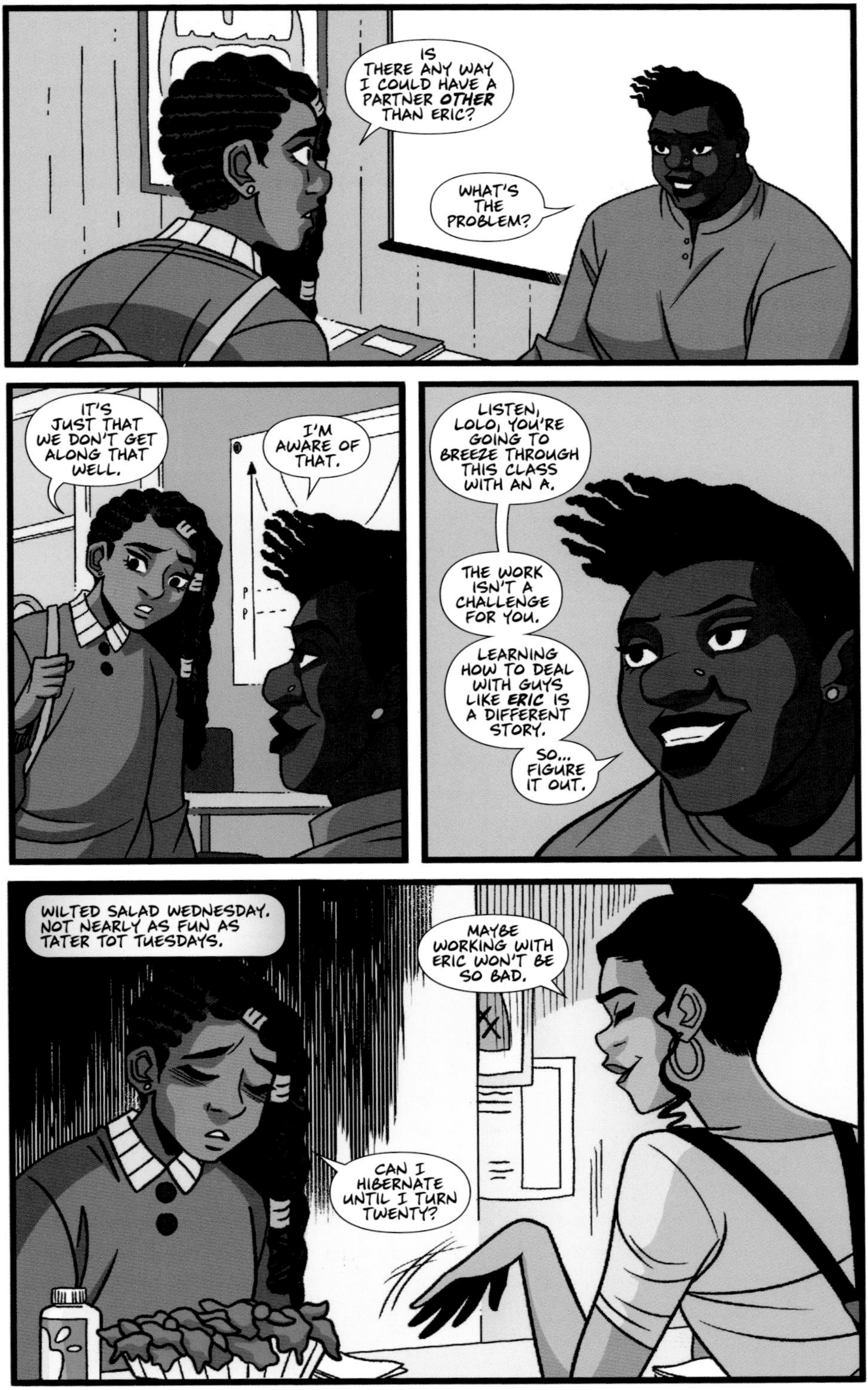
IS THERE ANY WAY I COULD HAVE A PARTNER OTHER THAN ERIC?
WHAT'S THE PROBLEM?
IT'S JUST THAT WE DON'T GET ALONG THAT WELL.
I'M AWARE OF THAT.
LISTEN, LOLO, YOU'RE GOING TO BREEZE THROUGH THIS CLASS WITH AN A.
THE WORK ISN'T A CHALLENGE FOR YOU.
LEARNING HOW TO DEAL WITH GUYS LIKE ERIC IS A DIFFERENT STORY.
SO... FIGURE IT OUT.
WILTED SALAD WEDNESDAY. NOT NEARLY AS FUN AS TATER TOT TUESDAYS.
MAYBE WORKING WITH ERIC WON'T BE SO BAD.
CAN I HIBERNATE UNTIL I TURN TWENTY?

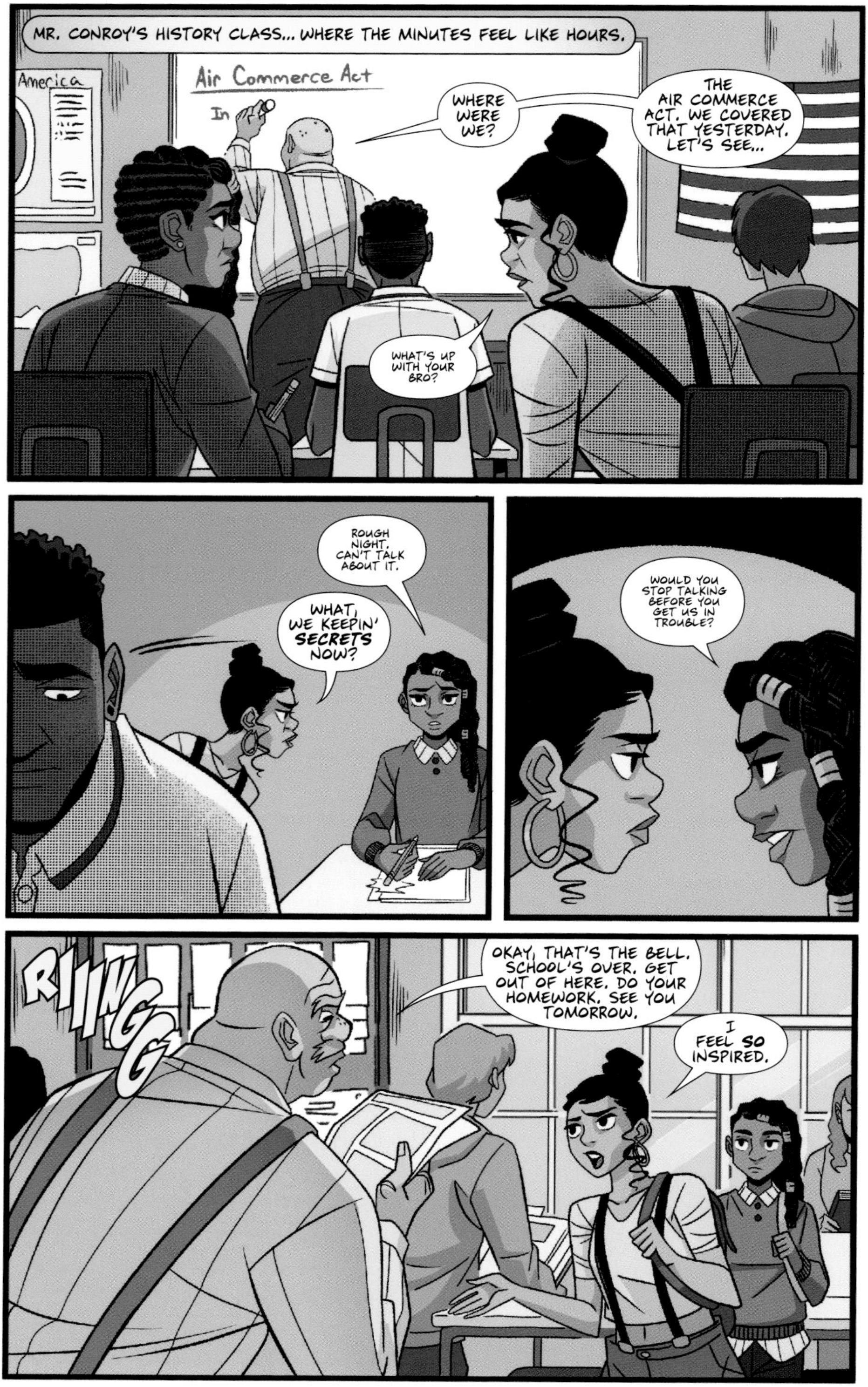
MR. CONROY'S HISTORY CLASS... WHERE THE MINUTES FEEL LIKE HOURS.
America
Air Commerce Act
In
WHERE WERE WE?
THE AIR COMMERCE ACT. WE COVERED THAT YESTERDAY. LET'S SEE...
WHAT'S UP WITH YOUR BRO?
ROUGH NIGHT. CAN'T TALK ABOUT IT.
WHAT, WE KEEPIN' **SECRETS** NOW?
WOULD YOU STOP TALKING BEFORE YOU GET US IN TROUBLE?
RIIINGG
OKAY, THAT'S THE BELL. SCHOOL'S OVER. GET OUT OF HERE. DO YOUR HOMEWORK. SEE YOU TOMORROW.
I FEEL **SO** INSPIRED.

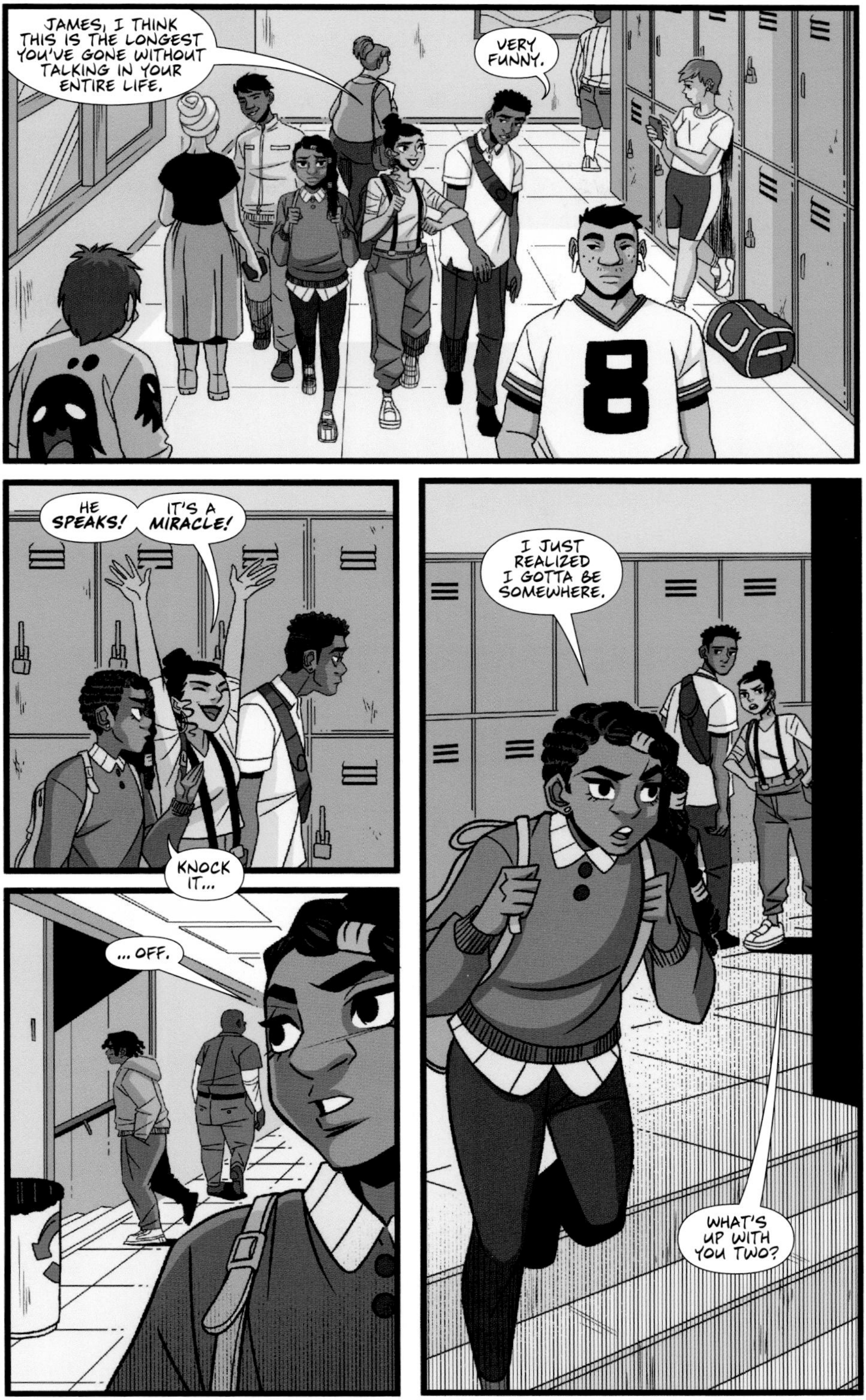
JAMES, I THINK THIS IS THE LONGEST YOU'VE GONE WITHOUT TALKING IN YOUR ENTIRE LIFE.
VERY FUNNY.
HE SPEAKS!
IT'S A MIRACLE!
KNOCK IT...
...OFF.
I JUST REALIZED I GOTTA BE SOMEWHERE.
WHAT'S UP WITH YOU TWO?

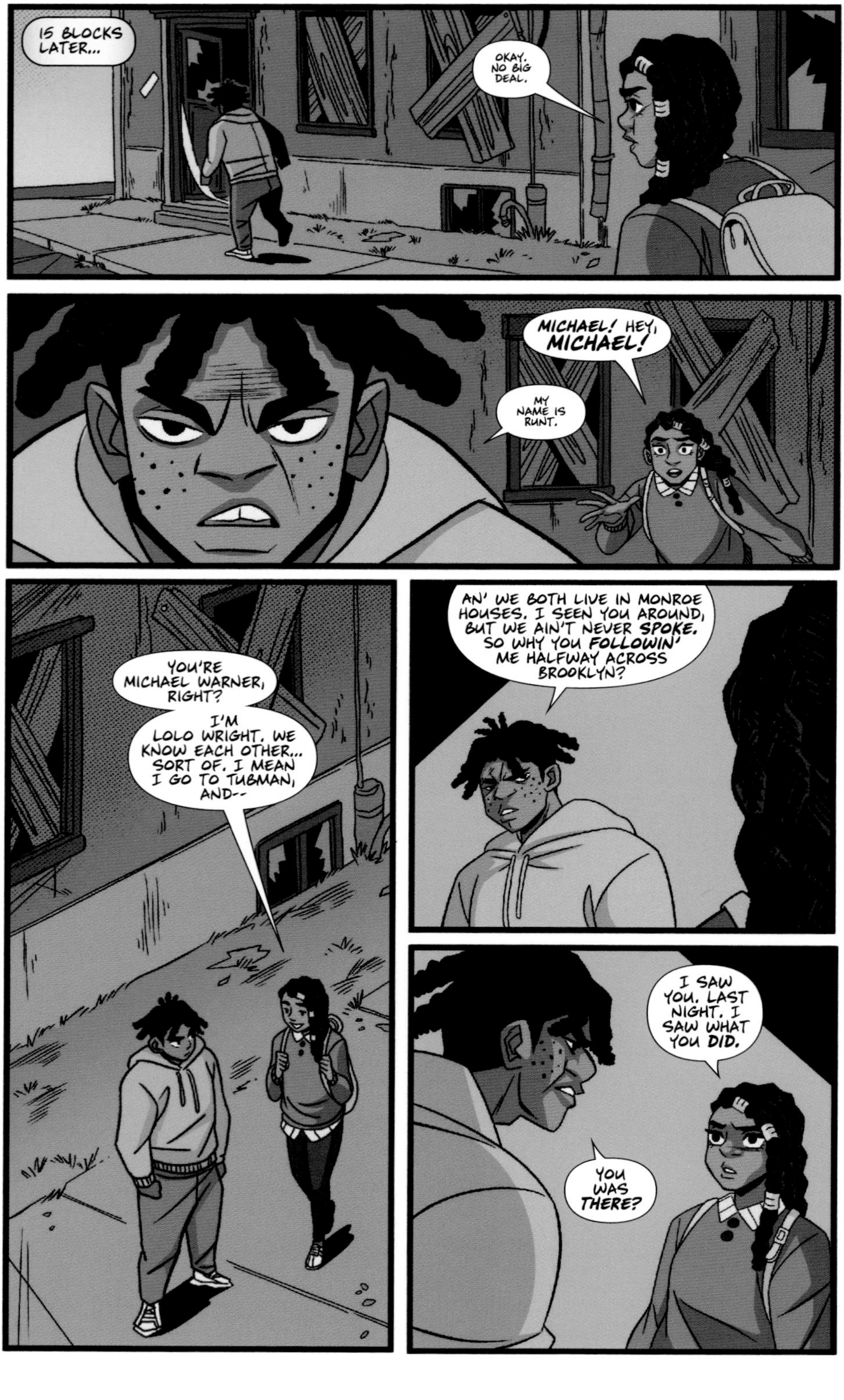
15 BLOCKS LATER...
OKAY. NO BIG DEAL.
MICHAEL! HEY, MICHAEL!
MY NAME IS RUNT.
YOU'RE MICHAEL WARNER, RIGHT?
I'M LOLO WRIGHT. WE KNOW EACH OTHER... SORT OF. I MEAN I GO TO TUBMAN, AND--
AN' WE BOTH LIVE IN MONROE HOUSES. I SEEN YOU AROUND, BUT WE AIN'T NEVER SPOKE. SO WHY YOU FOLLOWIN' ME HALFWAY ACROSS BROOKLYN?
I SAW YOU. LAST NIGHT. I SAW WHAT YOU DID.
YOU WAS THERE?

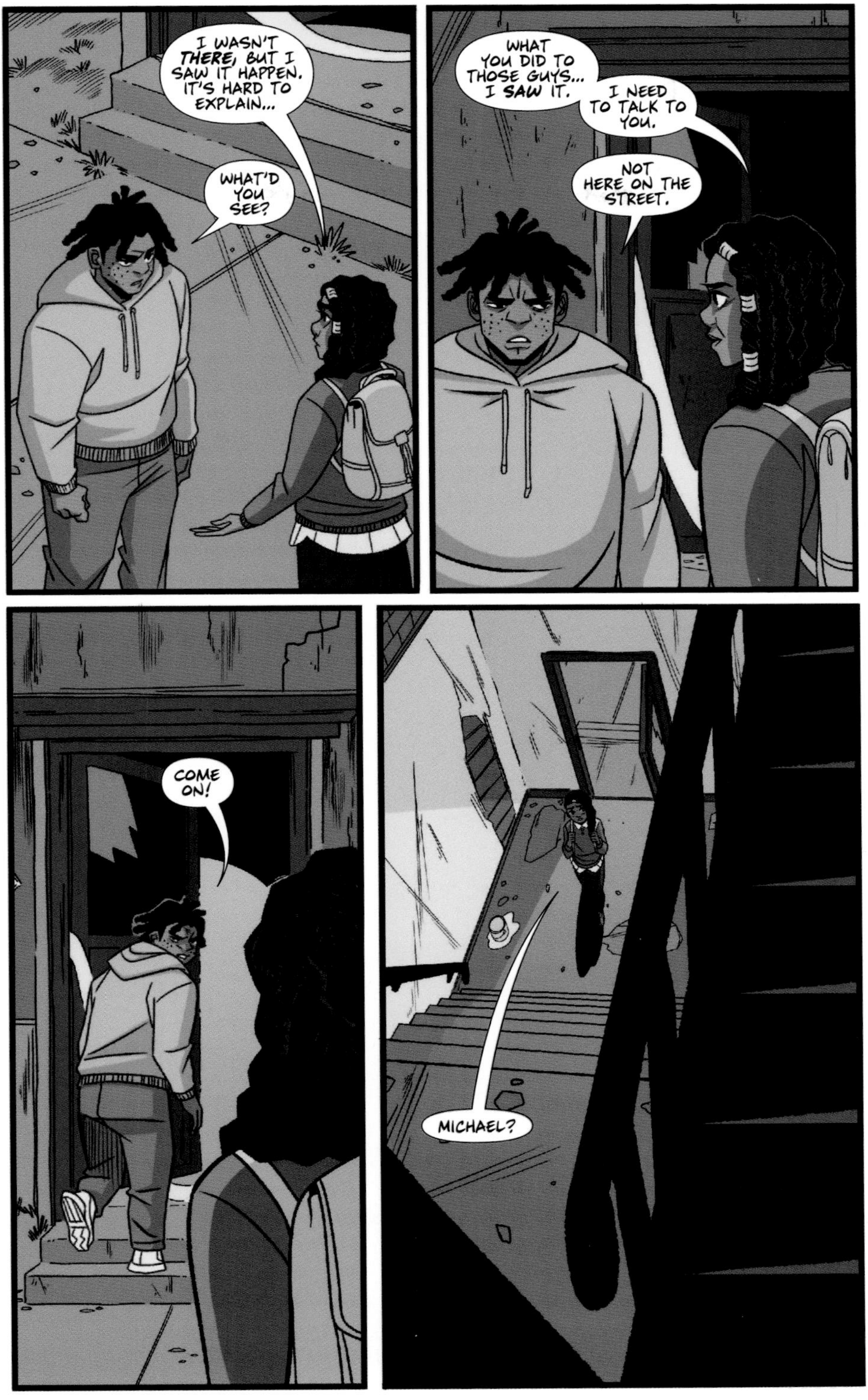
I WASN'T THERE, BUT I SAW IT HAPPEN. IT'S HARD TO EXPLAIN...
WHAT'D YOU SEE?
WHAT YOU DID TO THOSE GUYS... I SAW IT.
I NEED TO TALK TO YOU.
NOT HERE ON THE STREET.
COME ON!
MICHAEL?

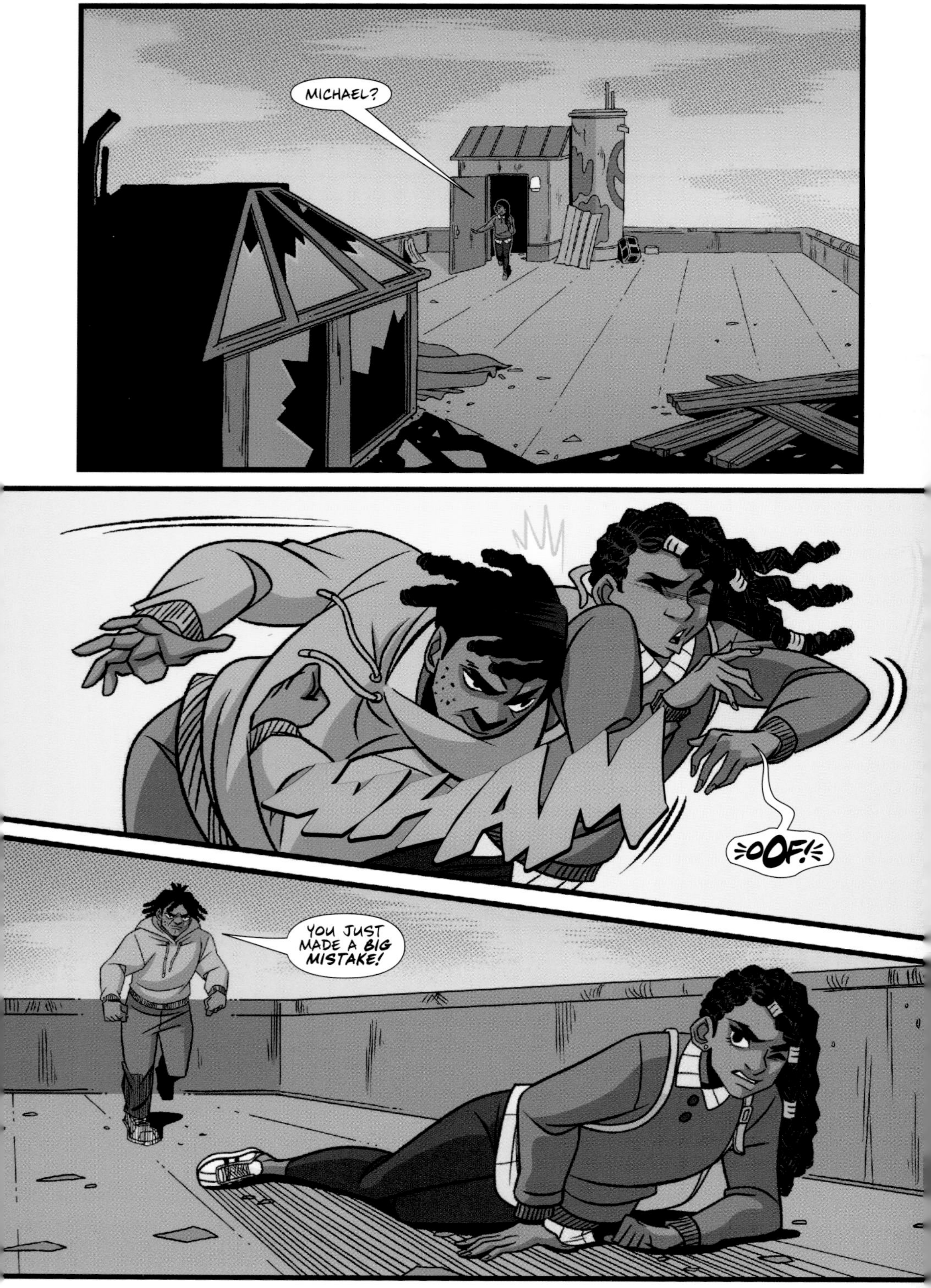
MICHAEL?
WHAM
OOF!
YOU JUST MADE A BIG MISTAKE!

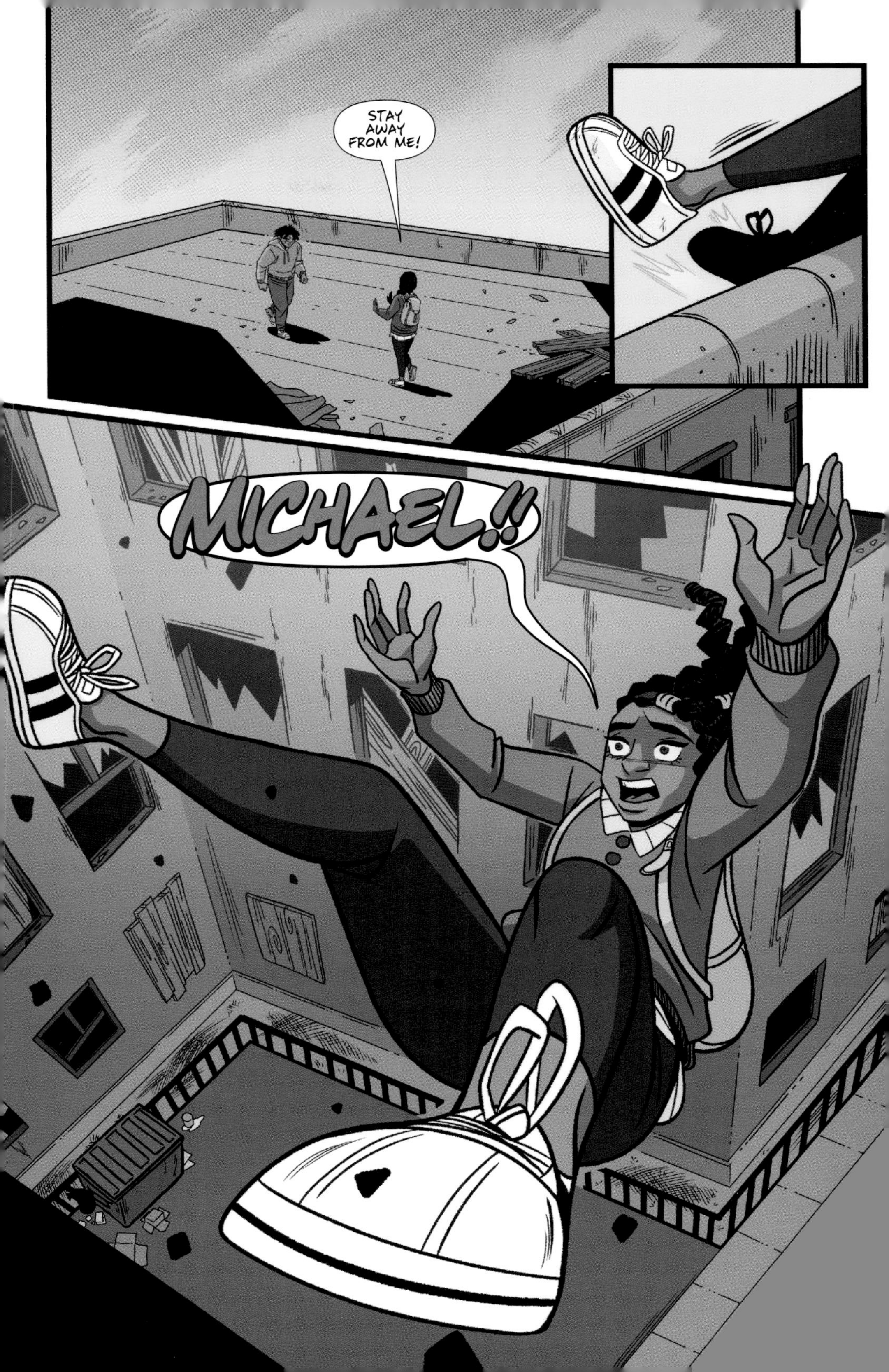
STAY AWAY FROM ME!
MICHAEL.!!

CHAPTER 3

YOU DON'T KNOW MY NAME

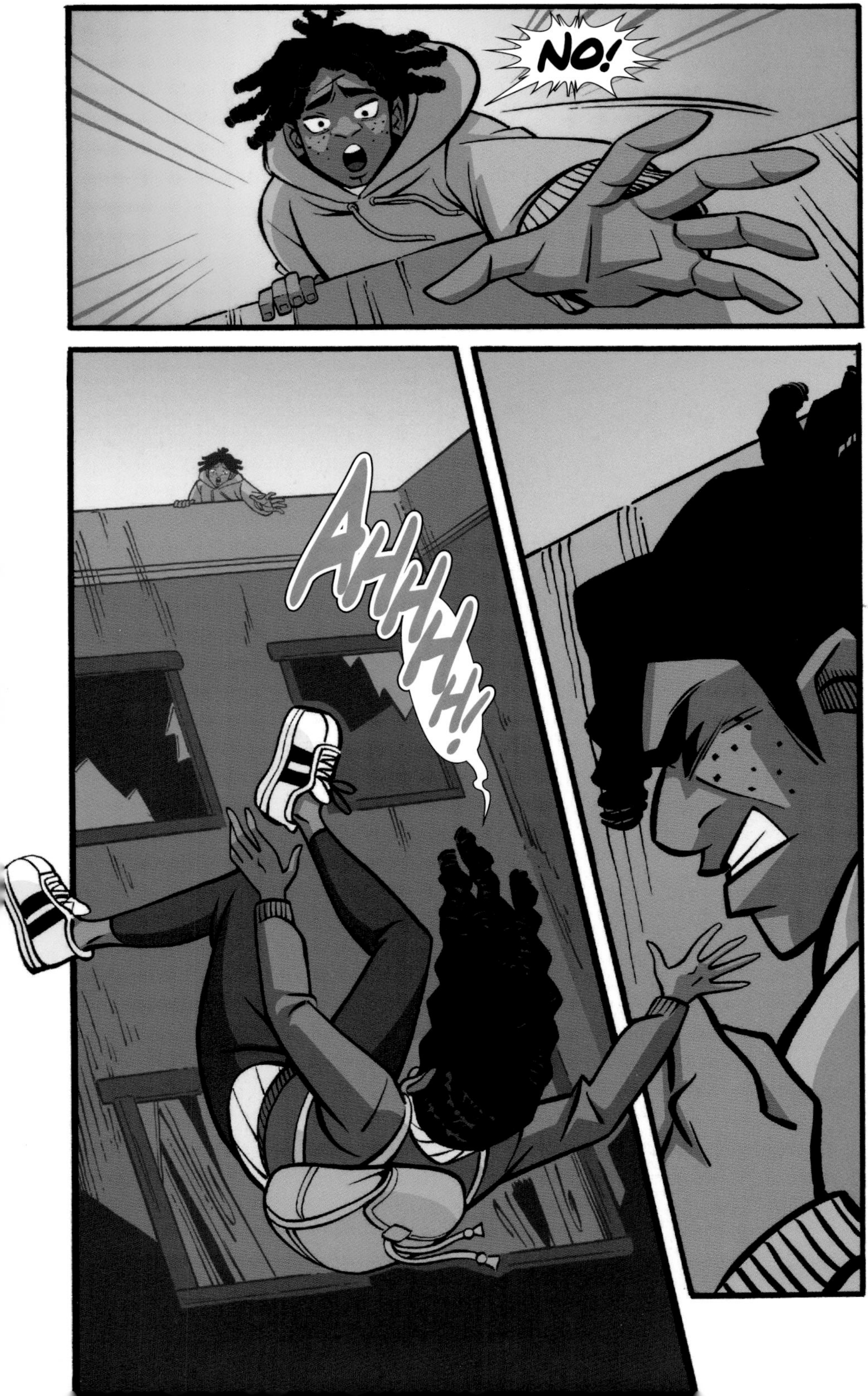
NO!
AHHHH!

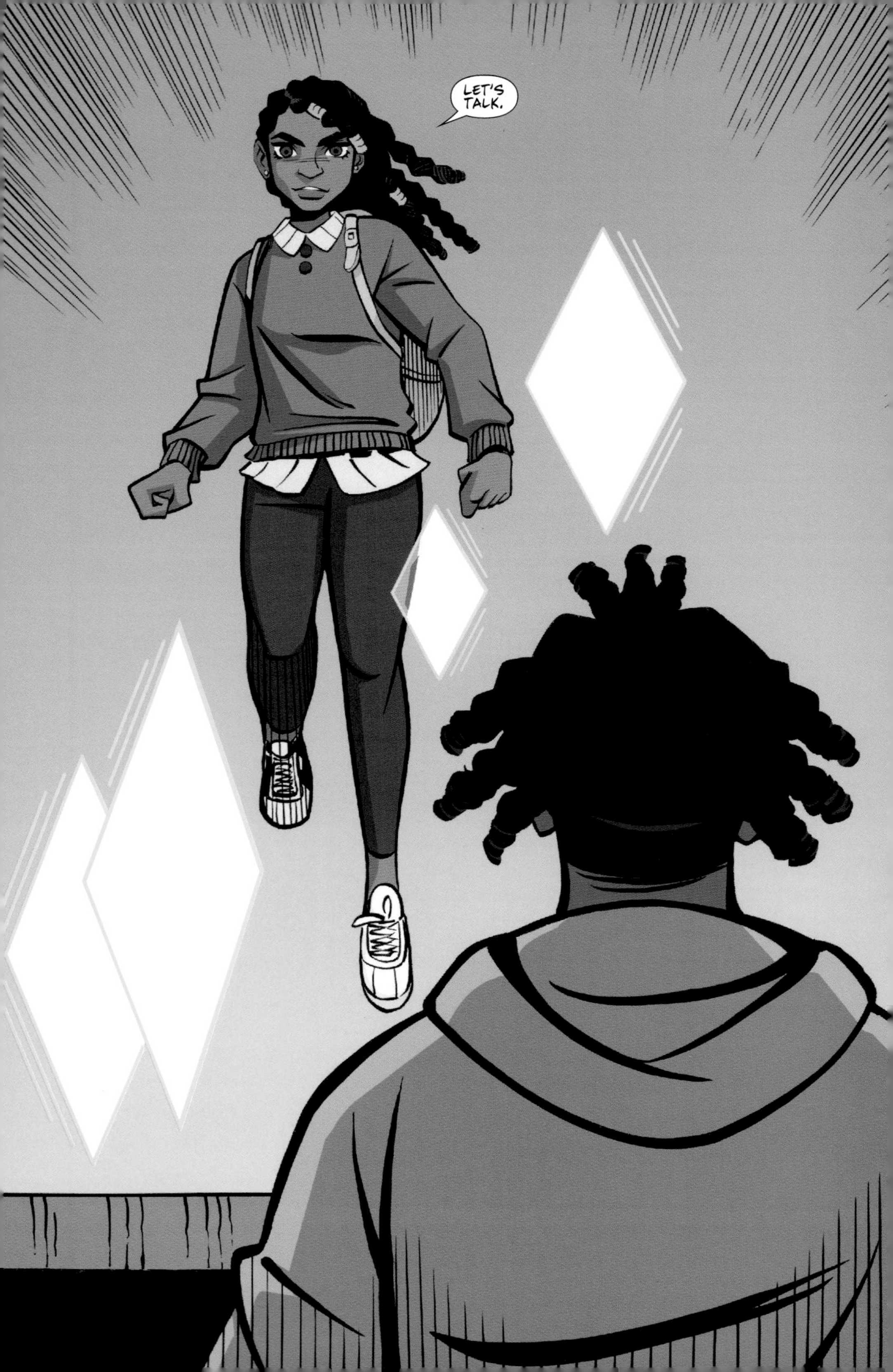
LET'S TALK.

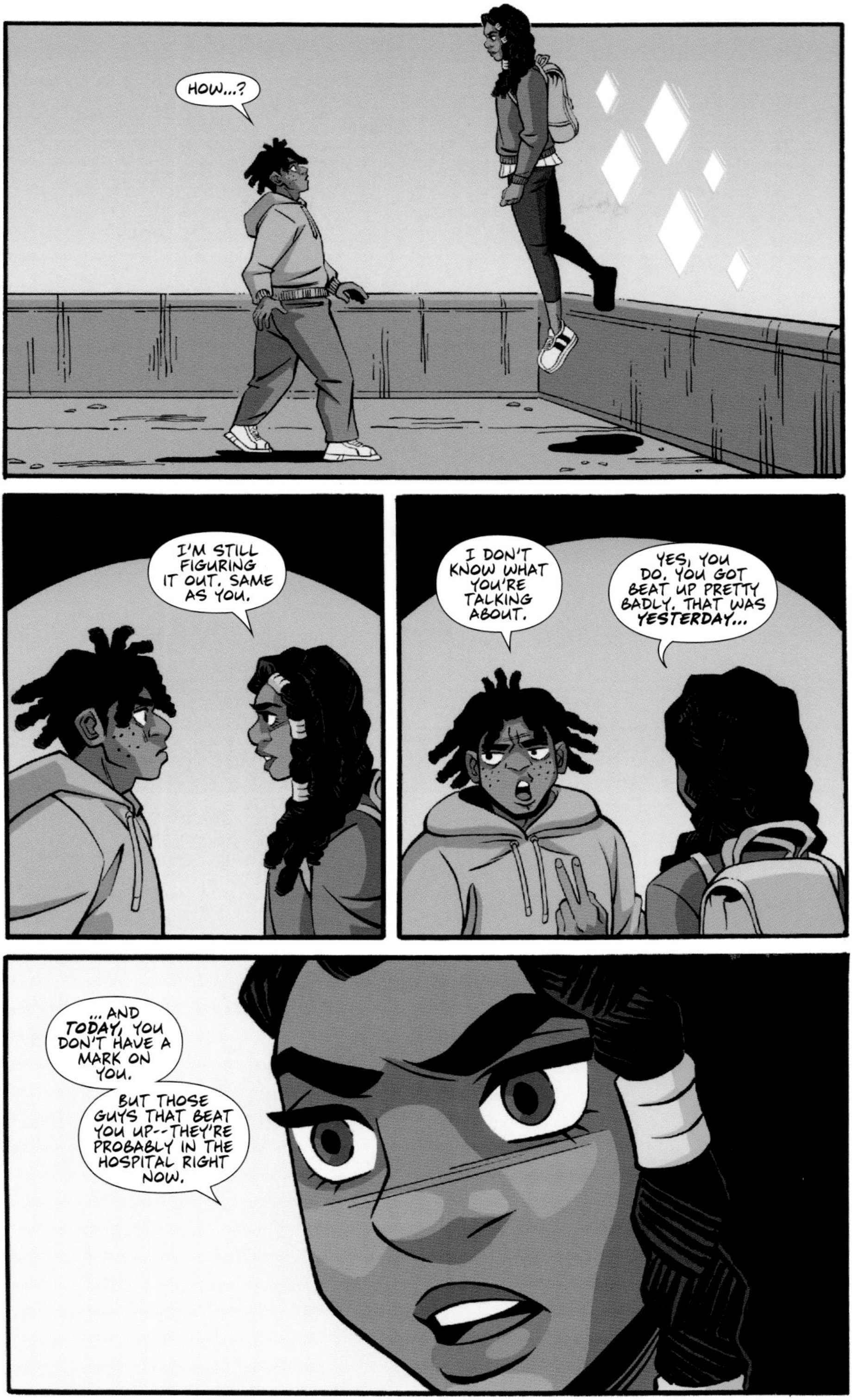
HOW...?
I'M STILL FIGURING IT OUT. SAME AS YOU.
I DON'T KNOW WHAT YOU'RE TALKING ABOUT.
YES, YOU DO. YOU GOT BEAT UP PRETTY BADLY. THAT WAS YESTERDAY...
...AND TODAY, YOU DON'T HAVE A MARK ON YOU.
BUT THOSE GUYS THAT BEAT YOU UP--THEY'RE PROBABLY IN THE HOSPITAL RIGHT NOW.

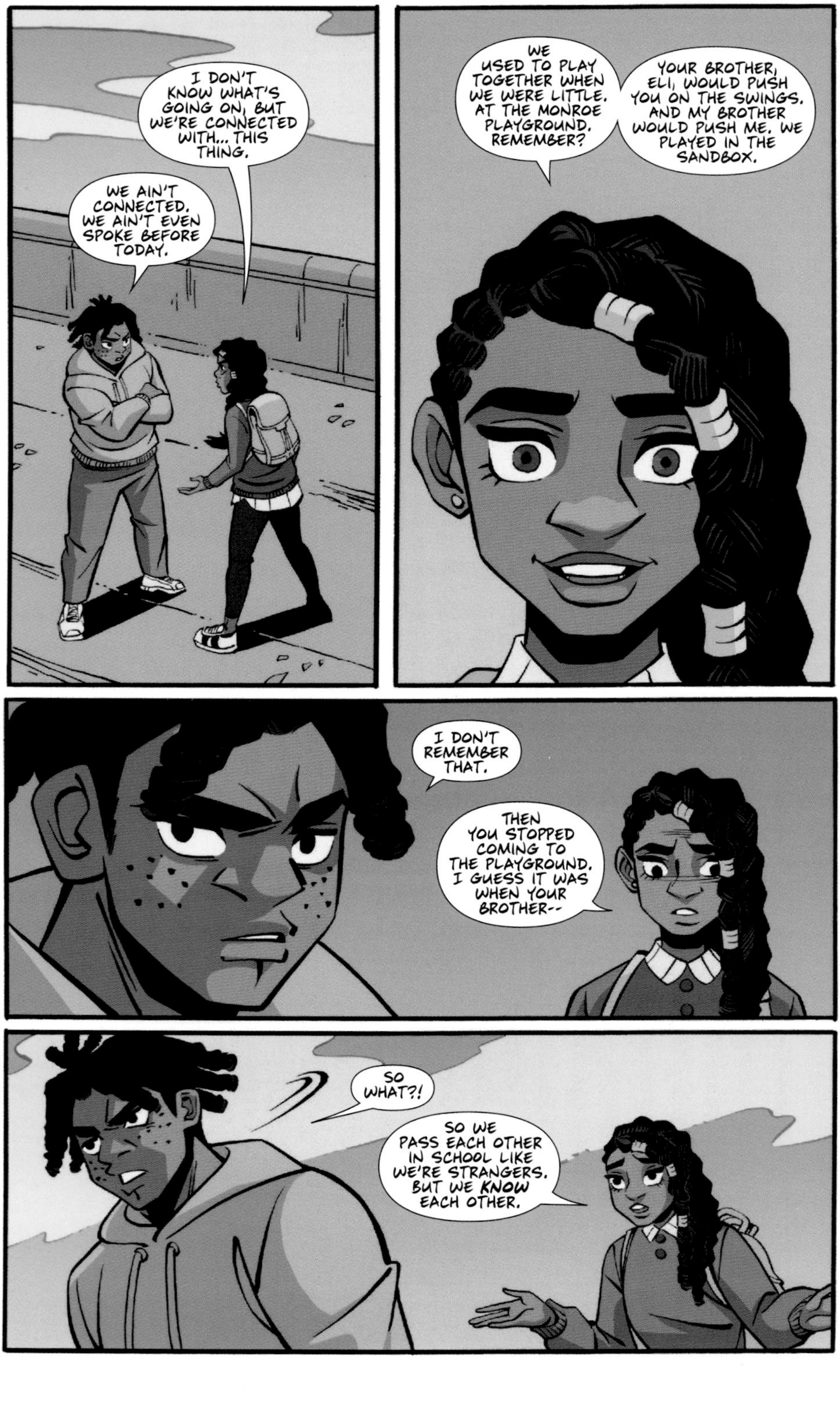
I DON'T KNOW WHAT'S GOING ON, BUT WE'RE CONNECTED WITH... THIS THING.
WE AIN'T CONNECTED. WE AIN'T EVEN SPOKE BEFORE TODAY.
WE USED TO PLAY TOGETHER WHEN WE WERE LITTLE. AT THE MONROE PLAYGROUND. REMEMBER?
YOUR BROTHER, ELI, WOULD PUSH YOU ON THE SWINGS. AND MY BROTHER WOULD PUSH ME. WE PLAYED IN THE SANDBOX.
I DON'T REMEMBER THAT.
THEN YOU STOPPED COMING TO THE PLAYGROUND. I GUESS IT WAS WHEN YOUR BROTHER--
SO WHAT?!
SO WE PASS EACH OTHER IN SCHOOL LIKE WE'RE STRANGERS. BUT WE *KNOW* EACH OTHER.

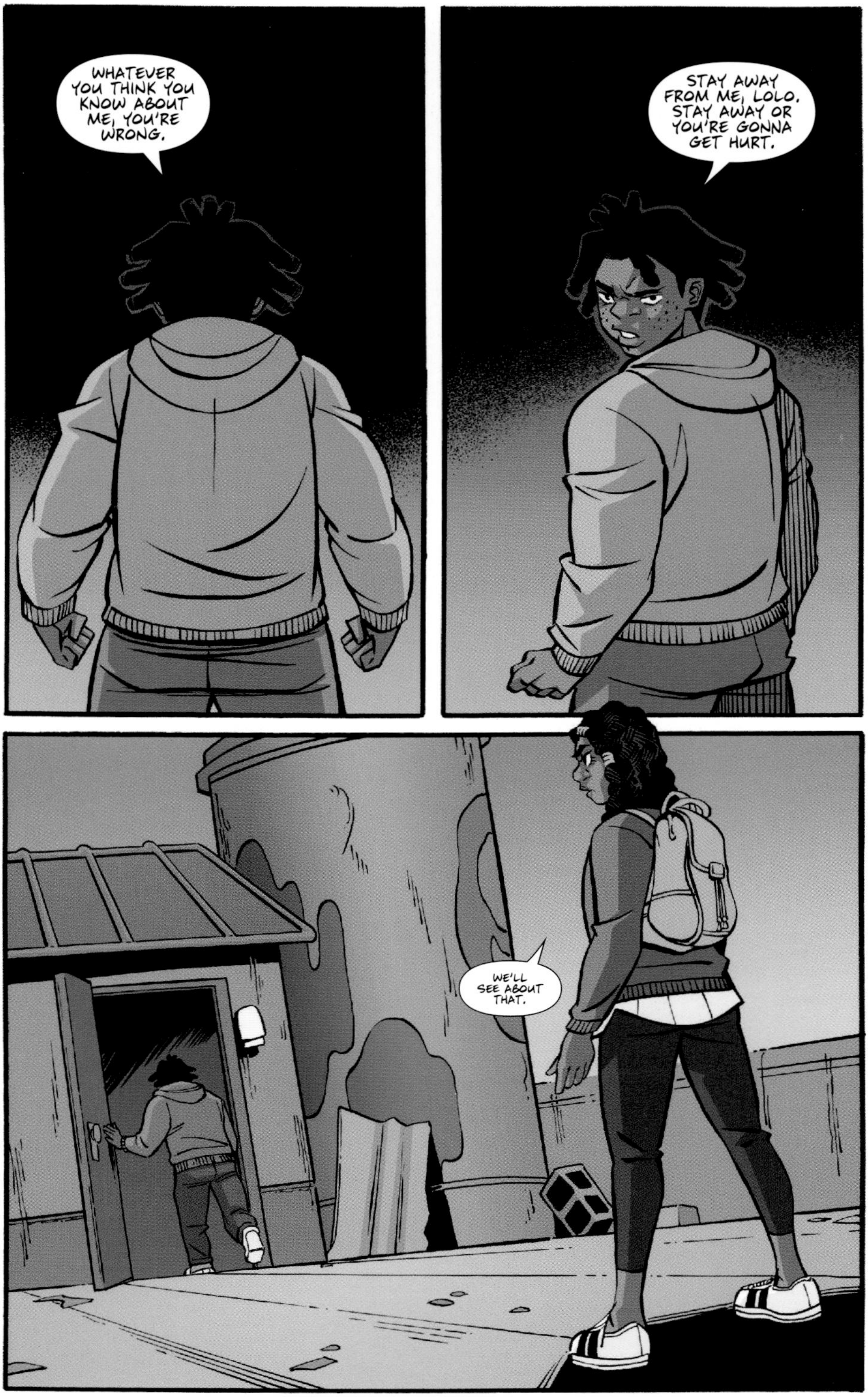
WHATEVER YOU THINK YOU KNOW ABOUT ME, YOU'RE WRONG.
STAY AWAY FROM ME, LOLO. STAY AWAY OR YOU'RE GONNA GET HURT.
WE'LL SEE ABOUT THAT.

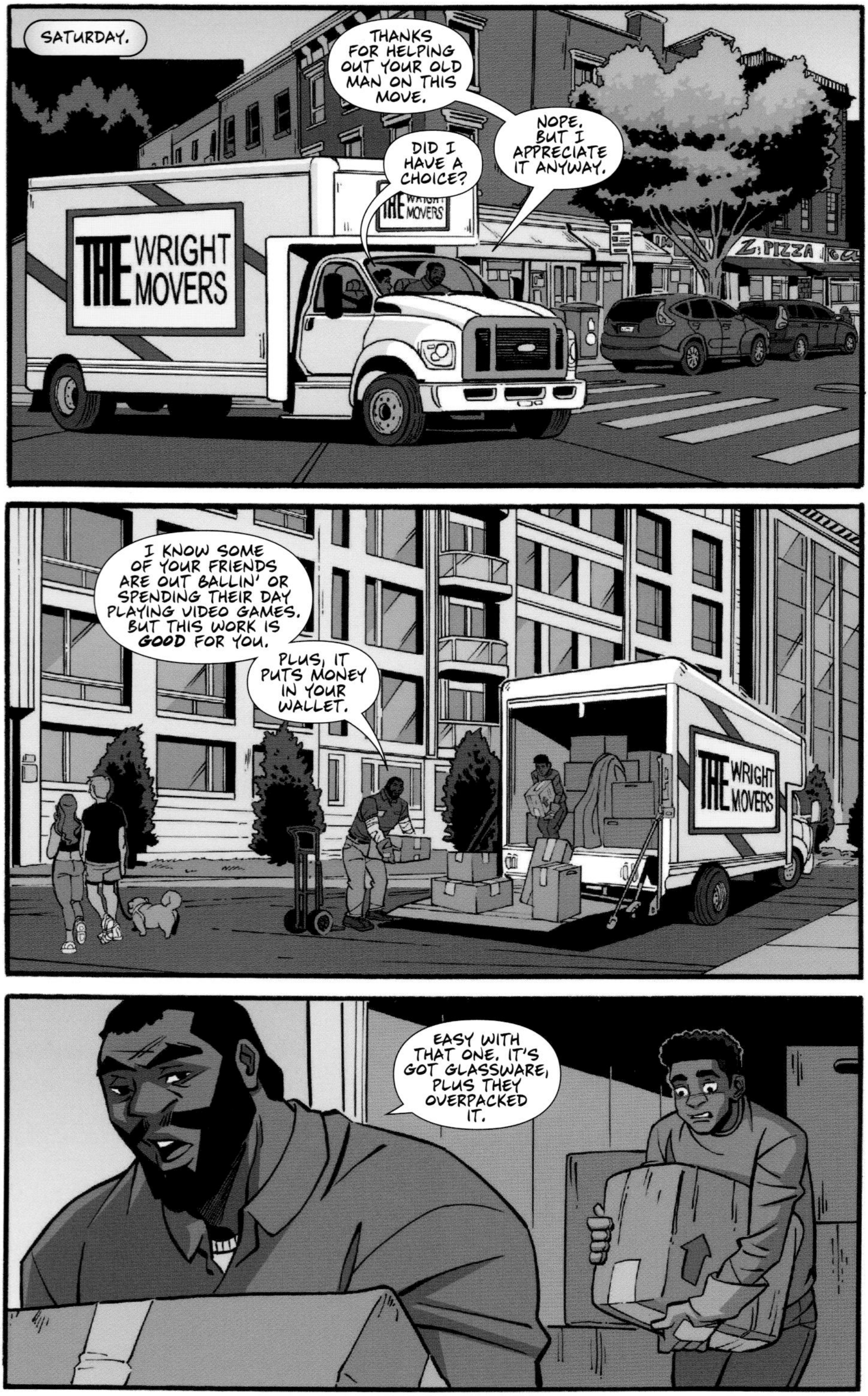
SATURDAY.
THANKS FOR HELPING OUT YOUR OLD MAN ON THIS MOVE.
DID I HAVE A CHOICE?
NOPE. BUT I APPRECIATE IT ANYWAY.
THE WRIGHT MOVERS
Z PIZZA
I KNOW SOME OF YOUR FRIENDS ARE OUT BALLIN' OR SPENDING THEIR DAY PLAYING VIDEO GAMES. BUT THIS WORK IS GOOD FOR YOU.
PLUS, IT PUTS MONEY IN YOUR WALLET.
EASY WITH THAT ONE. IT'S GOT GLASSWARE, PLUS THEY OVERPACKED IT.

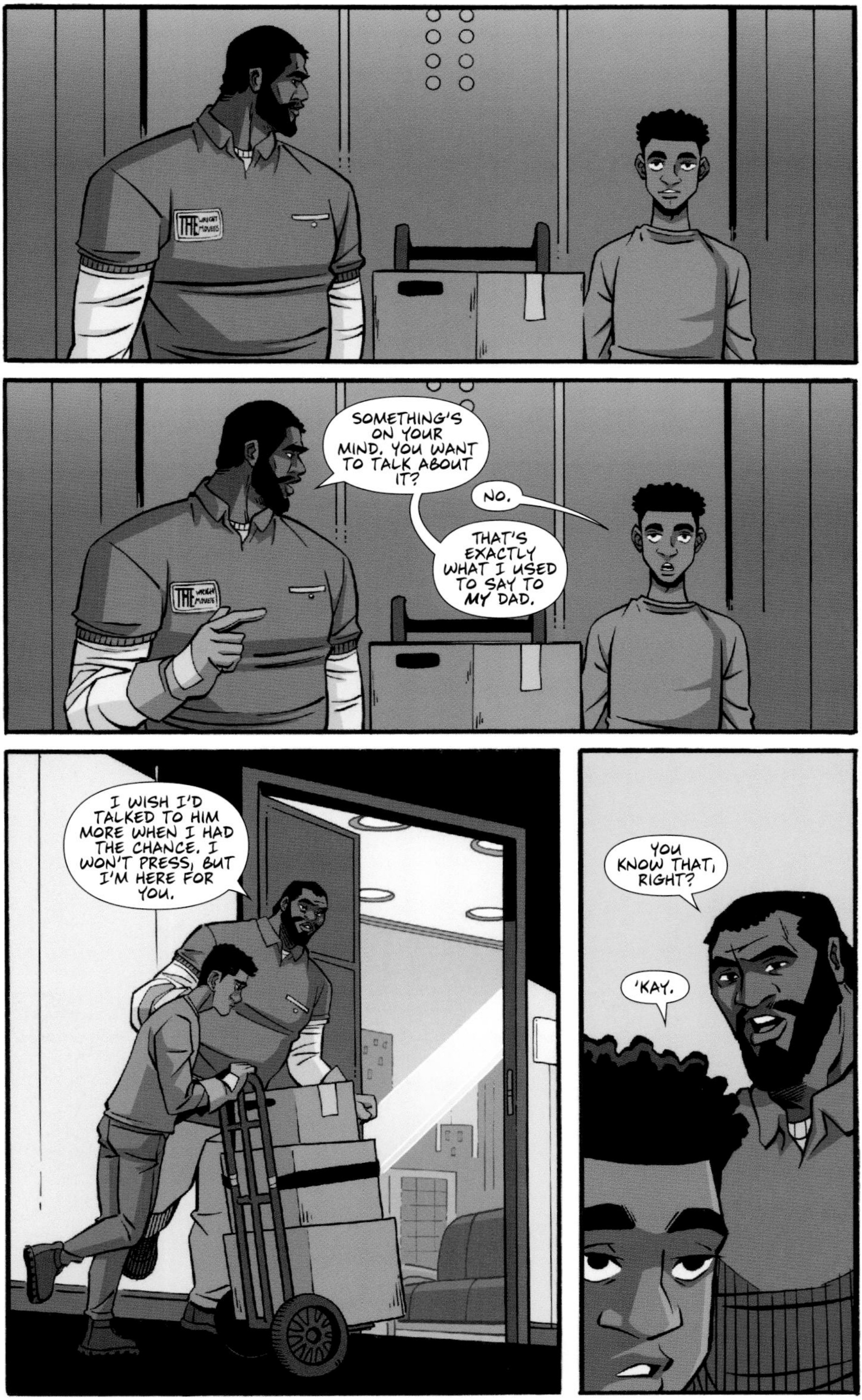

SOMETHING'S ON YOUR MIND. YOU WANT TO TALK ABOUT IT?
NO.
THAT'S EXACTLY WHAT I USED TO SAY TO MY DAD.
I WISH I'D TALKED TO HIM MORE WHEN I HAD THE CHANCE. I WON'T PRESS, BUT I'M HERE FOR YOU.
YOU KNOW THAT, RIGHT?
'KAY.

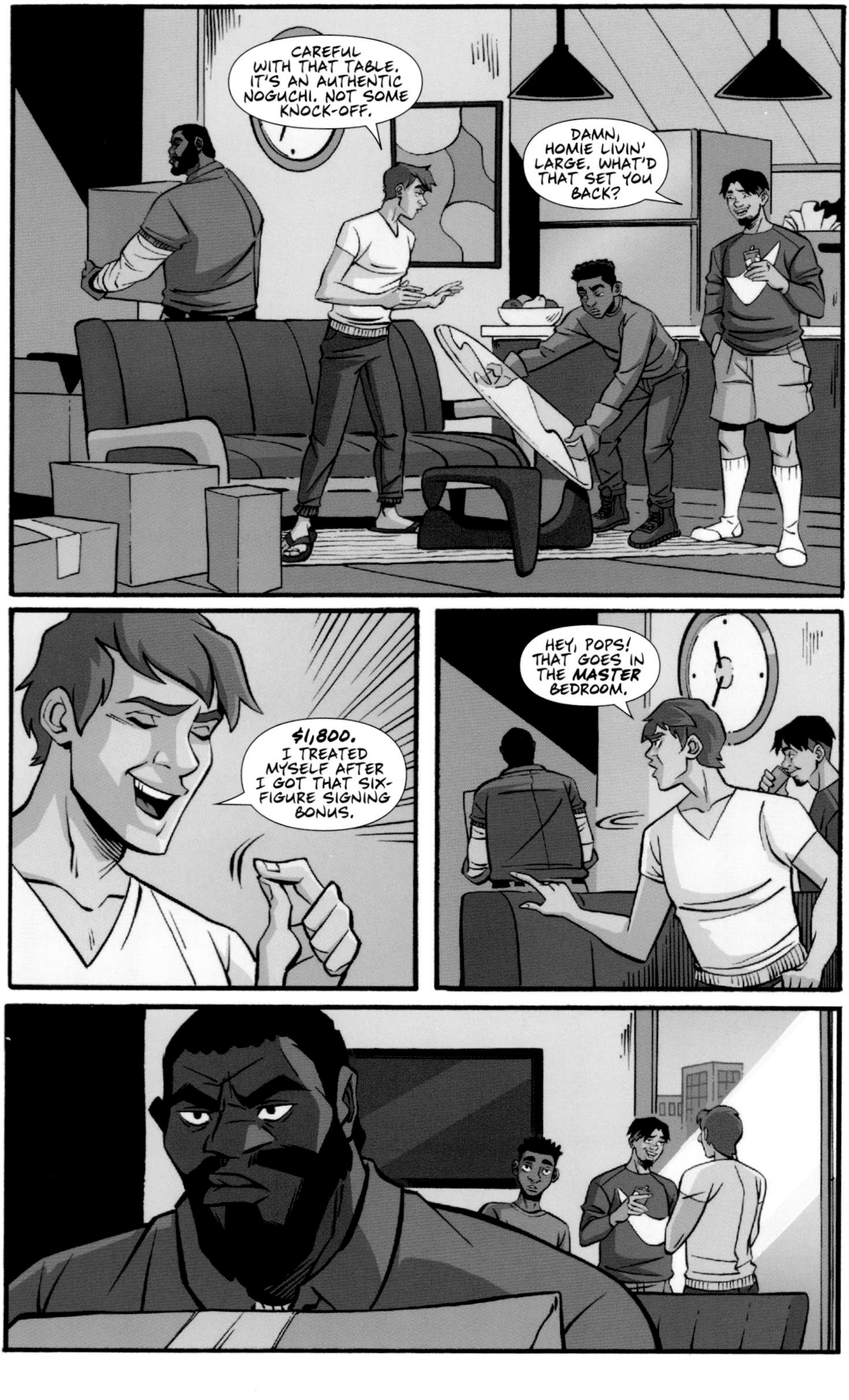
CAREFUL WITH THAT TABLE. IT'S AN AUTHENTIC NOGUCHI. NOT SOME KNOCK-OFF.
DAMN, HOMIE LIVIN' LARGE. WHAT'D THAT SET YOU BACK?
$1,800. I TREATED MYSELF AFTER I GOT THAT SIX-FIGURE SIGNING BONUS.
HEY, POPS! THAT GOES IN THE MASTER BEDROOM.

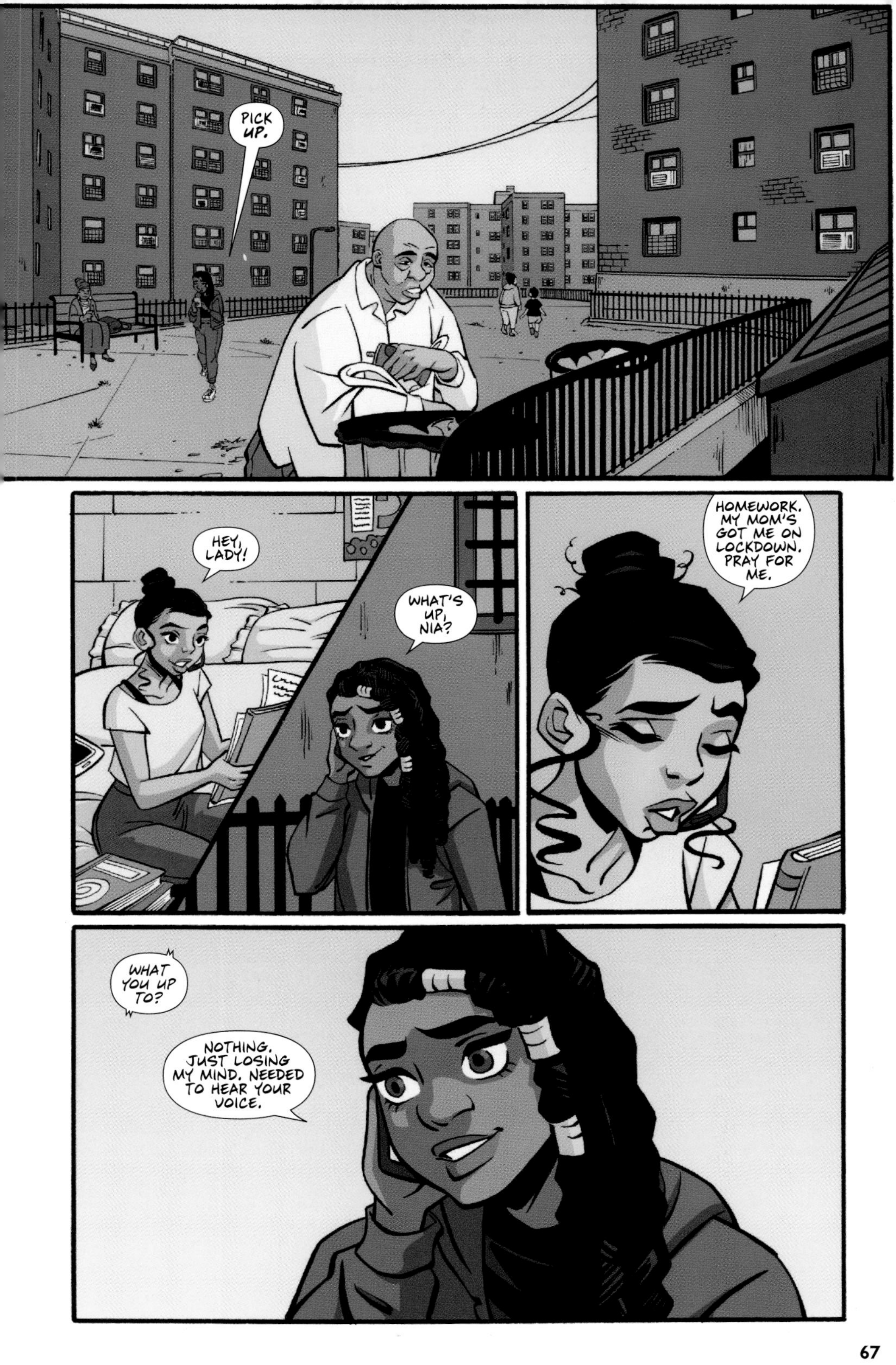
PICK UP.
HEY, LADY!
WHAT'S UP, NIA?
HOMEWORK. MY MOM'S GOT ME ON LOCKDOWN. PRAY FOR ME.
WHAT YOU UP TO?
NOTHING. JUST LOSING MY MIND. NEEDED TO HEAR YOUR VOICE.

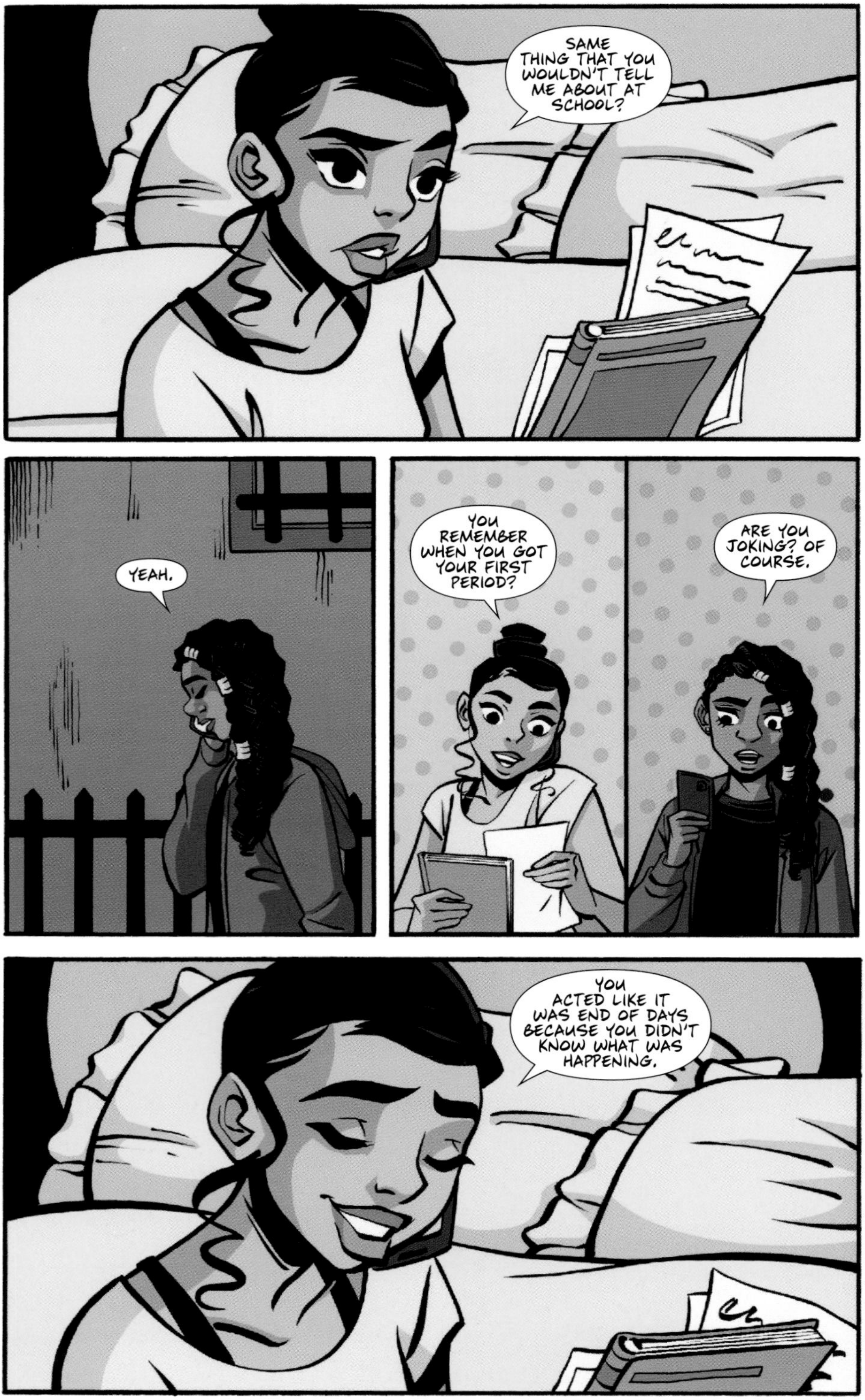
SAME THING THAT YOU WOULDN'T TELL ME ABOUT AT SCHOOL?
YEAH.
YOU REMEMBER WHEN YOU GOT YOUR FIRST PERIOD?
ARE YOU JOKING? OF COURSE.
YOU ACTED LIKE IT WAS END OF DAYS BECAUSE YOU DIDN'T KNOW WHAT WAS HAPPENING.

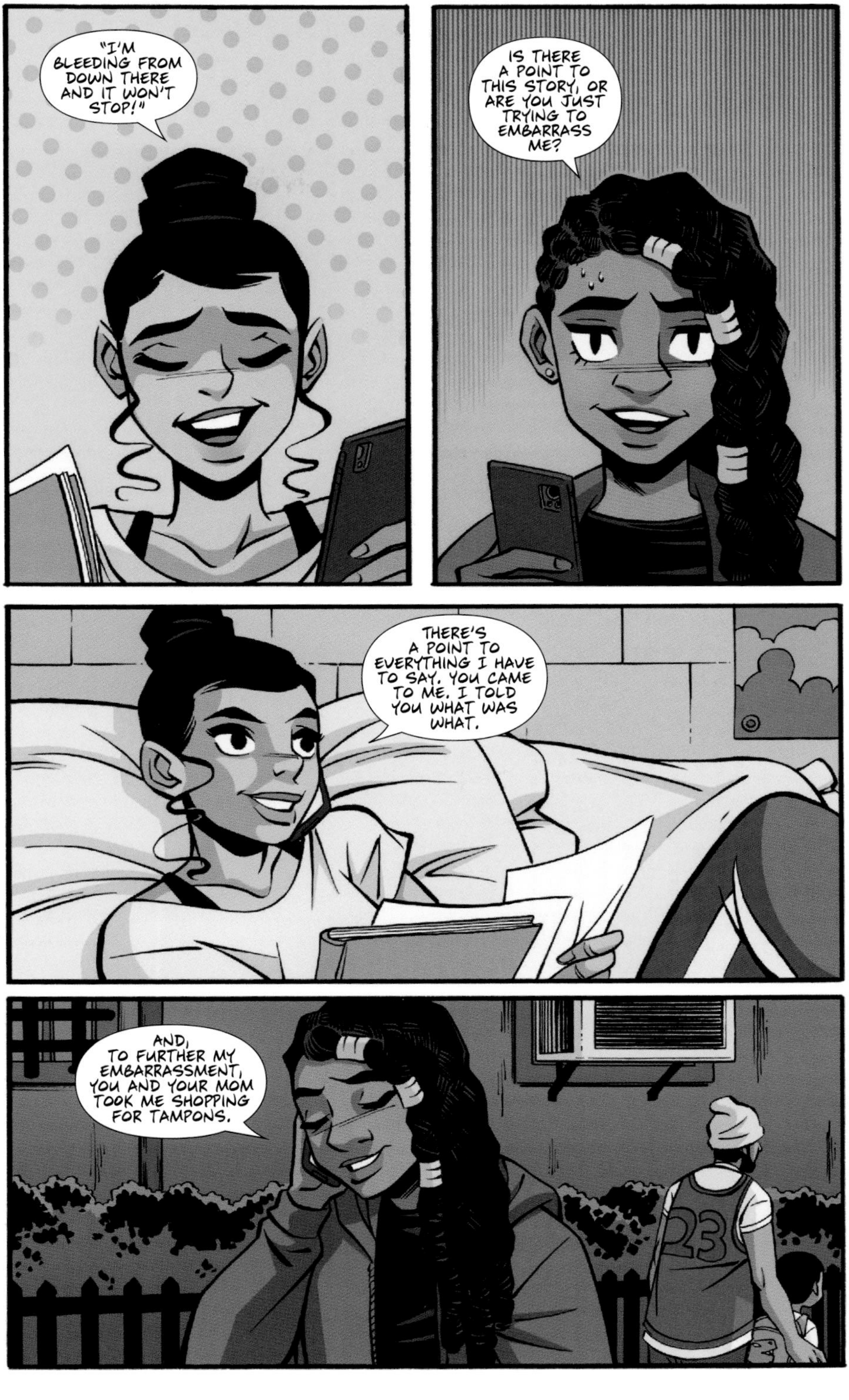
"I'M BLEEDING FROM DOWN THERE AND IT WON'T STOP!"
IS THERE A POINT TO THIS STORY, OR ARE YOU JUST TRYING TO EMBARRASS ME?
THERE'S A POINT TO EVERYTHING I HAVE TO SAY. YOU CAME TO ME. I TOLD YOU WHAT WAS WHAT.
AND, TO FURTHER MY EMBARRASSMENT, YOU AND YOUR MOM TOOK ME SHOPPING FOR TAMPONS.
23

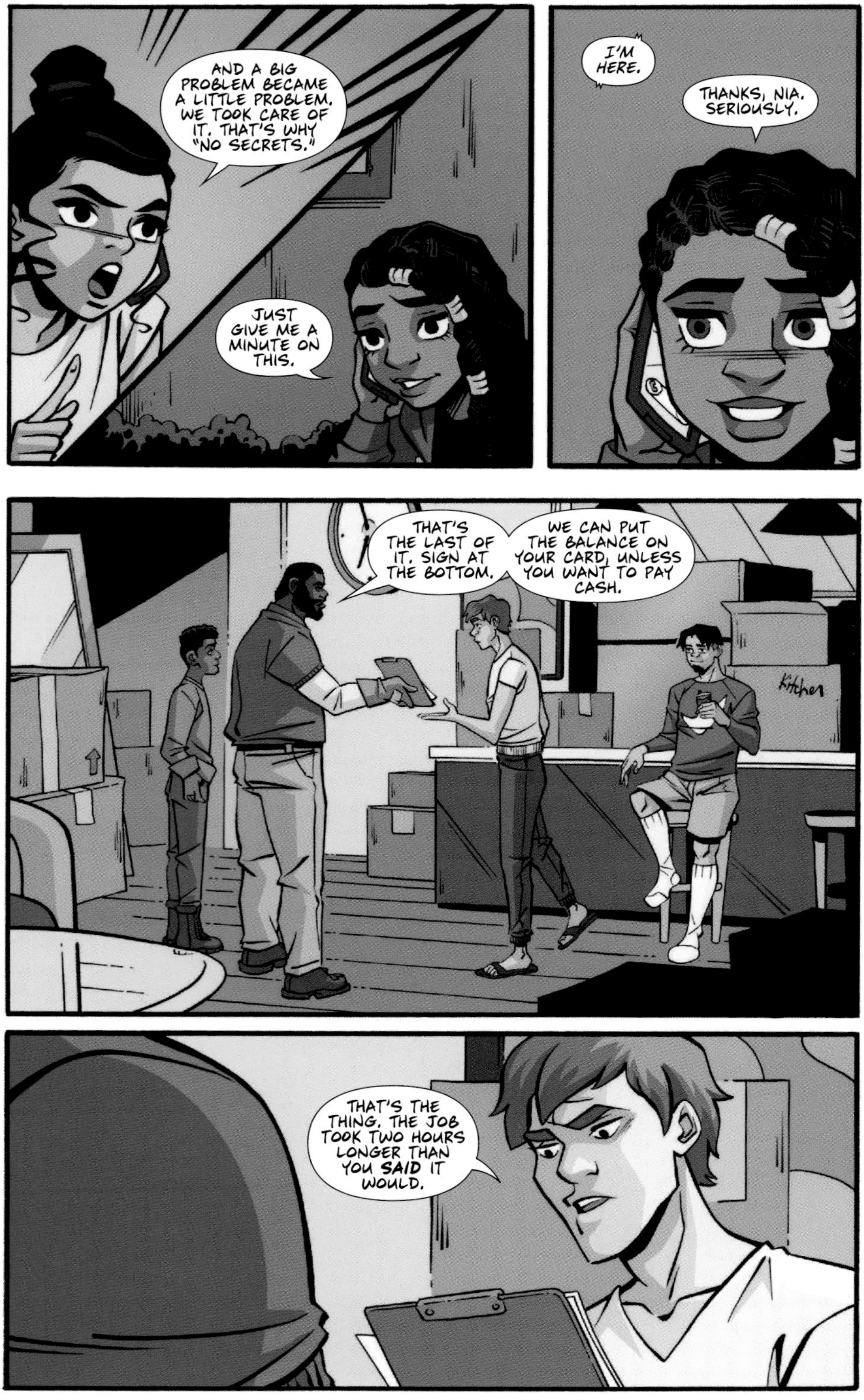
AND A BIG PROBLEM BECAME A LITTLE PROBLEM. WE TOOK CARE OF IT. THAT'S WHY "NO SECRETS."
JUST GIVE ME A MINUTE ON THIS.
I'M HERE.
THANKS, NIA. SERIOUSLY.
THAT'S THE LAST OF IT. SIGN AT THE BOTTOM.
WE CAN PUT THE BALANCE ON YOUR CARD, UNLESS YOU WANT TO PAY CASH.
Kitchen
THAT'S THE THING. THE JOB TOOK TWO HOURS LONGER THAN YOU **SAID** IT WOULD.

THERE WERE TWELVE MORE BOXES THAN YOU SAID THERE'D BE--AND THOSE WEREN'T PACKED.

I TOLD YOU THAT IF WE HAD TO DISASSEMBLE AND REASSEMBLE FURNITURE, THAT WOULD TAKE MORE TIME.

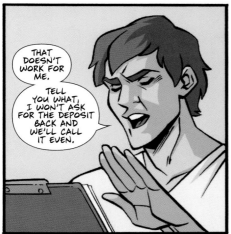

THAT DOESN'T WORK FOR ME.

TELL YOU WHAT, I WON'T ASK FOR THE DEPOSIT BACK AND WE'LL CALL IT EVEN.

YOU KIDDING ME? THE DEPOSIT WAS $200. YOU OWE ME ANOTHER $835.

I'M MAKING A REASONABLE OFFER, AND I PROMISE I WON'T WRITE NEGATIVE ONLINE REVIEWS OF YOUR SERVICES.

BAD WORD OF MOUTH. THAT CAN SINK A BUSINESS, RIGHT?

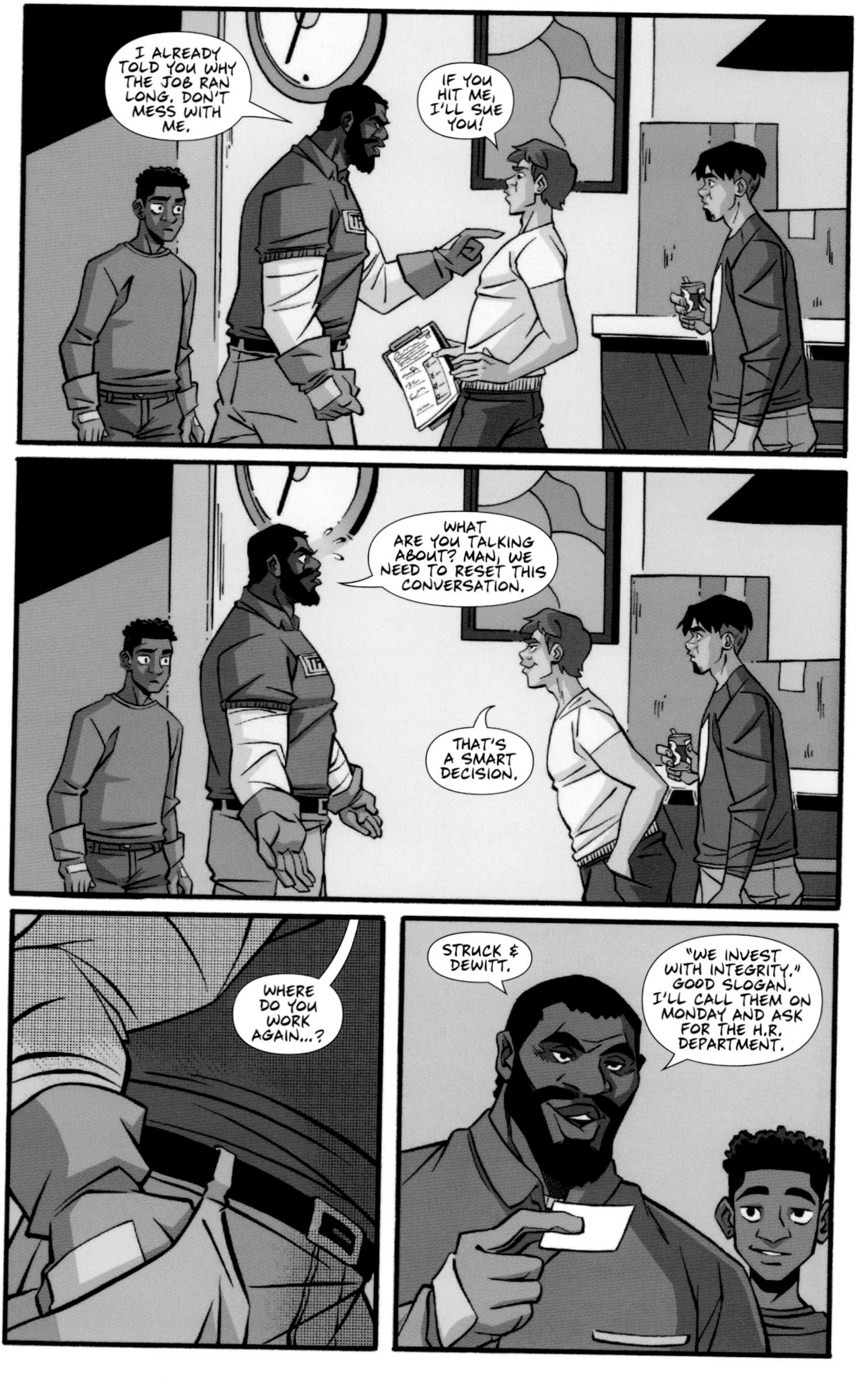
I ALREADY TOLD YOU WHY THE JOB RAN LONG. DON'T MESS WITH ME.
IF YOU HIT ME, I'LL SUE YOU!
WHAT ARE YOU TALKING ABOUT? MAN, WE NEED TO RESET THIS CONVERSATION.
THAT'S A SMART DECISION.
WHERE DO YOU WORK AGAIN...?
STRUCK & DEWITT.
"WE INVEST WITH INTEGRITY." GOOD SLOGAN. I'LL CALL THEM ON MONDAY AND ASK FOR THE H.R. DEPARTMENT.

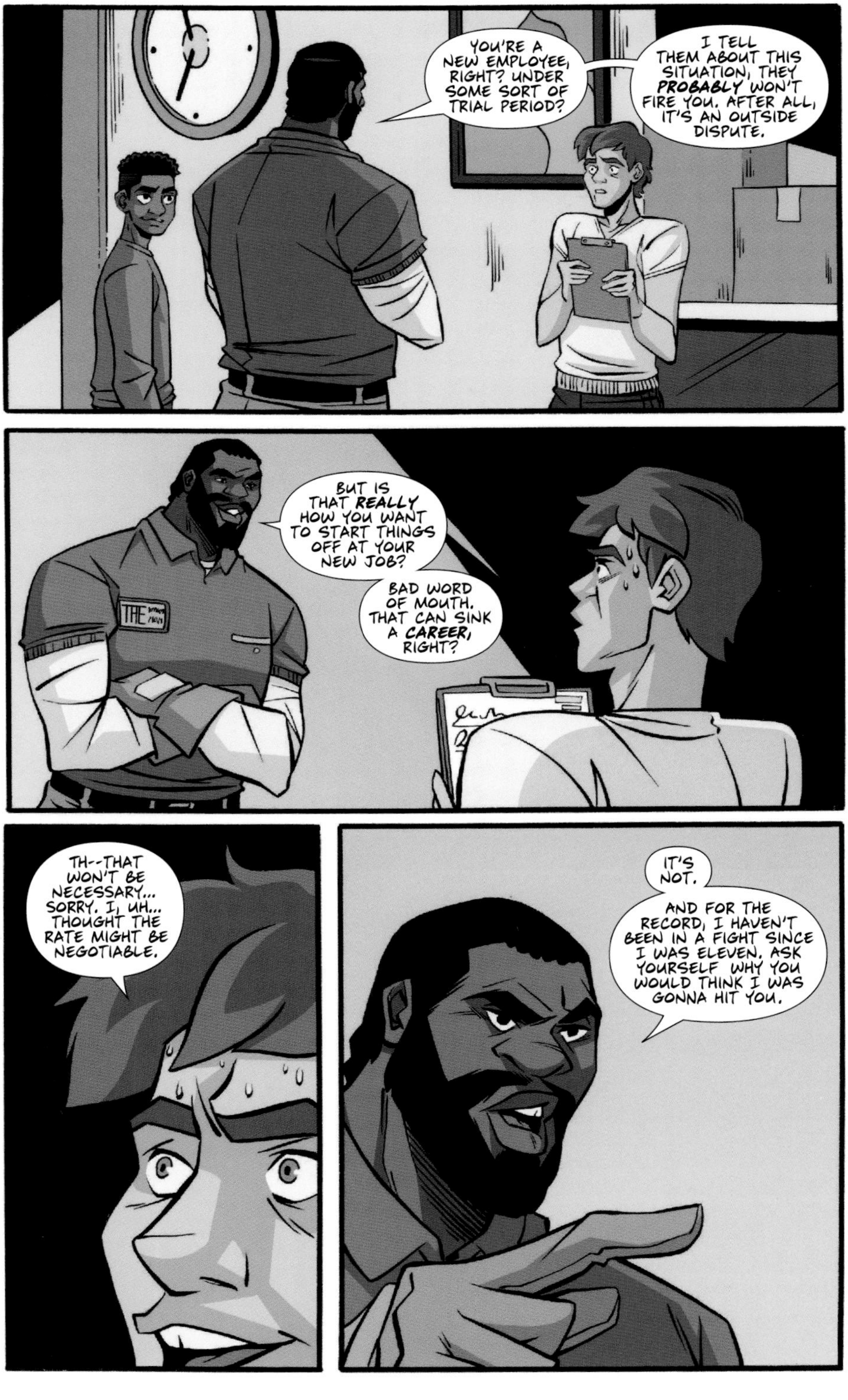
YOU'RE A NEW EMPLOYEE, RIGHT? UNDER SOME SORT OF TRIAL PERIOD?
I TELL THEM ABOUT THIS SITUATION, THEY **PROBABLY** WON'T FIRE YOU. AFTER ALL, IT'S AN OUTSIDE DISPUTE.
BUT IS THAT **REALLY** HOW YOU WANT TO START THINGS OFF AT YOUR NEW JOB?
BAD WORD OF MOUTH. THAT CAN SINK A **CAREER,** RIGHT?
TH--THAT WON'T BE NECESSARY... SORRY. I, UH... THOUGHT THE RATE MIGHT BE NEGOTIABLE.
IT'S NOT.
AND FOR THE RECORD, I HAVEN'T BEEN IN A FIGHT SINCE I WAS ELEVEN. ASK YOURSELF WHY YOU WOULD THINK I WAS GONNA HIT YOU.

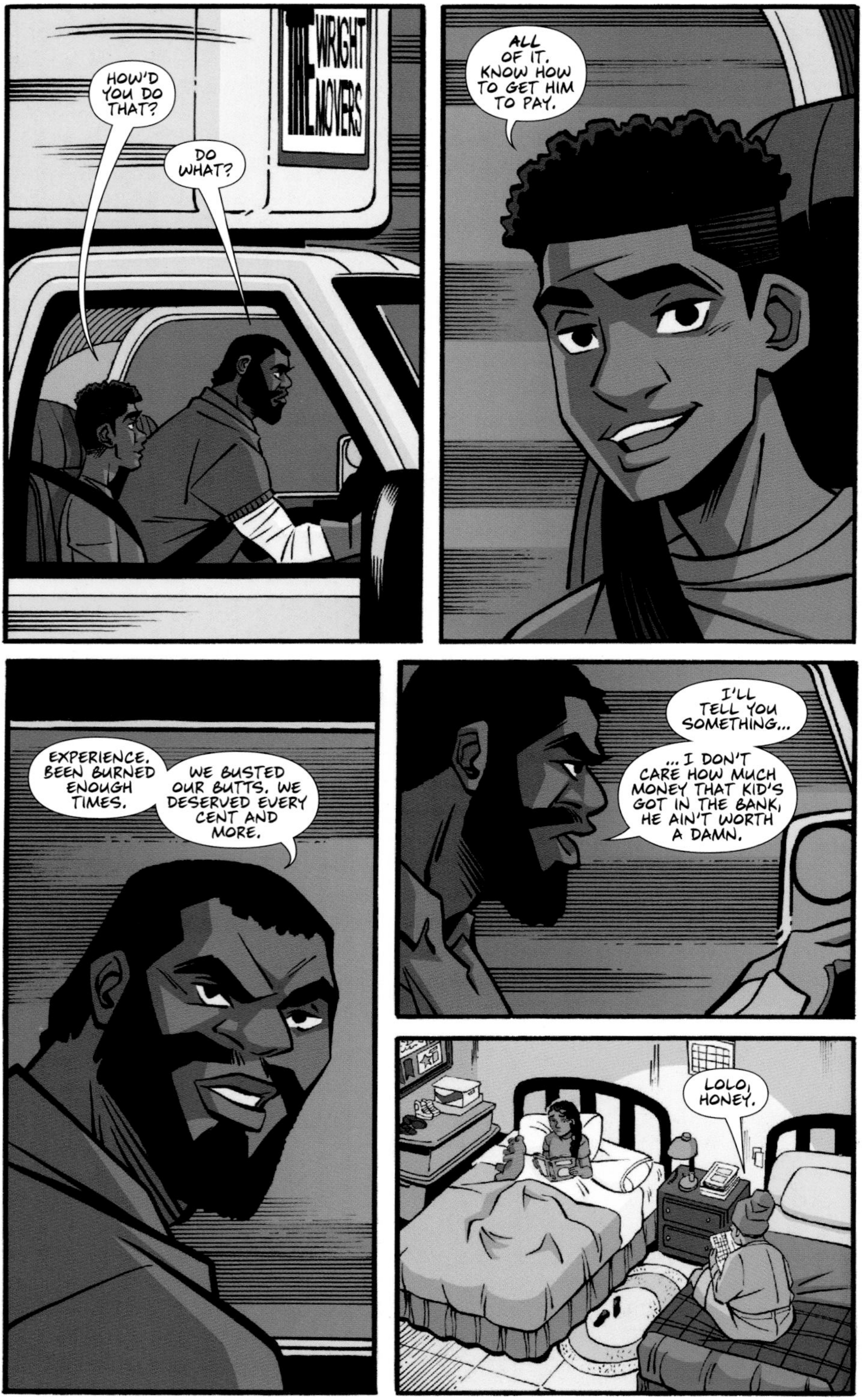
WRIGHT MOVERS
HOW'D YOU DO THAT?
DO WHAT?
ALL OF IT. KNOW HOW TO GET HIM TO PAY.
EXPERIENCE. BEEN BURNED ENOUGH TIMES.
WE BUSTED OUR BUTTS. WE DESERVED EVERY CENT AND MORE.
I'LL TELL YOU SOMETHING...
...I DON'T CARE HOW MUCH MONEY THAT KID'S GOT IN THE BANK, HE AIN'T WORTH A DAMN.
LOLO, HONEY.

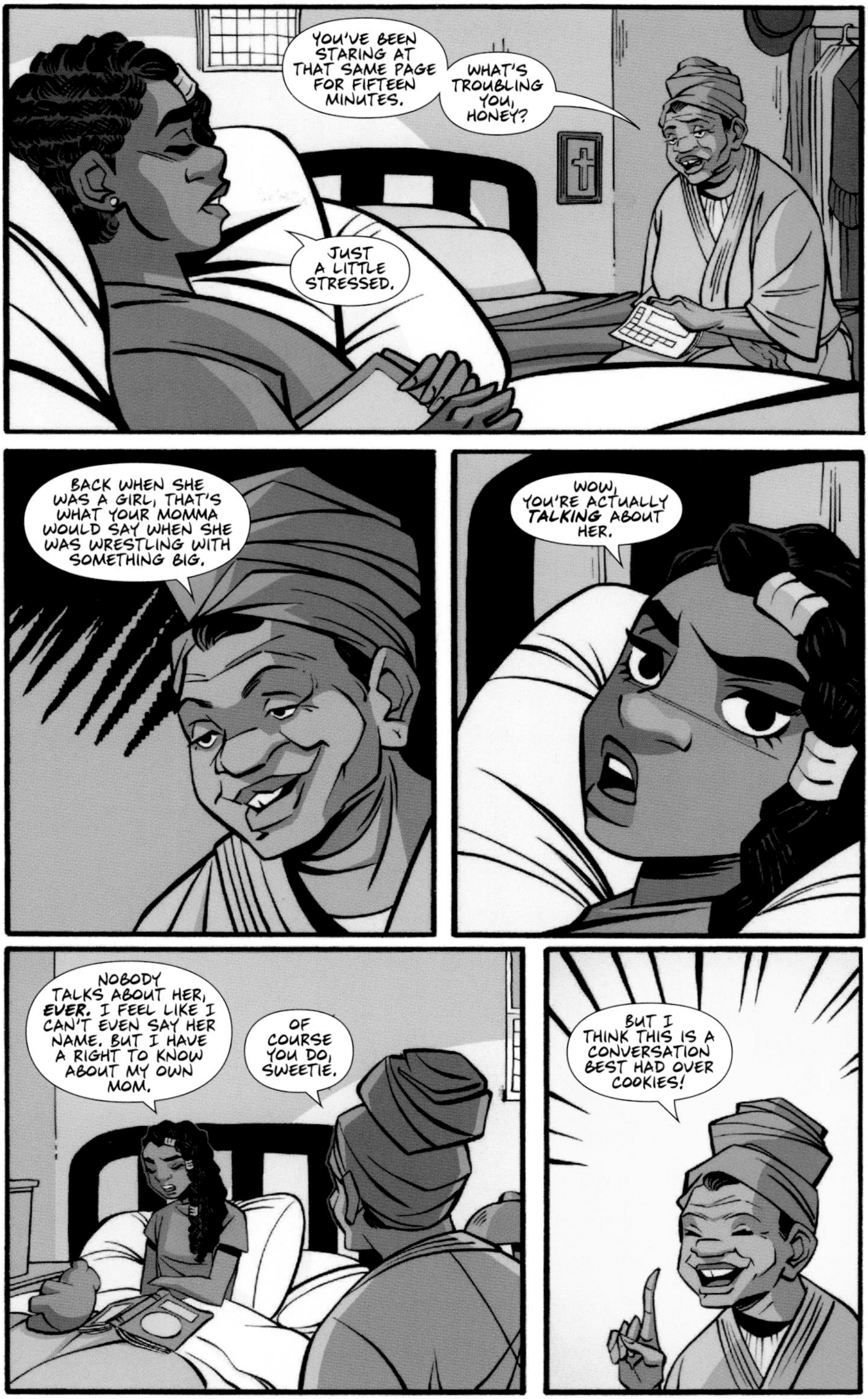
YOU'VE BEEN STARING AT THAT SAME PAGE FOR FIFTEEN MINUTES.
WHAT'S TROUBLING YOU, HONEY?
JUST A LITTLE STRESSED.
BACK WHEN SHE WAS A GIRL, THAT'S WHAT YOUR MOMMA WOULD SAY WHEN SHE WAS WRESTLING WITH SOMETHING BIG.
WOW, YOU'RE ACTUALLY *TALKING* ABOUT HER.
NOBODY TALKS ABOUT HER, **EVER.** I FEEL LIKE I CAN'T EVEN SAY HER NAME. BUT I HAVE A RIGHT TO KNOW ABOUT MY OWN MOM.
OF COURSE YOU DO, SWEETIE.
BUT I THINK THIS IS A CONVERSATION BEST HAD OVER COOKIES!

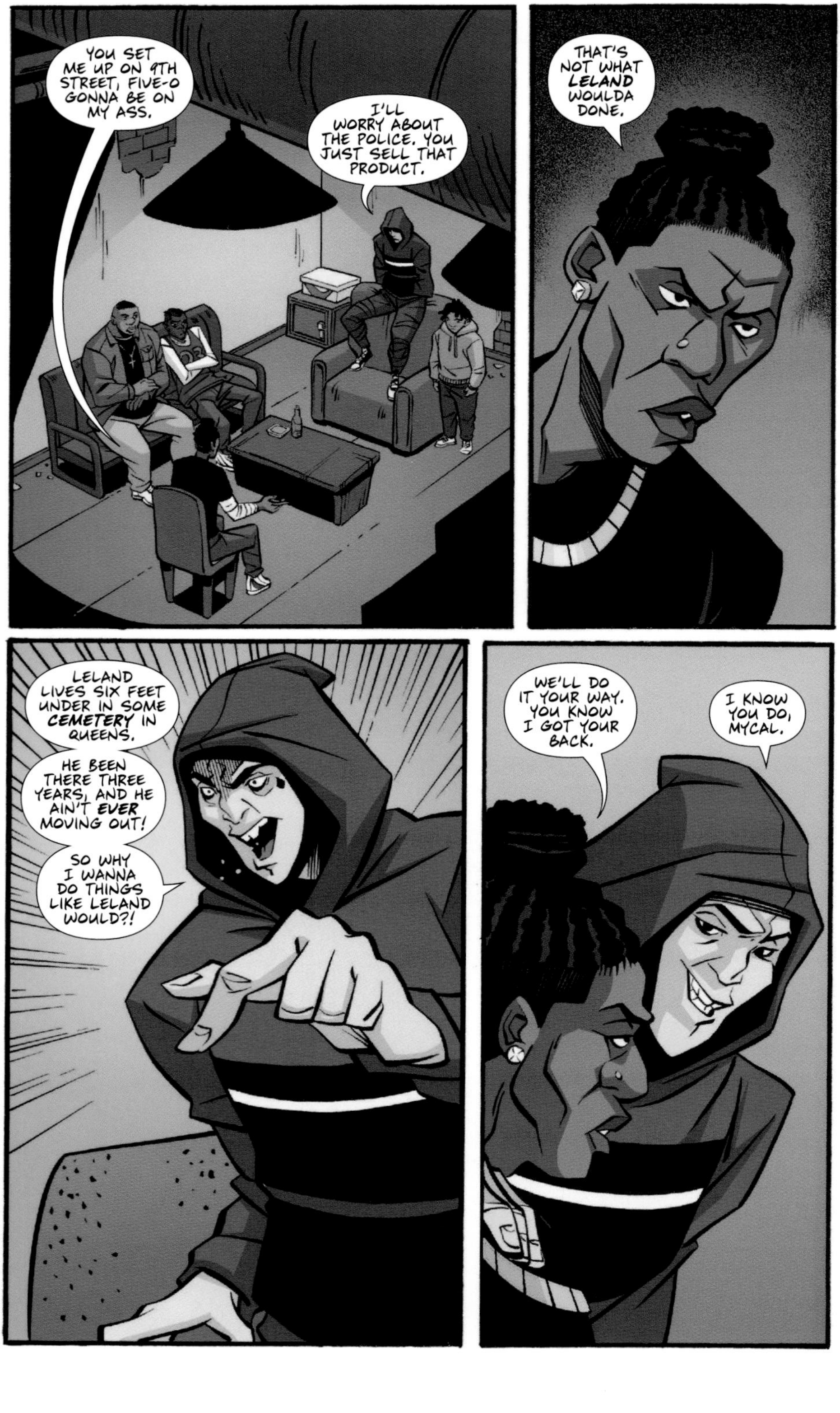
YOU SET ME UP ON 9TH STREET, FIVE-O GONNA BE ON MY ASS.
I'LL WORRY ABOUT THE POLICE. YOU JUST SELL THAT PRODUCT.
THAT'S NOT WHAT LELAND WOULDA DONE.
LELAND LIVES SIX FEET UNDER IN SOME CEMETERY IN QUEENS.
HE BEEN THERE THREE YEARS, AND HE AIN'T EVER MOVING OUT!
SO WHY I WANNA DO THINGS LIKE LELAND WOULD?!
WE'LL DO IT YOUR WAY. YOU KNOW I GOT YOUR BACK.
I KNOW YOU DO, MYCAL.

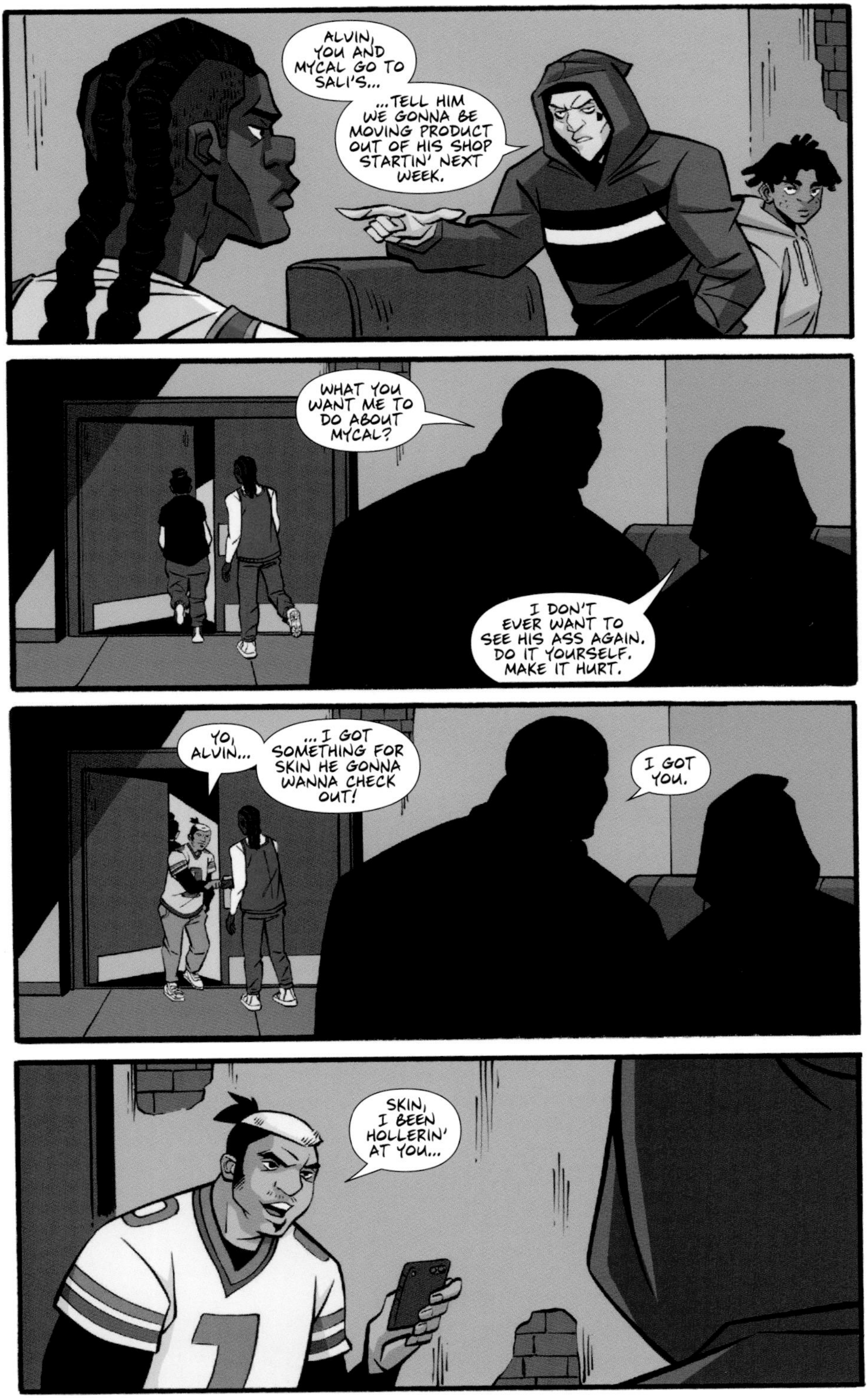
ALVIN, YOU AND MYCAL GO TO SALI'S...
...TELL HIM WE GONNA BE MOVING PRODUCT OUT OF HIS SHOP STARTIN' NEXT WEEK.
WHAT YOU WANT ME TO DO ABOUT MYCAL?
I DON'T EVER WANT TO SEE HIS ASS AGAIN. DO IT YOURSELF. MAKE IT HURT.
YO, ALVIN...
...I GOT SOMETHING FOR SKIN HE GONNA WANNA CHECK OUT!
I GOT YOU.
SKIN, I BEEN HOLLERIN' AT YOU...

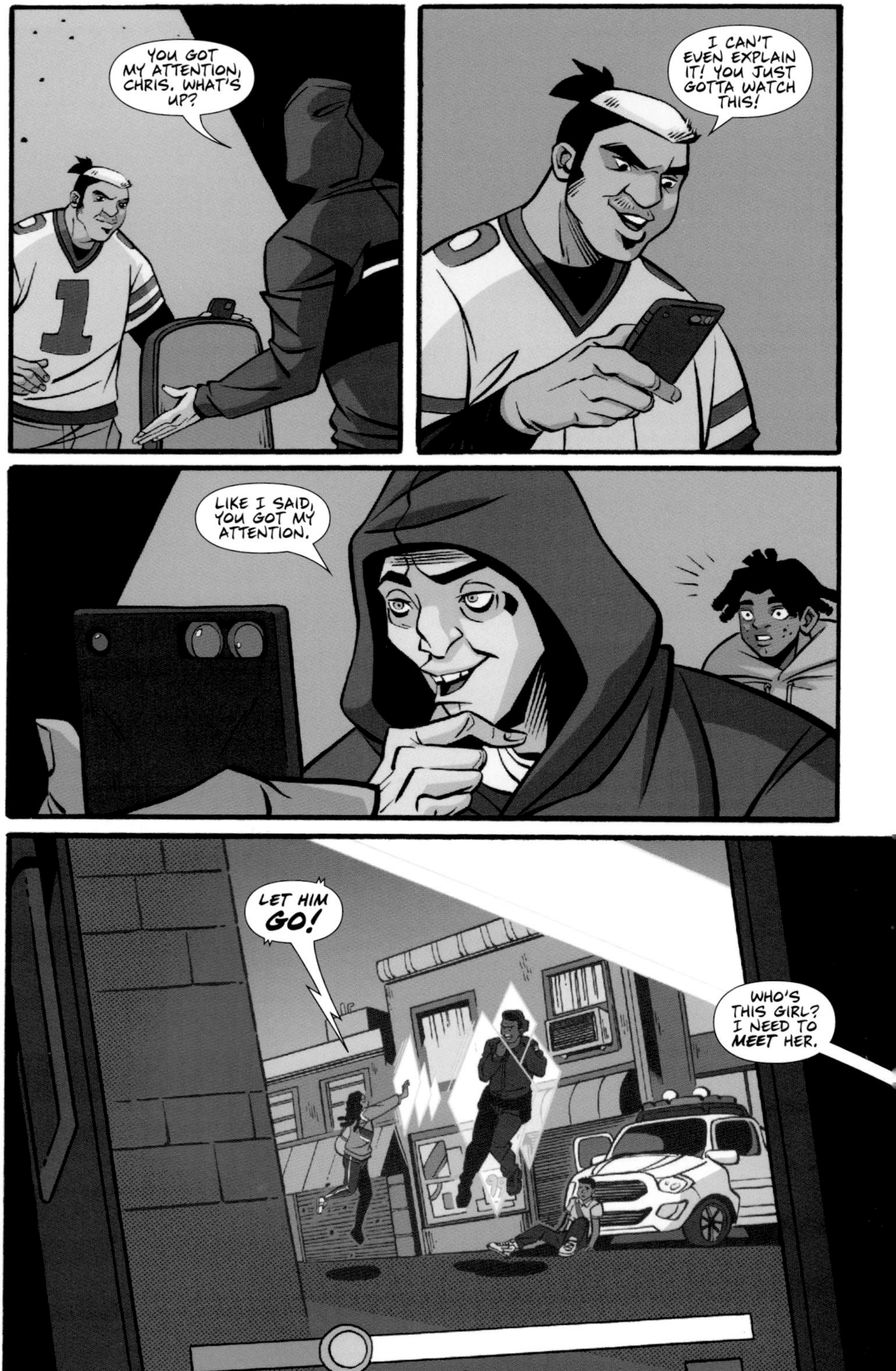
YOU GOT MY ATTENTION, CHRIS. WHAT'S UP?
I CAN'T EVEN EXPLAIN IT! YOU JUST GOTTA WATCH THIS!
LIKE I SAID, YOU GOT MY ATTENTION.
LET HIM GO!
WHO'S THIS GIRL? I NEED TO MEET HER.

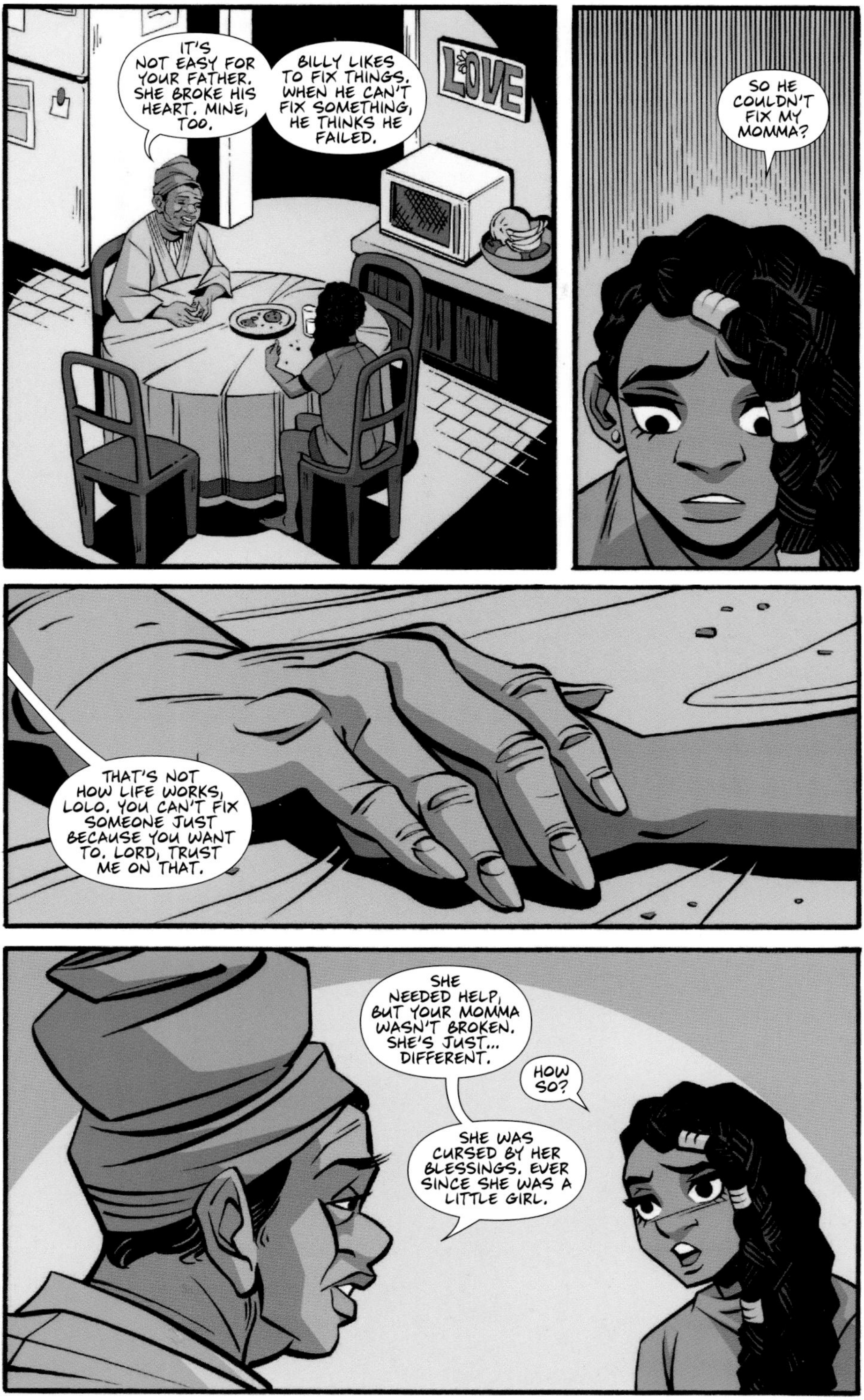
IT'S NOT EASY FOR YOUR FATHER. SHE BROKE HIS HEART. MINE, TOO.
BILLY LIKES TO FIX THINGS. WHEN HE CAN'T FIX SOMETHING, HE THINKS HE FAILED.
LOVE
SO HE COULDN'T FIX MY MOMMA?
THAT'S NOT HOW LIFE WORKS, LOLO. YOU CAN'T FIX SOMEONE JUST BECAUSE YOU WANT TO. LORD, TRUST ME ON THAT.
SHE NEEDED HELP, BUT YOUR MOMMA WASN'T BROKEN. SHE'S JUST... DIFFERENT.
HOW SO?
SHE WAS CURSED BY HER BLESSINGS. EVER SINCE SHE WAS A LITTLE GIRL.

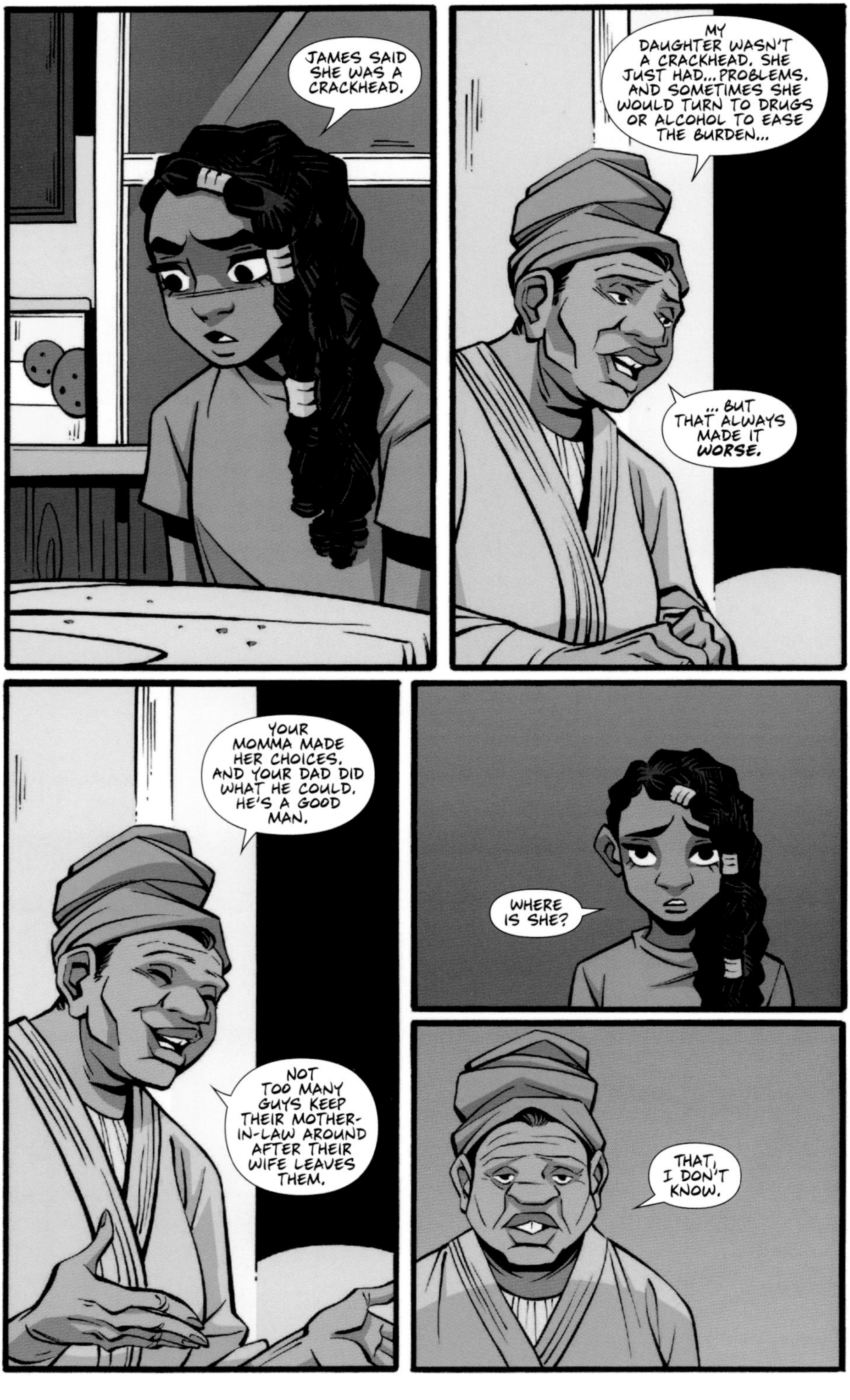
JAMES SAID SHE WAS A CRACKHEAD.
MY DAUGHTER WASN'T A CRACKHEAD. SHE JUST HAD...PROBLEMS. AND SOMETIMES SHE WOULD TURN TO DRUGS OR ALCOHOL TO EASE THE BURDEN...
...BUT THAT ALWAYS MADE IT WORSE.
YOUR MOMMA MADE HER CHOICES. AND YOUR DAD DID WHAT HE COULD. HE'S A GOOD MAN.
NOT TOO MANY GUYS KEEP THEIR MOTHER-IN-LAW AROUND AFTER THEIR WIFE LEAVES THEM.
WHERE IS SHE?
THAT, I DON'T KNOW.

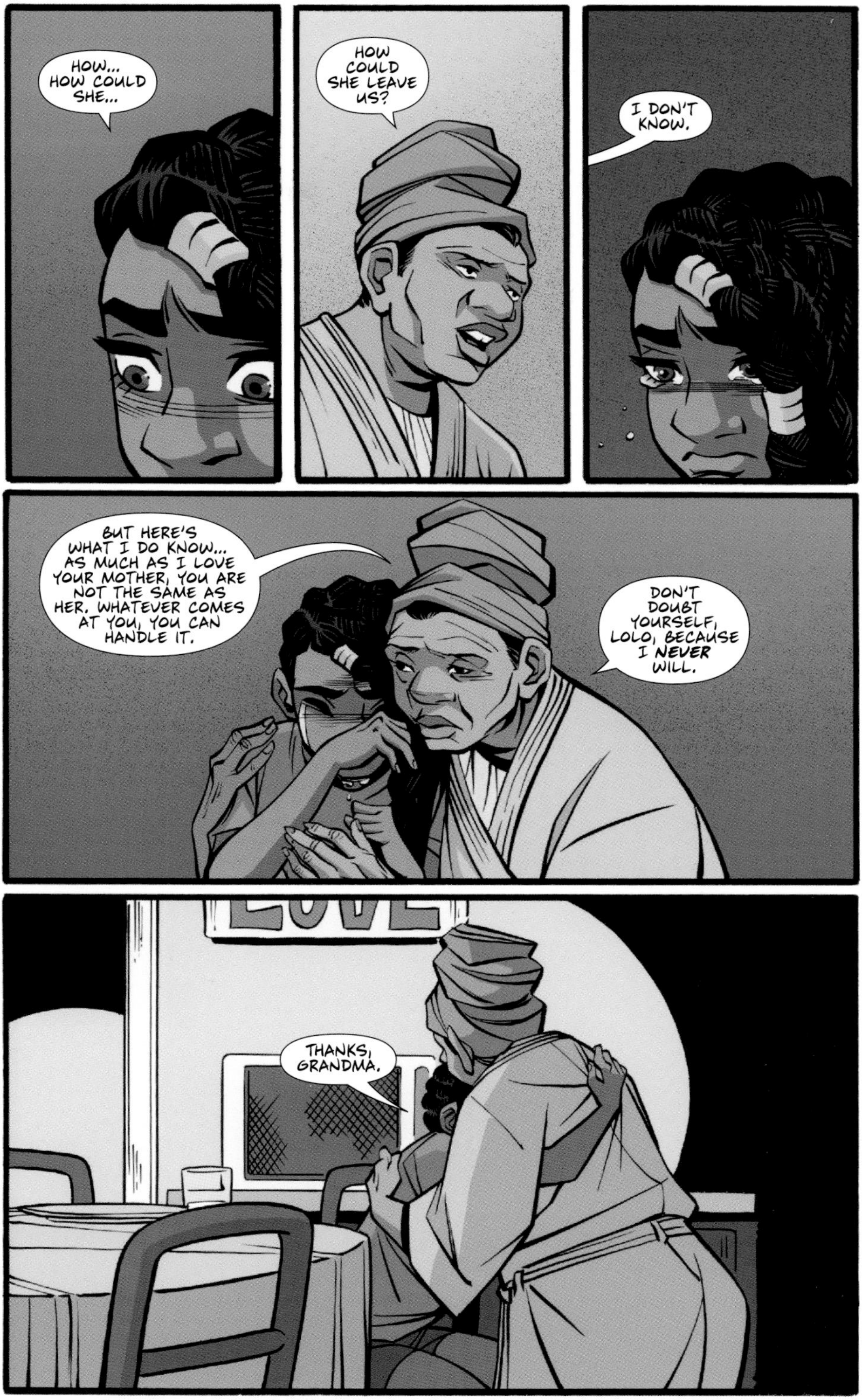
HOW... HOW COULD SHE...
HOW COULD SHE LEAVE US?
I DON'T KNOW.
BUT HERE'S WHAT I DO KNOW... AS MUCH AS I LOVE YOUR MOTHER, YOU ARE NOT THE SAME AS HER. WHATEVER COMES AT YOU, YOU CAN HANDLE IT.
DON'T DOUBT YOURSELF, LOLO, BECAUSE I **NEVER** WILL.
LOVE
THANKS, GRANDMA.

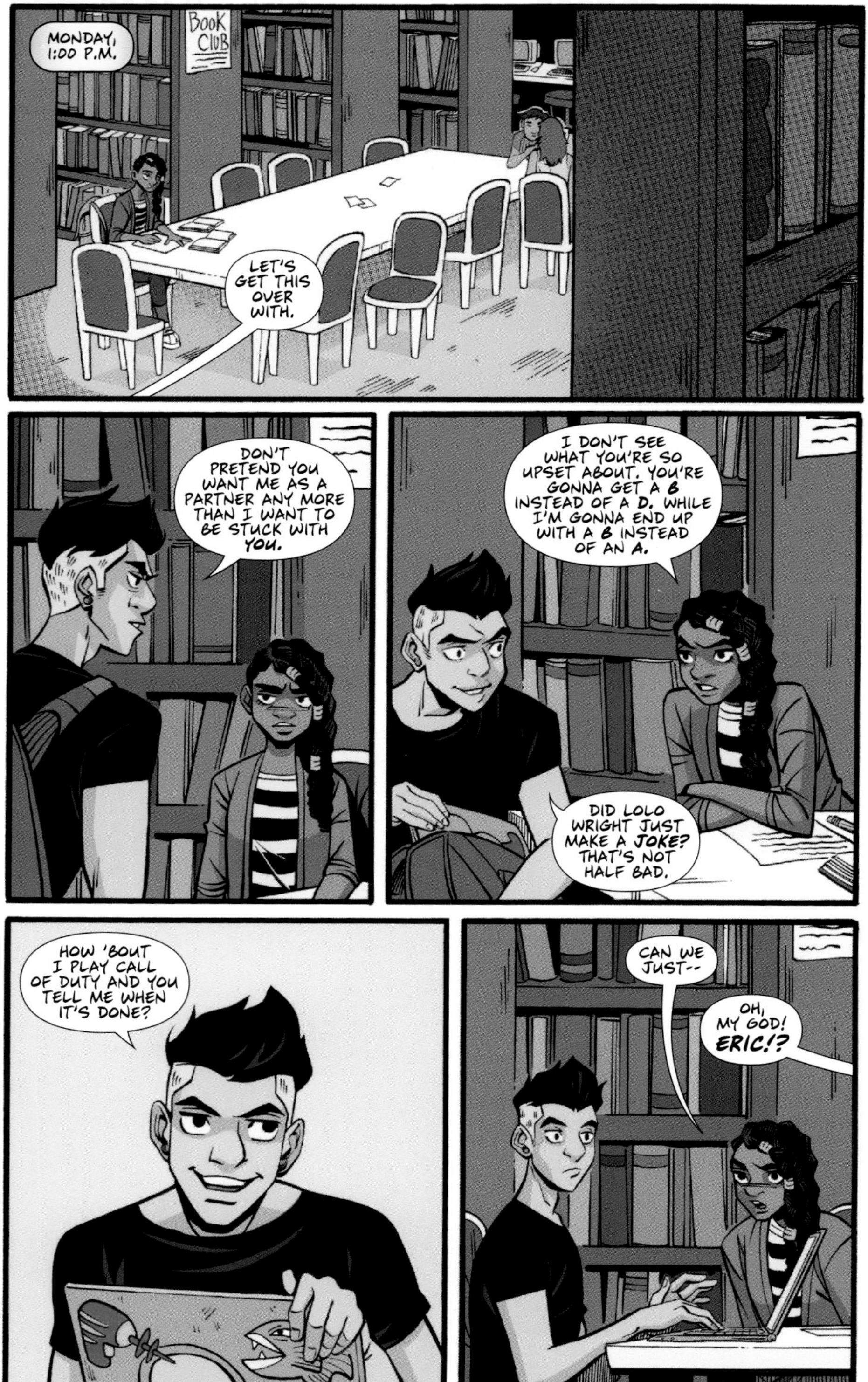
MONDAY, 1:00 P.M.
BOOK CLUB
LET'S GET THIS OVER WITH.
DON'T PRETEND YOU WANT ME AS A PARTNER ANY MORE THAN I WANT TO BE STUCK WITH YOU.
I DON'T SEE WHAT YOU'RE SO UPSET ABOUT. YOU'RE GONNA GET A B INSTEAD OF A D, WHILE I'M GONNA END UP WITH A B INSTEAD OF AN A.
DID LOLO WRIGHT JUST MAKE A JOKE? THAT'S NOT HALF BAD.
HOW 'BOUT I PLAY CALL OF DUTY AND YOU TELL ME WHEN IT'S DONE?
CAN WE JUST--
OH, MY GOD! ERIC!?

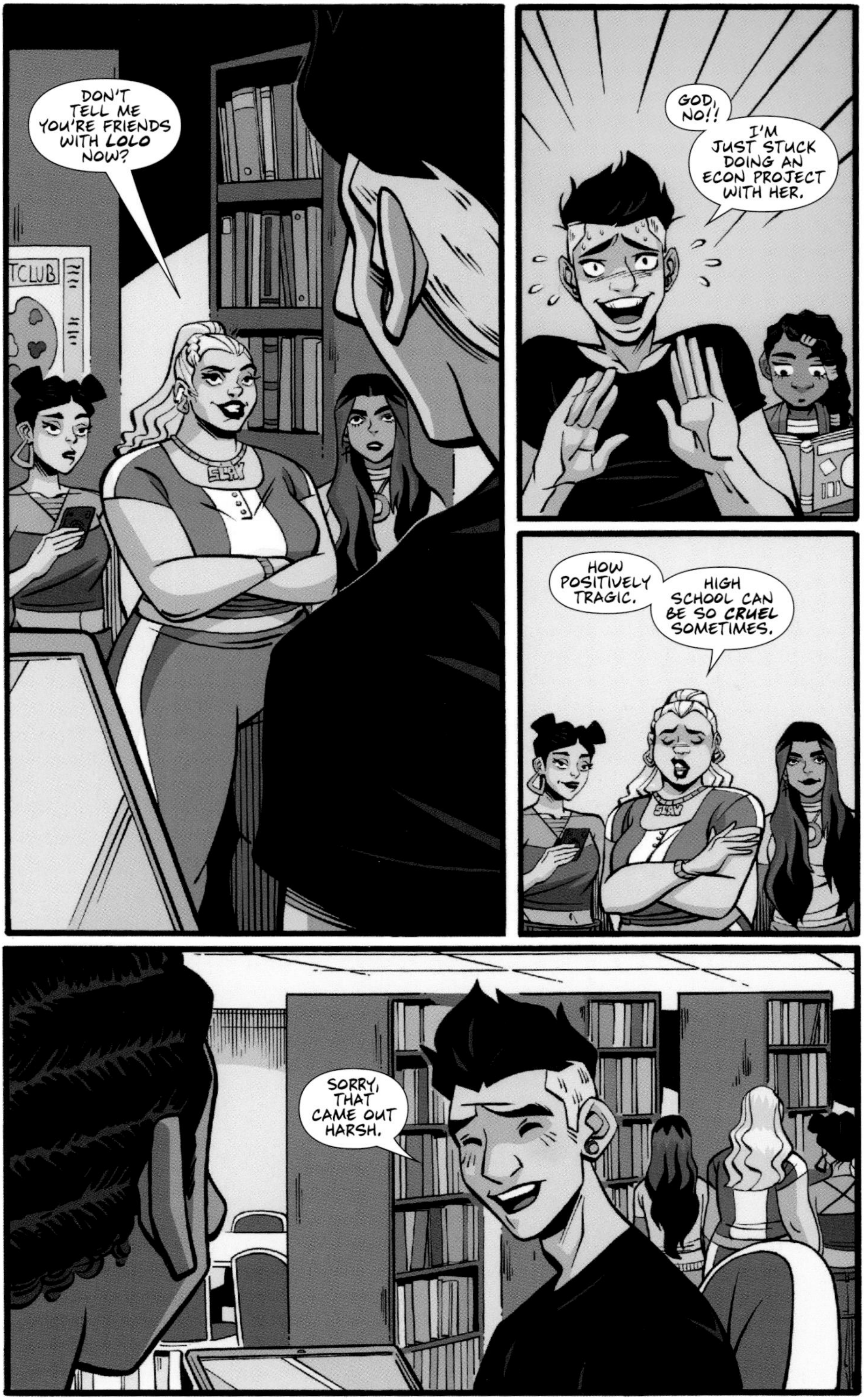
DON'T TELL ME YOU'RE FRIENDS WITH LOLO NOW?
TCLUB
SLAY
GOD, NO!!
I'M JUST STUCK DOING AN ECON PROJECT WITH HER.
HOW POSITIVELY TRAGIC.
HIGH SCHOOL CAN BE SO CRUEL SOMETIMES.
SLAY
SORRY, THAT CAME OUT HARSH.

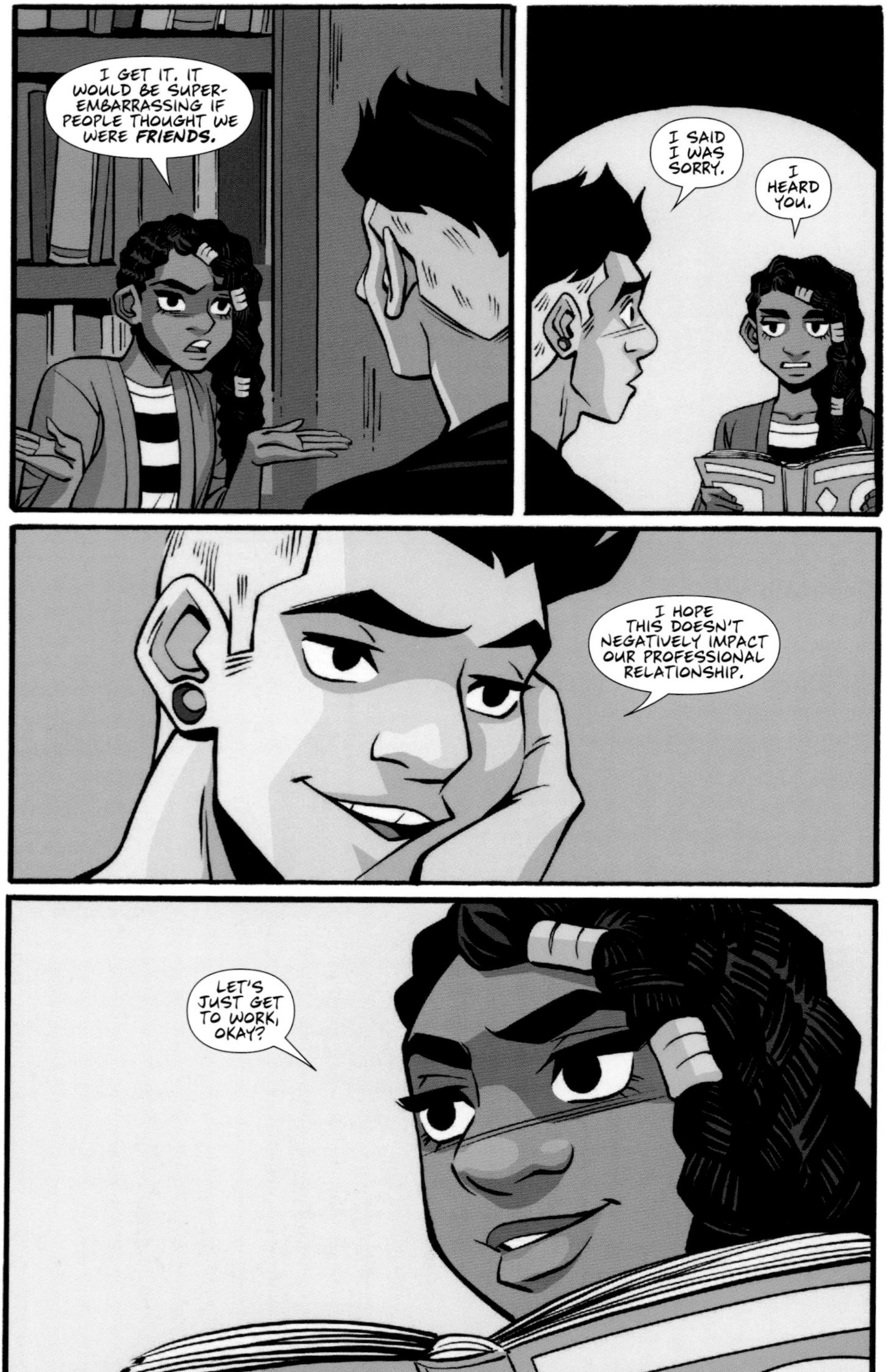

I GET IT. IT WOULD BE SUPER-EMBARRASSING IF PEOPLE THOUGHT WE WERE **FRIENDS.**
I SAID I WAS SORRY.
I HEARD YOU.
I HOPE THIS DOESN'T NEGATIVELY IMPACT OUR PROFESSIONAL RELATIONSHIP.
LET'S JUST GET TO WORK, OKAY?

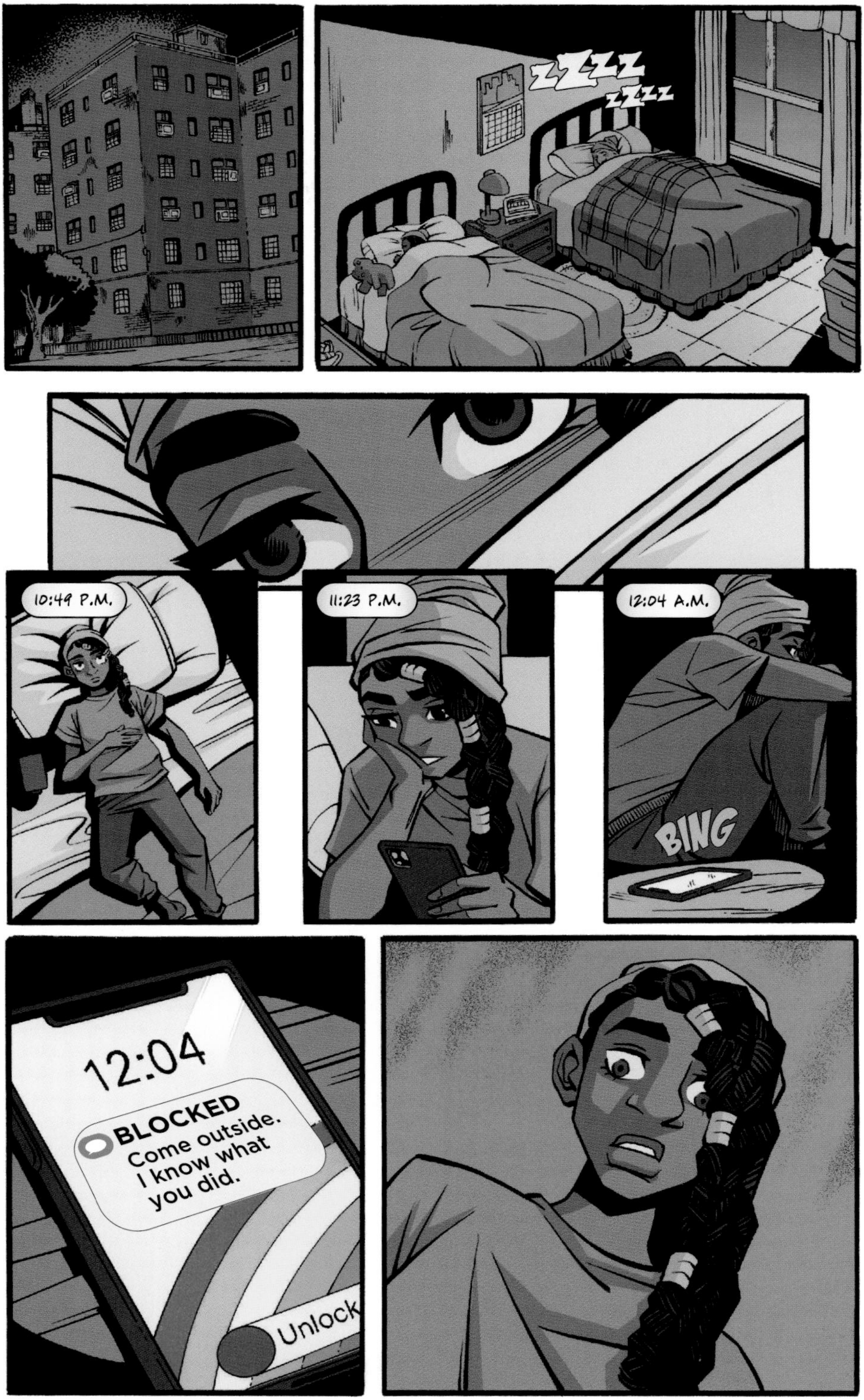
ZZZZ
ZZZZ
10:49 P.M.
11:23 P.M.
12:04 A.M.
BING
12:04
BLOCKED
Come outside. I know what you did.
Unlock

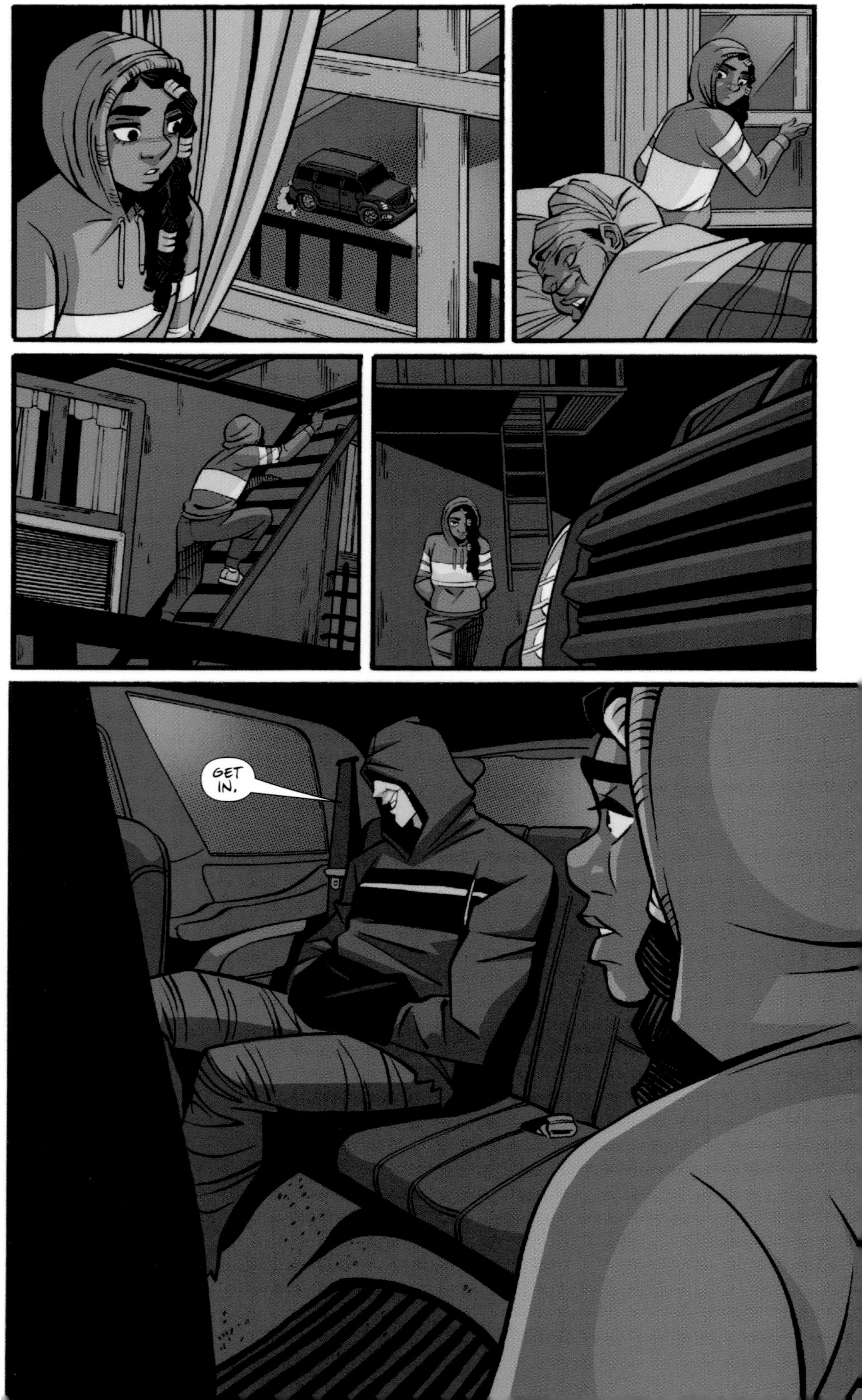
GET IN.

CHAPTER 4

BRAND NEW ME

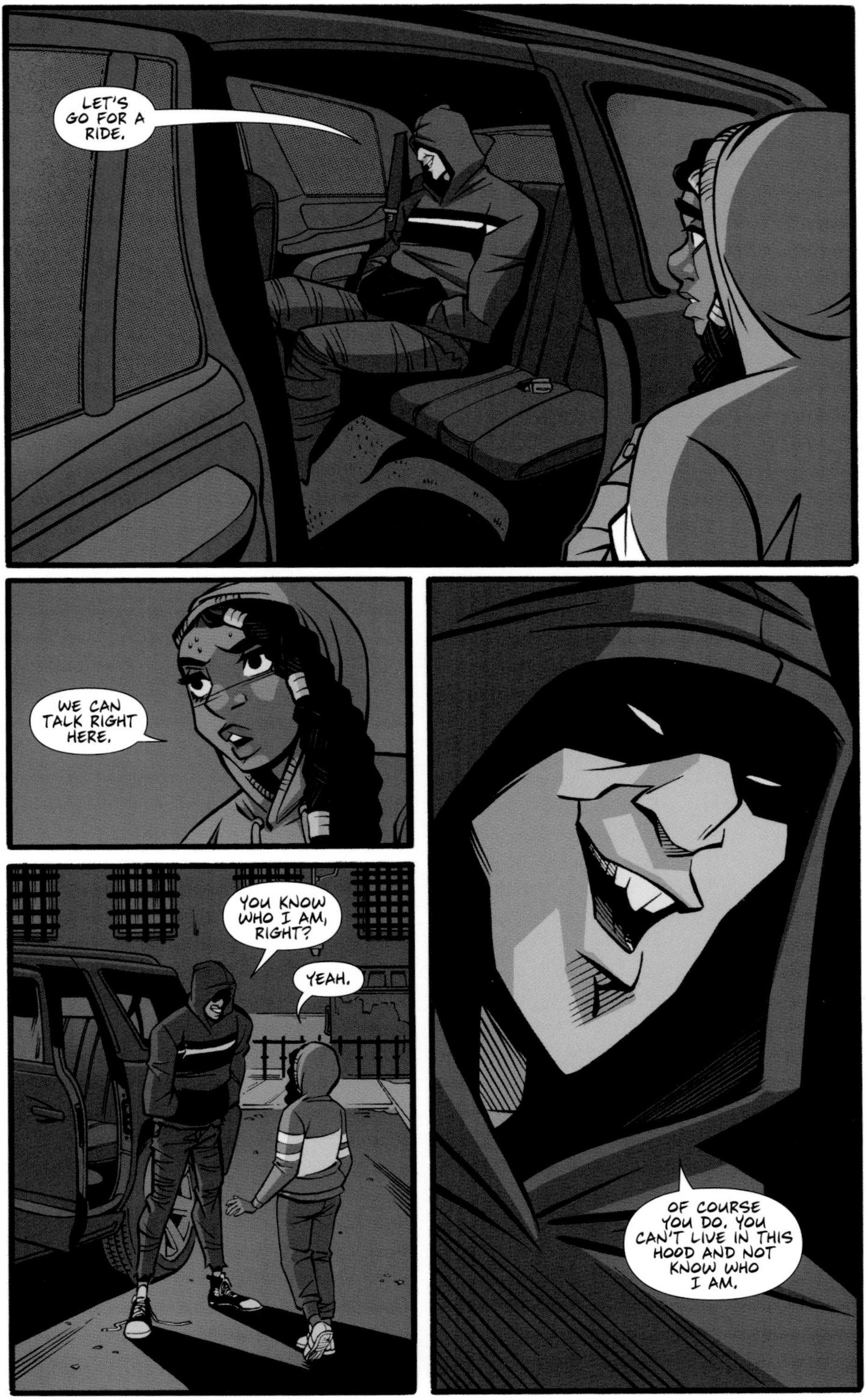
LET'S GO FOR A RIDE.
WE CAN TALK RIGHT HERE.
YOU KNOW WHO I AM, RIGHT?
YEAH.
OF COURSE YOU DO. YOU CAN'T LIVE IN THIS HOOD AND NOT KNOW WHO I AM.

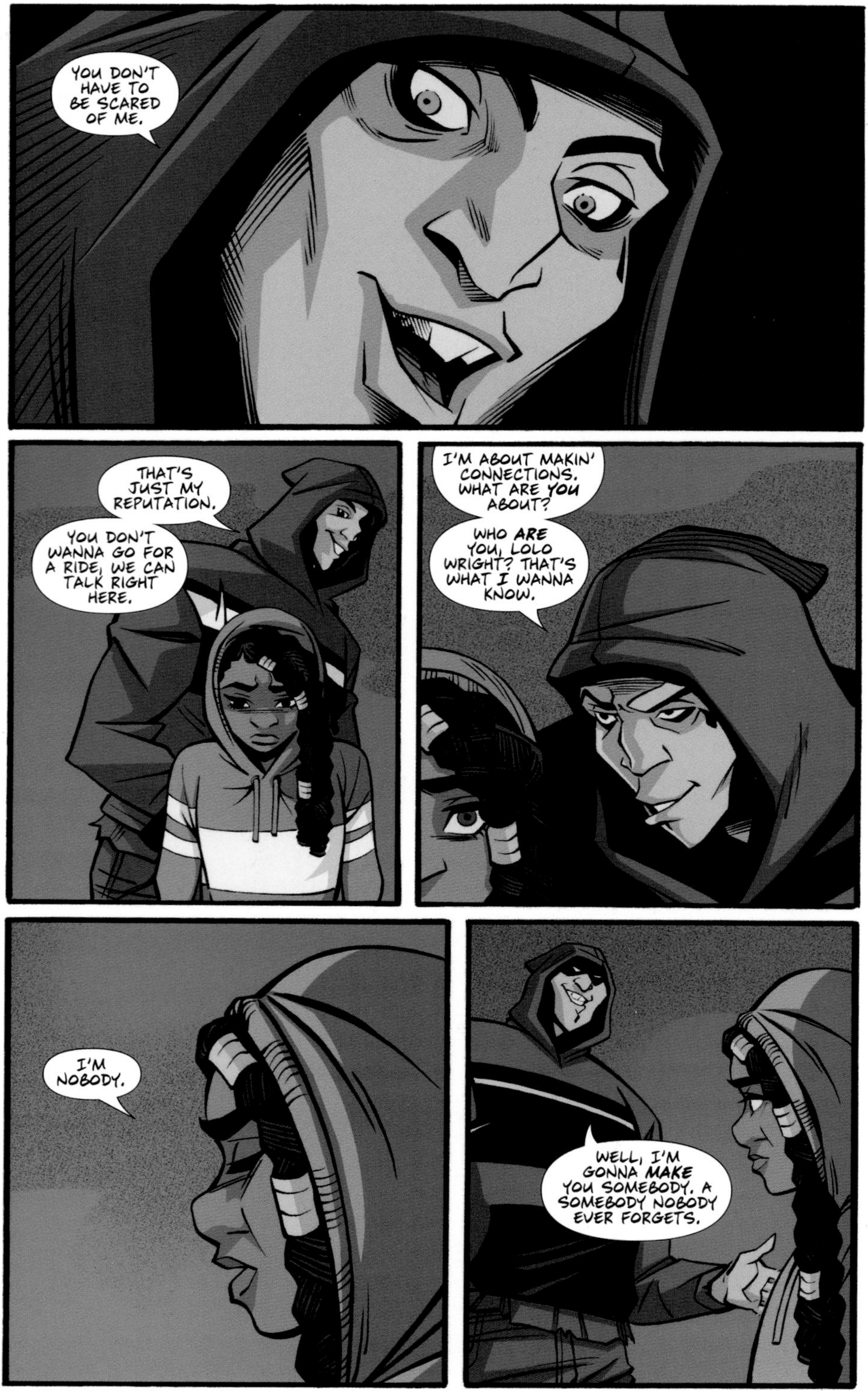
YOU DON'T HAVE TO BE SCARED OF ME.
THAT'S JUST MY REPUTATION.
YOU DON'T WANNA GO FOR A RIDE, WE CAN TALK RIGHT HERE.
I'M ABOUT MAKIN' CONNECTIONS. WHAT ARE **YOU** ABOUT?
WHO **ARE** YOU, LOLO WRIGHT? THAT'S WHAT *I* WANNA KNOW.
I'M NOBODY.
WELL, I'M GONNA **MAKE** YOU SOMEBODY. A SOMEBODY NOBODY EVER FORGETS.

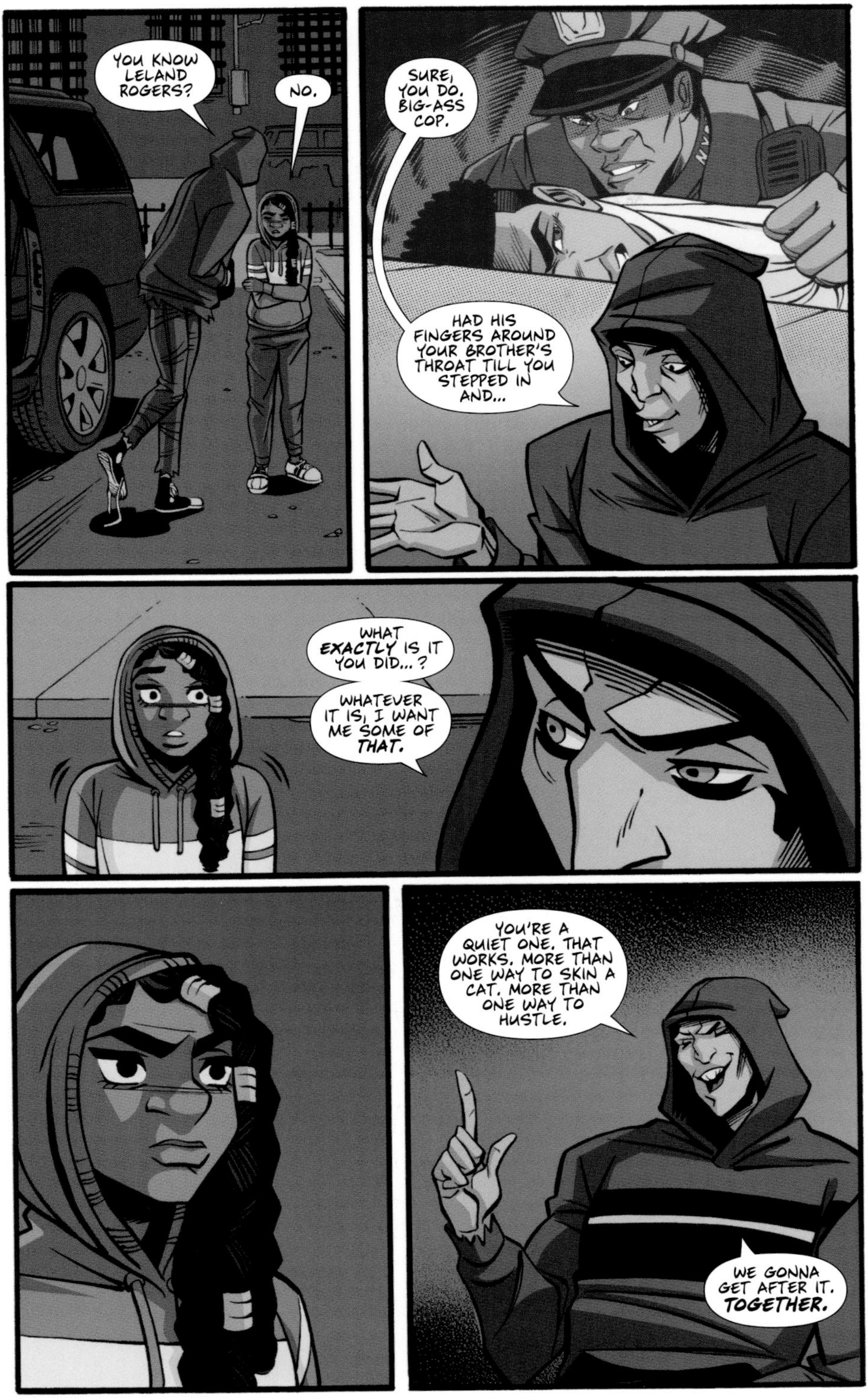
YOU KNOW LELAND ROGERS?
NO.
SURE, YOU DO. BIG-ASS COP.
HAD HIS FINGERS AROUND YOUR BROTHER'S THROAT TILL YOU STEPPED IN AND...
WHAT **EXACTLY** IS IT YOU DID...?
WHATEVER IT IS, I WANT ME SOME OF **THAT.**
YOU'RE A QUIET ONE. THAT WORKS. MORE THAN ONE WAY TO SKIN A CAT. MORE THAN ONE WAY TO HUSTLE.
WE GONNA GET AFTER IT. **TOGETHER.**

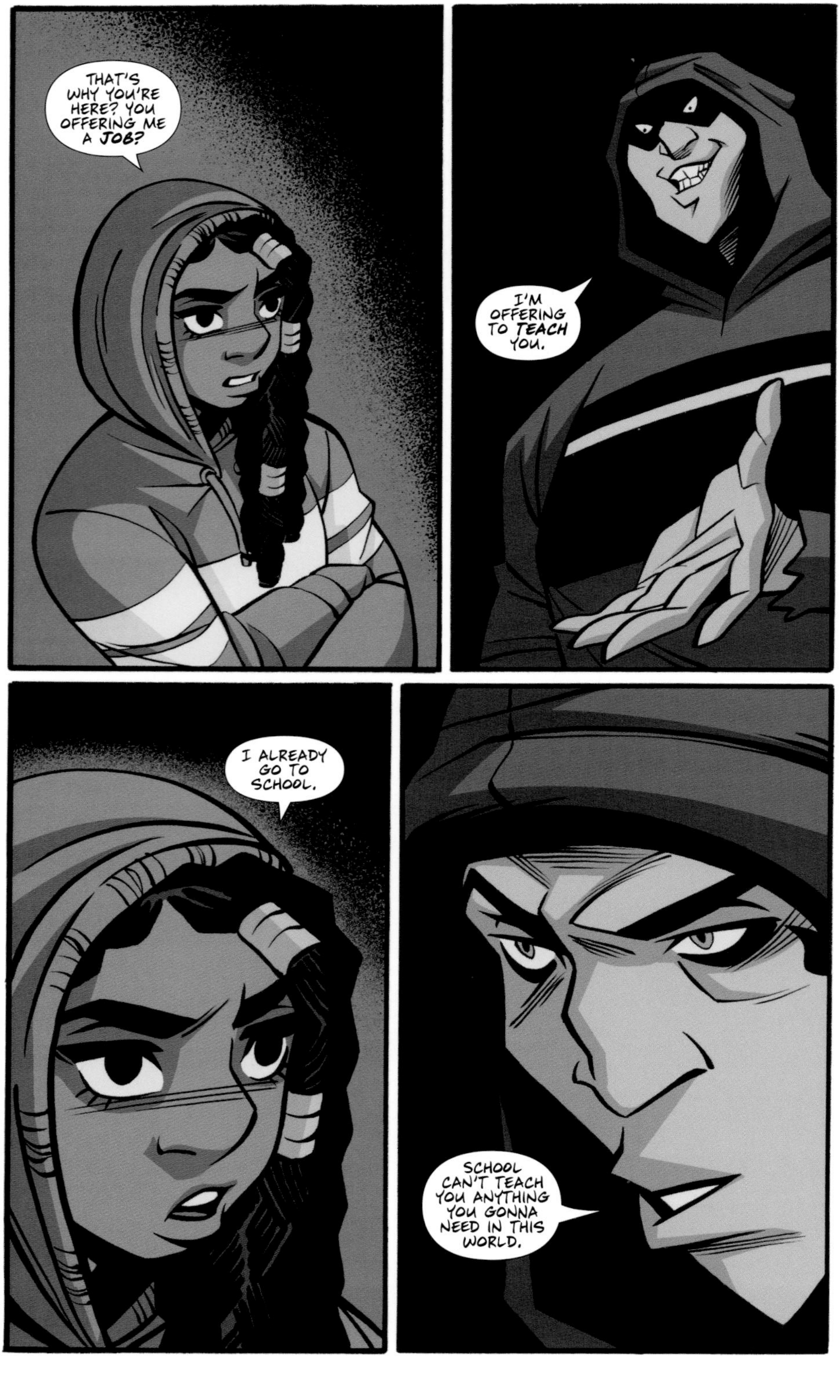
THAT'S WHY YOU'RE HERE? YOU OFFERING ME A **JOB**?
I'M OFFERING TO ***TEACH*** YOU.
I ALREADY GO TO SCHOOL.
SCHOOL CAN'T TEACH YOU ANYTHING YOU GONNA NEED IN THIS WORLD.

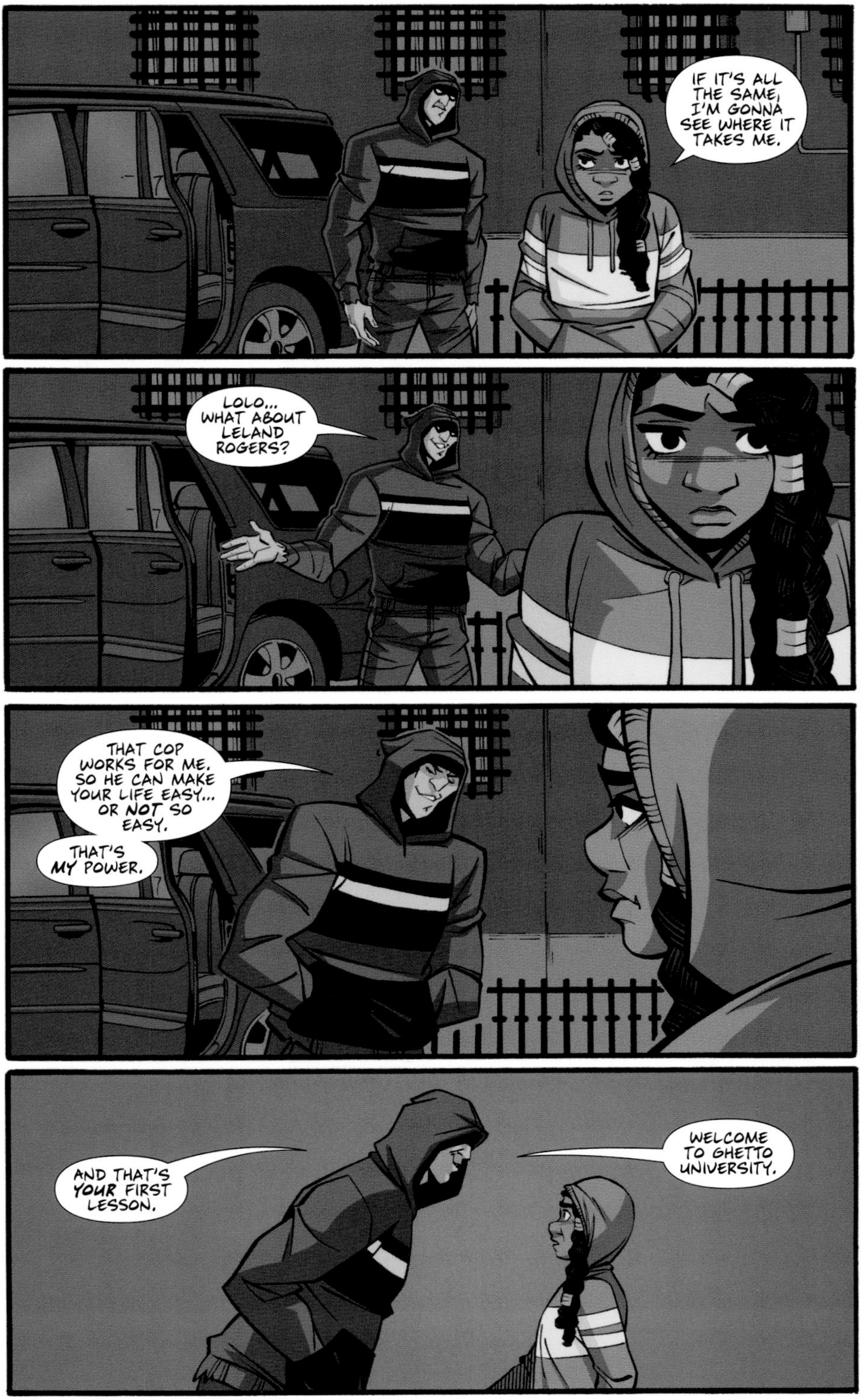
IF IT'S ALL THE SAME, I'M GONNA SEE WHERE IT TAKES ME.
LOLO... WHAT ABOUT LELAND ROGERS?
THAT COP WORKS FOR ME. SO HE CAN MAKE YOUR LIFE EASY... OR **NOT** SO EASY.
THAT'S **MY** POWER.
AND THAT'S **YOUR** FIRST LESSON.
WELCOME TO GHETTO UNIVERSITY.

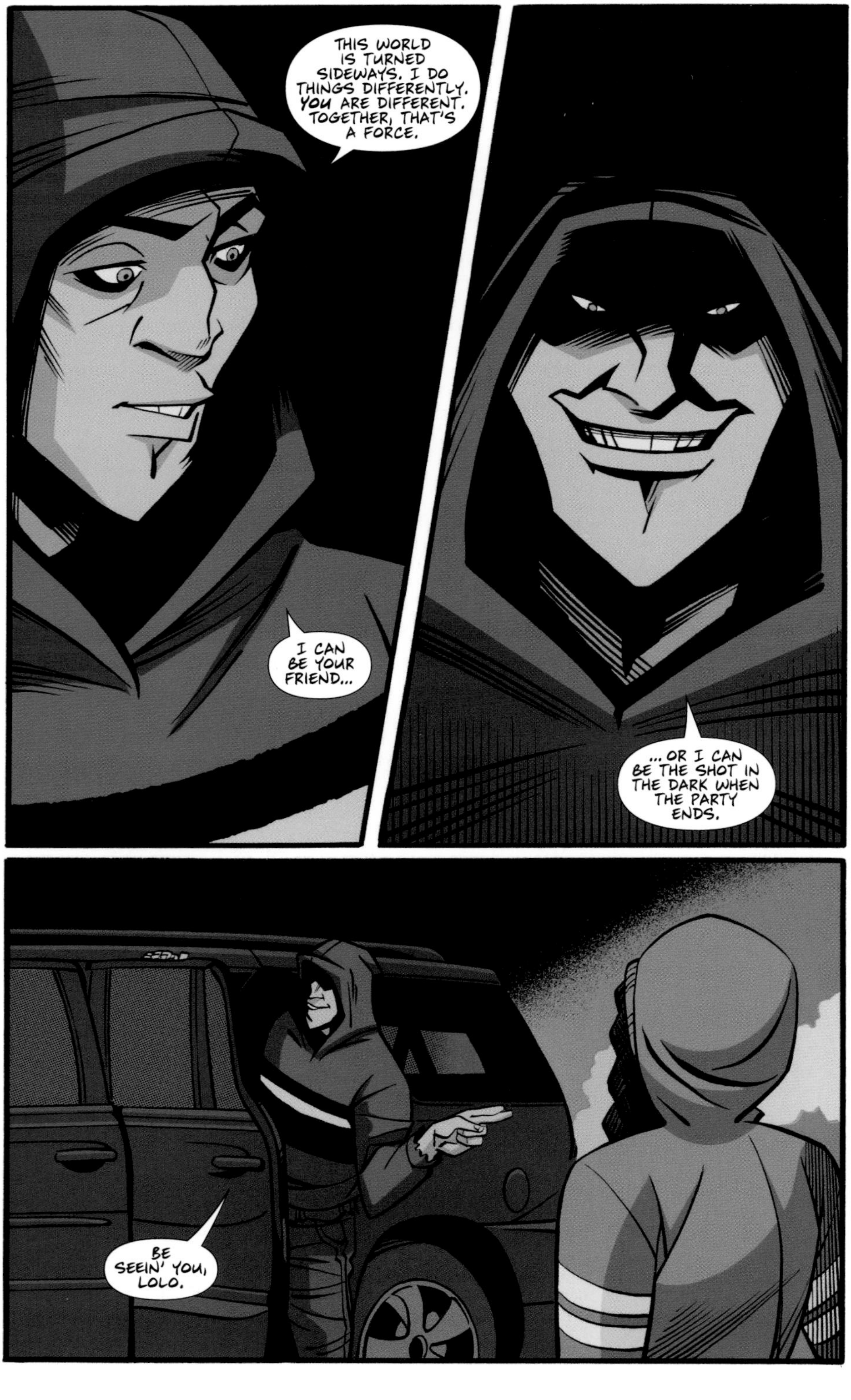
THIS WORLD IS TURNED SIDEWAYS. I DO THINGS DIFFERENTLY. YOU ARE DIFFERENT. TOGETHER, THAT'S A FORCE.
I CAN BE YOUR FRIEND...
...OR I CAN BE THE SHOT IN THE DARK WHEN THE PARTY ENDS.
BE SEEIN' YOU, LOLO.

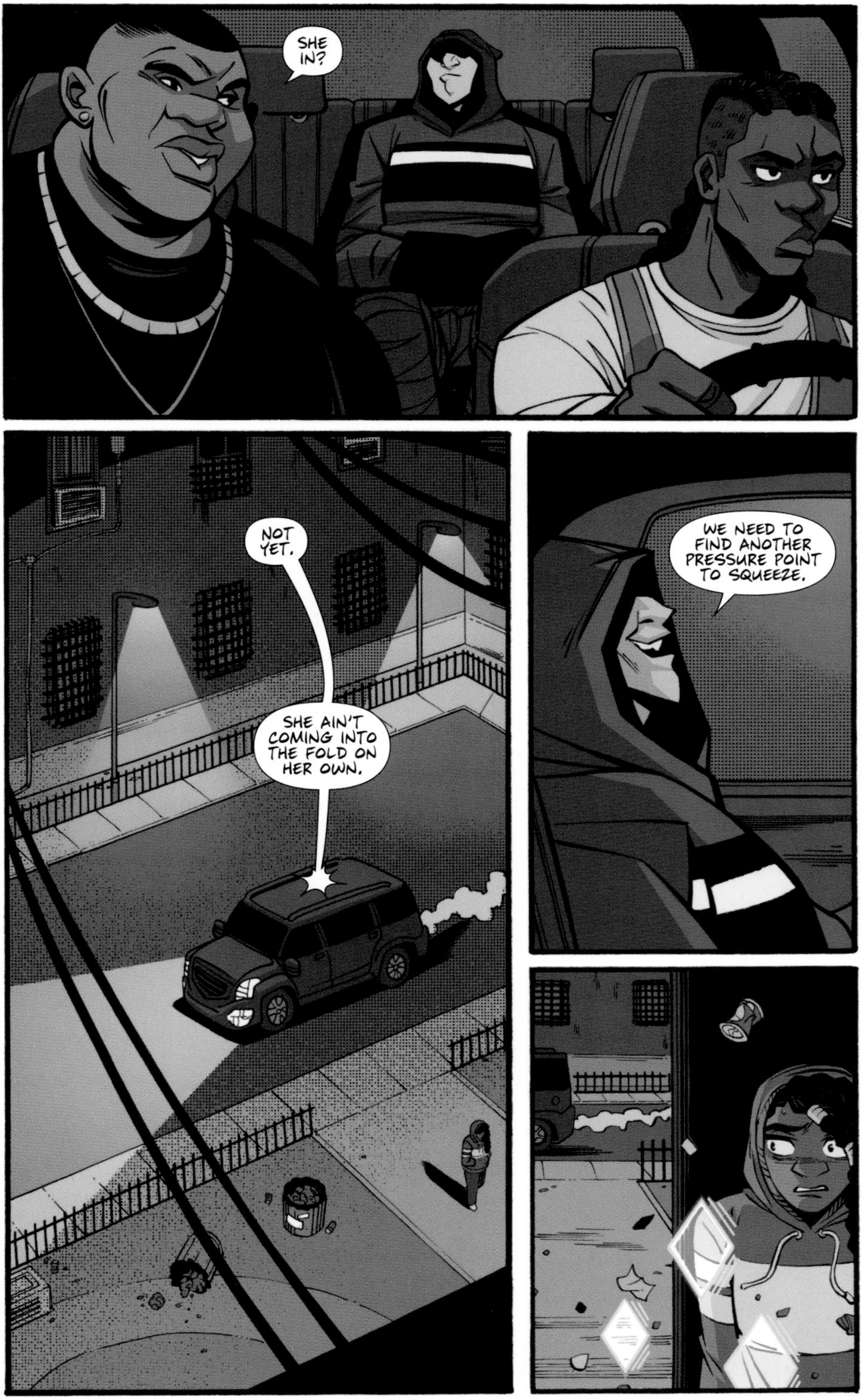
SHE IN?
NOT YET.
SHE AIN'T COMING INTO THE FOLD ON HER OWN.
WE NEED TO FIND ANOTHER PRESSURE POINT TO SQUEEZE.

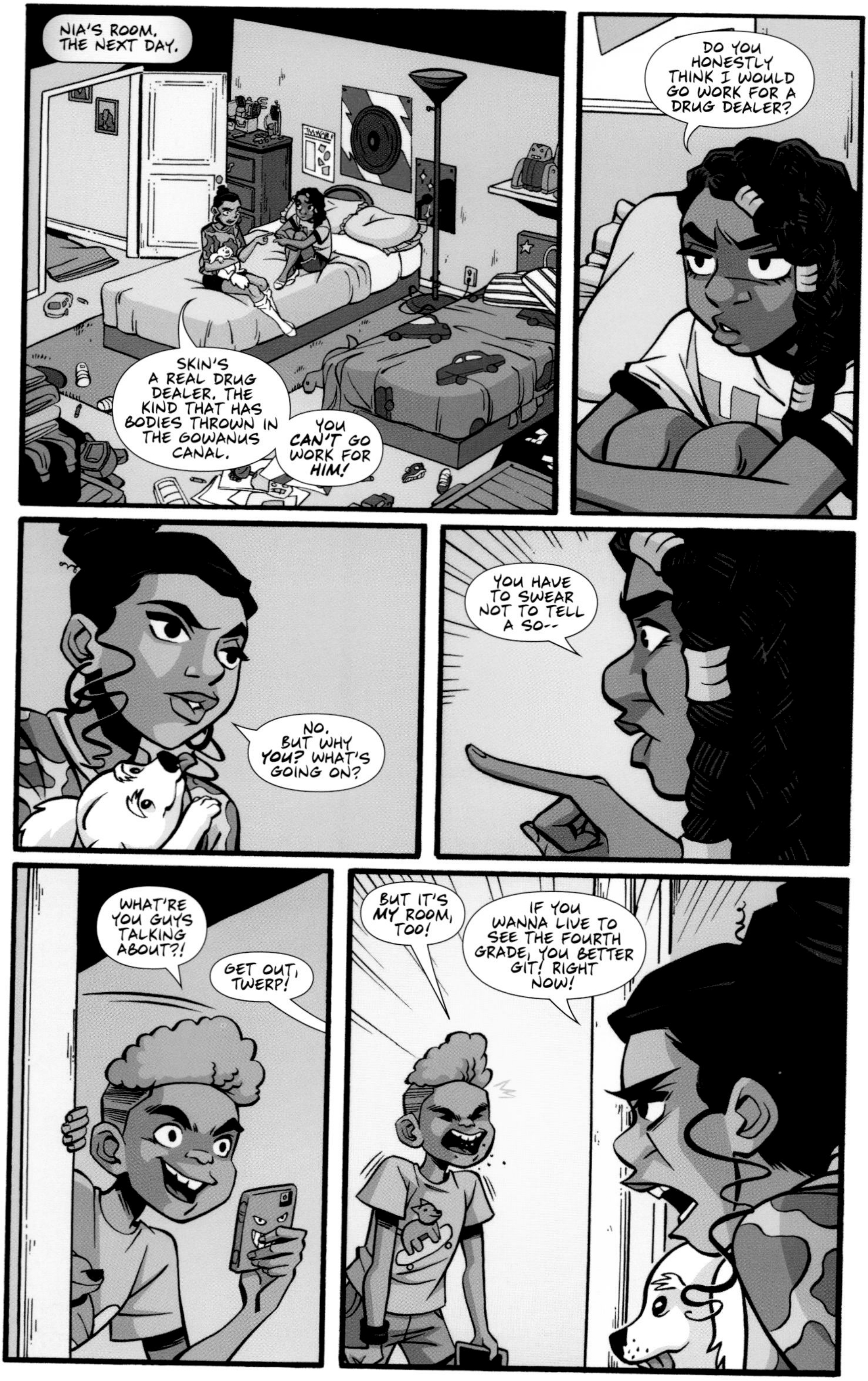
NIA'S ROOM, THE NEXT DAY.
SKIN'S A REAL DRUG DEALER. THE KIND THAT HAS BODIES THROWN IN THE GOWANUS CANAL.
YOU CAN'T GO WORK FOR HIM!
DO YOU HONESTLY THINK I WOULD GO WORK FOR A DRUG DEALER?
NO. BUT WHY YOU? WHAT'S GOING ON?
YOU HAVE TO SWEAR NOT TO TELL A SO--
WHAT'RE YOU GUYS TALKING ABOUT?!
GET OUT, TWERP!
BUT IT'S MY ROOM, TOO!
IF YOU WANNA LIVE TO SEE THE FOURTH GRADE, YOU BETTER GIT! RIGHT NOW!

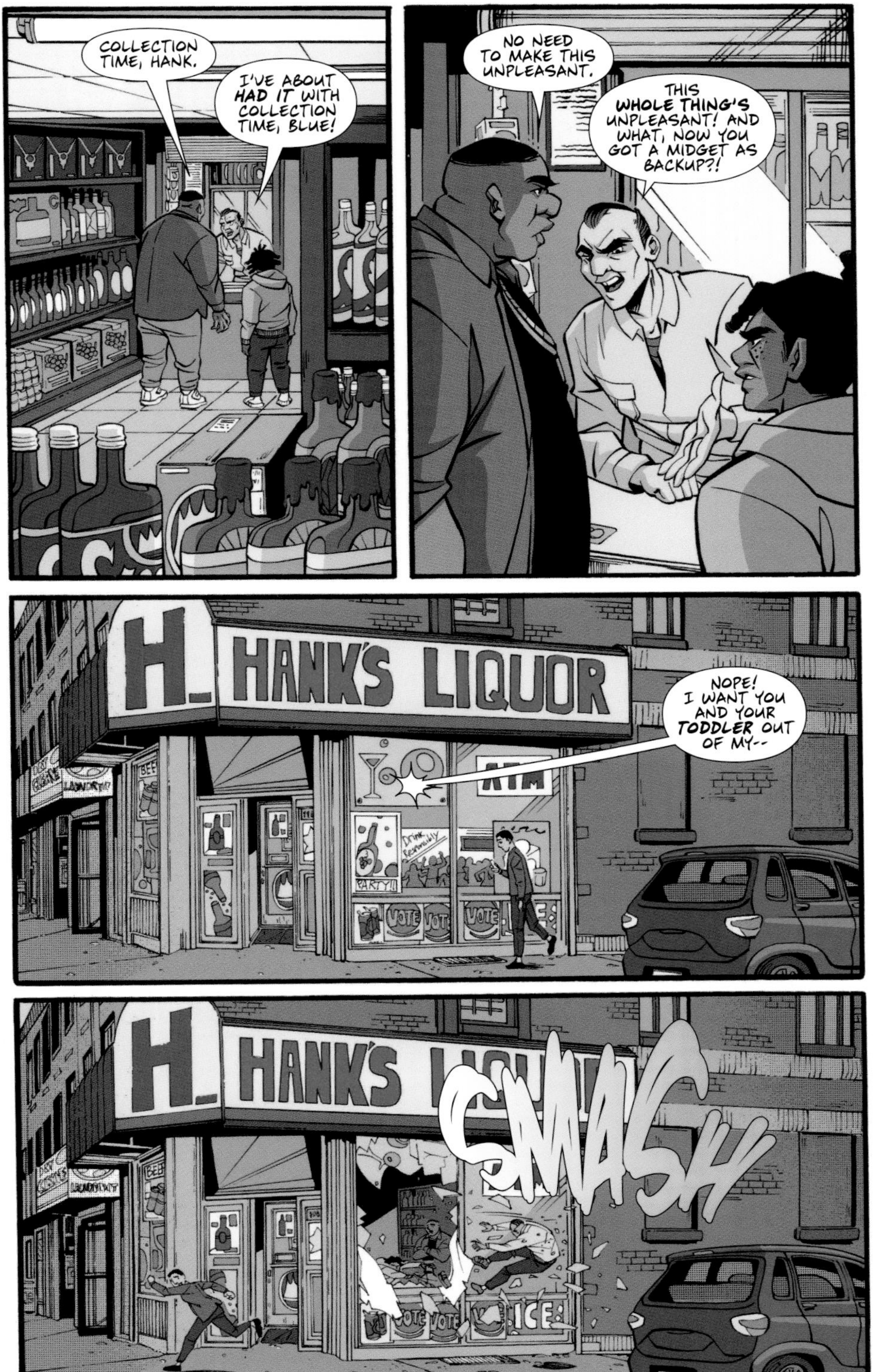
COLLECTION TIME, HANK.
I'VE ABOUT **HAD IT** WITH COLLECTION TIME, BLUE!
NO NEED TO MAKE THIS UNPLEASANT.
THIS **WHOLE THING'S** UNPLEASANT! AND WHAT, NOW YOU GOT A MIDGET AS BACKUP?!
H.
HANK'S LIQUOR
ATM
VOTE
NOPE! I WANT YOU AND YOUR **TODDLER** OUT OF MY--
HANK'S
SMASH
ICE

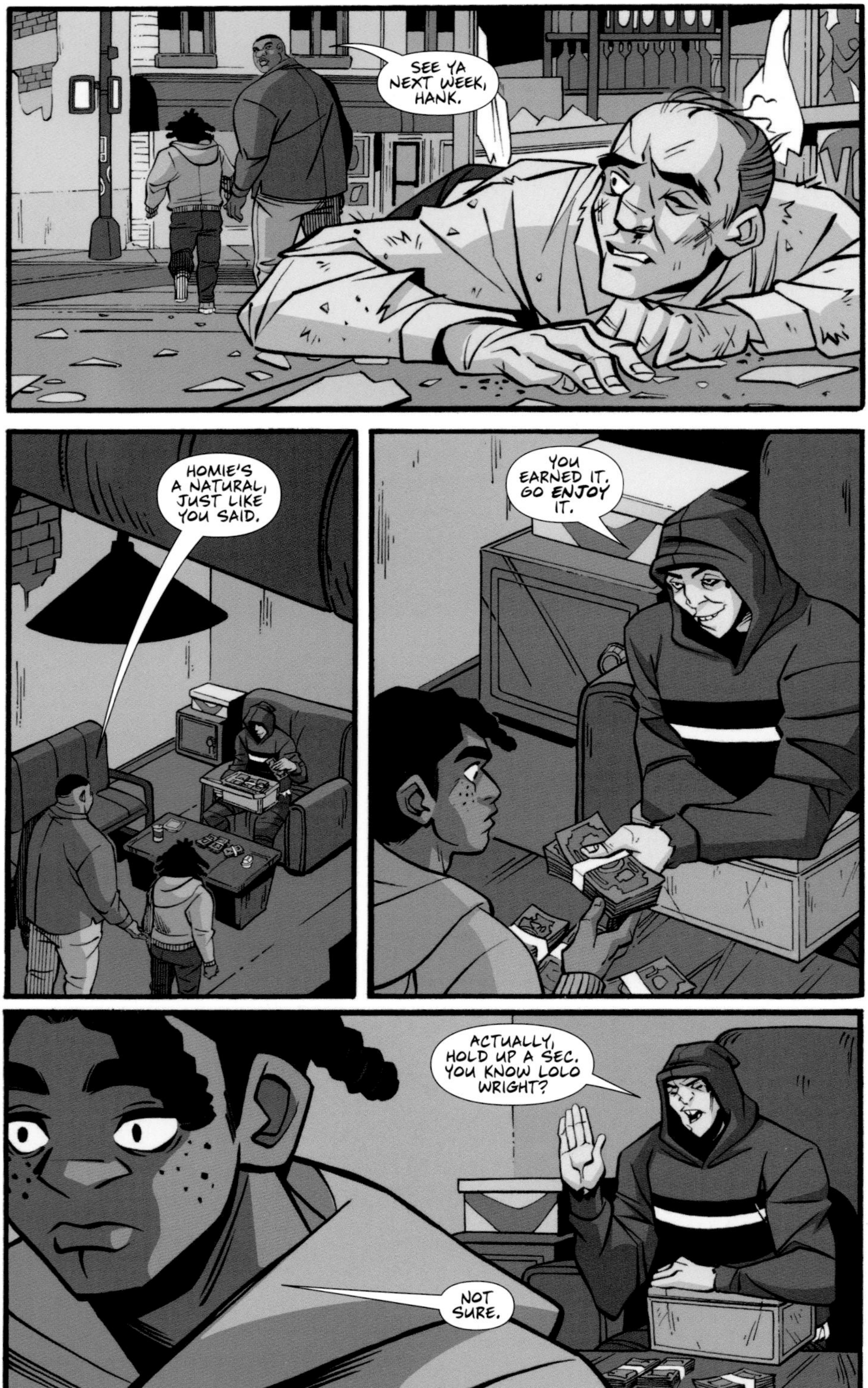
SEE YA NEXT WEEK, HANK.
HOMIE'S A NATURAL, JUST LIKE YOU SAID.
YOU EARNED IT. GO ENJOY IT.
ACTUALLY, HOLD UP A SEC. YOU KNOW LOLO WRIGHT?
NOT SURE.

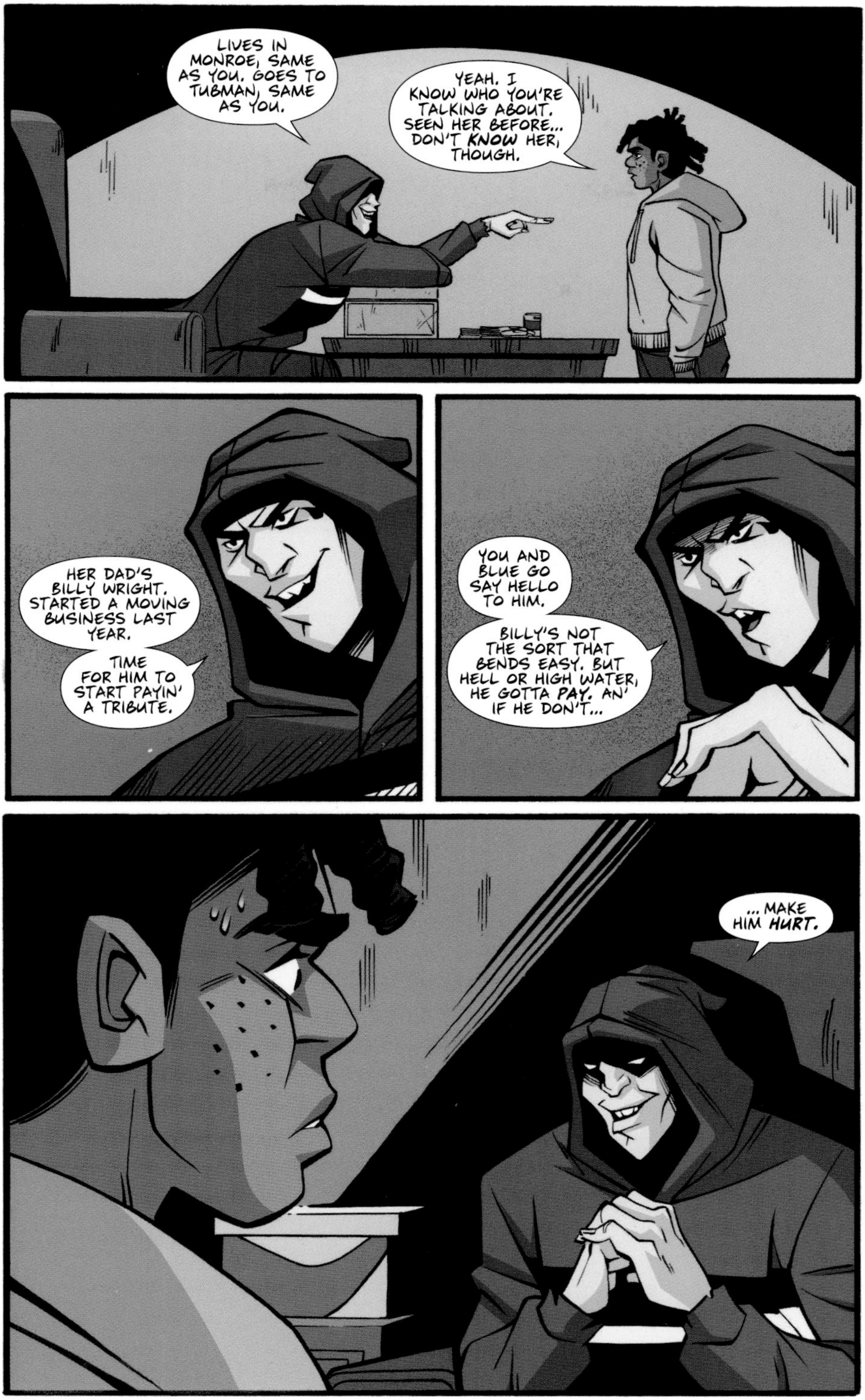
LIVES IN MONROE, SAME AS YOU. GOES TO TUBMAN, SAME AS YOU.
YEAH. I KNOW WHO YOU'RE TALKING ABOUT. SEEN HER BEFORE... DON'T KNOW HER, THOUGH.
HER DAD'S BILLY WRIGHT. STARTED A MOVING BUSINESS LAST YEAR.
TIME FOR HIM TO START PAYIN' A TRIBUTE.
YOU AND BLUE GO SAY HELLO TO HIM.
BILLY'S NOT THE SORT THAT BENDS EASY. BUT HELL OR HIGH WATER, HE GOTTA PAY. AN' IF HE DON'T...
...MAKE HIM HURT.

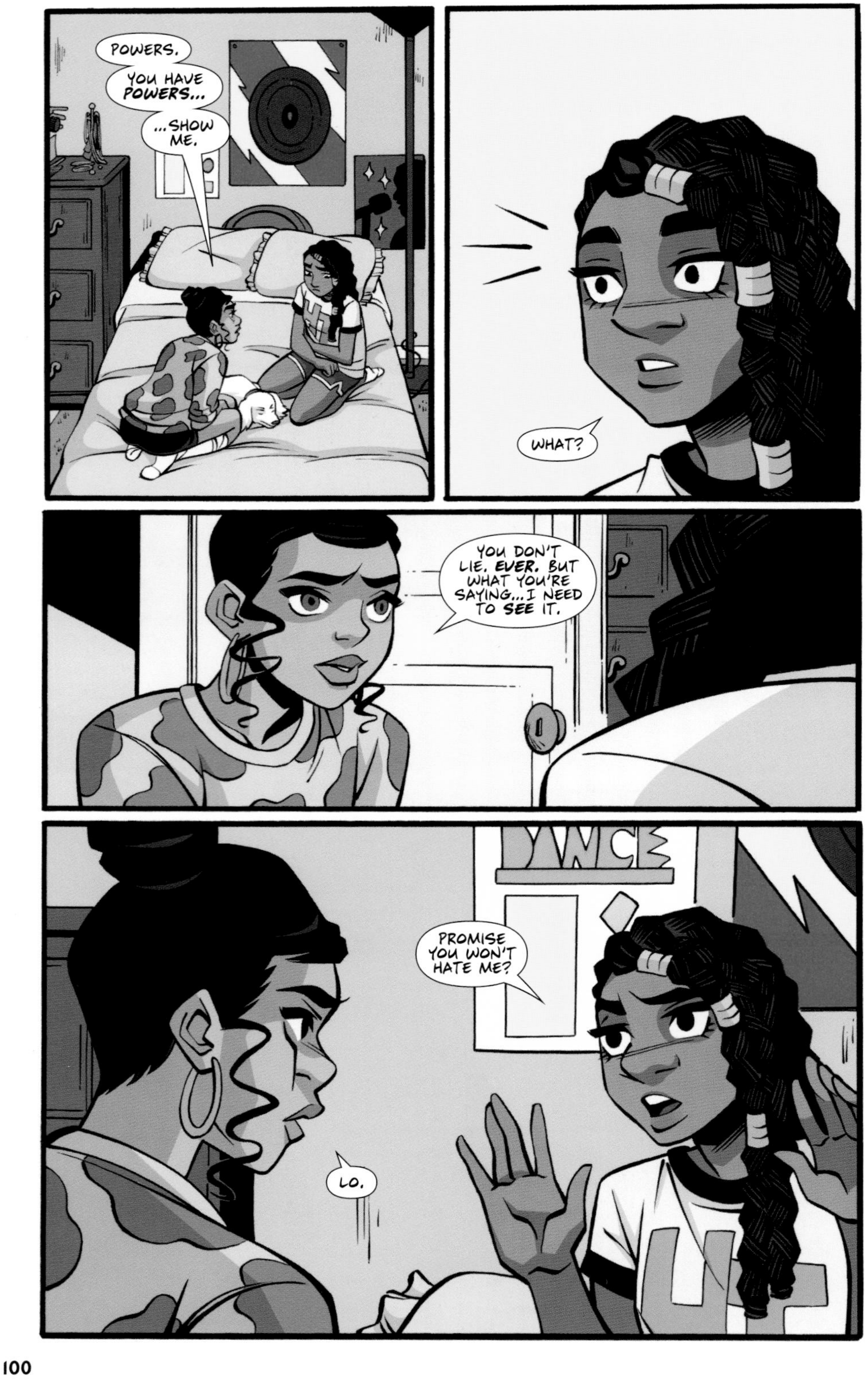
POWERS.
YOU HAVE POWERS...
...SHOW ME.
WHAT?
YOU DON'T LIE. EVER. BUT WHAT YOU'RE SAYING...I NEED TO SEE IT.
DANCE
PROMISE YOU WON'T HATE ME?
LO.

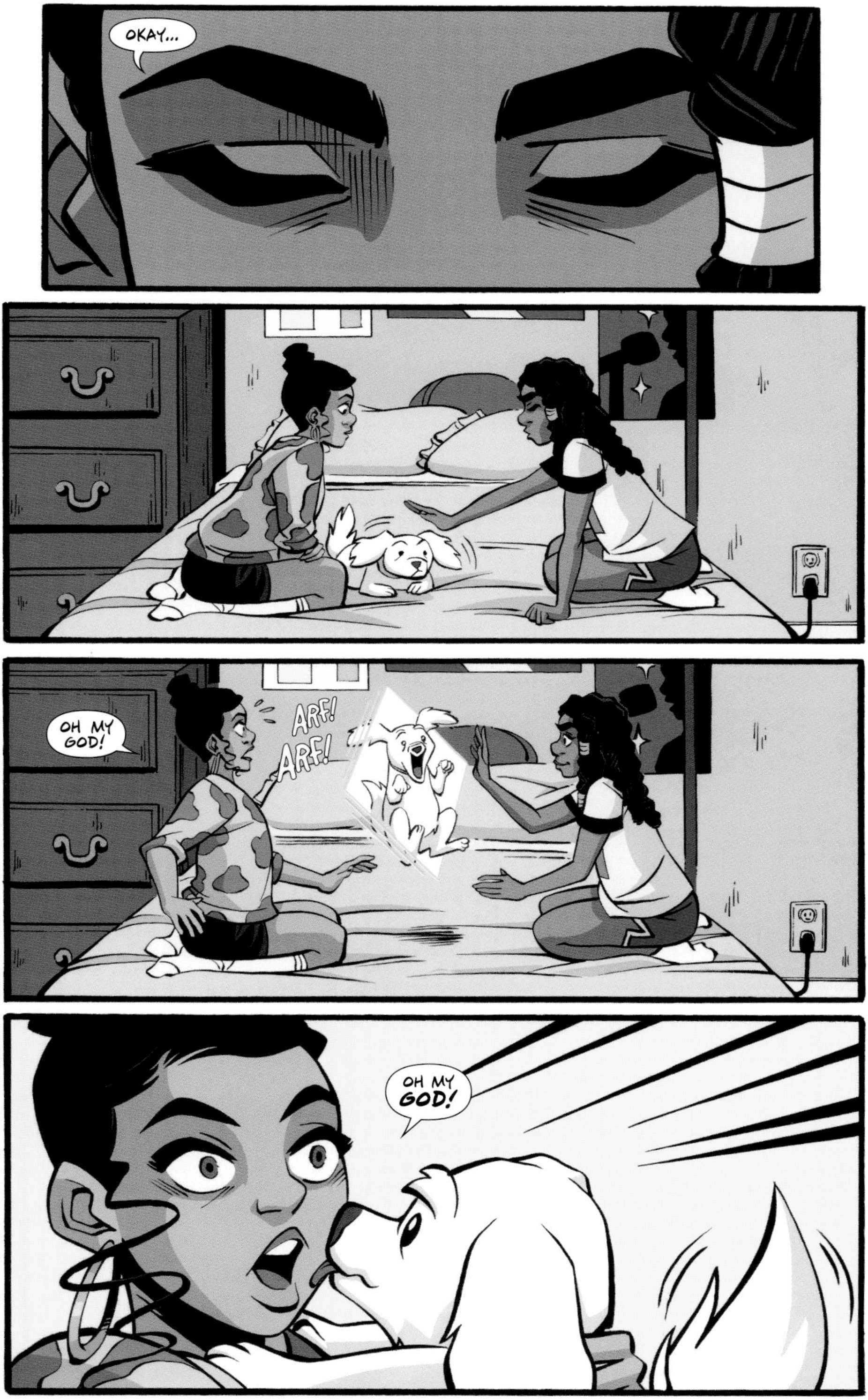
OKAY...
OH MY GOD!
ARF!
ARF!
OH MY GOD!

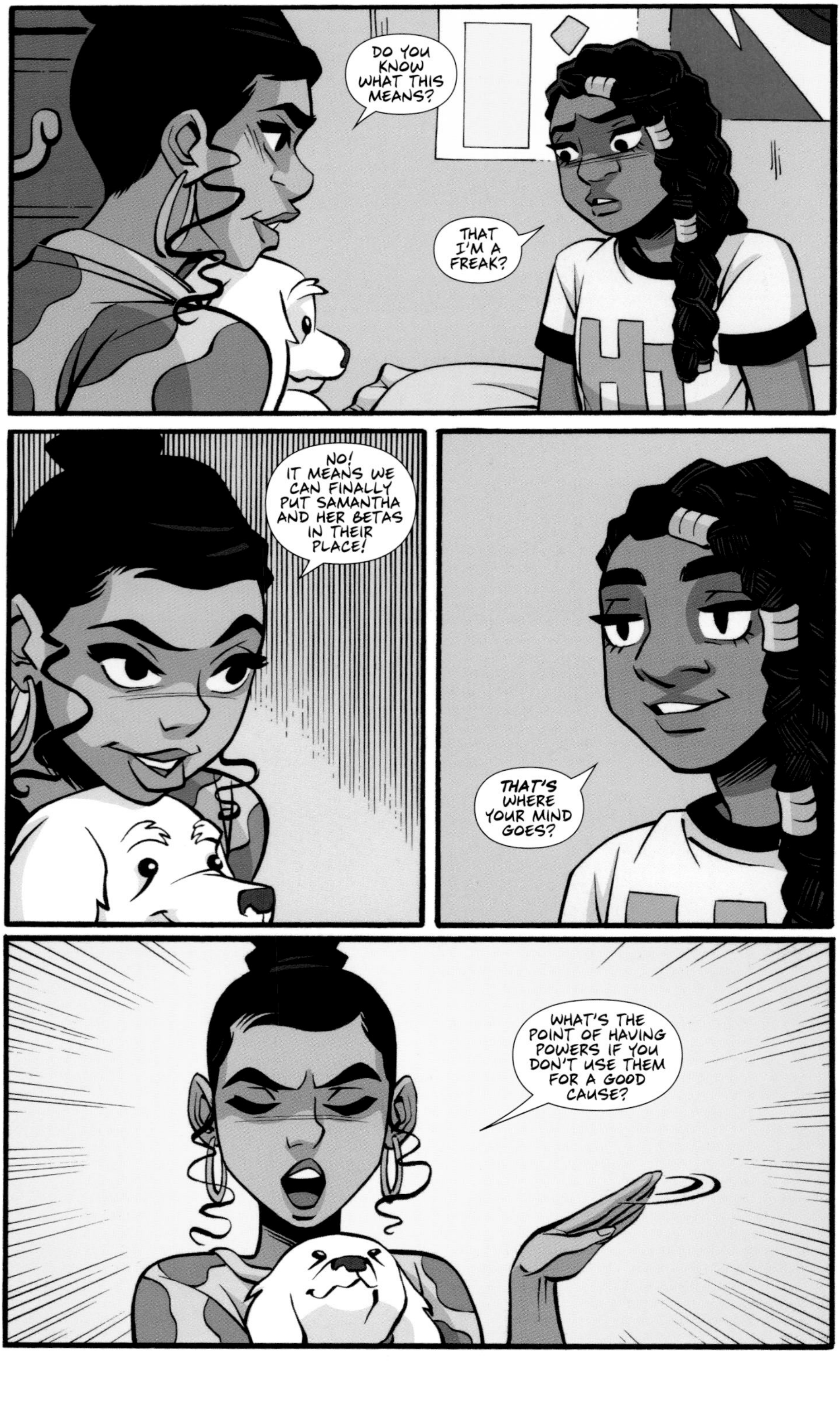
DO YOU KNOW WHAT THIS MEANS?
THAT I'M A FREAK?
NO! IT MEANS WE CAN FINALLY PUT SAMANTHA AND HER BETAS IN THEIR PLACE!
THAT'S WHERE YOUR MIND GOES?
WHAT'S THE POINT OF HAVING POWERS IF YOU DON'T USE THEM FOR A GOOD CAUSE?

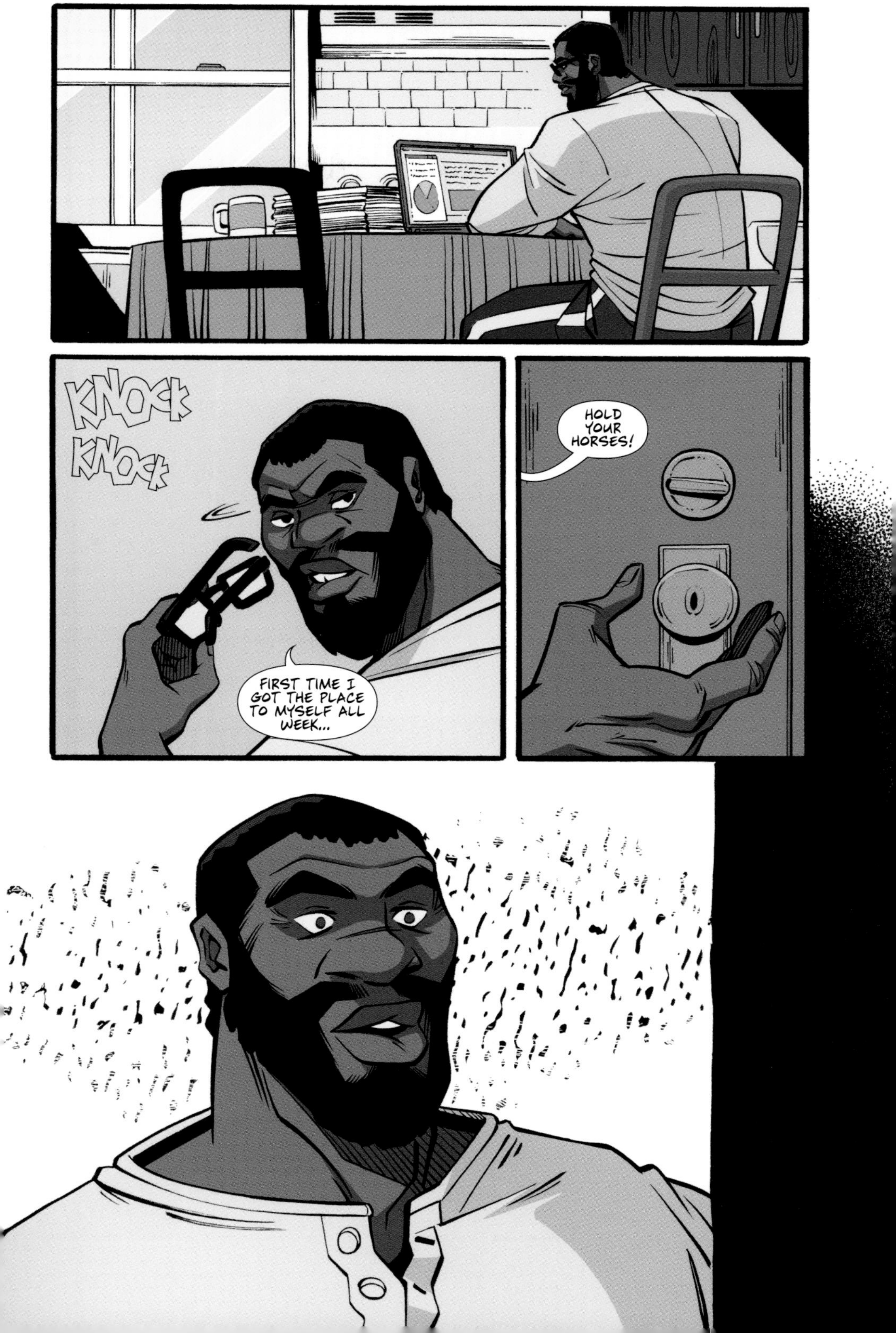
KNOCK
KNOCK
FIRST TIME I GOT THE PLACE TO MYSELF ALL WEEK...
HOLD YOUR HORSES!

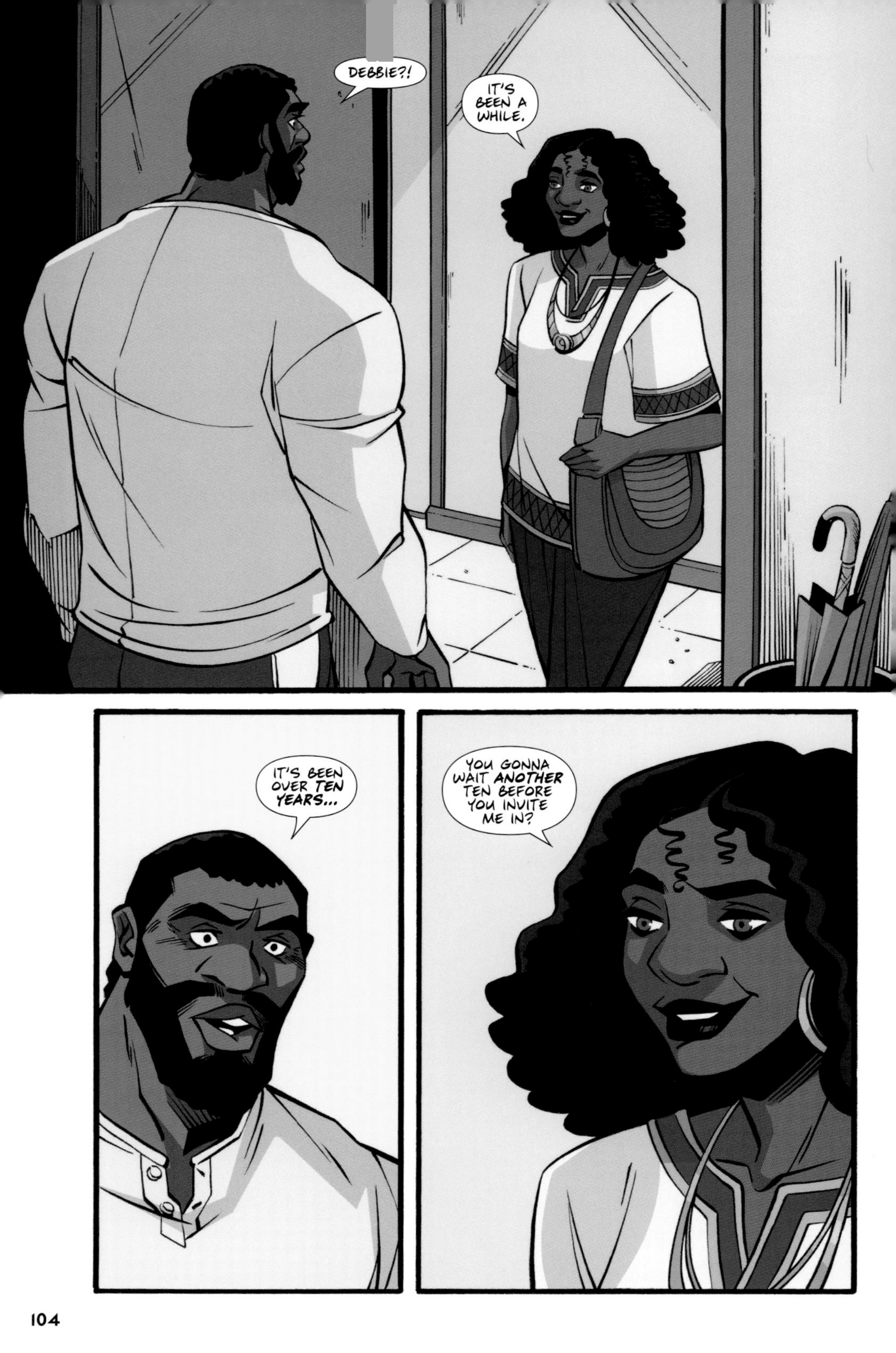
DEBBIE?!
IT'S BEEN A WHILE.
IT'S BEEN OVER TEN YEARS...
YOU GONNA WAIT ANOTHER TEN BEFORE YOU INVITE ME IN?

CHAPTER 5

SO
DONE

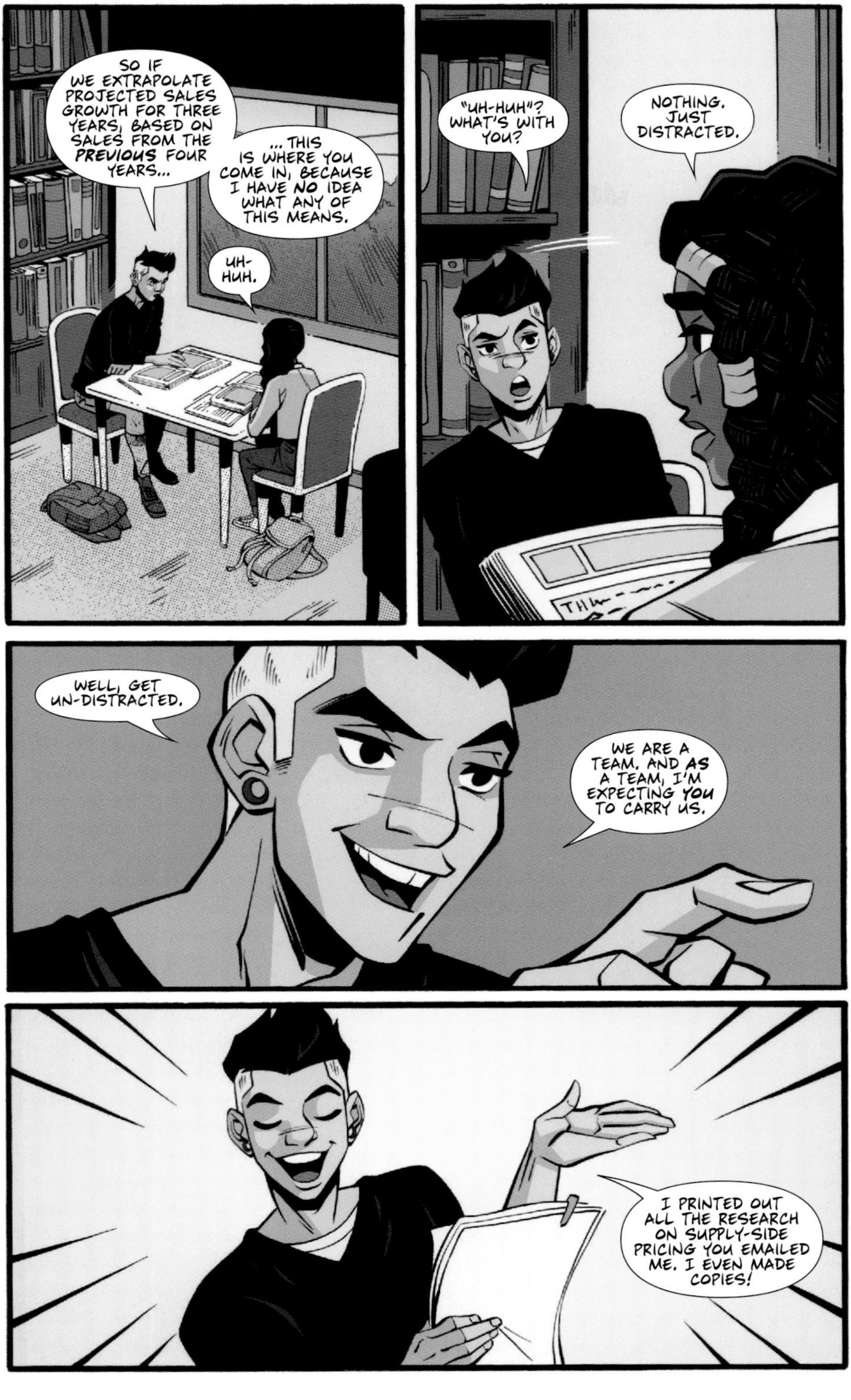
SO IF WE EXTRAPOLATE PROJECTED SALES GROWTH FOR THREE YEARS, BASED ON SALES FROM THE PREVIOUS FOUR YEARS...
... THIS IS WHERE YOU COME IN, BECAUSE I HAVE NO IDEA WHAT ANY OF THIS MEANS.
UH-HUH.
"UH-HUH"? WHAT'S WITH YOU?
NOTHING. JUST DISTRACTED.
WELL, GET UN-DISTRACTED.
WE ARE A TEAM. AND AS A TEAM, I'M EXPECTING YOU TO CARRY US.
I PRINTED OUT ALL THE RESEARCH ON SUPPLY-SIDE PRICING YOU EMAILED ME. I EVEN MADE COPIES!

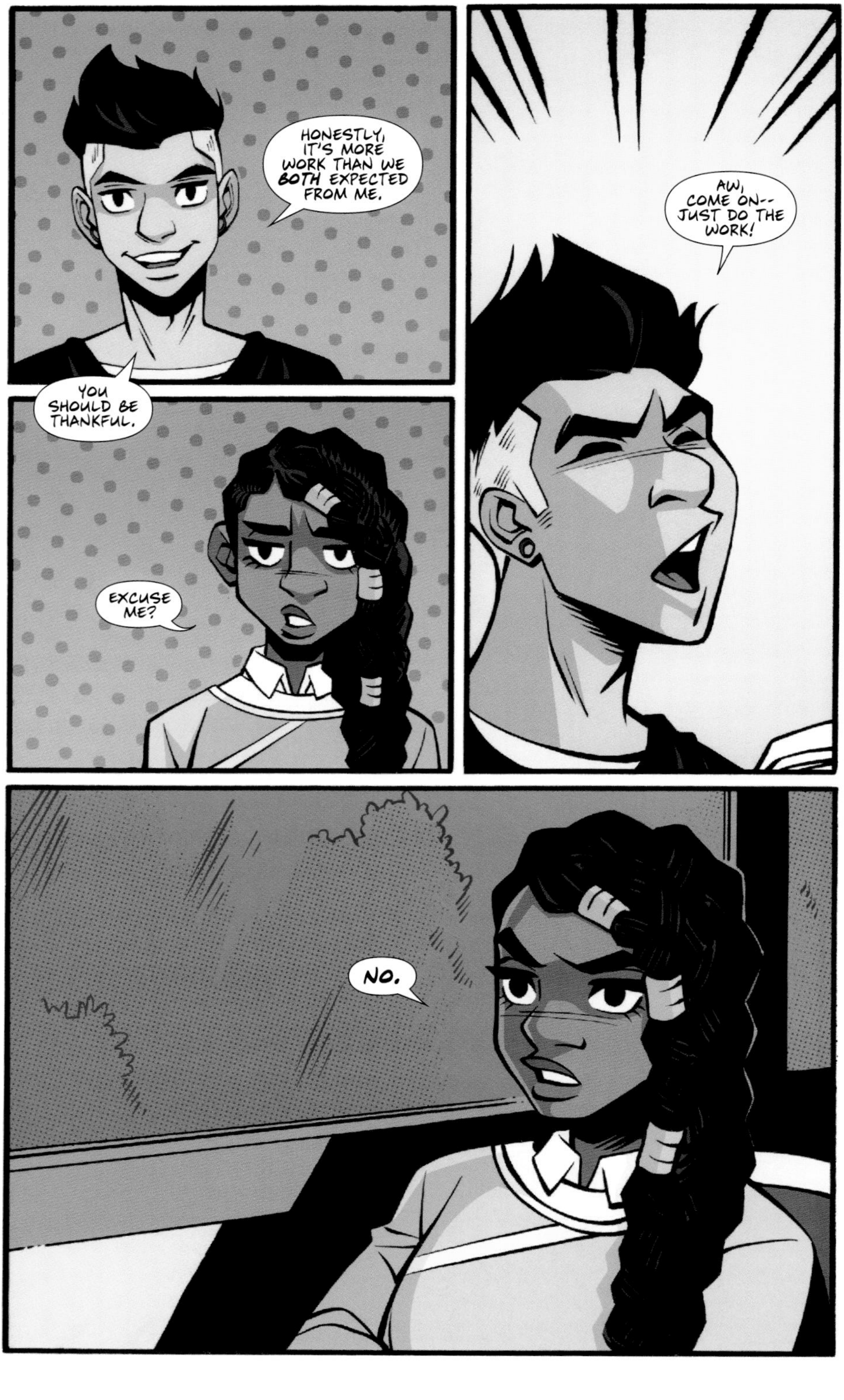
HONESTLY, IT'S MORE WORK THAN WE *BOTH* EXPECTED FROM ME.
YOU SHOULD BE THANKFUL.
EXCUSE ME?
AW, COME ON-- JUST DO THE WORK!
NO.

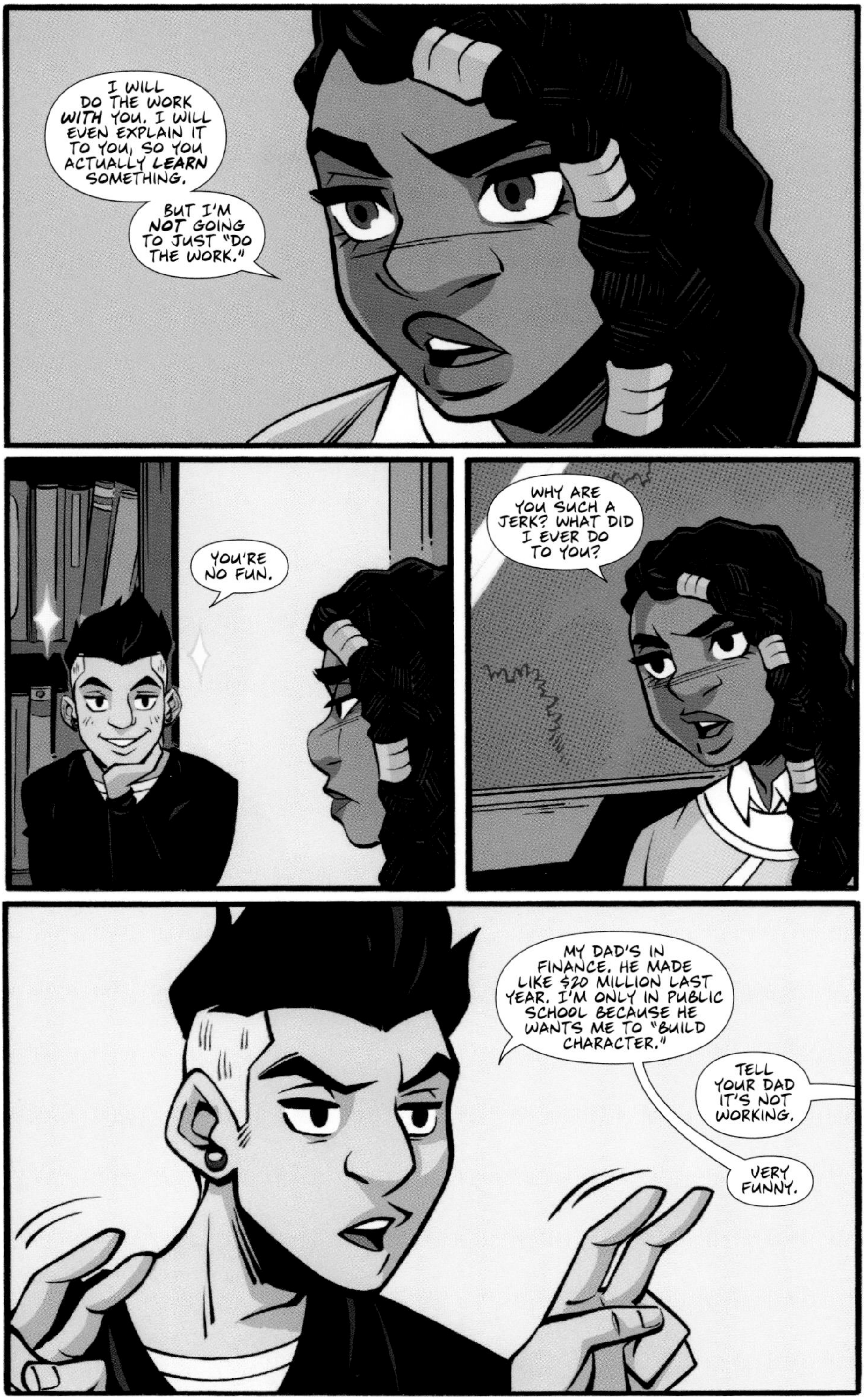
I WILL DO THE WORK WITH YOU. I WILL EVEN EXPLAIN IT TO YOU, SO YOU ACTUALLY LEARN SOMETHING.
BUT I'M NOT GOING TO JUST "DO THE WORK."
YOU'RE NO FUN.
WHY ARE YOU SUCH A JERK? WHAT DID I EVER DO TO YOU?
MY DAD'S IN FINANCE. HE MADE LIKE $20 MILLION LAST YEAR. I'M ONLY IN PUBLIC SCHOOL BECAUSE HE WANTS ME TO "BUILD CHARACTER."
TELL YOUR DAD IT'S NOT WORKING.
VERY FUNNY.

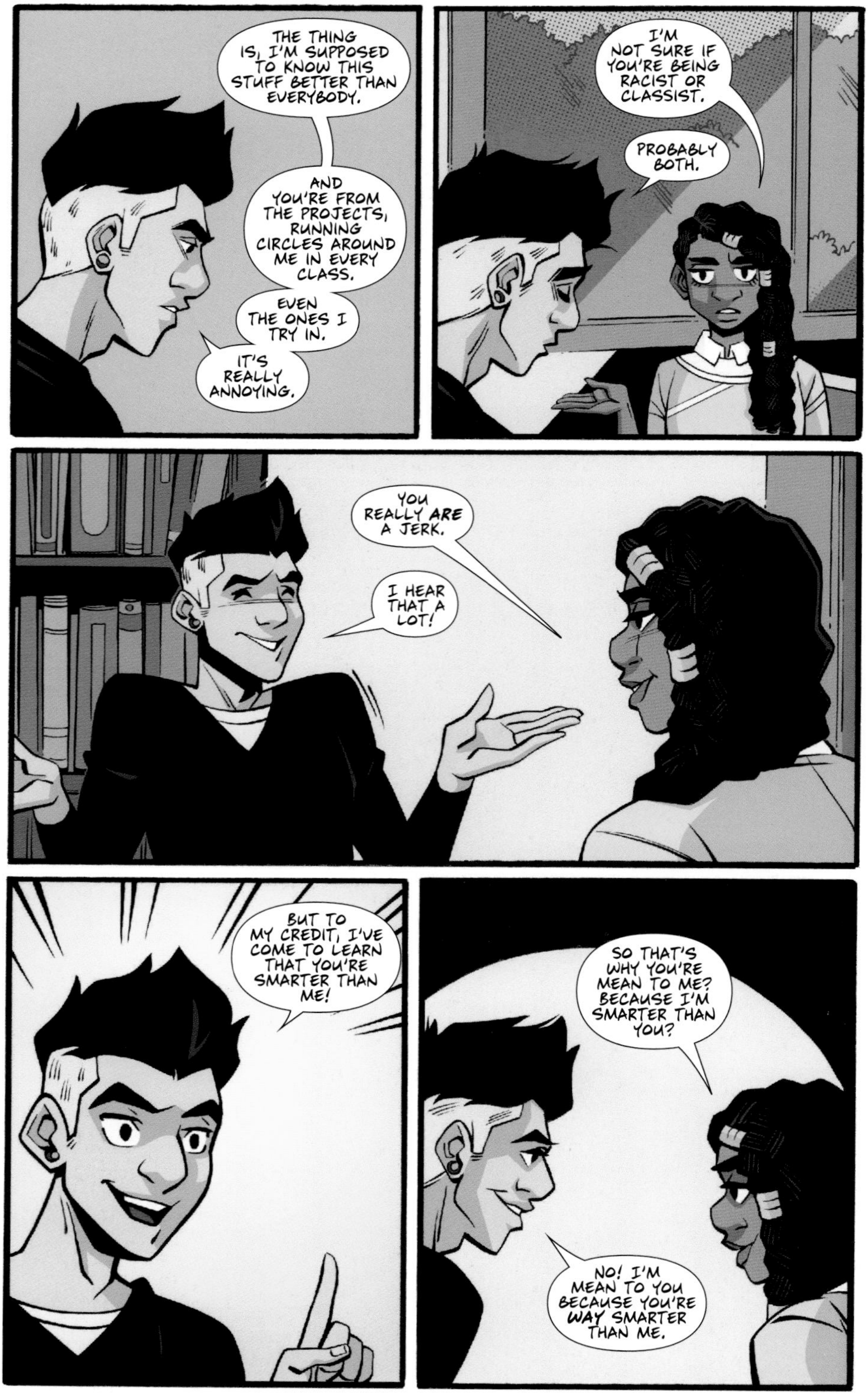

THE THING IS, I'M SUPPOSED TO KNOW THIS STUFF BETTER THAN EVERYBODY.
AND YOU'RE FROM THE PROJECTS, RUNNING CIRCLES AROUND ME IN EVERY CLASS.
EVEN THE ONES I TRY IN.
IT'S REALLY ANNOYING.
I'M NOT SURE IF YOU'RE BEING RACIST OR CLASSIST.
PROBABLY BOTH.
YOU REALLY ARE A JERK.
I HEAR THAT A LOT!
BUT TO MY CREDIT, I'VE COME TO LEARN THAT YOU'RE SMARTER THAN ME!
SO THAT'S WHY YOU'RE MEAN TO ME? BECAUSE I'M SMARTER THAN YOU?
NO! I'M MEAN TO YOU BECAUSE YOU'RE WAY SMARTER THAN ME.

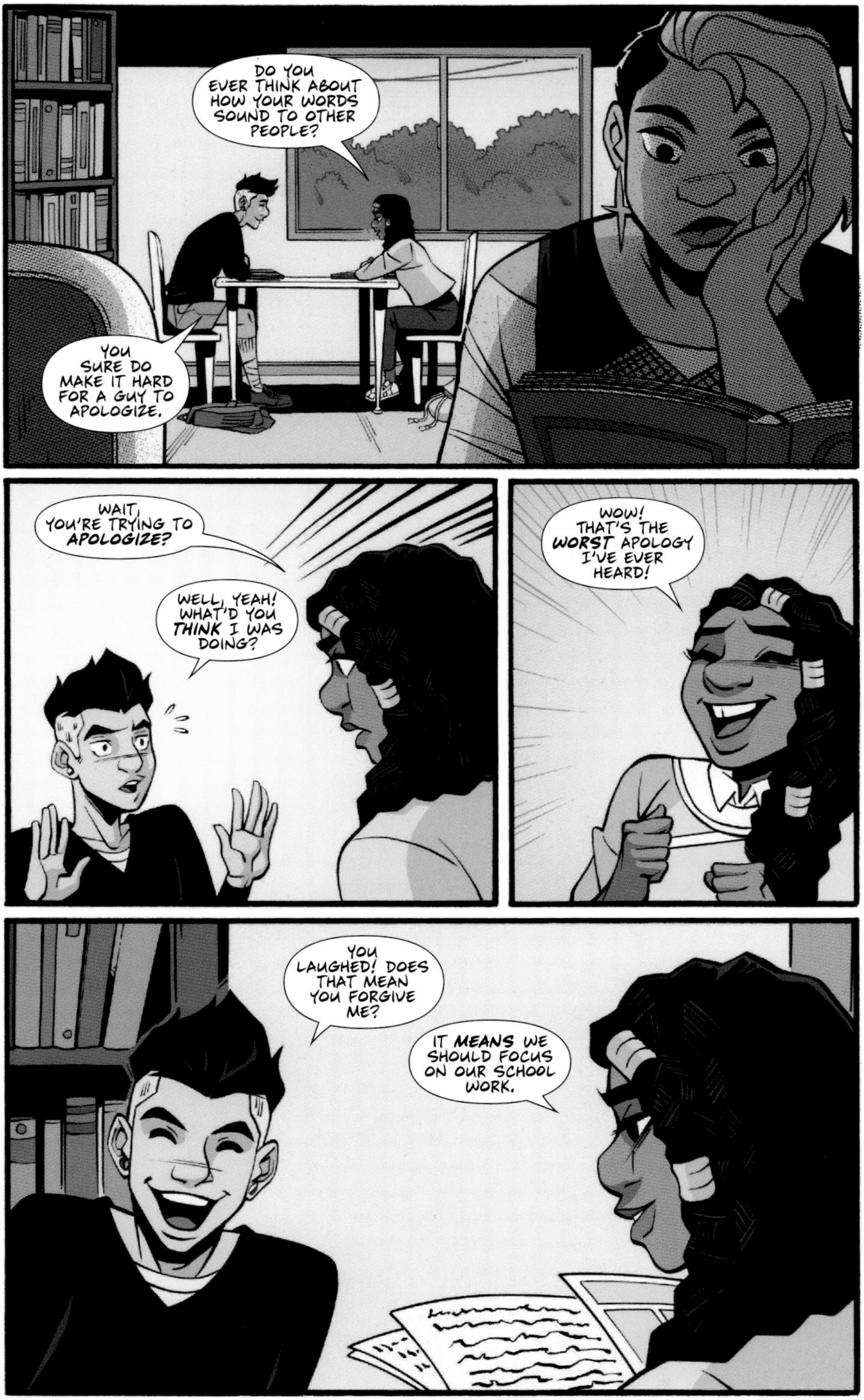
DO YOU EVER THINK ABOUT HOW YOUR WORDS SOUND TO OTHER PEOPLE?
YOU SURE DO MAKE IT HARD FOR A GUY TO APOLOGIZE.
WAIT, YOU'RE TRYING TO APOLOGIZE?
WELL, YEAH! WHAT'D YOU THINK I WAS DOING?
WOW! THAT'S THE WORST APOLOGY I'VE EVER HEARD!
YOU LAUGHED! DOES THAT MEAN YOU FORGIVE ME?
IT MEANS WE SHOULD FOCUS ON OUR SCHOOL WORK.

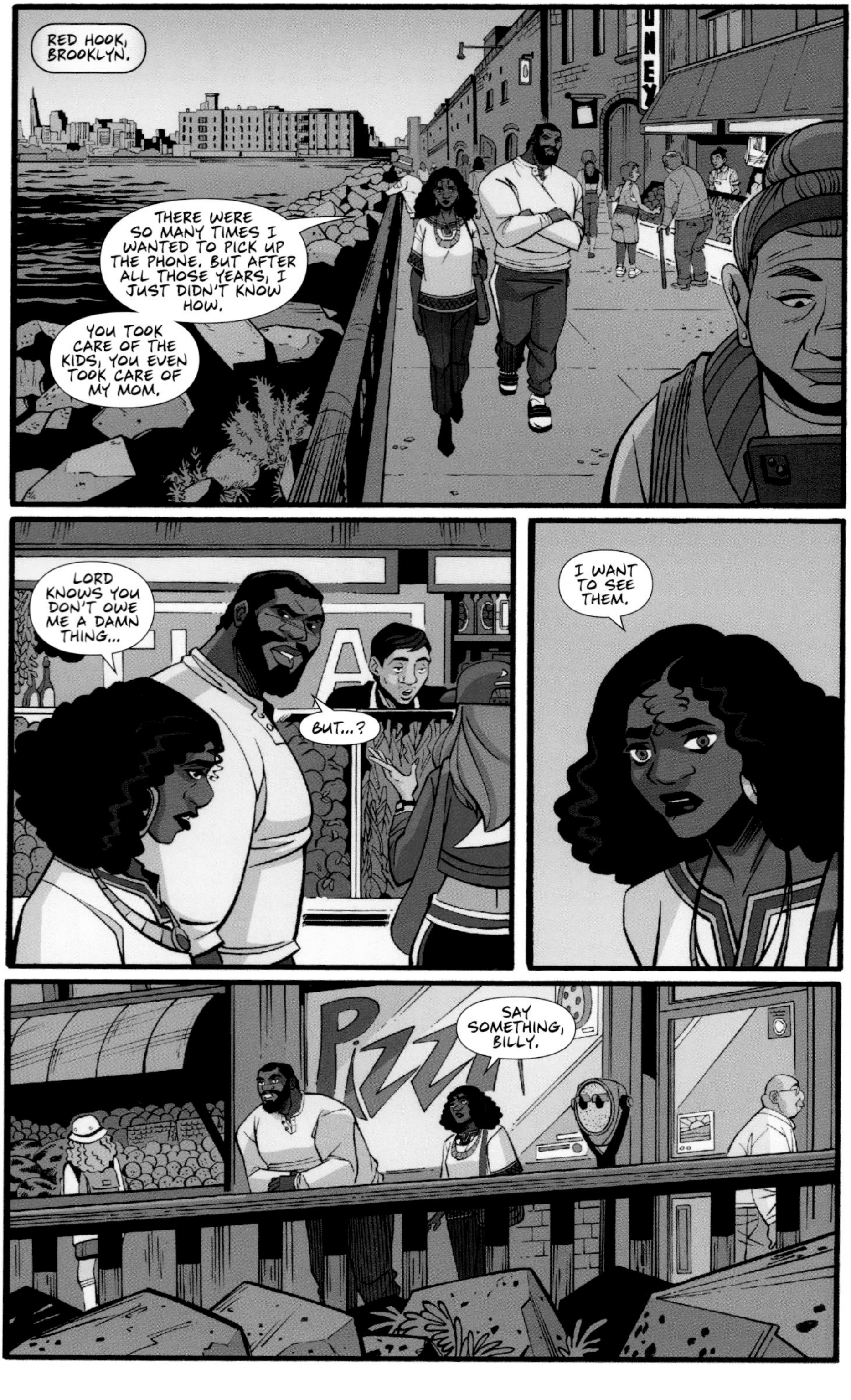
RED HOOK, BROOKLYN.
THERE WERE SO MANY TIMES I WANTED TO PICK UP THE PHONE. BUT AFTER ALL THOSE YEARS, I JUST DIDN'T KNOW HOW.
YOU TOOK CARE OF THE KIDS, YOU EVEN TOOK CARE OF MY MOM.
LORD KNOWS YOU DON'T OWE ME A DAMN THING...
BUT...?
I WANT TO SEE THEM.
SAY SOMETHING, BILLY.

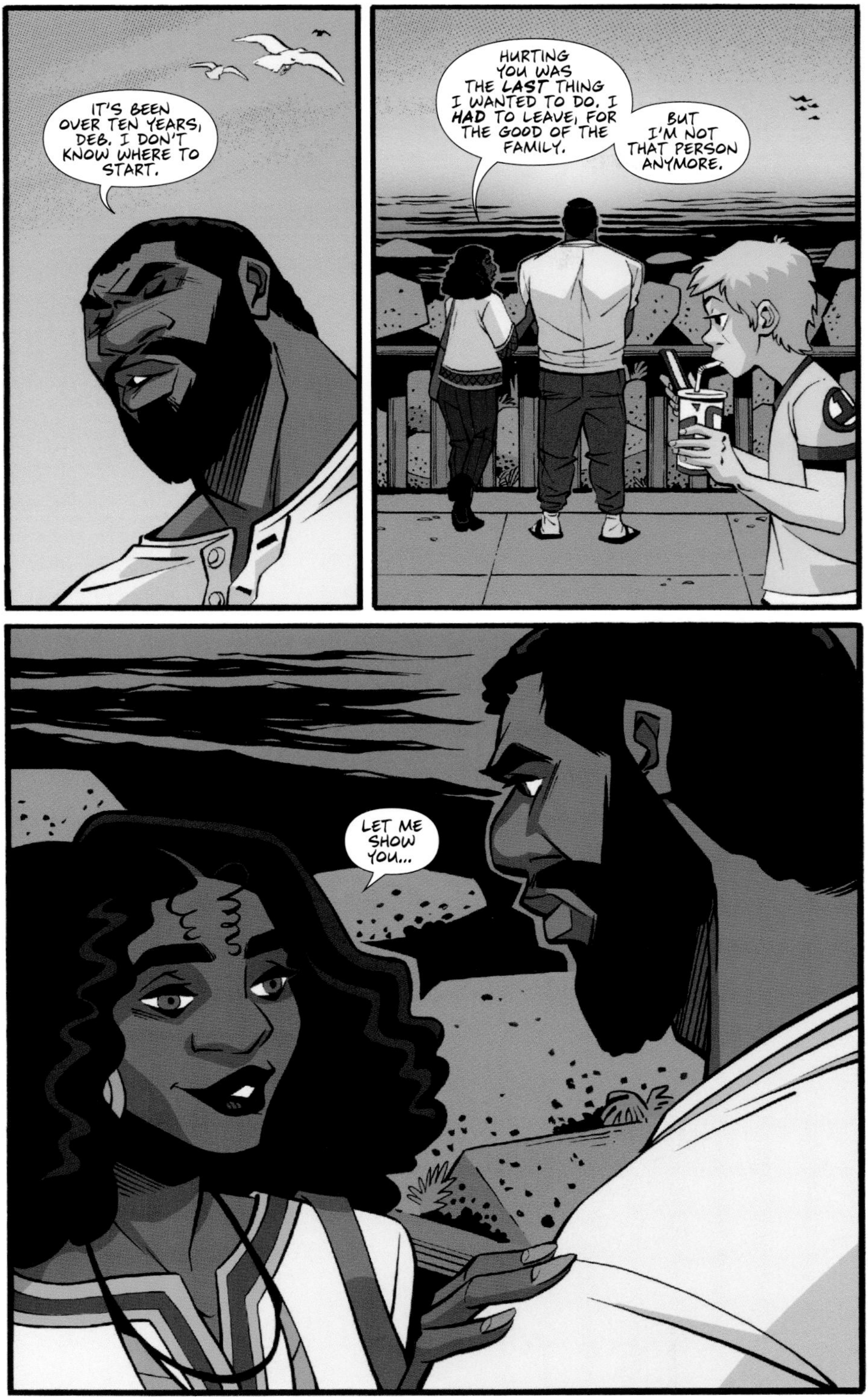
IT'S BEEN OVER TEN YEARS, DEB. I DON'T KNOW WHERE TO START.
HURTING YOU WAS THE LAST THING I WANTED TO DO. I HAD TO LEAVE, FOR THE GOOD OF THE FAMILY.
BUT I'M NOT THAT PERSON ANYMORE.
LET ME SHOW YOU...

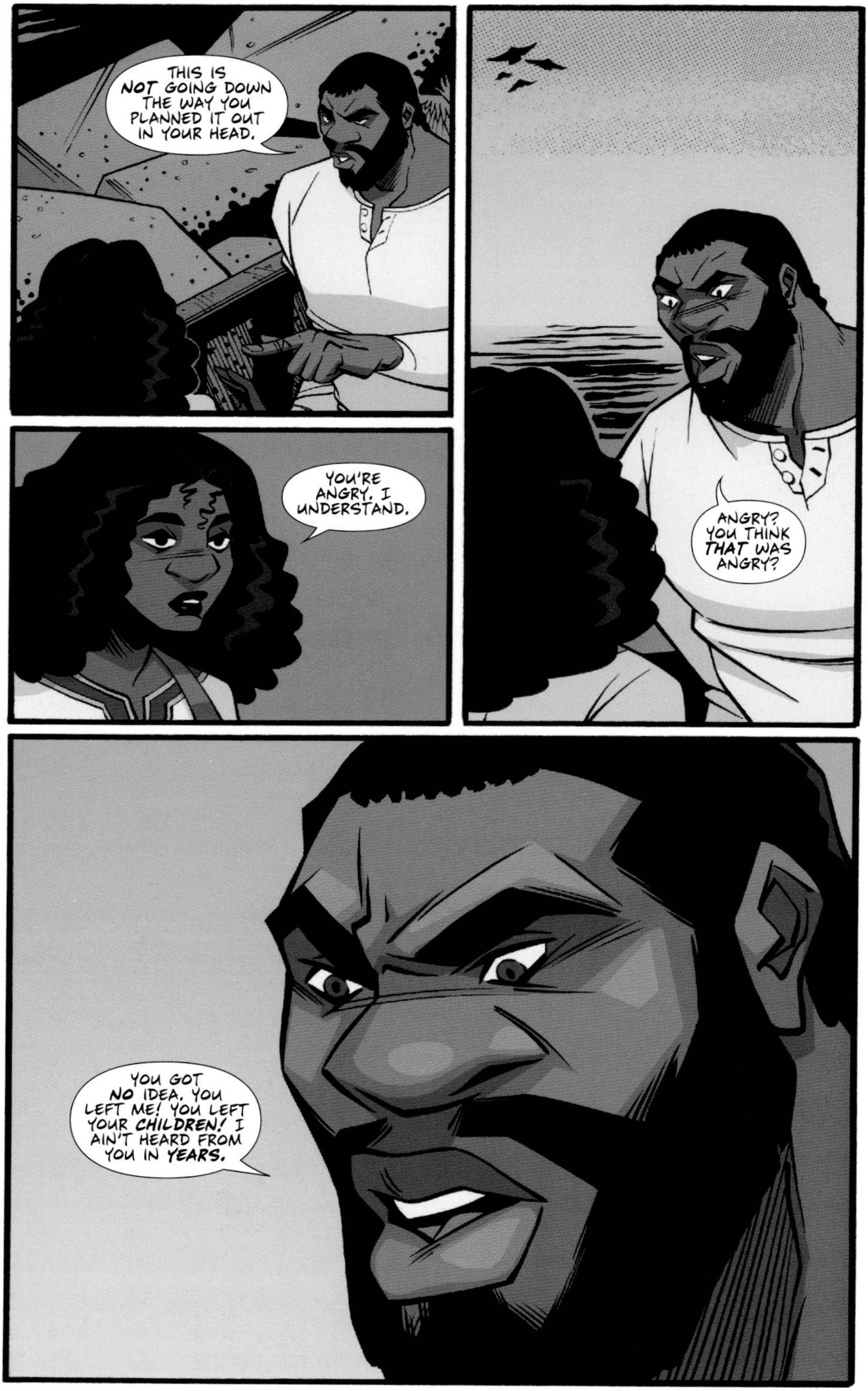
THIS IS NOT GOING DOWN THE WAY YOU PLANNED IT OUT IN YOUR HEAD.
YOU'RE ANGRY. I UNDERSTAND.
ANGRY? YOU THINK THAT WAS ANGRY?
YOU GOT NO IDEA. YOU LEFT ME! YOU LEFT YOUR CHILDREN! I AIN'T HEARD FROM YOU IN YEARS.

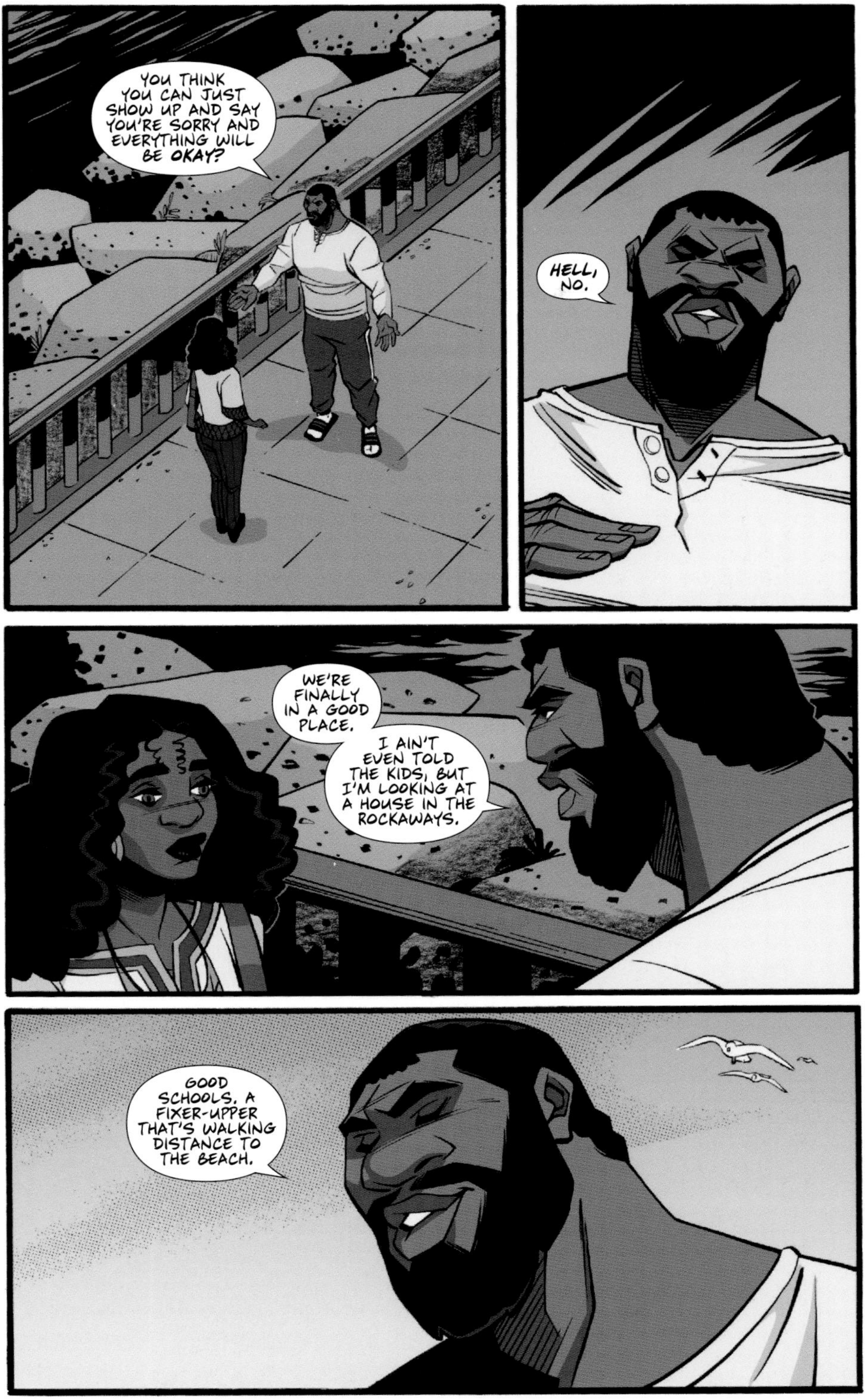
YOU THINK YOU CAN JUST SHOW UP AND SAY YOU'RE SORRY AND EVERYTHING WILL BE OKAY?
HELL, NO.
WE'RE FINALLY IN A GOOD PLACE.
I AIN'T EVEN TOLD THE KIDS, BUT I'M LOOKING AT A HOUSE IN THE ROCKAWAYS.
GOOD SCHOOLS. A FIXER-UPPER THAT'S WALKING DISTANCE TO THE BEACH.

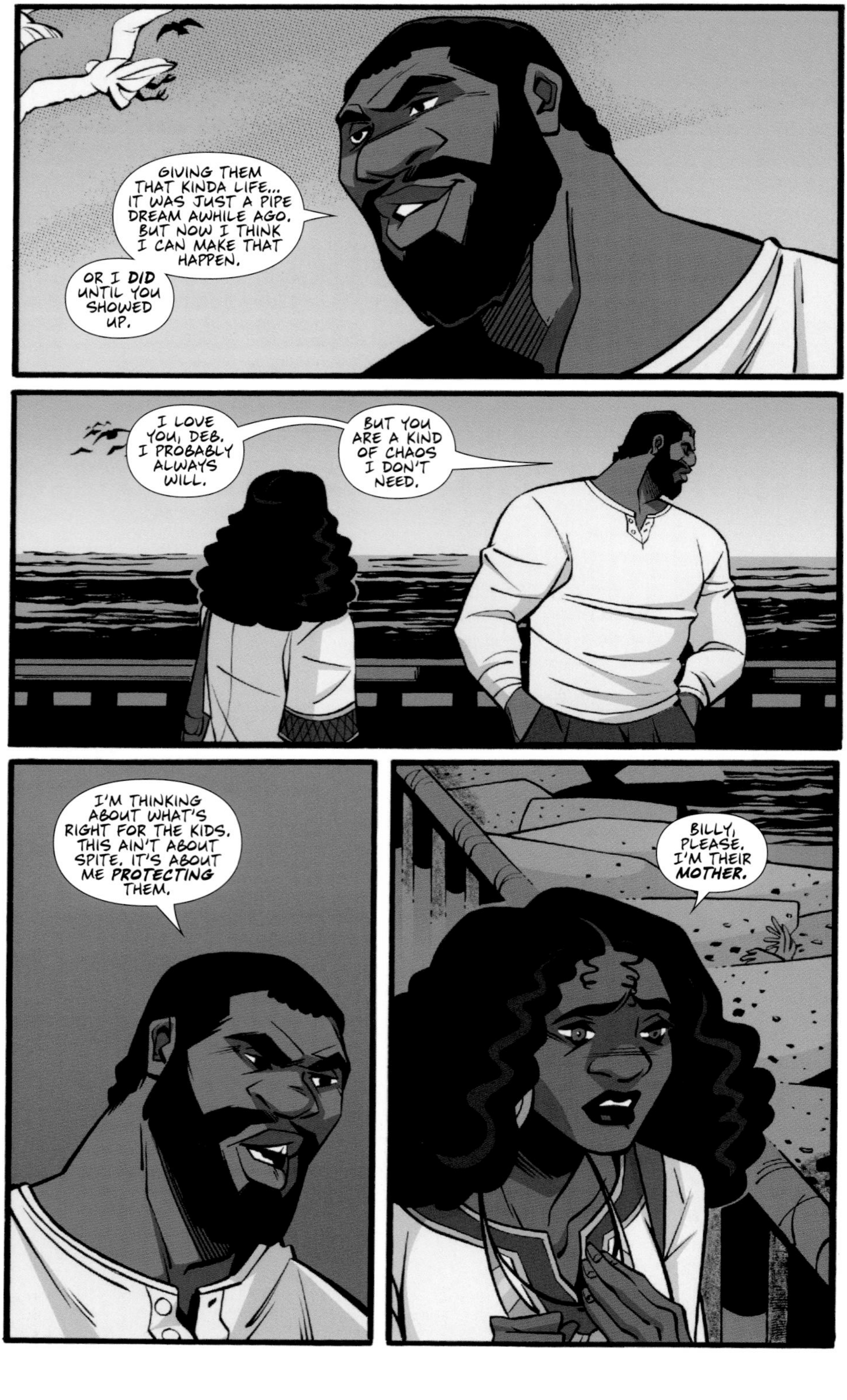
GIVING THEM THAT KINDA LIFE... IT WAS JUST A PIPE DREAM AWHILE AGO. BUT NOW I THINK I CAN MAKE THAT HAPPEN.
OR I **DID** UNTIL YOU SHOWED UP.
I LOVE YOU, DEB. I PROBABLY ALWAYS WILL.
BUT YOU ARE A KIND OF CHAOS I DON'T NEED.
I'M THINKING ABOUT WHAT'S RIGHT FOR THE KIDS. THIS AIN'T ABOUT SPITE. IT'S ABOUT ME **PROTECTING** THEM.
BILLY, PLEASE. I'M THEIR **MOTHER.**

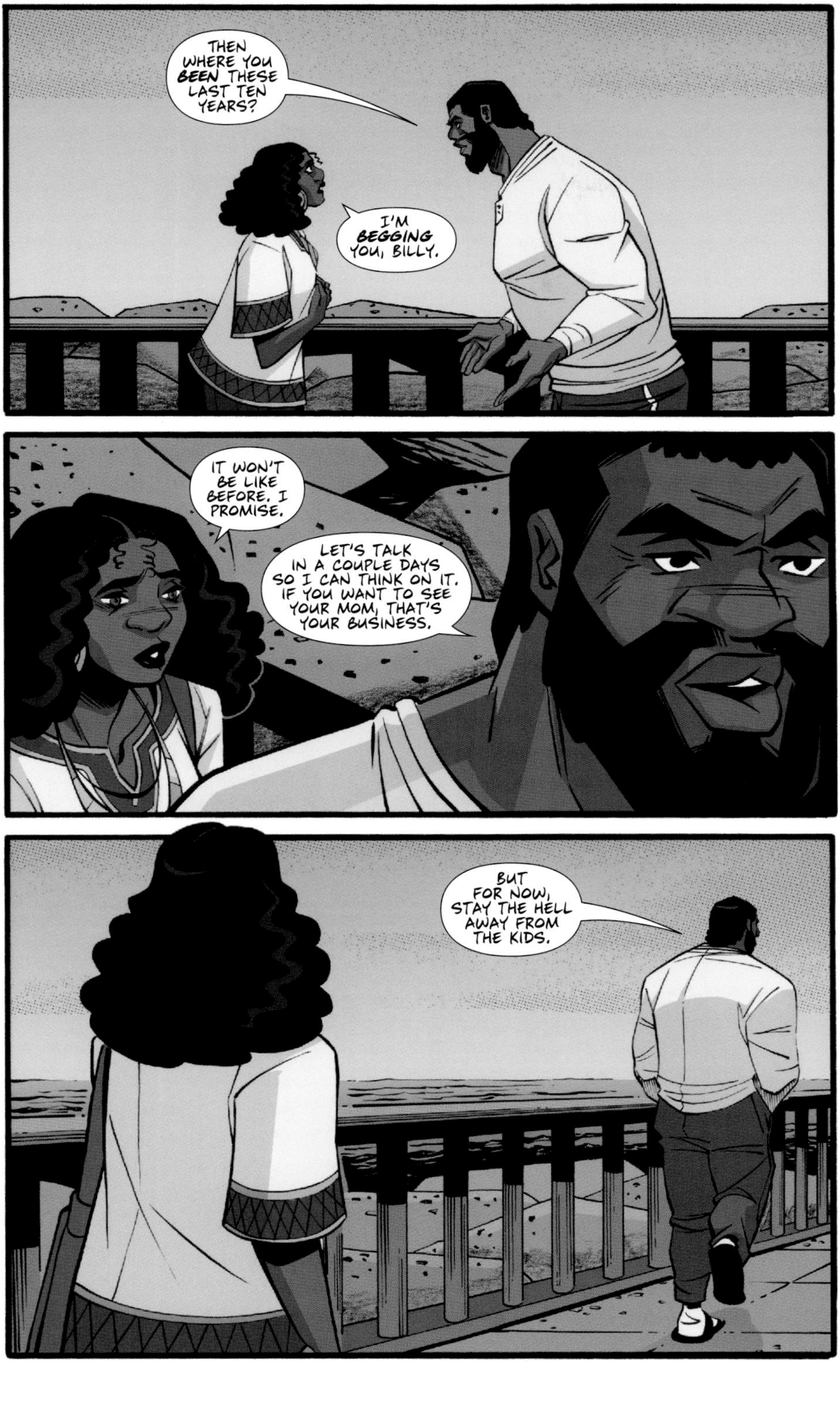
THEN WHERE YOU BEEN THESE LAST TEN YEARS?
I'M BEGGING YOU, BILLY.
IT WON'T BE LIKE BEFORE. I PROMISE.
LET'S TALK IN A COUPLE DAYS SO I CAN THINK ON IT. IF YOU WANT TO SEE YOUR MOM, THAT'S YOUR BUSINESS.
BUT FOR NOW, STAY THE HELL AWAY FROM THE KIDS.

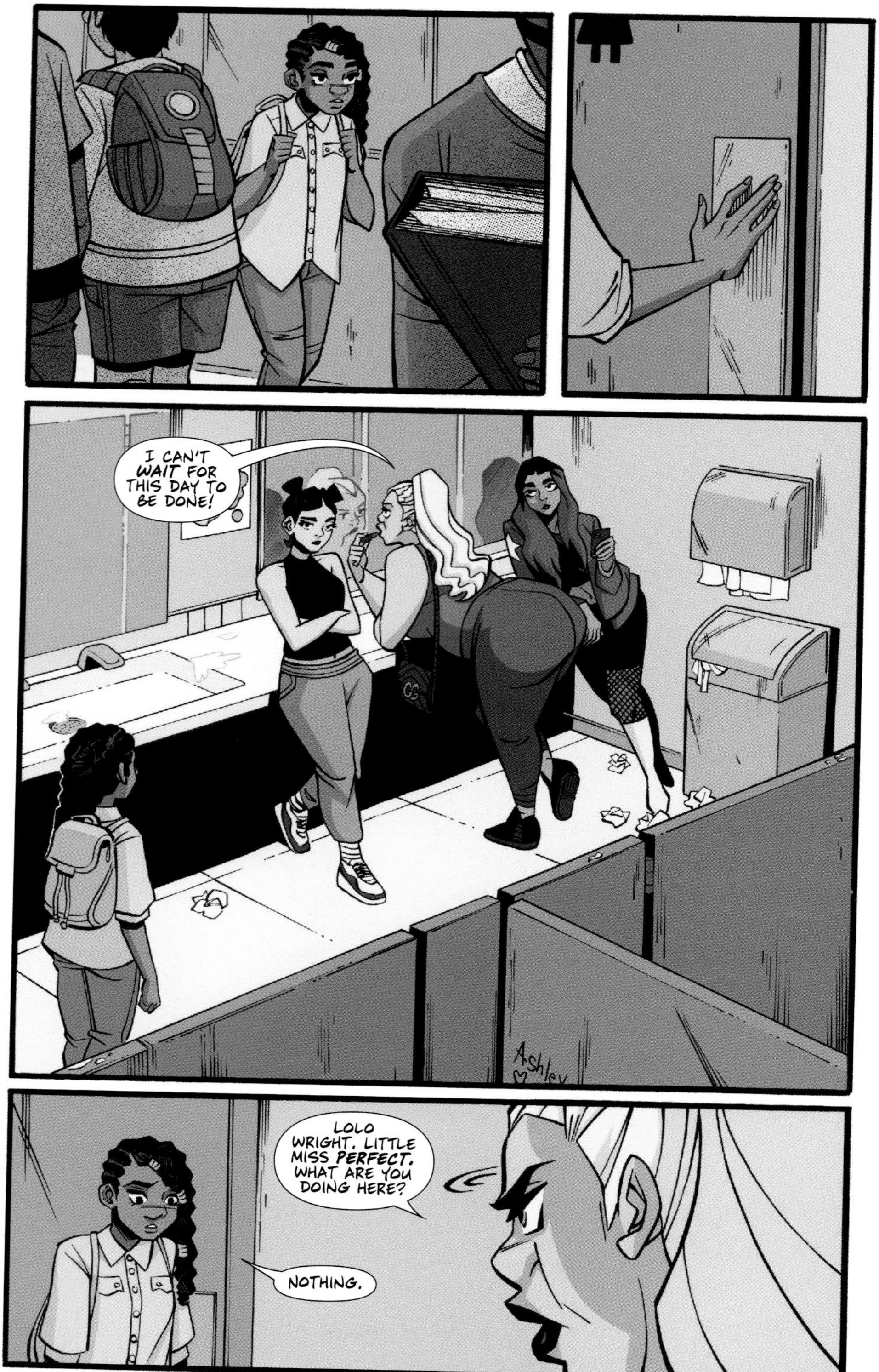
I CAN'T WAIT FOR THIS DAY TO BE DONE!
Ashley
LOLO WRIGHT. LITTLE MISS PERFECT. WHAT ARE YOU DOING HERE?
NOTHING.

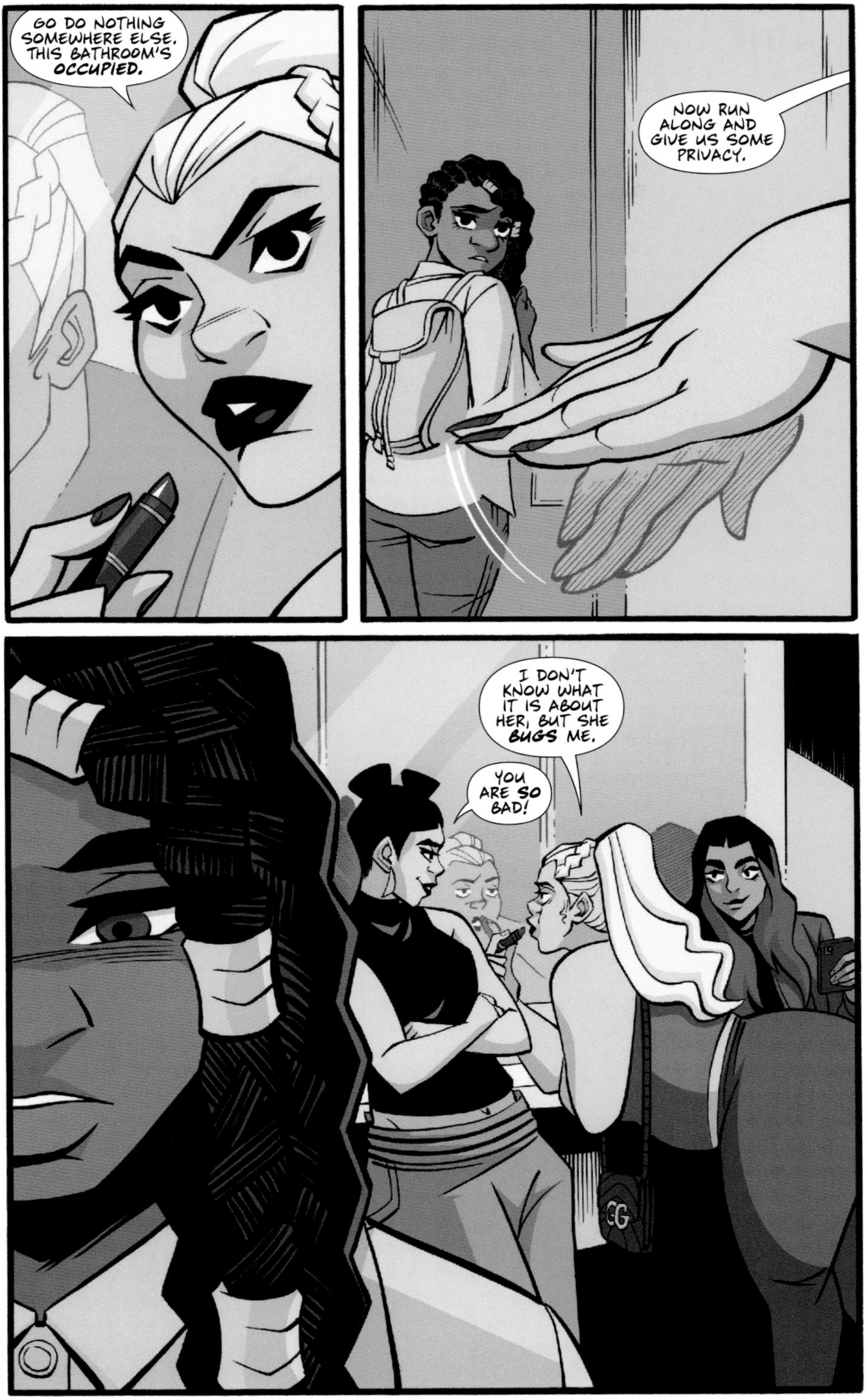
GO DO NOTHING SOMEWHERE ELSE. THIS BATHROOM'S OCCUPIED.
NOW RUN ALONG AND GIVE US SOME PRIVACY.
I DON'T KNOW WHAT IT IS ABOUT HER, BUT SHE BUGS ME.
YOU ARE SO BAD!
GG

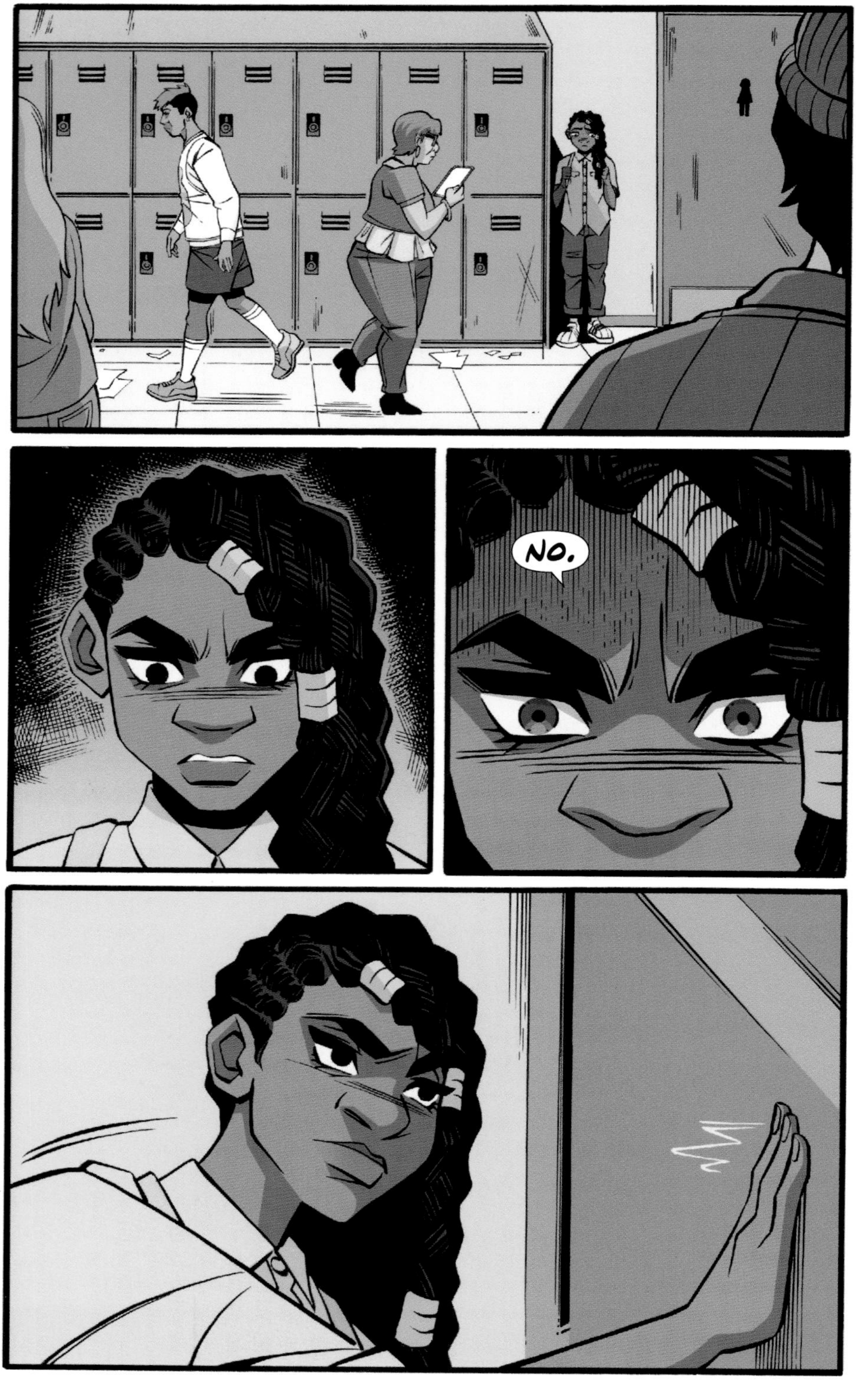
NO.

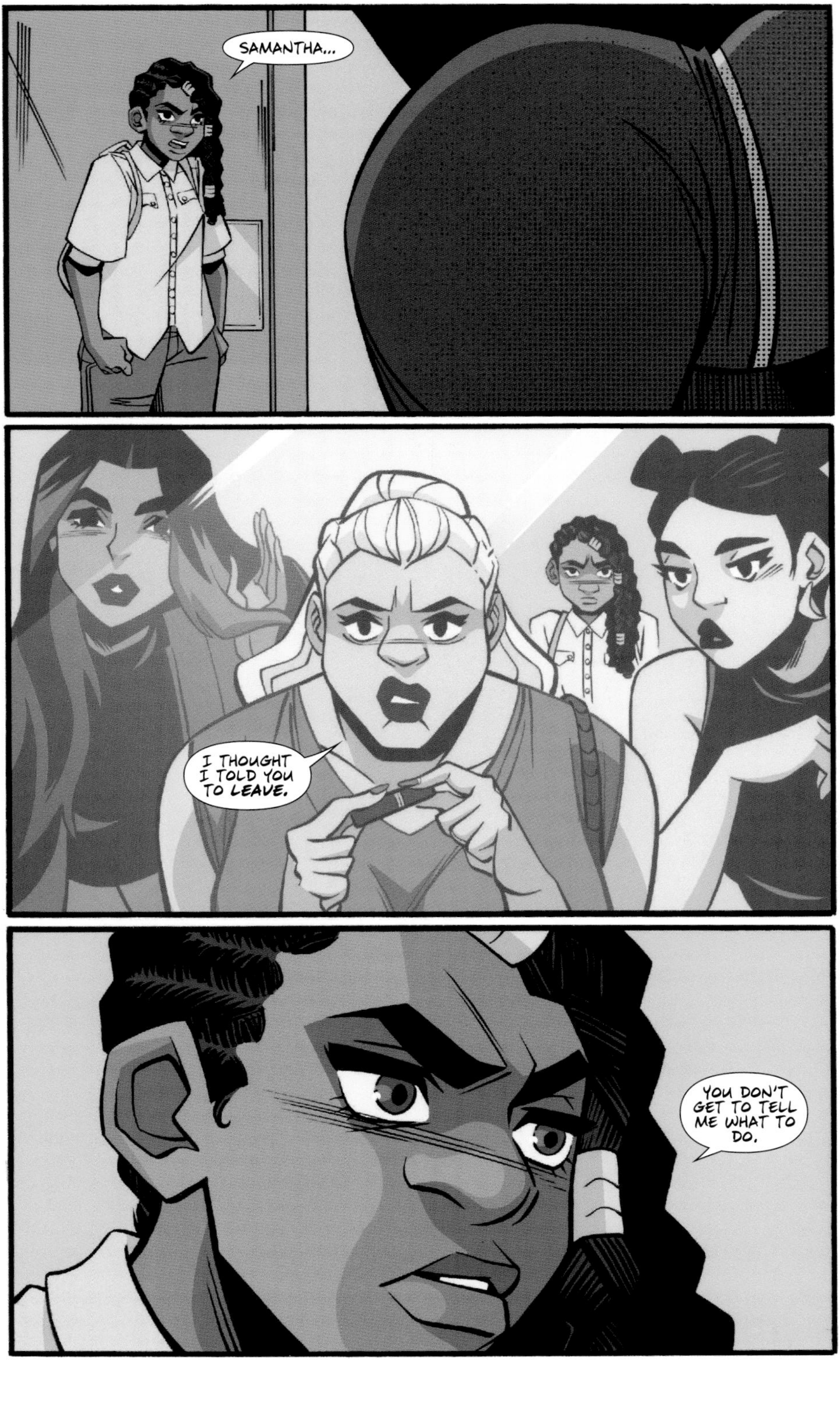
SAMANTHA...
I THOUGHT I TOLD YOU TO LEAVE.
YOU DON'T GET TO TELL ME WHAT TO DO.

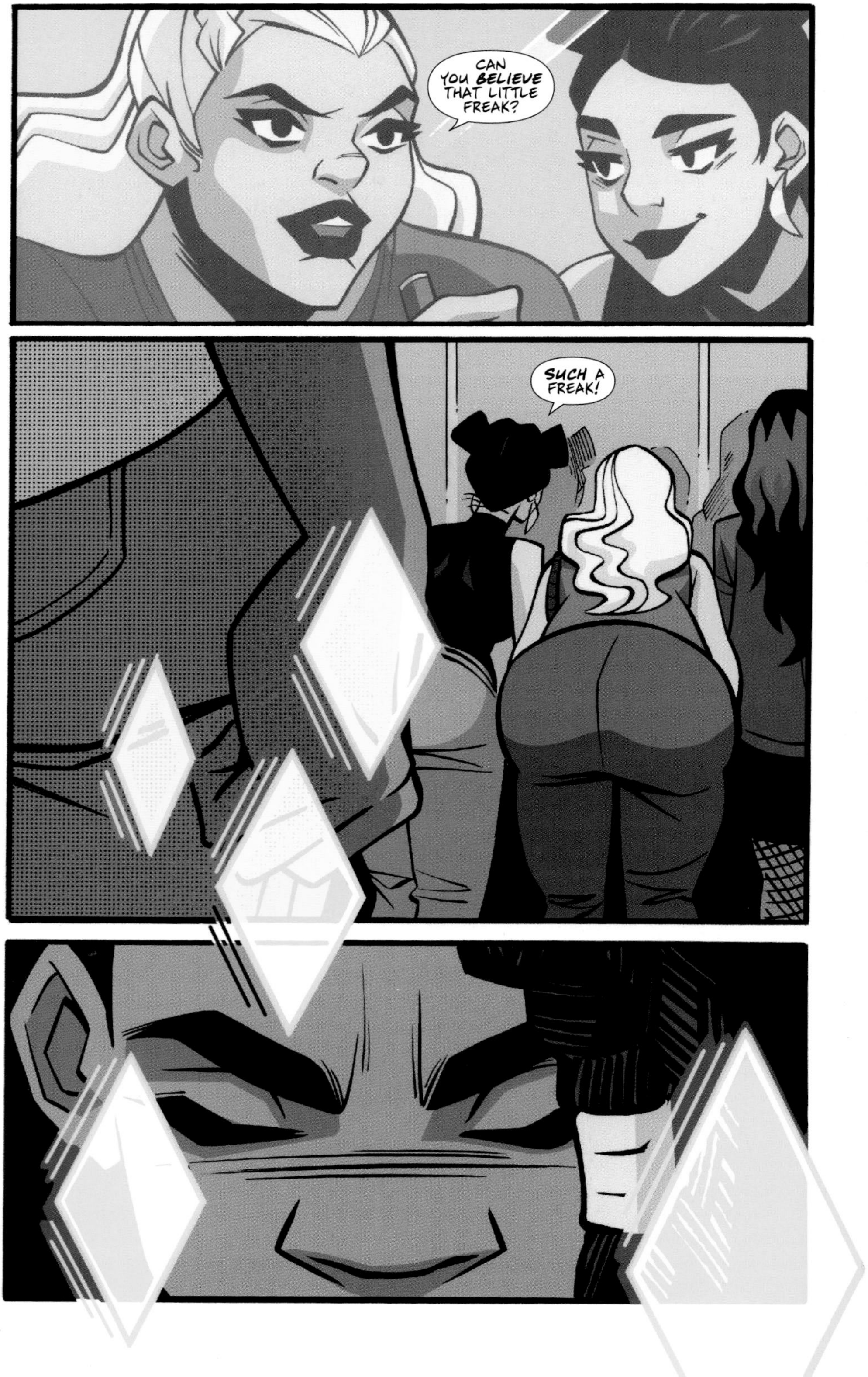
CAN YOU BELIEVE THAT LITTLE FREAK?
SUCH A FREAK!

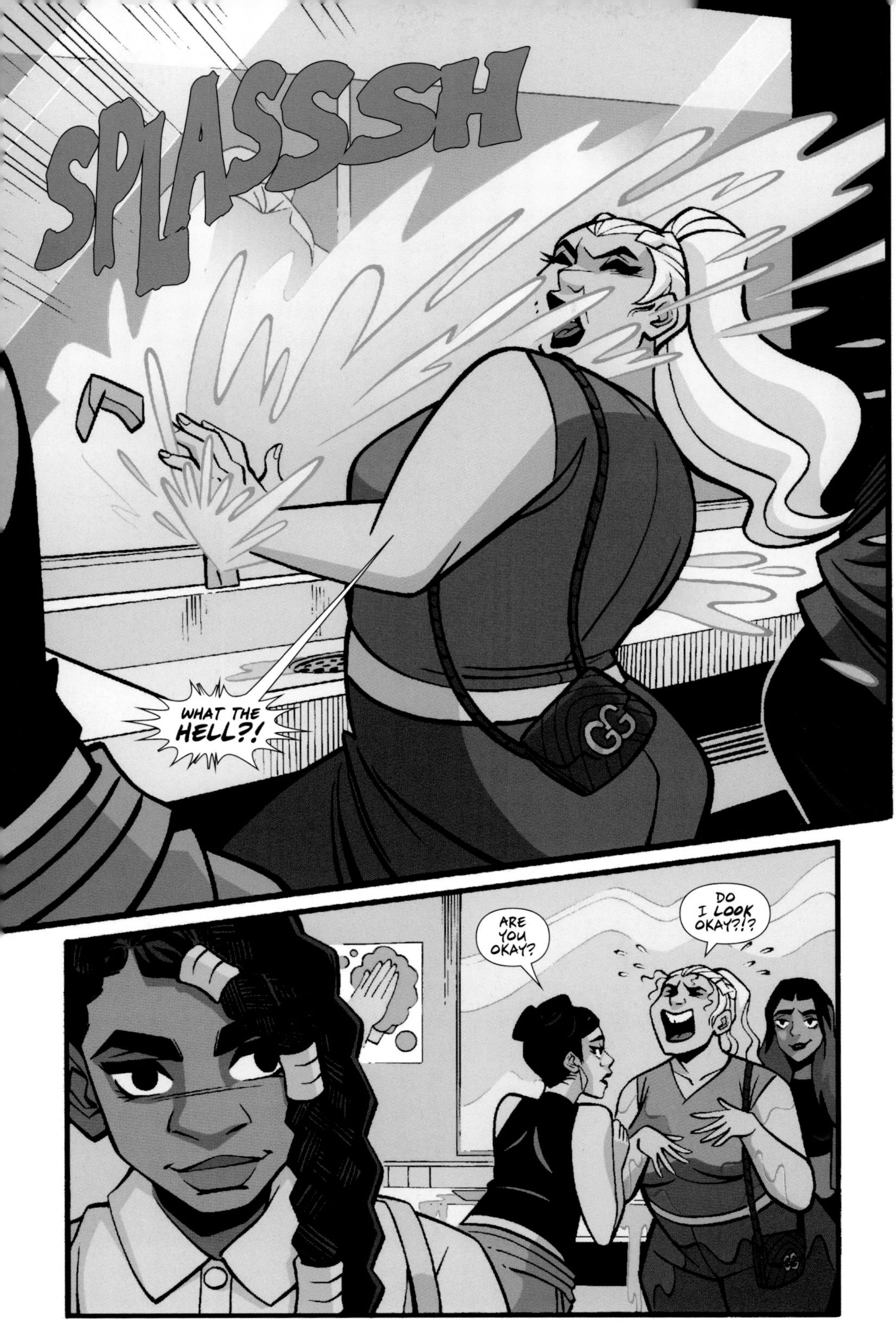
SPLASSSH
WHAT THE HELL?!
ARE YOU OKAY?
DO I LOOK OKAY?!?

CHAPTER 6

UNDER-DOG

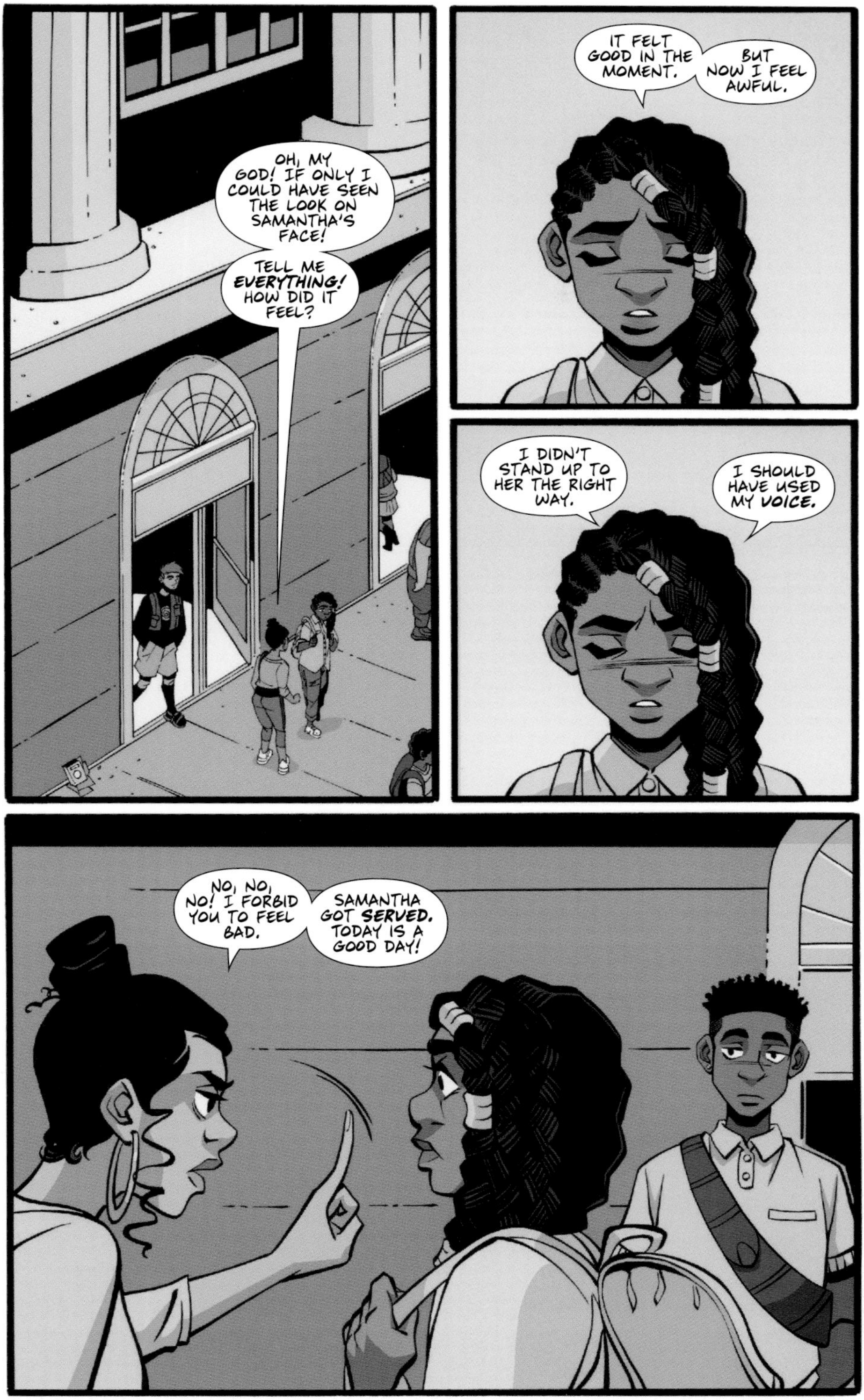
OH, MY GOD! IF ONLY I COULD HAVE SEEN THE LOOK ON SAMANTHA'S FACE!
TELL ME **EVERYTHING!** HOW DID IT FEEL?
IT FELT GOOD IN THE MOMENT.
BUT NOW I FEEL AWFUL.
I DIDN'T STAND UP TO HER THE RIGHT WAY.
I SHOULD HAVE USED MY **VOICE.**
NO, NO, NO! I FORBID YOU TO FEEL BAD.
SAMANTHA GOT **SERVED.** TODAY IS A GOOD DAY!

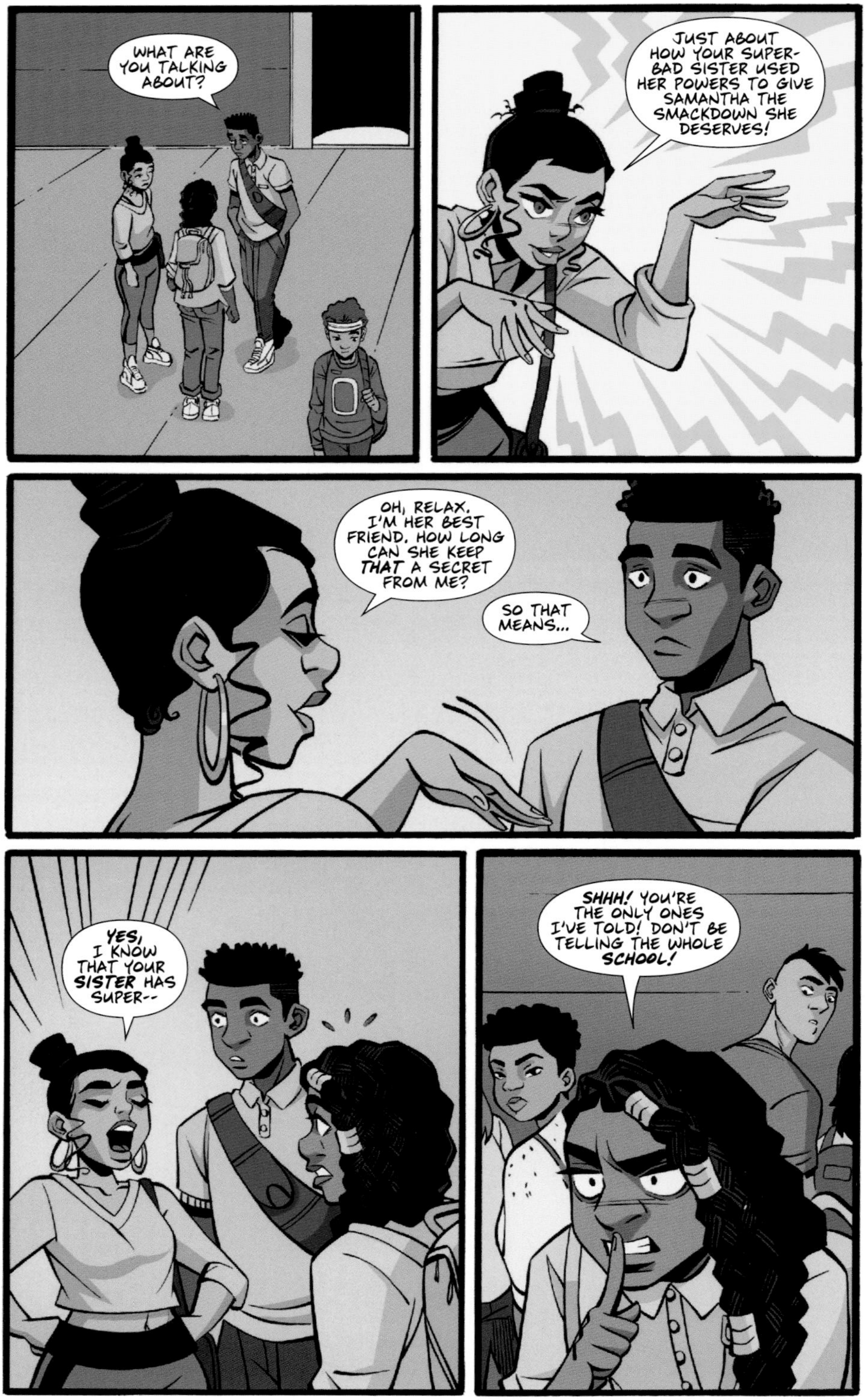

WHAT ARE YOU TALKING ABOUT?
JUST ABOUT HOW YOUR SUPER-BAD SISTER USED HER POWERS TO GIVE SAMANTHA THE SMACKDOWN SHE DESERVES!
OH, RELAX. I'M HER BEST FRIEND. HOW LONG CAN SHE KEEP THAT A SECRET FROM ME?
SO THAT MEANS...
YES, I KNOW THAT YOUR SISTER HAS SUPER--
SHHH! YOU'RE THE ONLY ONES I'VE TOLD! DON'T BE TELLING THE WHOLE SCHOOL!

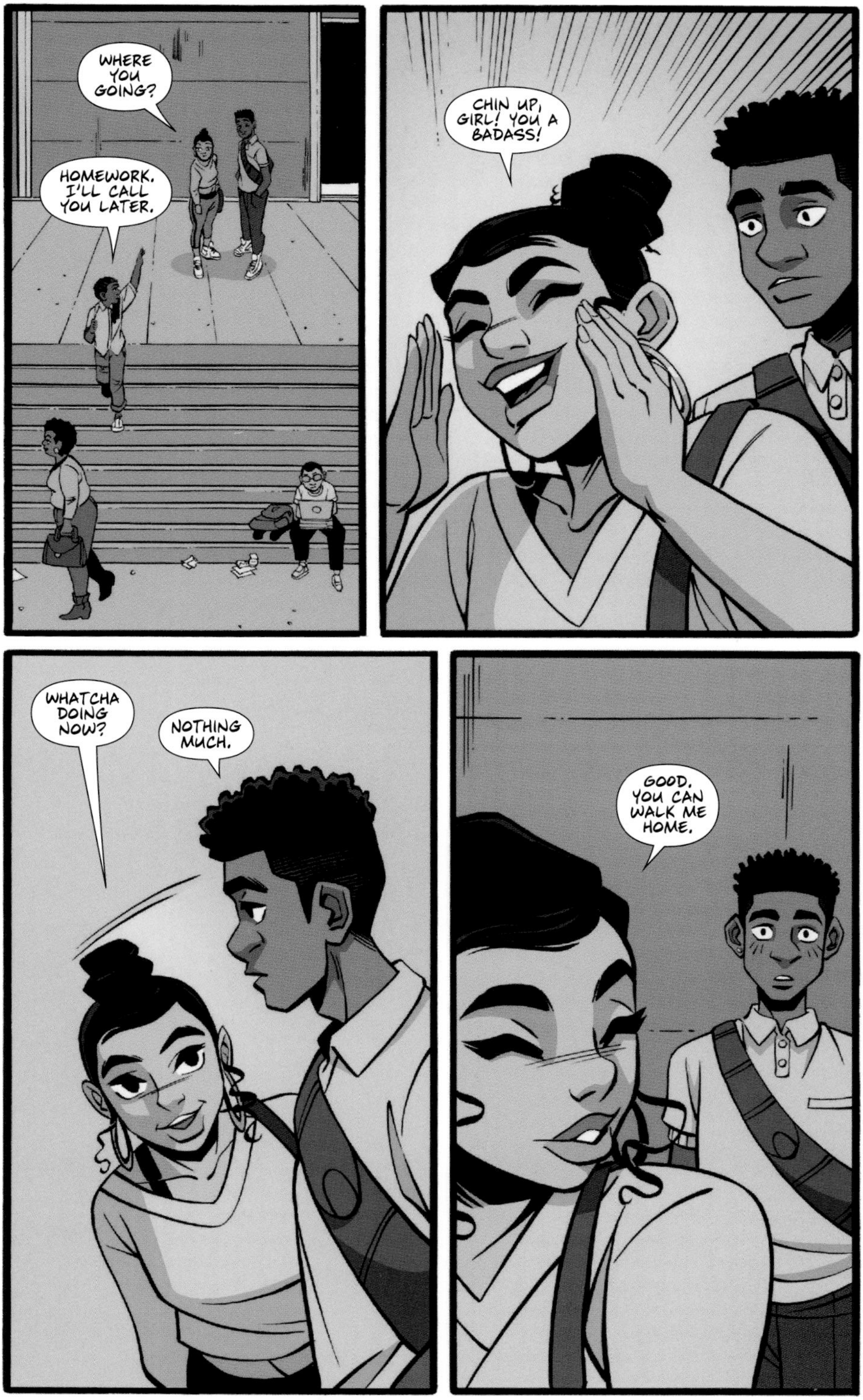
WHERE YOU GOING?
HOMEWORK. I'LL CALL YOU LATER.
CHIN UP, GIRL! YOU A BADASS!
WHATCHA DOING NOW?
NOTHING MUCH.
GOOD. YOU CAN WALK ME HOME.

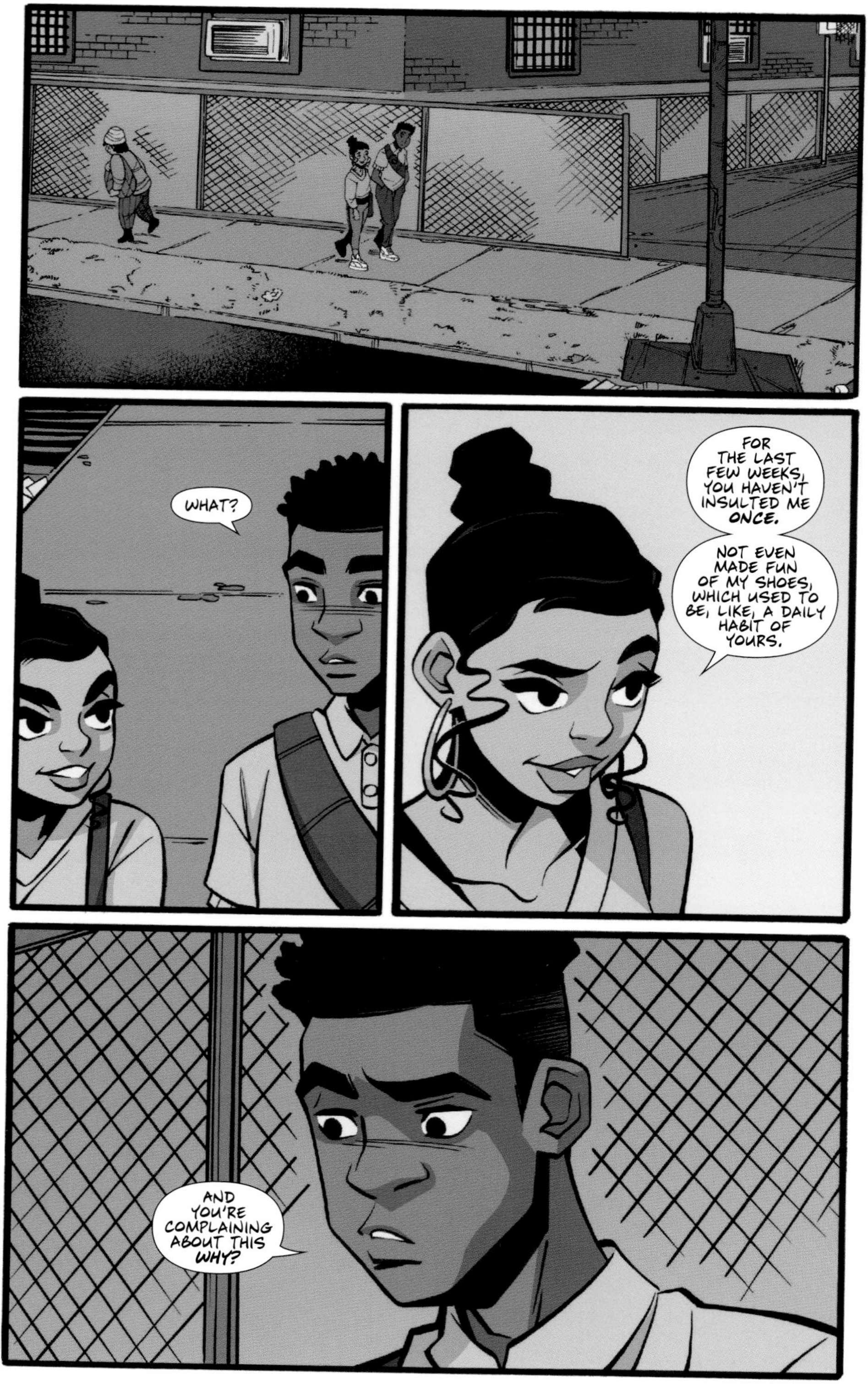
WHAT?
FOR THE LAST FEW WEEKS, YOU HAVEN'T INSULTED ME ONCE.
NOT EVEN MADE FUN OF MY SHOES, WHICH USED TO BE, LIKE, A DAILY HABIT OF YOURS.
AND YOU'RE COMPLAINING ABOUT THIS WHY?

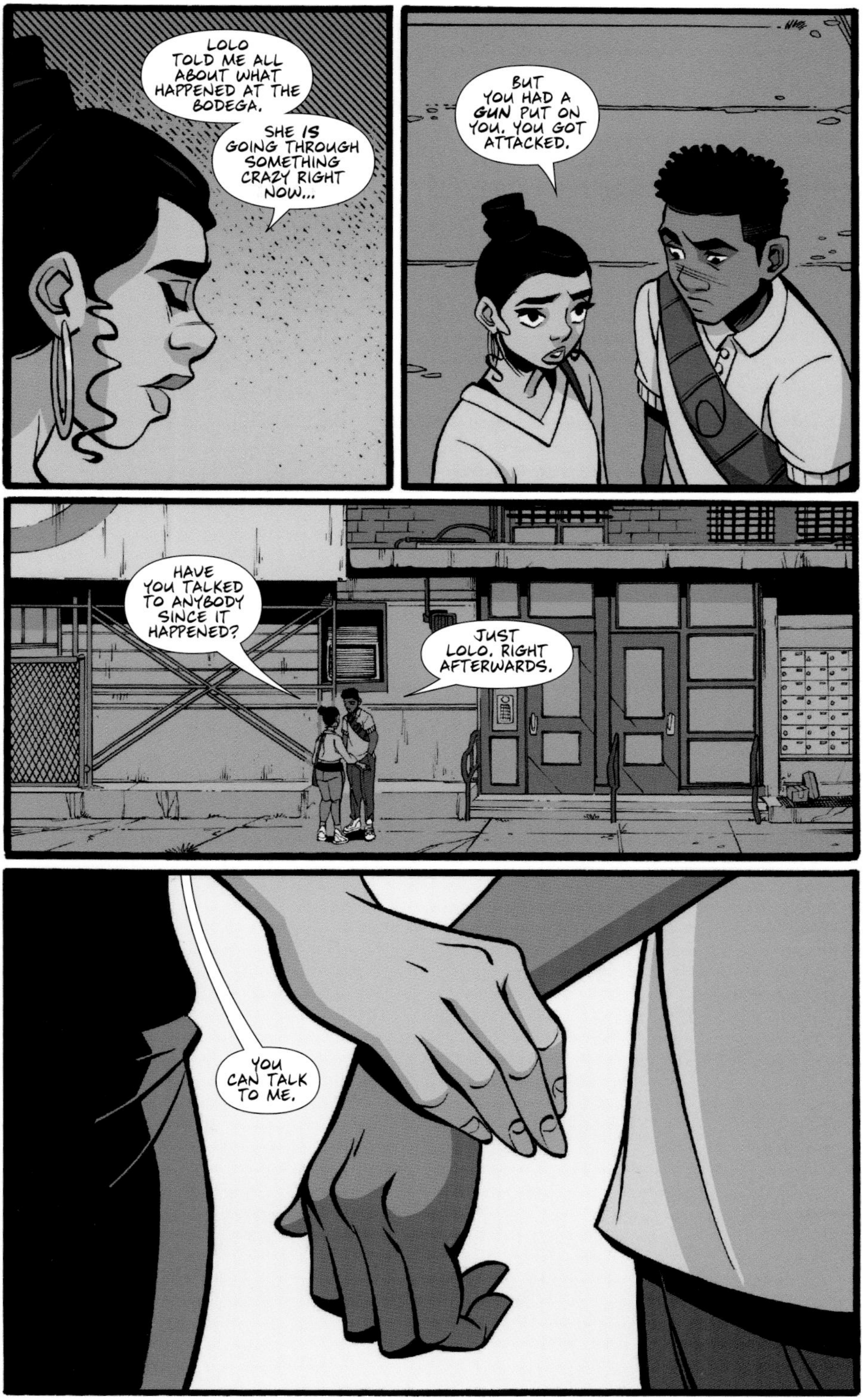
LOLO TOLD ME ALL ABOUT WHAT HAPPENED AT THE BODEGA.
SHE IS GOING THROUGH SOMETHING CRAZY RIGHT NOW...
BUT YOU HAD A GUN PUT ON YOU. YOU GOT ATTACKED.
HAVE YOU TALKED TO ANYBODY SINCE IT HAPPENED?
JUST LOLO. RIGHT AFTERWARDS.
YOU CAN TALK TO ME.

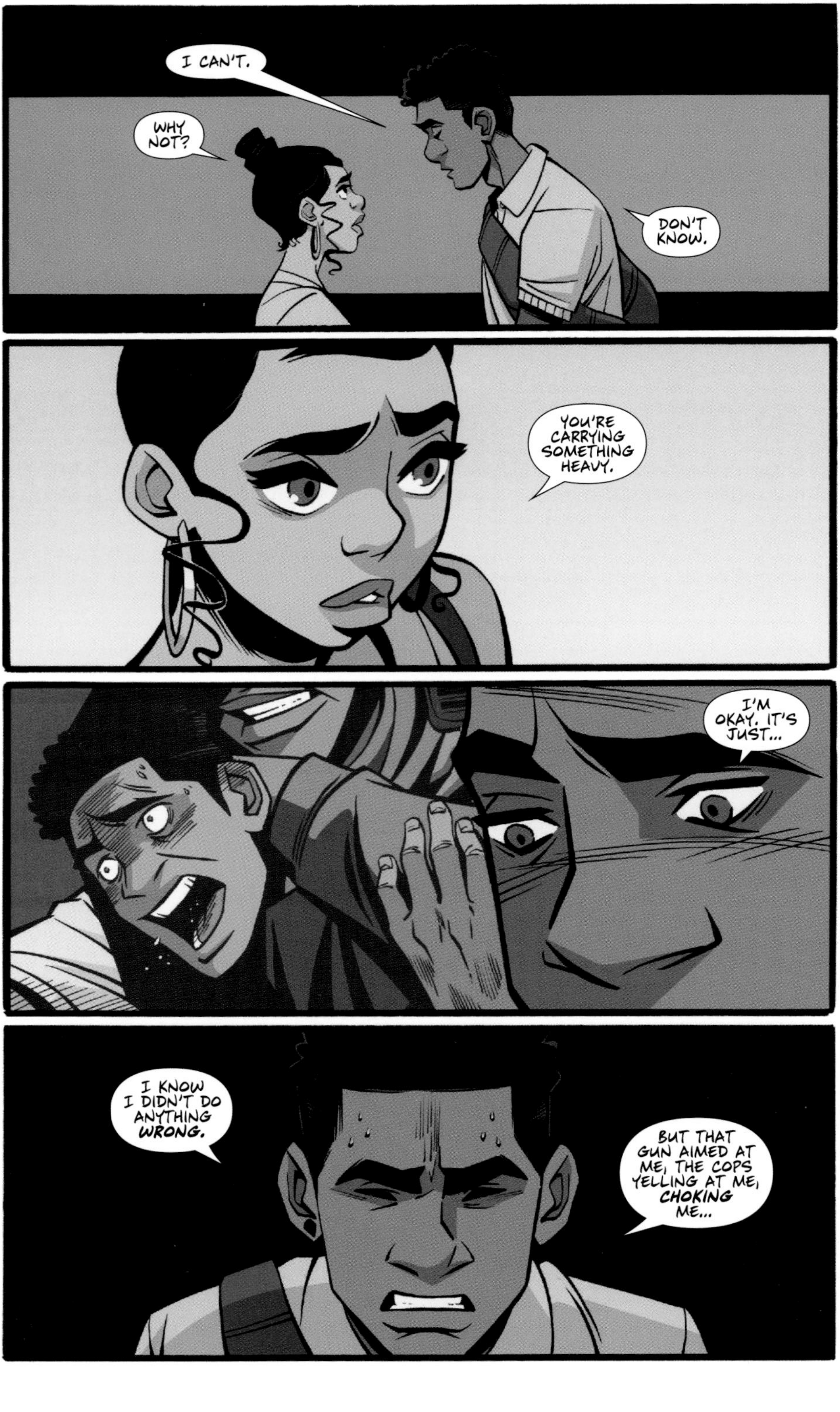
I CAN'T.
WHY NOT?
DON'T KNOW.
YOU'RE CARRYING SOMETHING HEAVY.
I'M OKAY. IT'S JUST...
I KNOW I DIDN'T DO ANYTHING WRONG.
BUT THAT GUN AIMED AT ME, THE COPS YELLING AT ME, CHOKING ME...

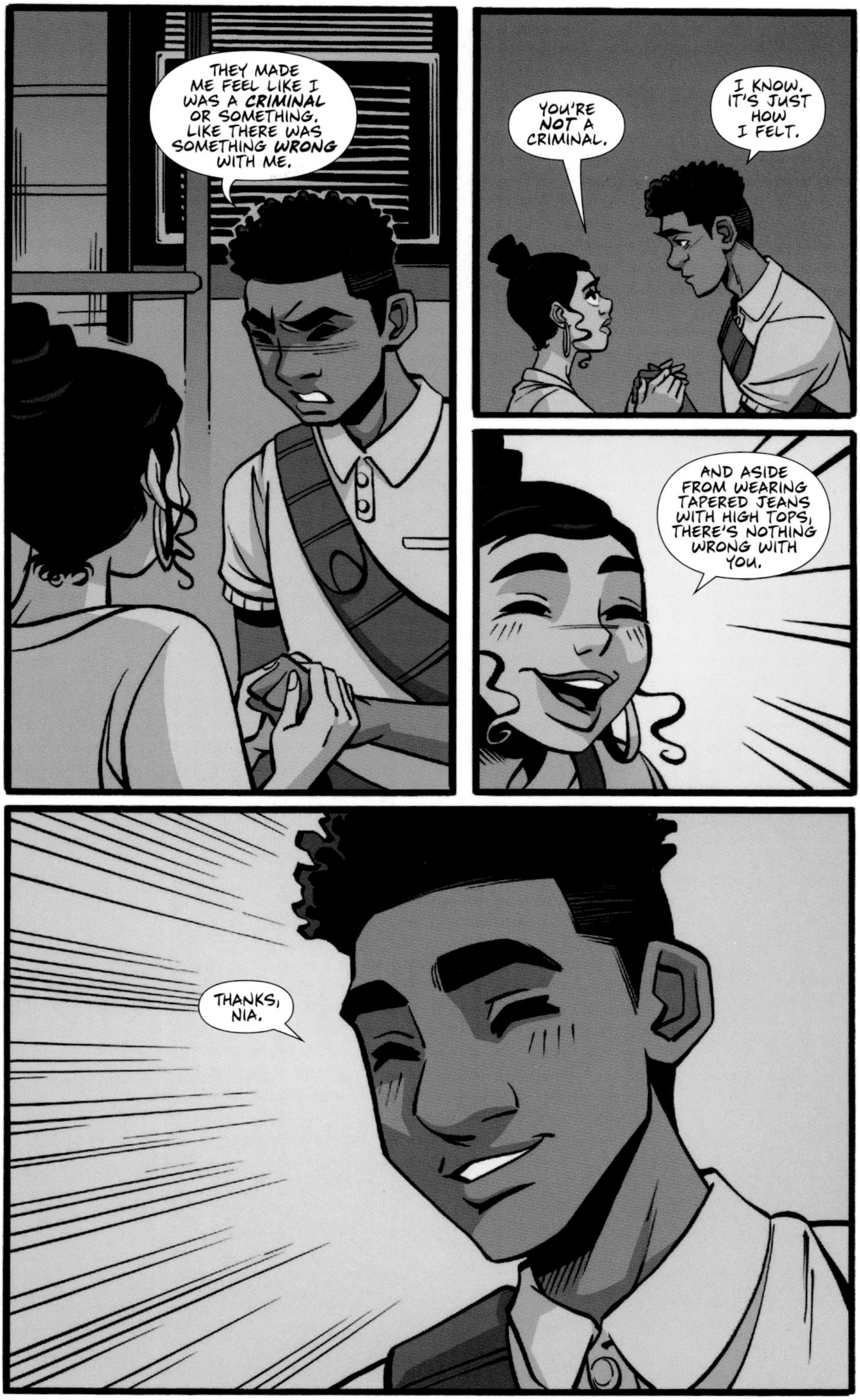
THEY MADE ME FEEL LIKE I WAS A CRIMINAL OR SOMETHING. LIKE THERE WAS SOMETHING WRONG WITH ME.
YOU'RE NOT A CRIMINAL.
I KNOW. IT'S JUST HOW I FELT.
AND ASIDE FROM WEARING TAPERED JEANS WITH HIGH TOPS, THERE'S NOTHING WRONG WITH YOU.
THANKS, NIA.

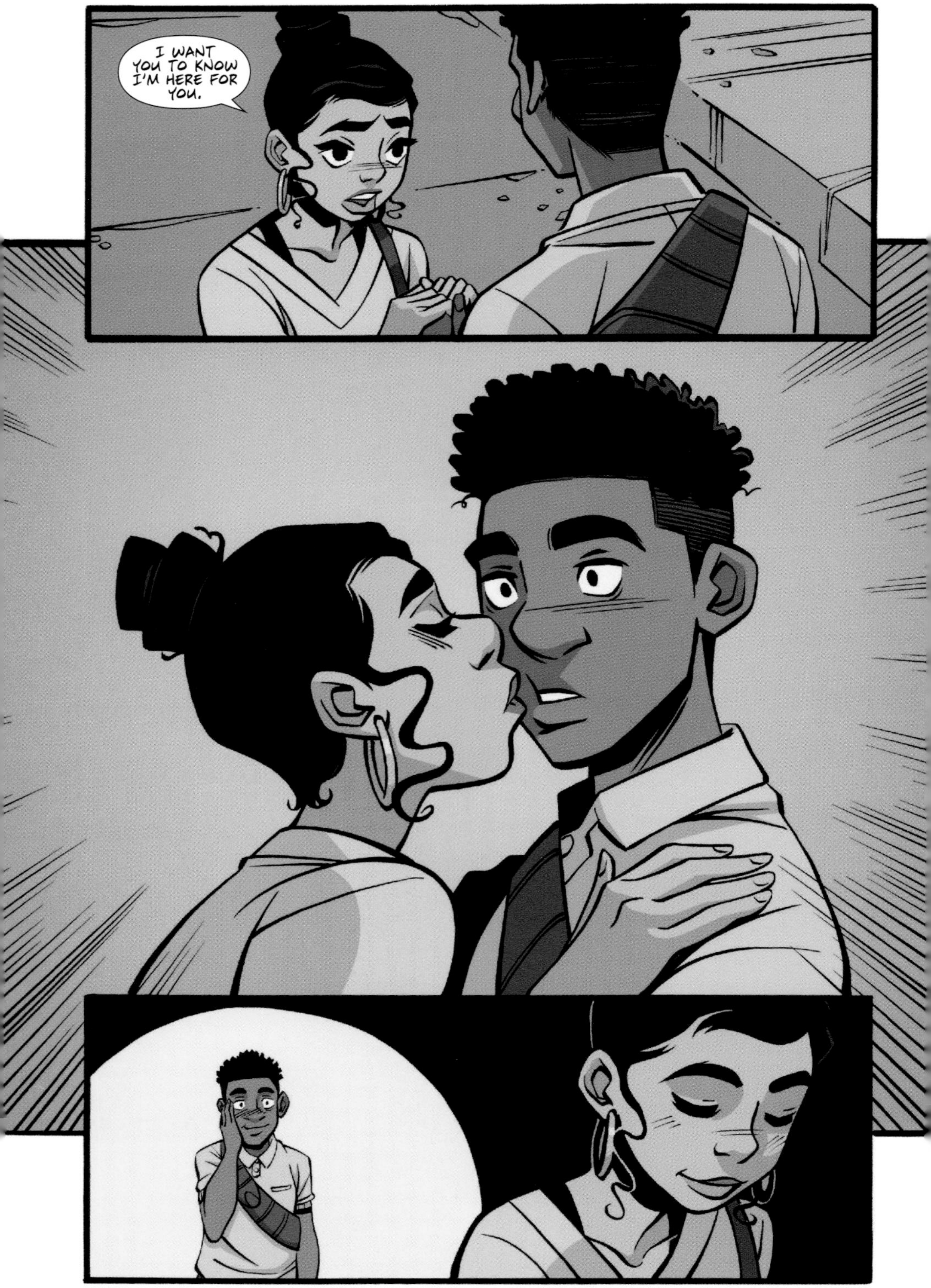
I WANT YOU TO KNOW I'M HERE FOR YOU.

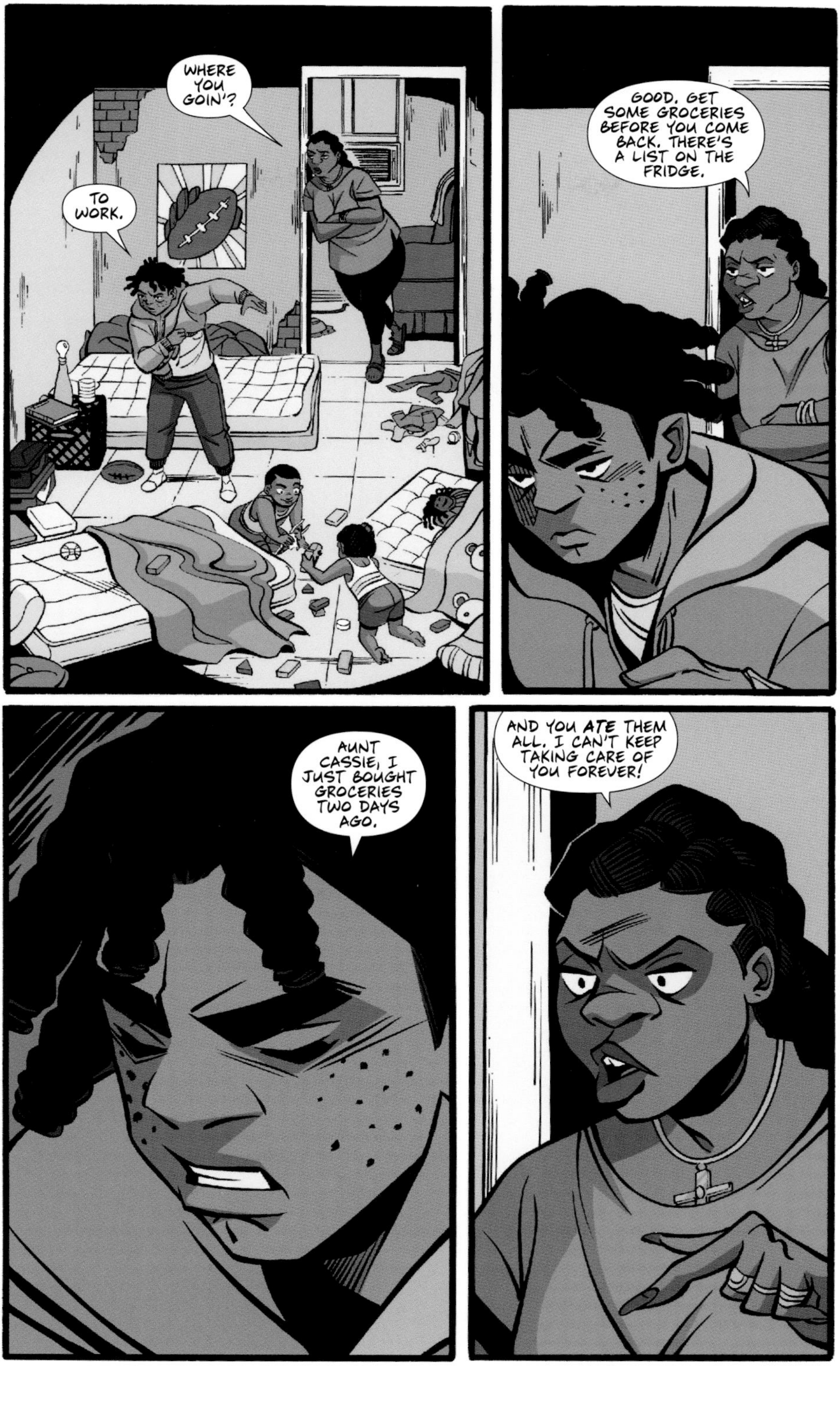
WHERE YOU GOIN'?
TO WORK.
GOOD. GET SOME GROCERIES BEFORE YOU COME BACK. THERE'S A LIST ON THE FRIDGE.
AUNT CASSIE, I JUST BOUGHT GROCERIES TWO DAYS AGO.
AND YOU ATE THEM ALL. I CAN'T KEEP TAKING CARE OF YOU FOREVER!

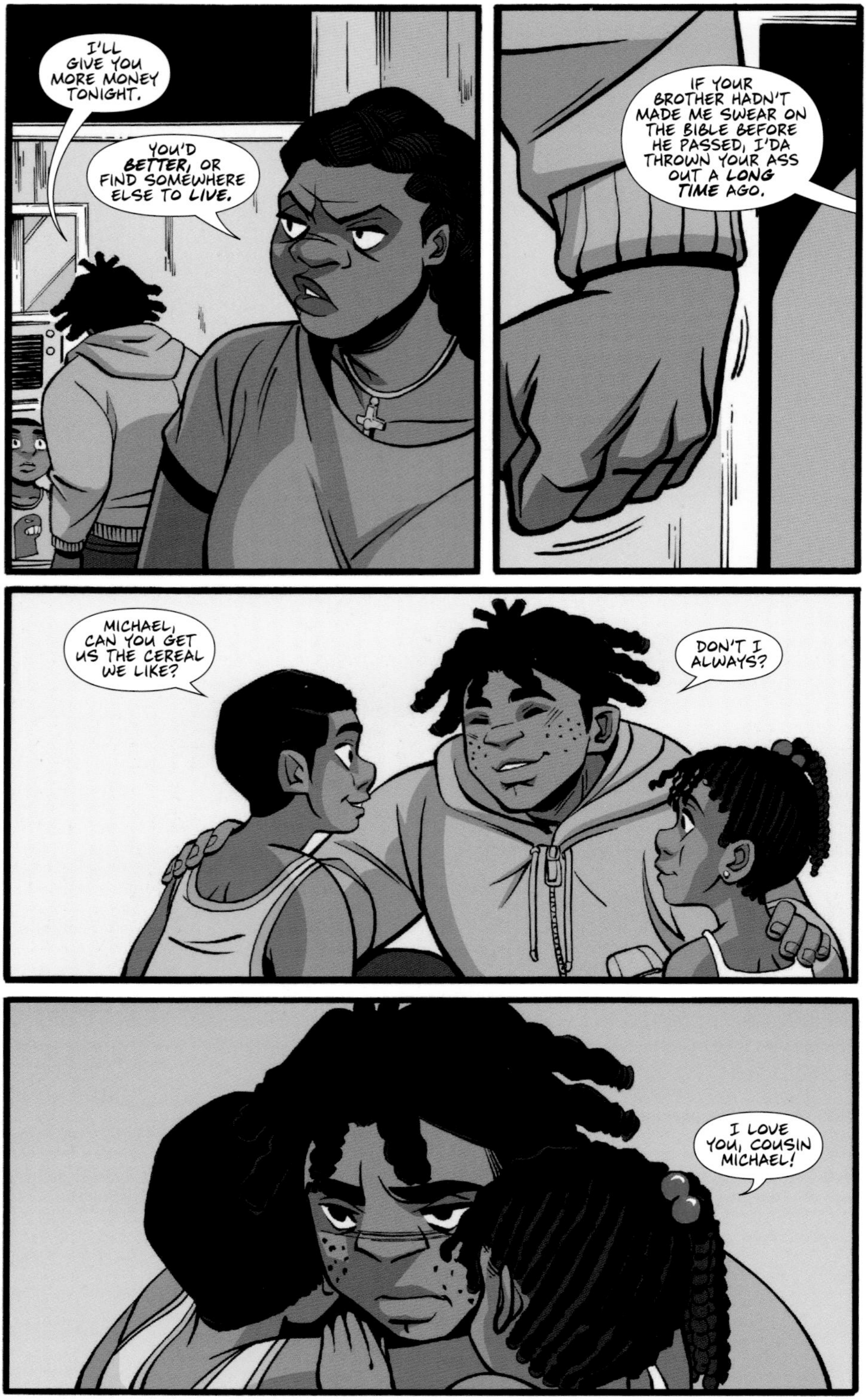
I'LL GIVE YOU MORE MONEY TONIGHT.
YOU'D BETTER, OR FIND SOMEWHERE ELSE TO LIVE.
IF YOUR BROTHER HADN'T MADE ME SWEAR ON THE BIBLE BEFORE HE PASSED, I'DA THROWN YOUR ASS OUT A LONG TIME AGO.
MICHAEL, CAN YOU GET US THE CEREAL WE LIKE?
DON'T I ALWAYS?
I LOVE YOU, COUSIN MICHAEL!

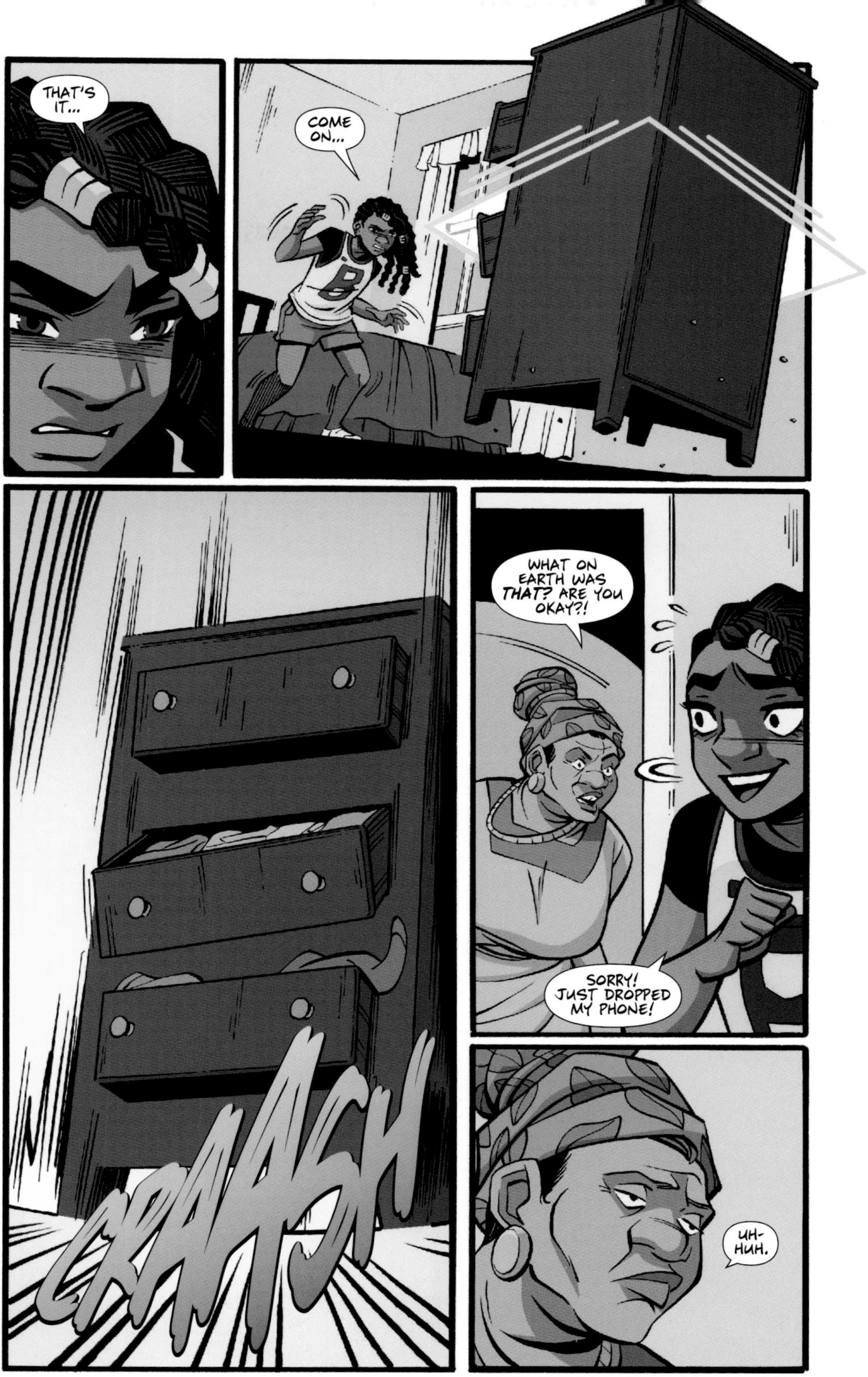
THAT'S IT...
COME ON...
CRAASH
WHAT ON EARTH WAS THAT? ARE YOU OKAY?!
SORRY! JUST DROPPED MY PHONE!
UH-HUH.

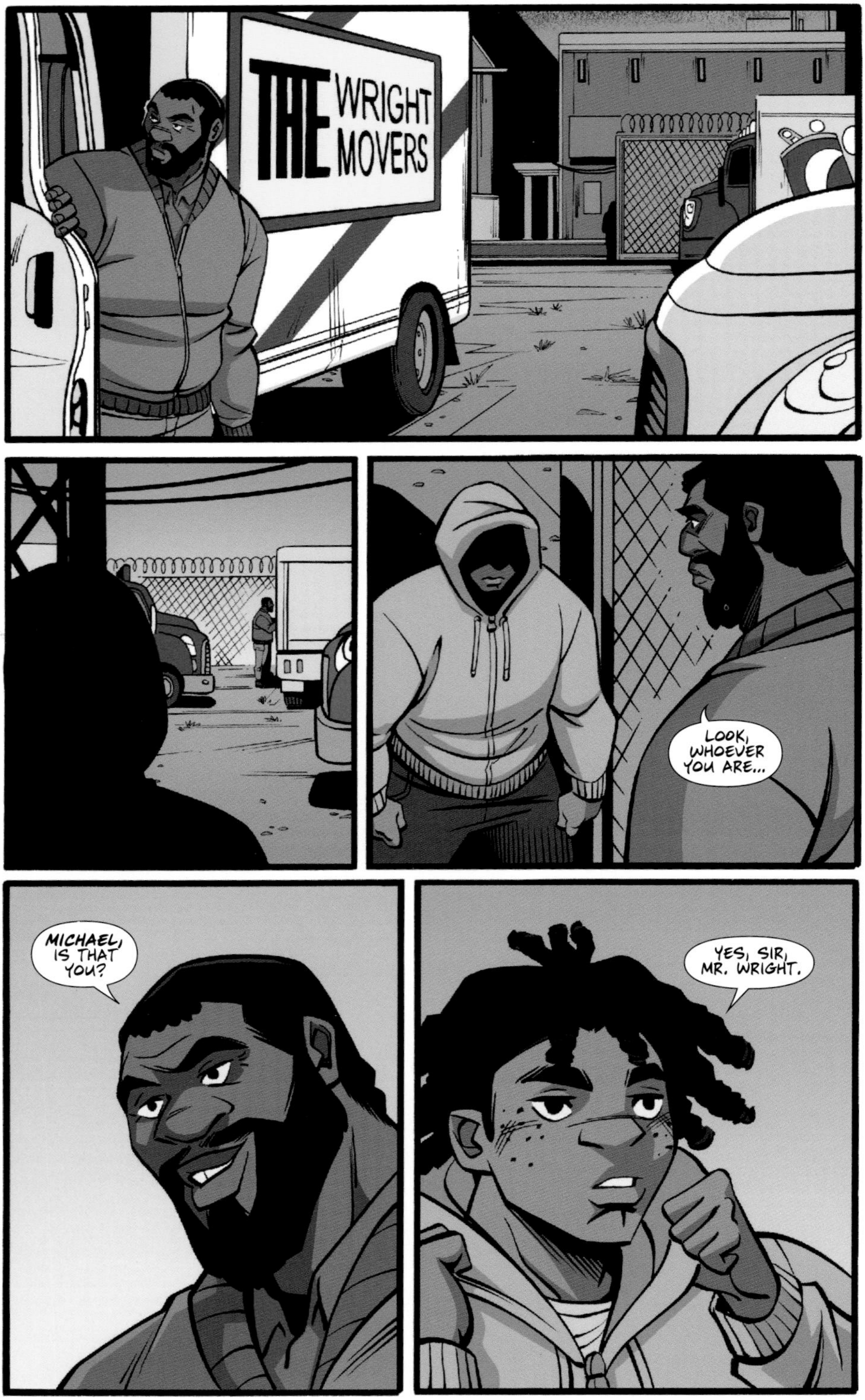
THE WRIGHT MOVERS
LOOK, WHOEVER YOU ARE...
MICHAEL, IS THAT YOU?
YES, SIR, MR. WRIGHT.

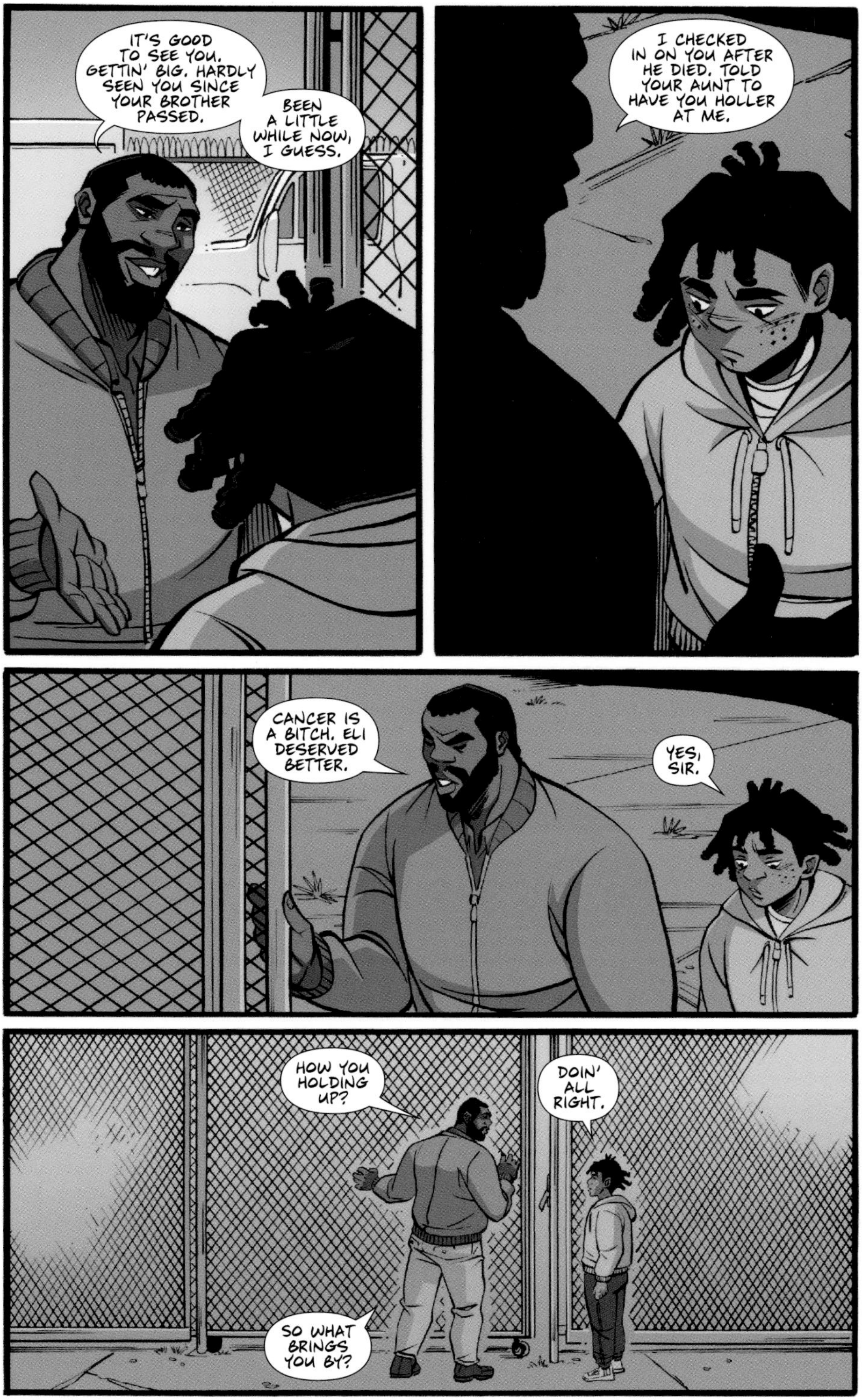
IT'S GOOD TO SEE YOU. GETTIN' BIG. HARDLY SEEN YOU SINCE YOUR BROTHER PASSED.
BEEN A LITTLE WHILE NOW, I GUESS.
I CHECKED IN ON YOU AFTER HE DIED. TOLD YOUR AUNT TO HAVE YOU HOLLER AT ME.
CANCER IS A BITCH. ELI DESERVED BETTER.
YES, SIR.
HOW YOU HOLDING UP?
DOIN' ALL RIGHT.
SO WHAT BRINGS YOU BY?

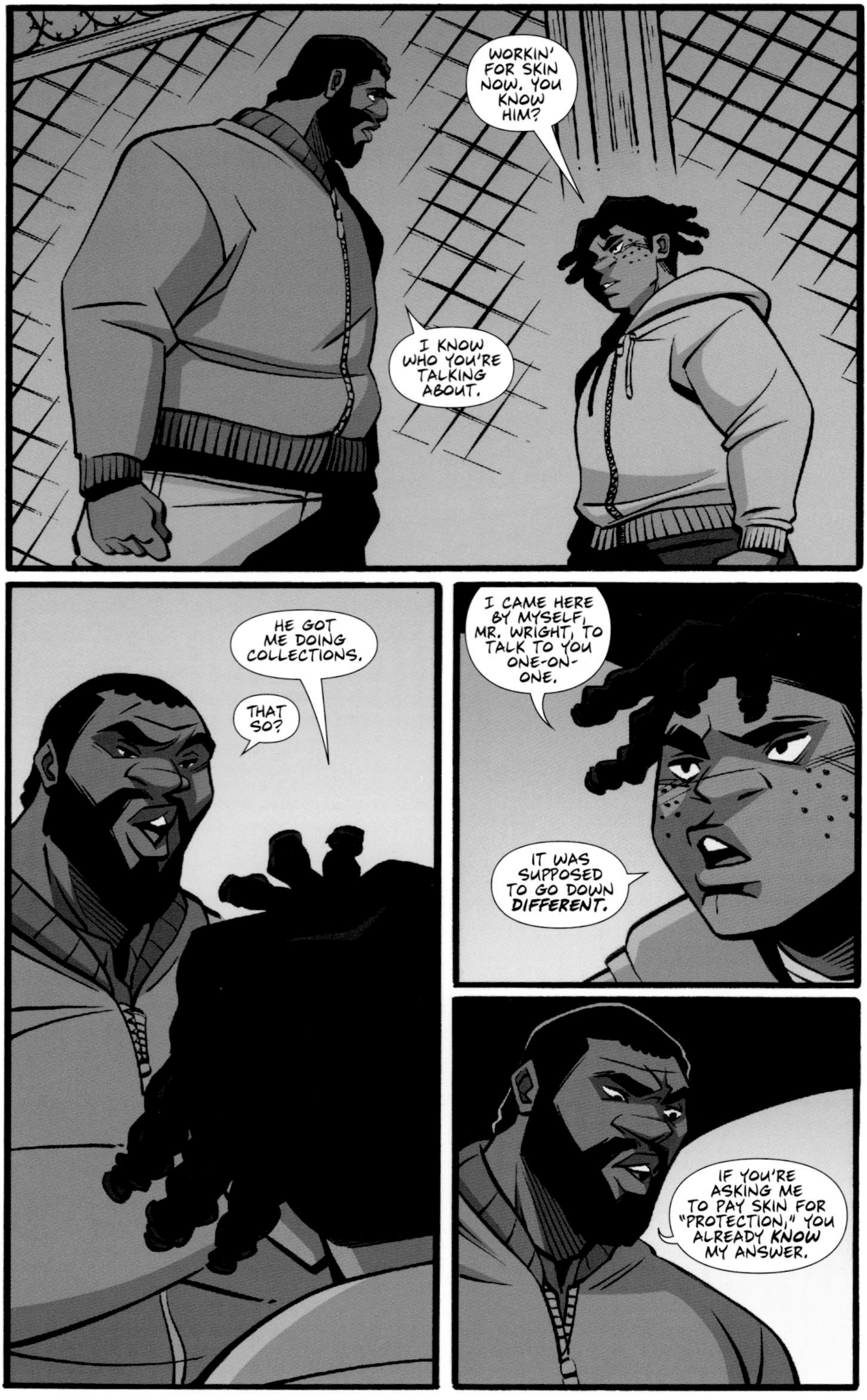
WORKIN' FOR SKIN NOW. YOU KNOW HIM?
I KNOW WHO YOU'RE TALKING ABOUT.
HE GOT ME DOING COLLECTIONS.
THAT SO?
I CAME HERE BY MYSELF, MR. WRIGHT, TO TALK TO YOU ONE-ON-ONE.
IT WAS SUPPOSED TO GO DOWN **DIFFERENT**.
IF YOU'RE ASKING ME TO PAY SKIN FOR "PROTECTION," YOU ALREADY **KNOW** MY ANSWER.

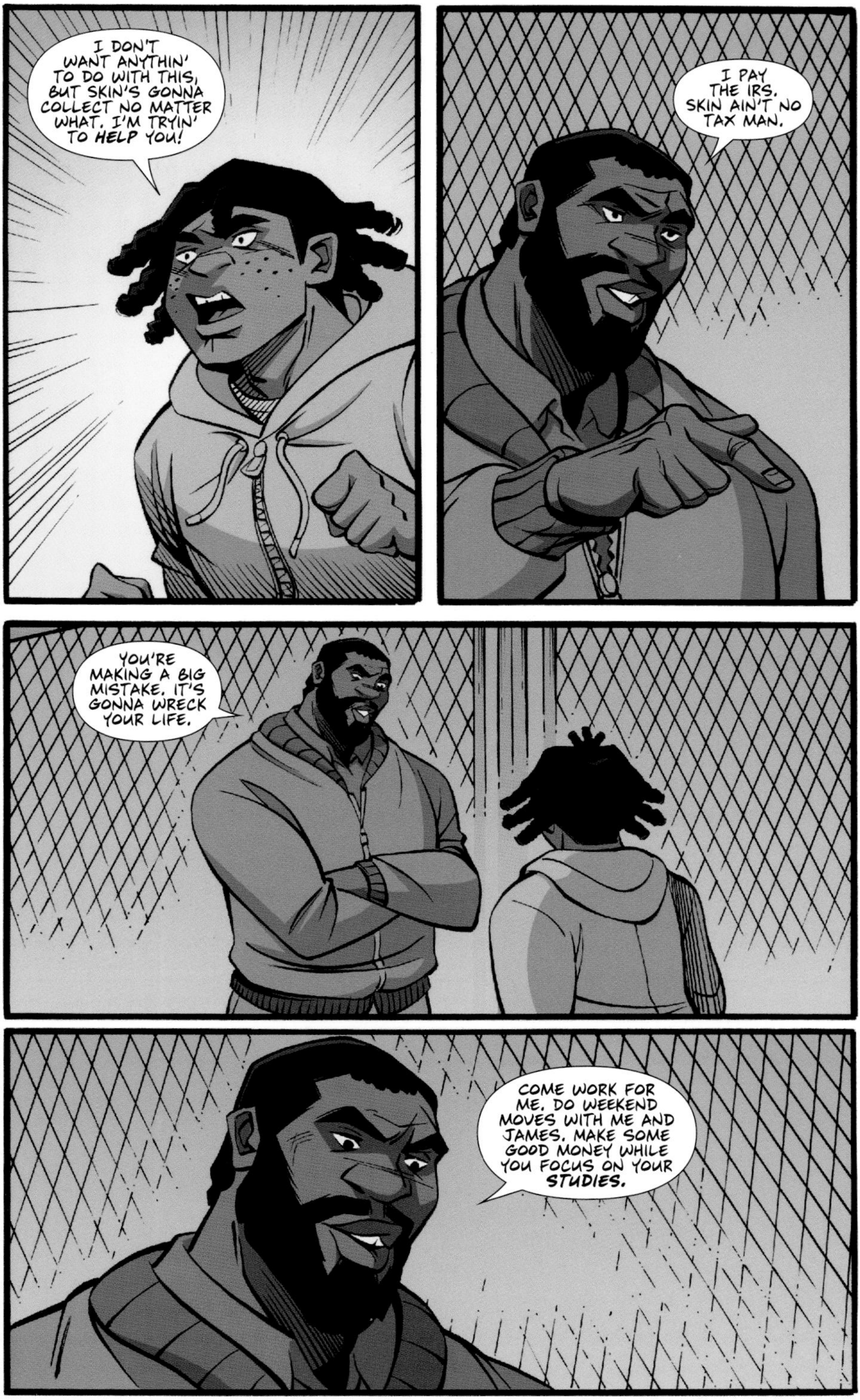
I DON'T WANT ANYTHIN' TO DO WITH THIS, BUT SKIN'S GONNA COLLECT NO MATTER WHAT. I'M TRYIN' TO HELP YOU!
I PAY THE IRS. SKIN AIN'T NO TAX MAN.
YOU'RE MAKING A BIG MISTAKE. IT'S GONNA WRECK YOUR LIFE.
COME WORK FOR ME. DO WEEKEND MOVES WITH ME AND JAMES. MAKE SOME GOOD MONEY WHILE YOU FOCUS ON YOUR STUDIES.

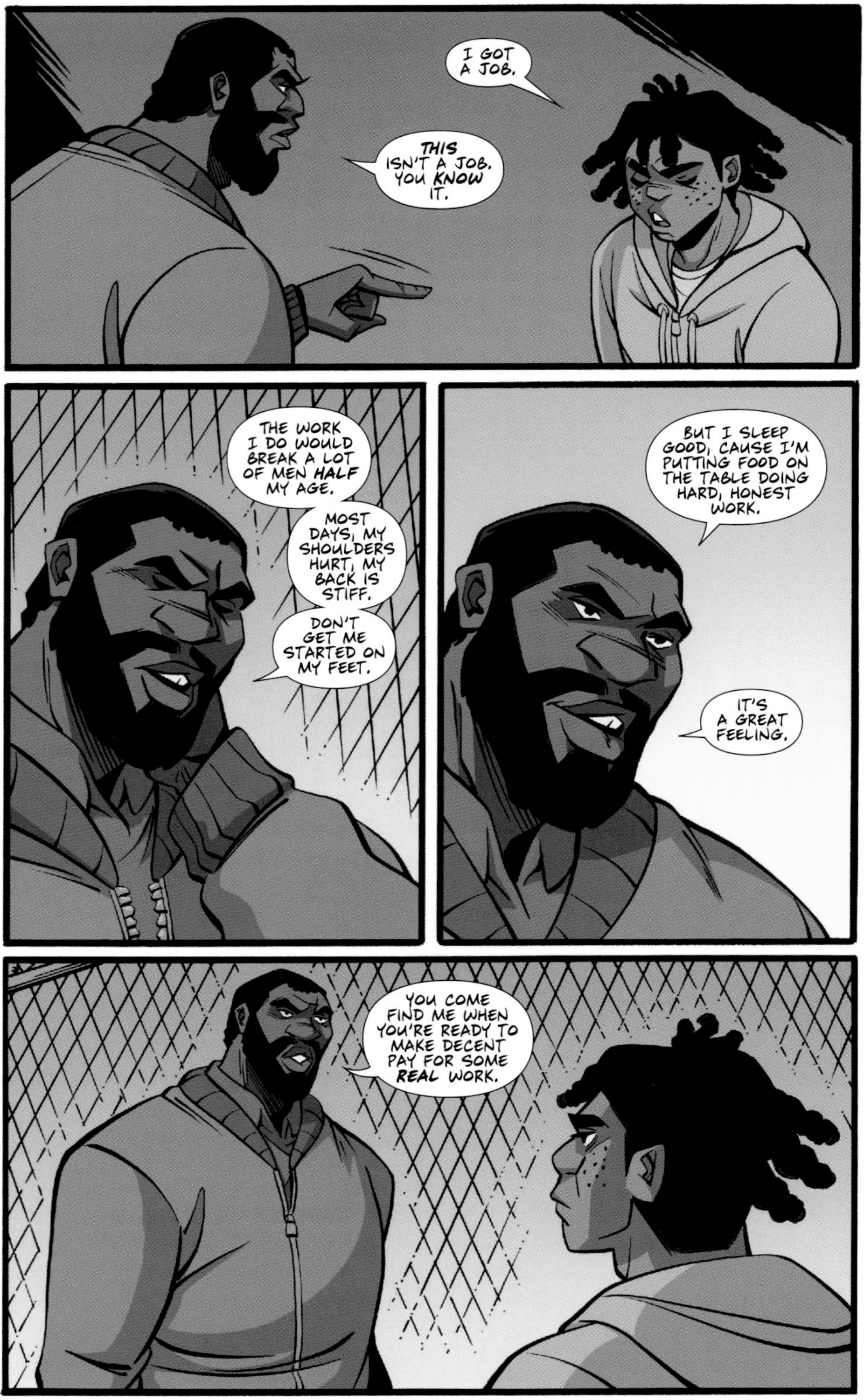
I GOT A JOB.
THIS ISN'T A JOB. YOU KNOW IT.
THE WORK I DO WOULD BREAK A LOT OF MEN HALF MY AGE.
MOST DAYS, MY SHOULDERS HURT, MY BACK IS STIFF.
DON'T GET ME STARTED ON MY FEET.
BUT I SLEEP GOOD, CAUSE I'M PUTTING FOOD ON THE TABLE DOING HARD, HONEST WORK.
IT'S A GREAT FEELING.
YOU COME FIND ME WHEN YOU'RE READY TO MAKE DECENT PAY FOR SOME REAL WORK.

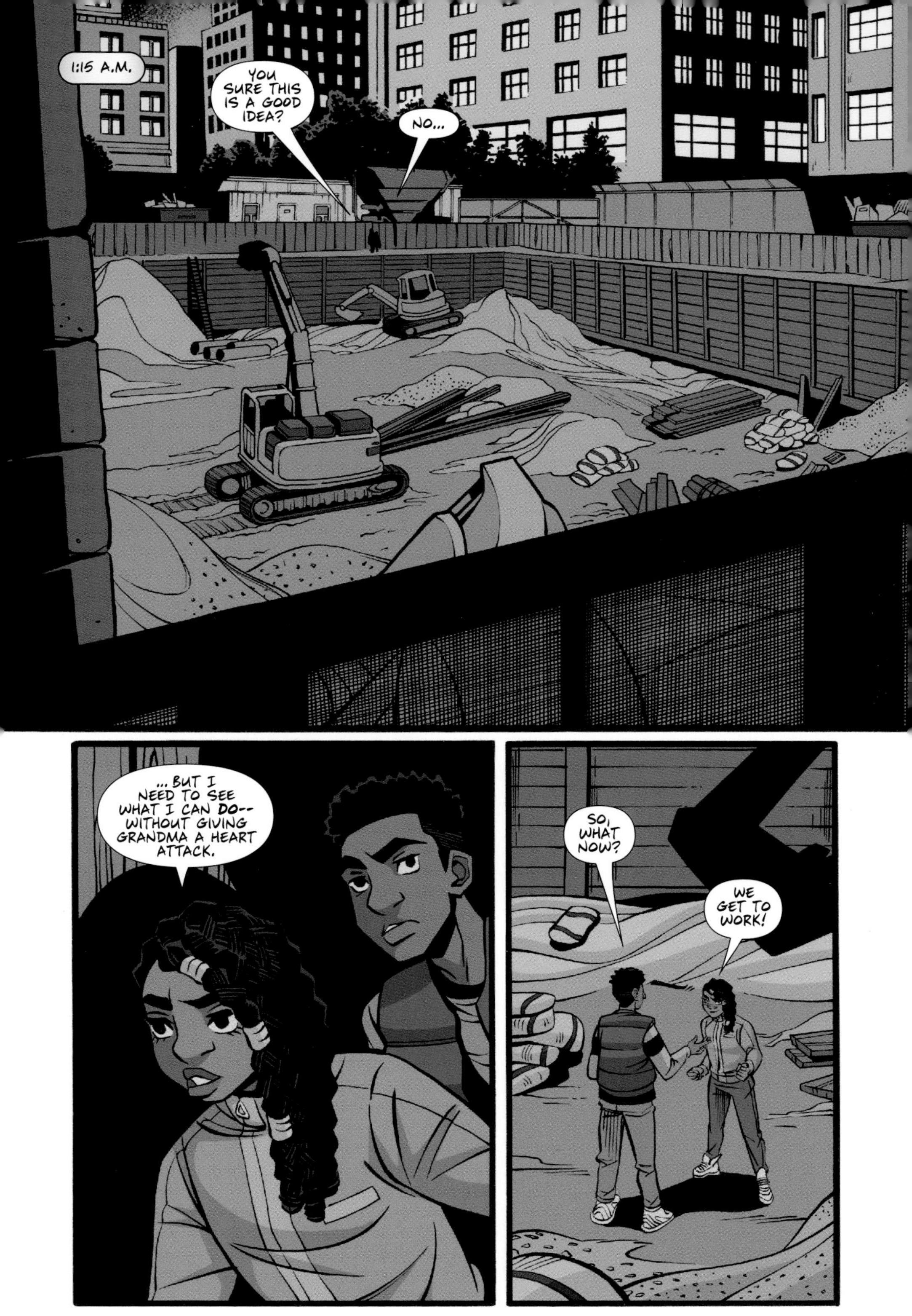
1:15 A.M.
YOU SURE THIS IS A GOOD IDEA?
NO...
...BUT I NEED TO SEE WHAT I CAN DO-- WITHOUT GIVING GRANDMA A HEART ATTACK.
SO, WHAT NOW?
WE GET TO WORK!

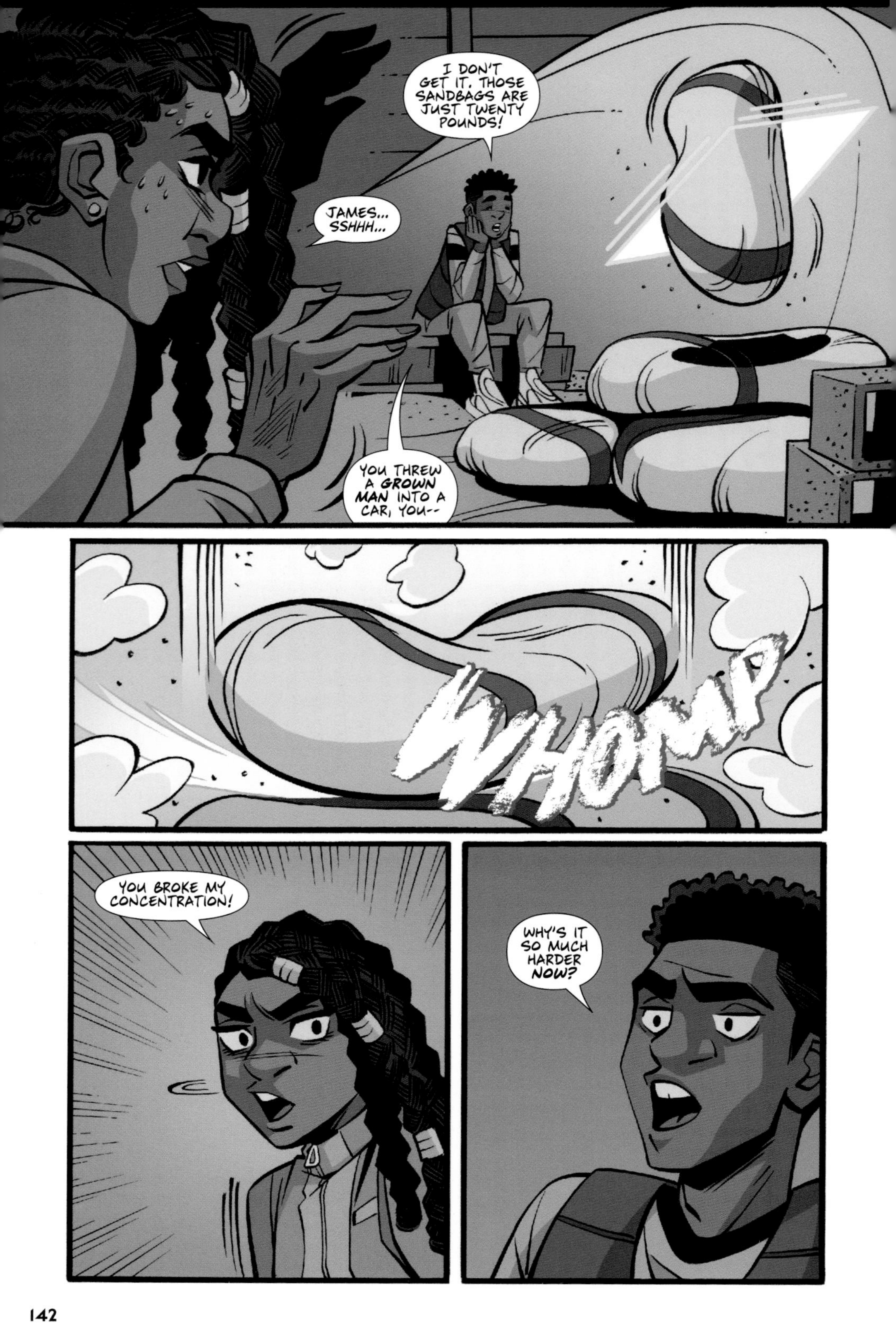

I DON'T GET IT. THOSE SANDBAGS ARE JUST TWENTY POUNDS!
JAMES... SSHHH...
YOU THREW A GROWN MAN INTO A CAR, YOU--
WHOMP
YOU BROKE MY CONCENTRATION!
WHY'S IT SO MUCH HARDER NOW?

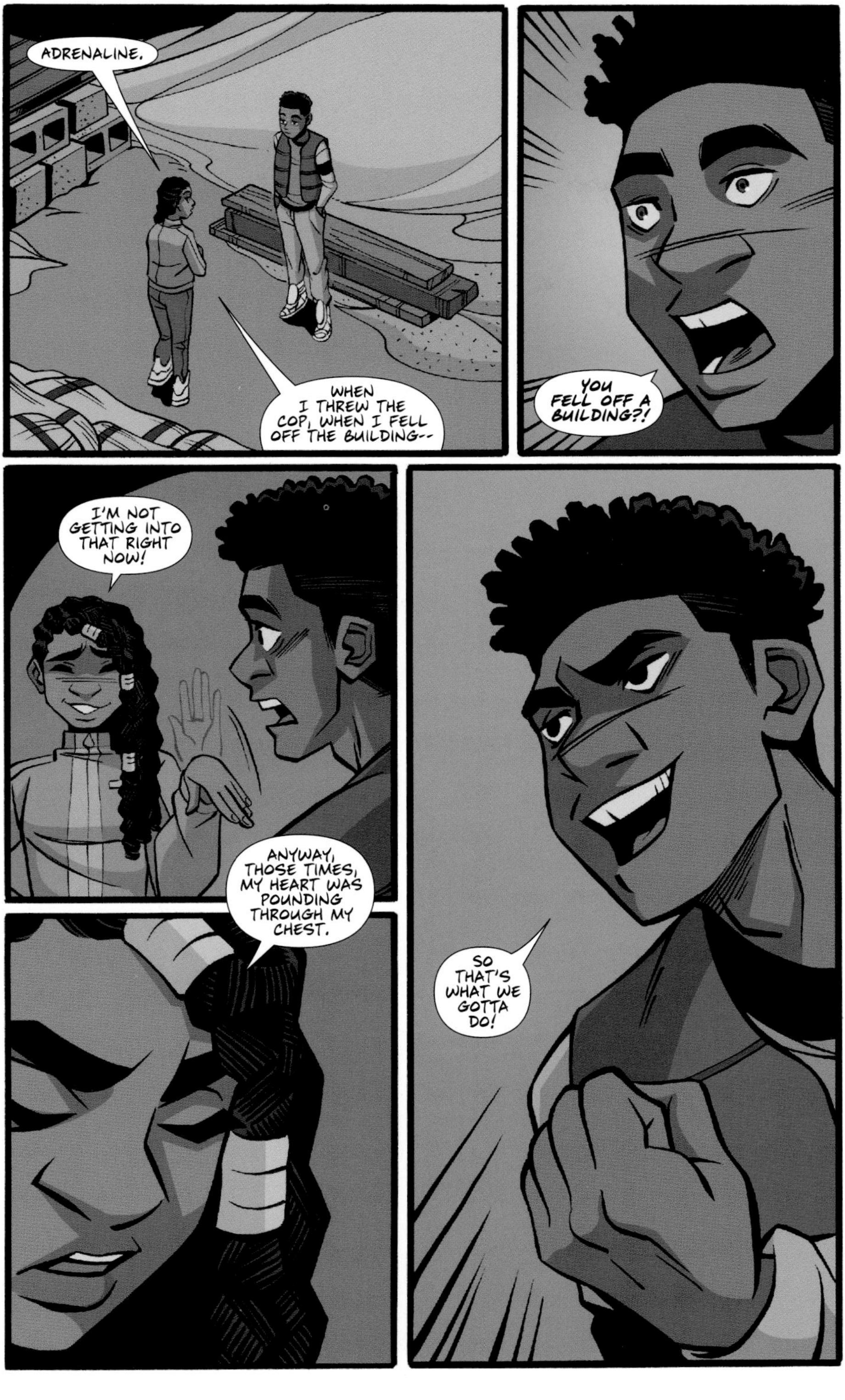
ADRENALINE.
WHEN I THREW THE COP, WHEN I FELL OFF THE BUILDING--
YOU FELL OFF A BUILDING?!
I'M NOT GETTING INTO THAT RIGHT NOW!
ANYWAY, THOSE TIMES, MY HEART WAS POUNDING THROUGH MY CHEST.
SO THAT'S WHAT WE GOTTA DO!

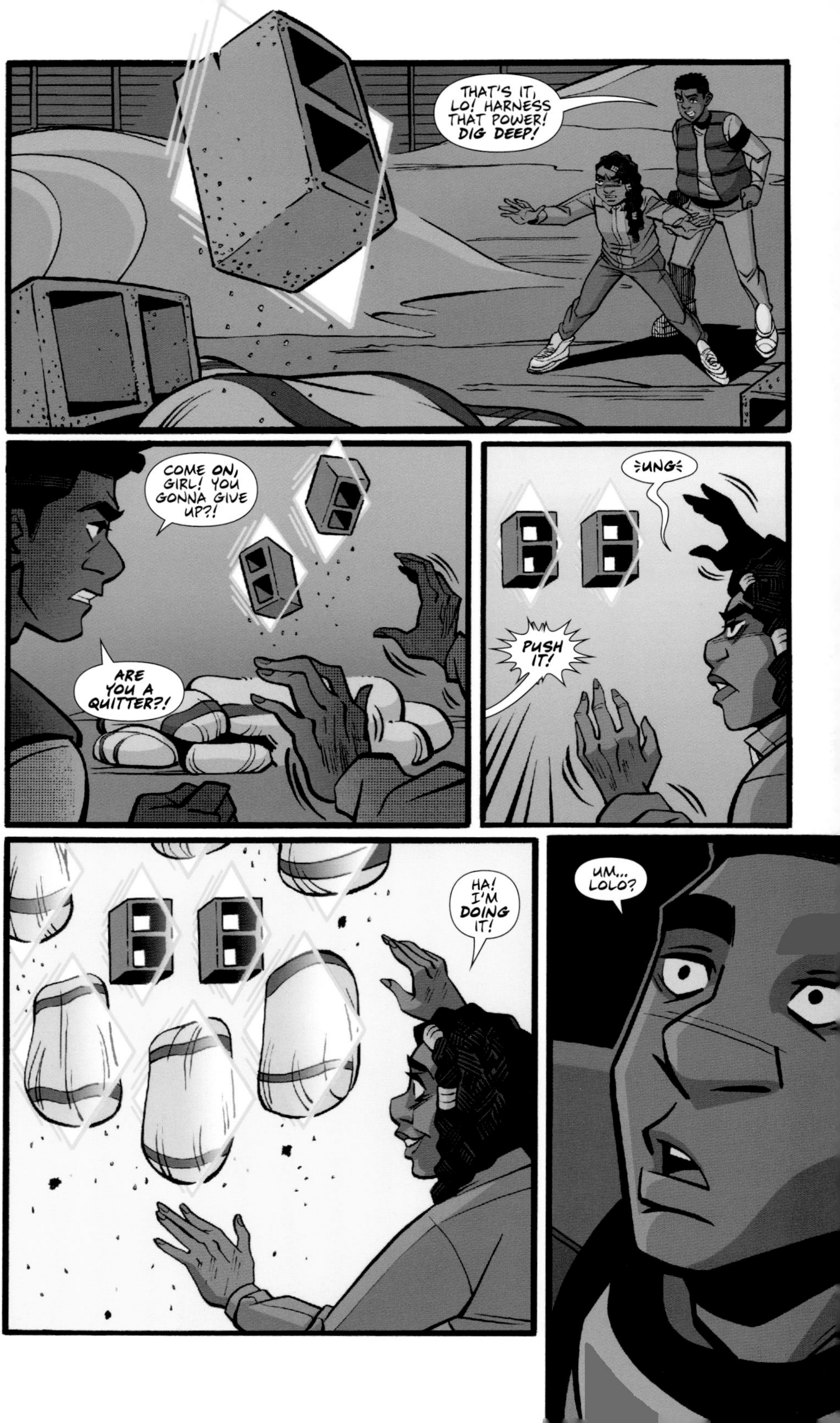
THAT'S IT, LO! HARNESS THAT POWER! DIG DEEP!
COME ON, GIRL! YOU GONNA GIVE UP?!
ARE YOU A QUITTER?!
UNG
PUSH IT!
HA! I'M DOING IT!
UM... LOLO?

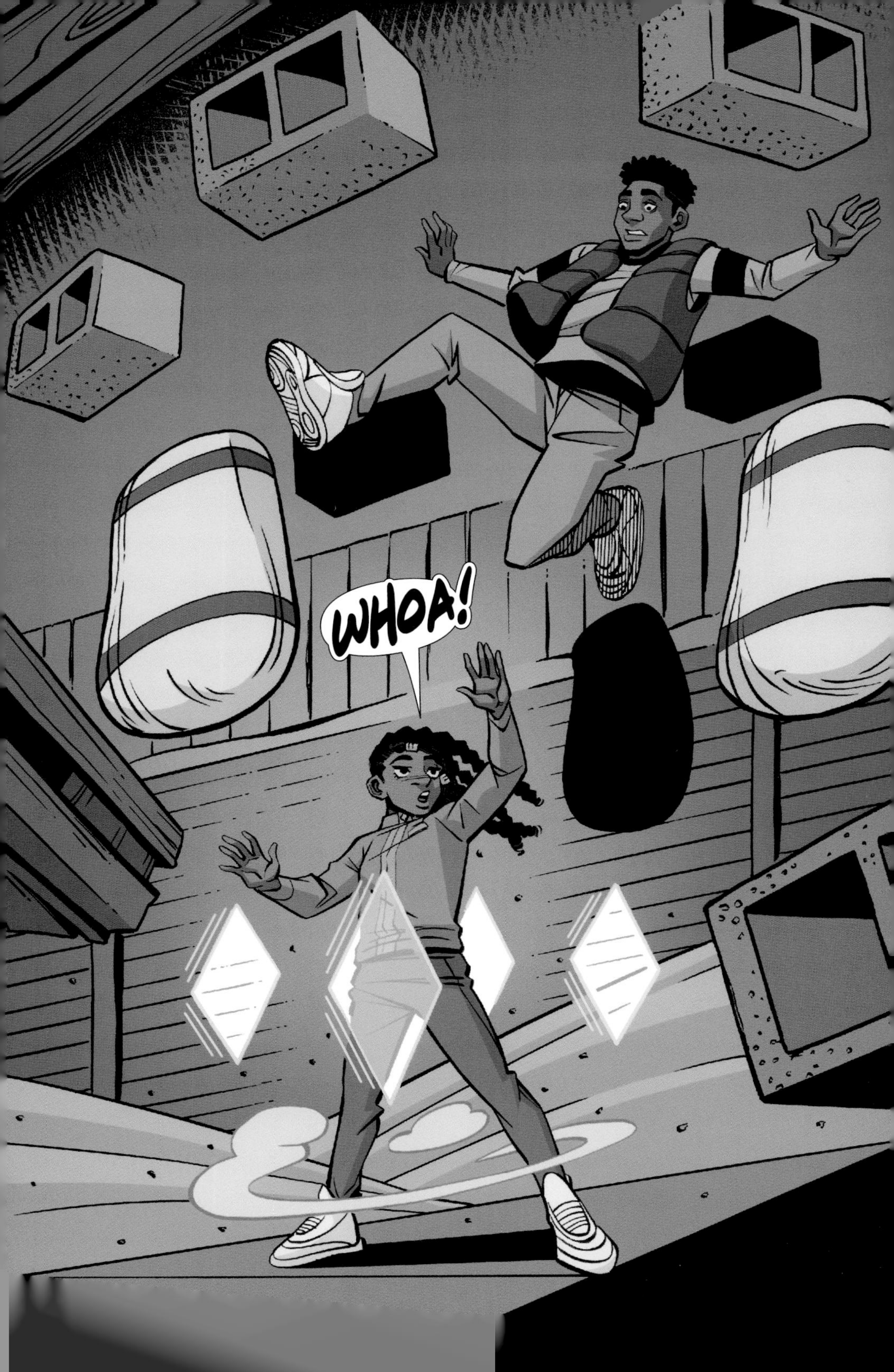
WHOA!

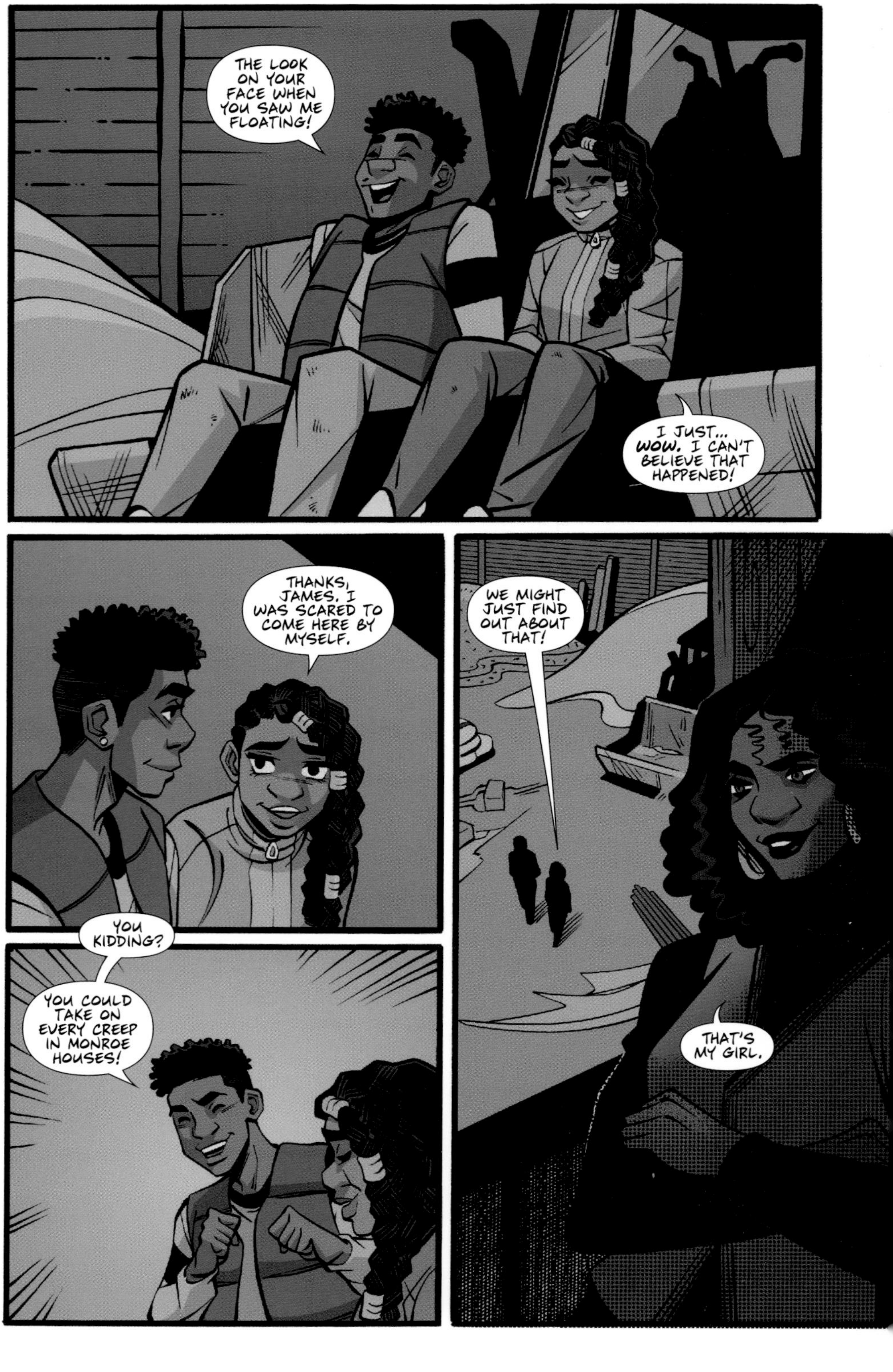
THE LOOK ON YOUR FACE WHEN YOU SAW ME FLOATING!
I JUST... **WOW.** I CAN'T BELIEVE THAT HAPPENED!
THANKS, JAMES. I WAS SCARED TO COME HERE BY MYSELF.
YOU KIDDING?
YOU COULD TAKE ON EVERY CREEP IN MONROE HOUSES!
WE MIGHT JUST FIND OUT ABOUT THAT!
THAT'S MY GIRL.

CHAPTER 7

WHERE DO WE GO FROM HERE?

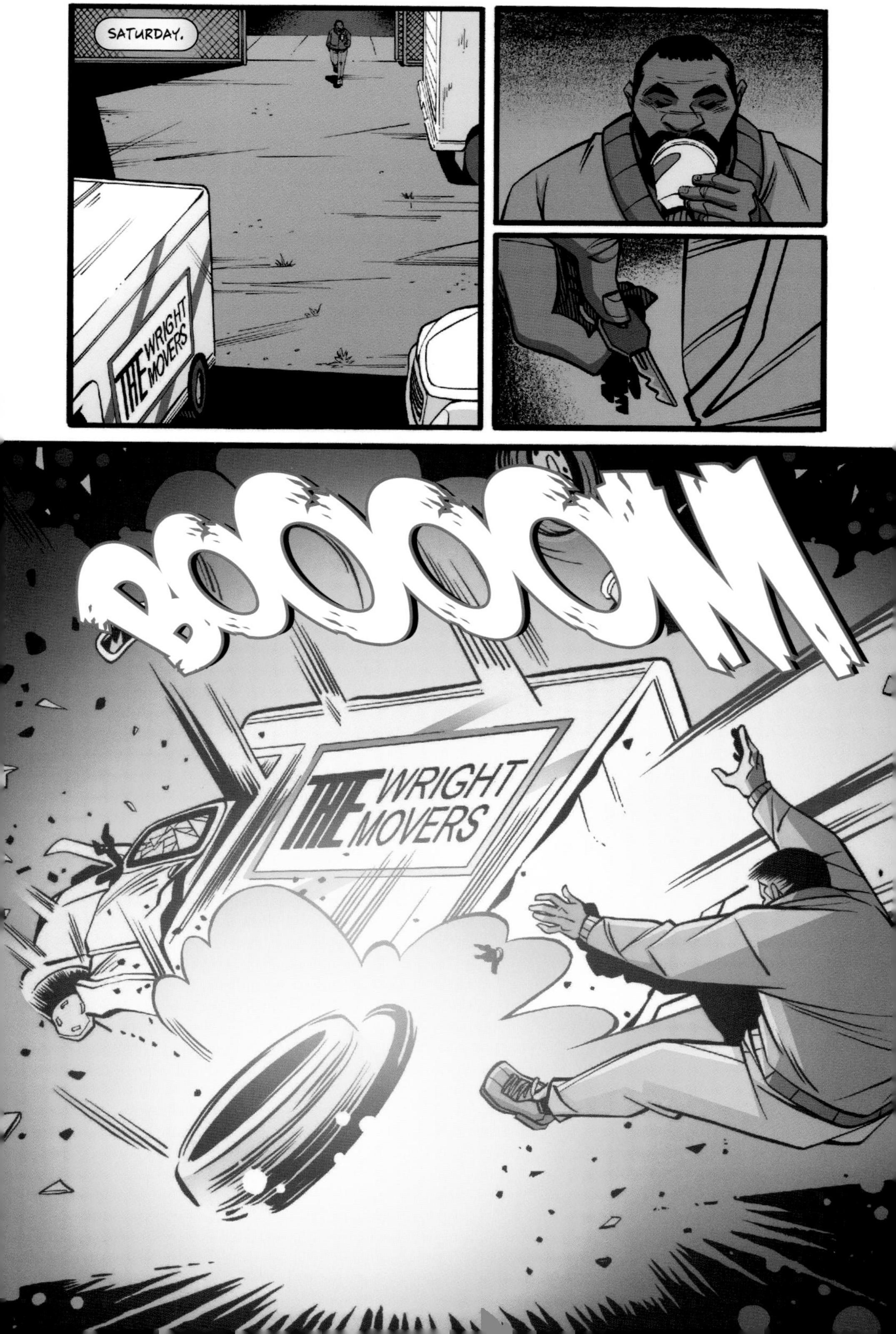
SATURDAY.
THE WRIGHT MOVERS
BOOOOOM
THE WRIGHT MOVERS

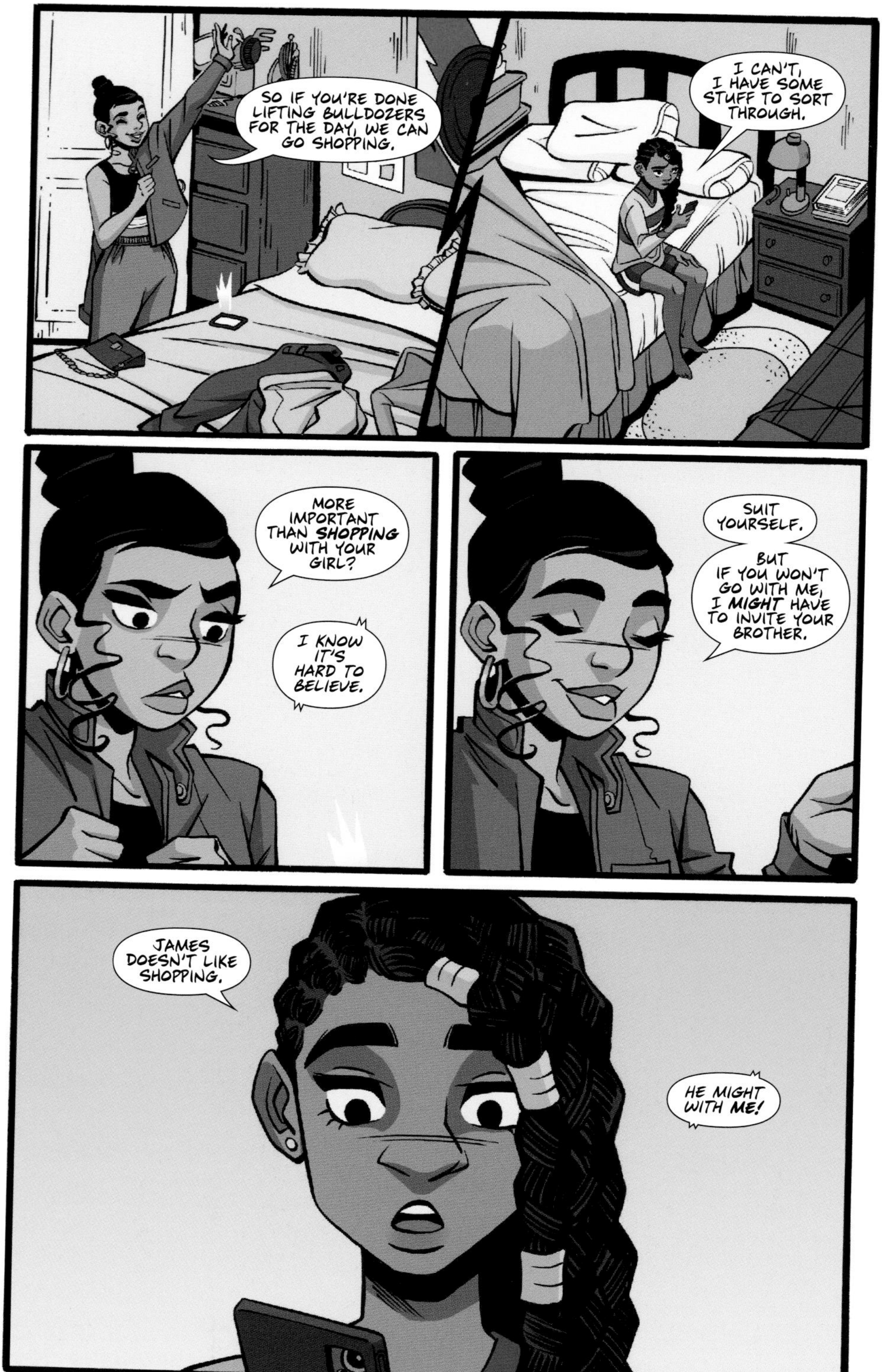
SO IF YOU'RE DONE LIFTING BULLDOZERS FOR THE DAY, WE CAN GO SHOPPING.
I CAN'T, I HAVE SOME STUFF TO SORT THROUGH.
MORE IMPORTANT THAN SHOPPING WITH YOUR GIRL?
I KNOW IT'S HARD TO BELIEVE.
SUIT YOURSELF.
BUT IF YOU WON'T GO WITH ME, I MIGHT HAVE TO INVITE YOUR BROTHER.
JAMES DOESN'T LIKE SHOPPING.
HE MIGHT WITH ME!

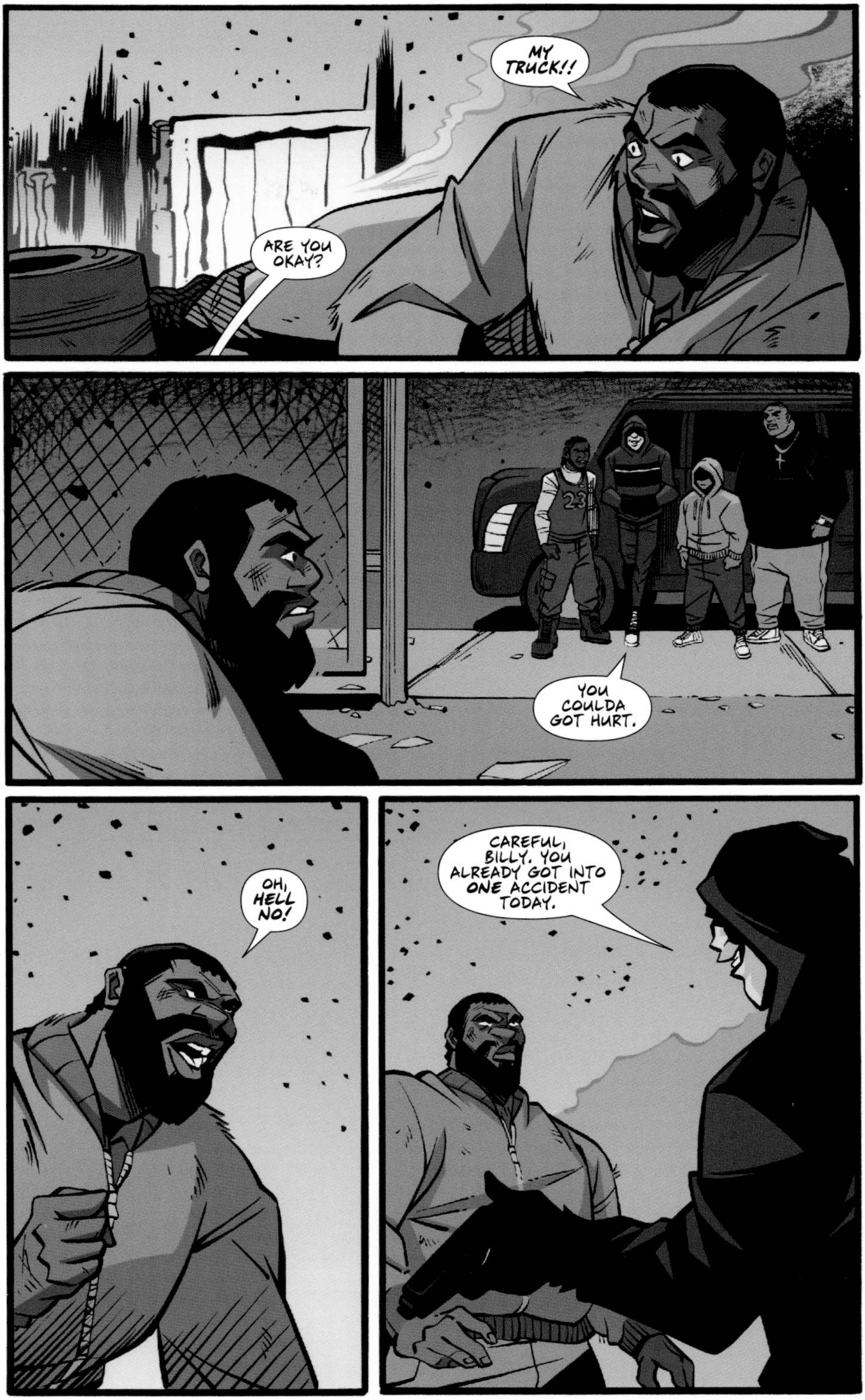
MY TRUCK!!
ARE YOU OKAY?
YOU COULDA GOT HURT.
OH, HELL NO!
CAREFUL, BILLY. YOU ALREADY GOT INTO ONE ACCIDENT TODAY.

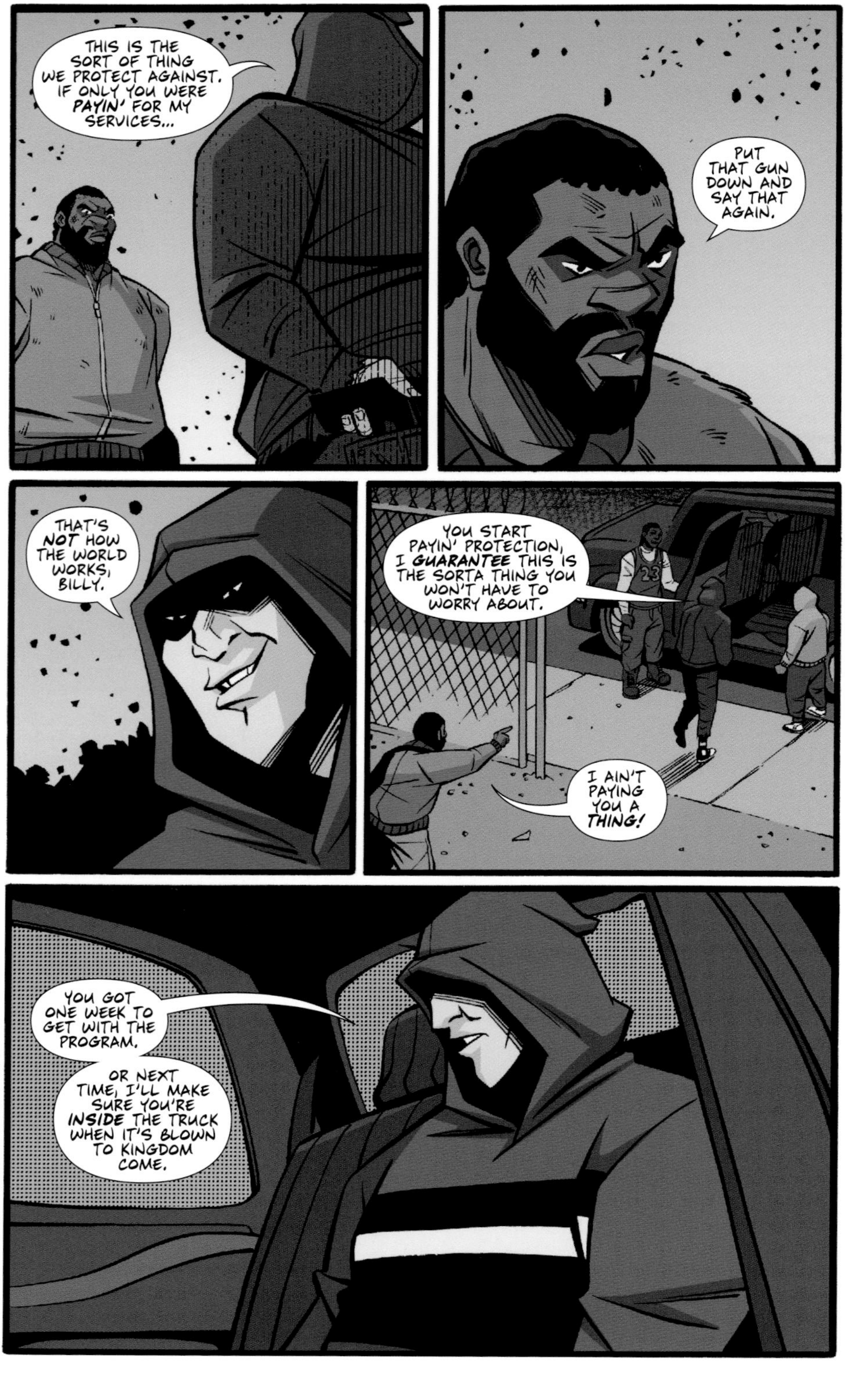
THIS IS THE SORT OF THING WE PROTECT AGAINST. IF ONLY YOU WERE PAYIN' FOR MY SERVICES...
PUT THAT GUN DOWN AND SAY THAT AGAIN.
THAT'S NOT HOW THE WORLD WORKS, BILLY.
YOU START PAYIN' PROTECTION, I GUARANTEE THIS IS THE SORTA THING YOU WON'T HAVE TO WORRY ABOUT.
I AIN'T PAYING YOU A THING!
YOU GOT ONE WEEK TO GET WITH THE PROGRAM.
OR NEXT TIME, I'LL MAKE SURE YOU'RE INSIDE THE TRUCK WHEN IT'S BLOWN TO KINGDOM COME.

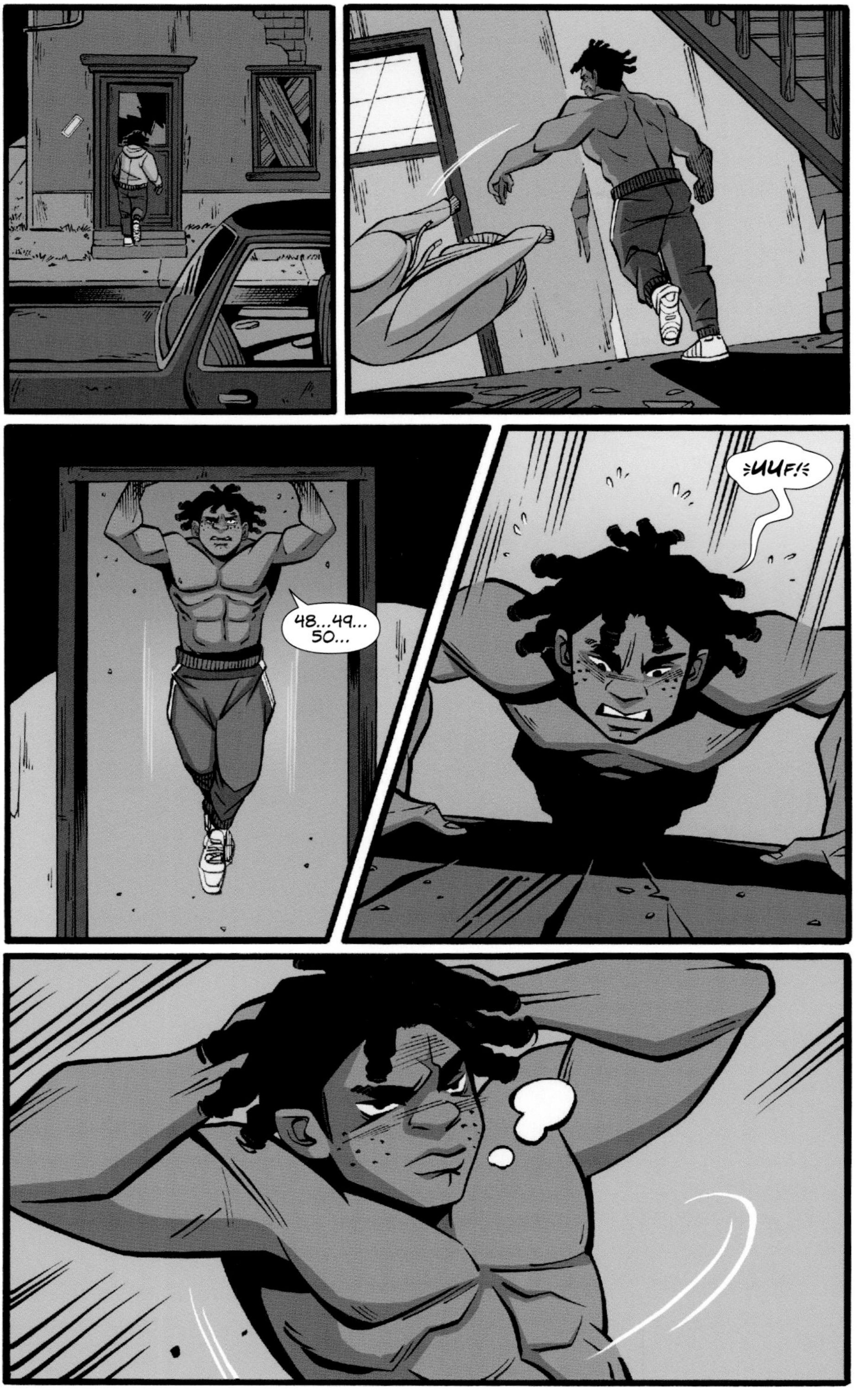
48...49...
50...
UUF!

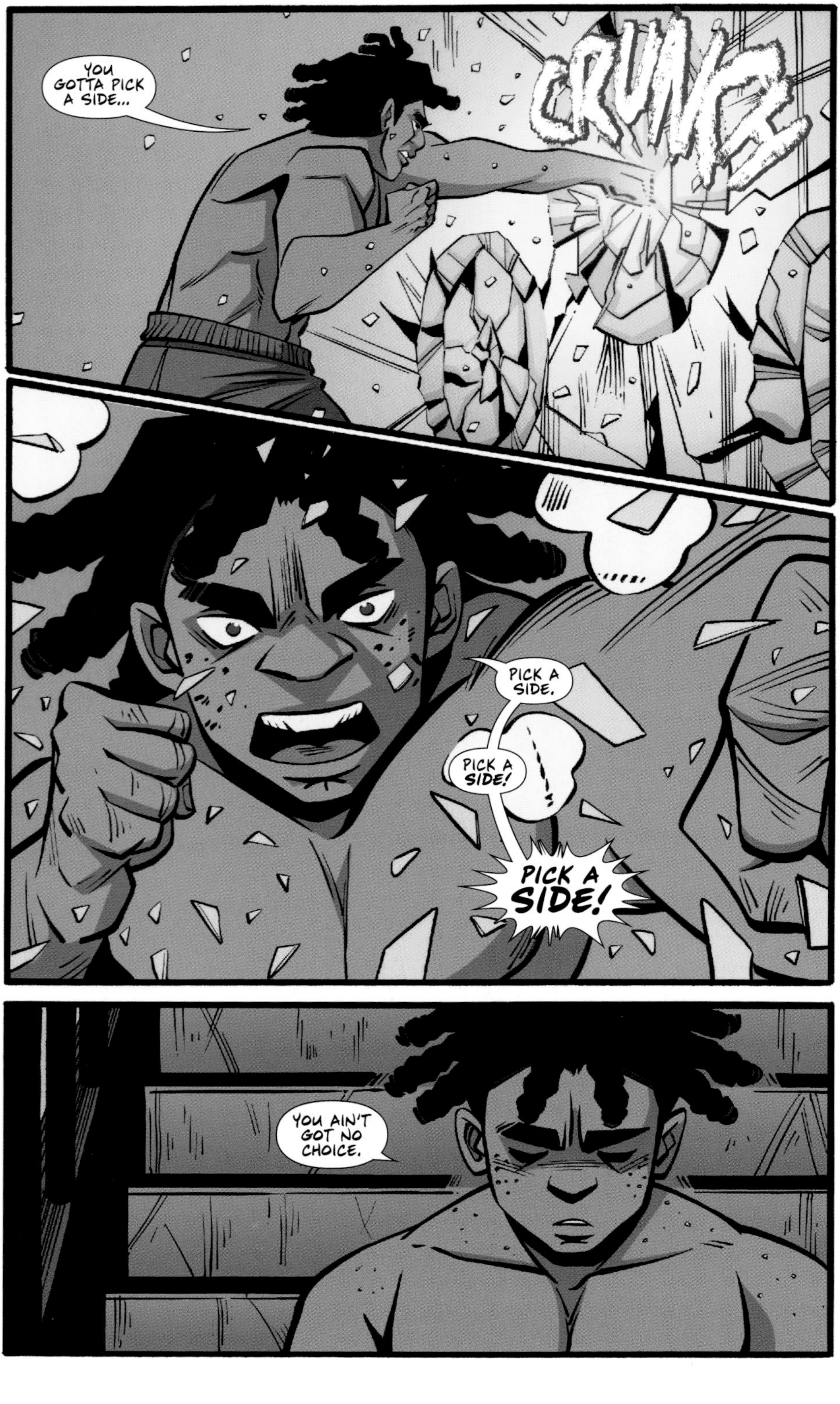
YOU GOTTA PICK A SIDE...
CRUNCH
PICK A SIDE.
PICK A SIDE!
PICK A SIDE!
YOU AIN'T GOT NO CHOICE.

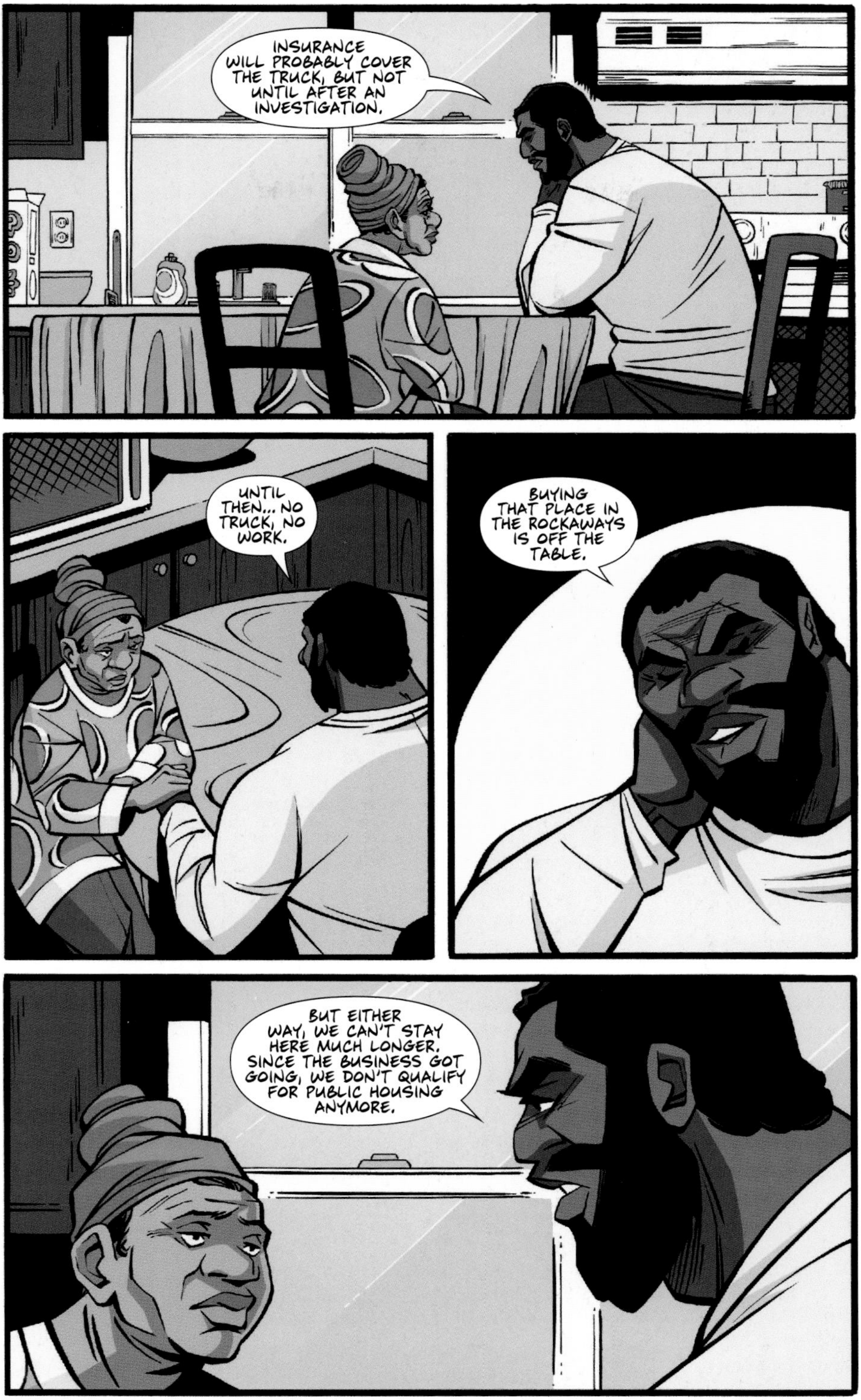

INSURANCE WILL PROBABLY COVER THE TRUCK, BUT NOT UNTIL AFTER AN INVESTIGATION.
UNTIL THEN... NO TRUCK, NO WORK.
BUYING THAT PLACE IN THE ROCKAWAYS IS OFF THE TABLE.
BUT EITHER WAY, WE CAN'T STAY HERE MUCH LONGER. SINCE THE BUSINESS GOT GOING, WE DON'T QUALIFY FOR PUBLIC HOUSING ANYMORE.

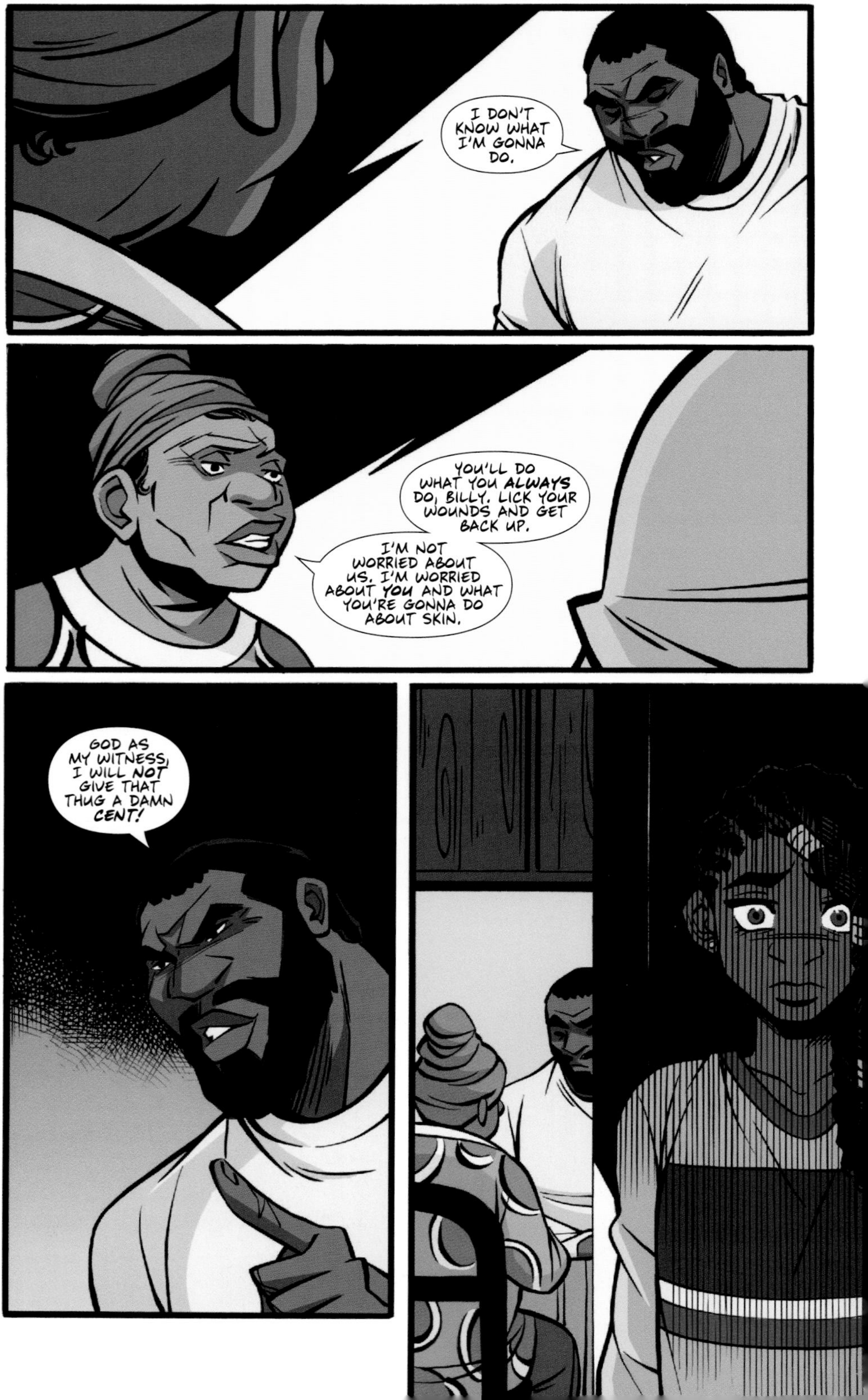
I DON'T KNOW WHAT I'M GONNA DO.
YOU'LL DO WHAT YOU **ALWAYS** DO, BILLY. LICK YOUR WOUNDS AND GET BACK UP.
I'M NOT WORRIED ABOUT US. I'M WORRIED ABOUT **YOU** AND WHAT YOU'RE GONNA DO ABOUT SKIN.
GOD AS MY WITNESS, I WILL **NOT** GIVE THAT THUG A DAMN **CENT!**

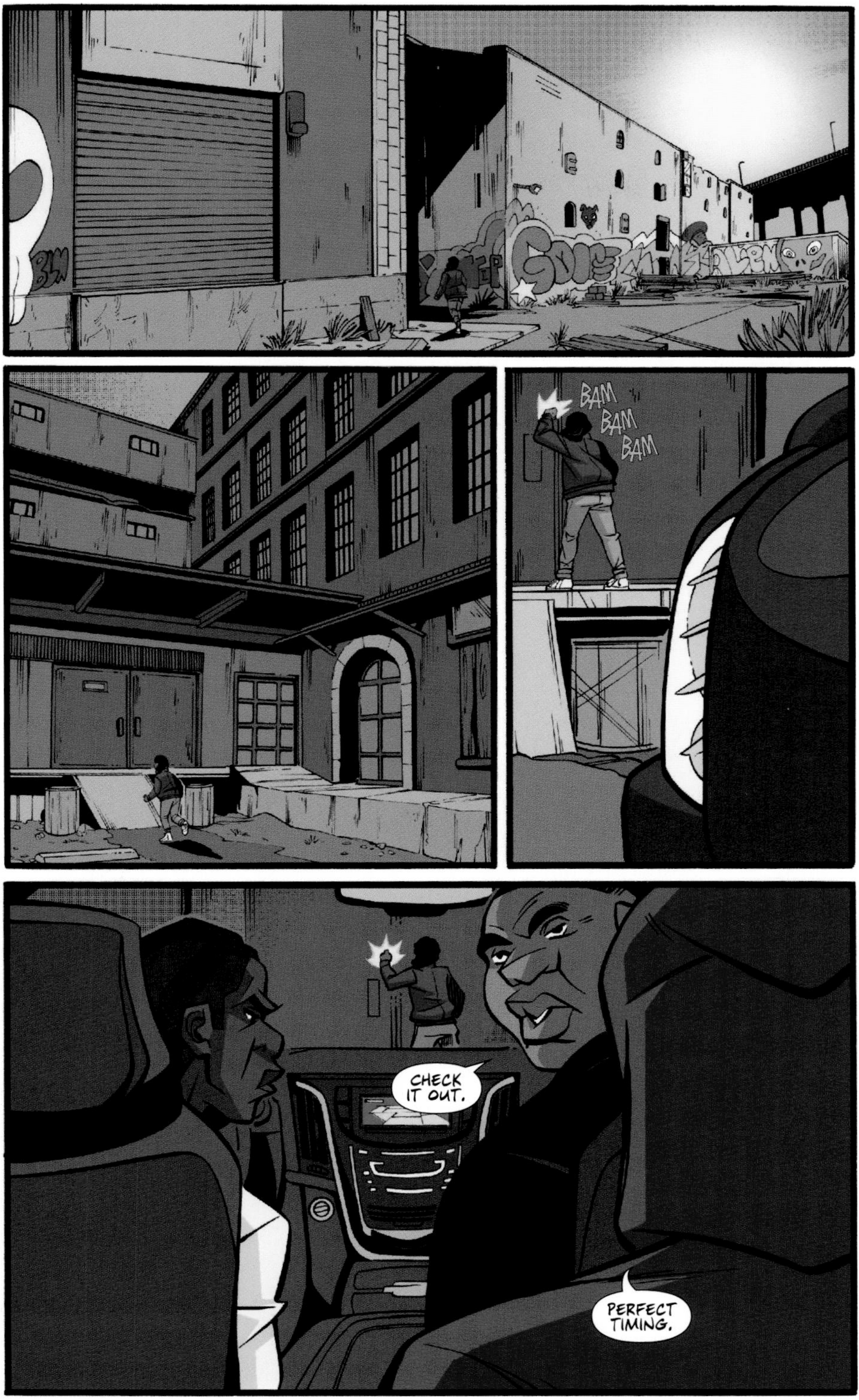
BAM
BAM
BAM
CHECK IT OUT.
PERFECT TIMING.

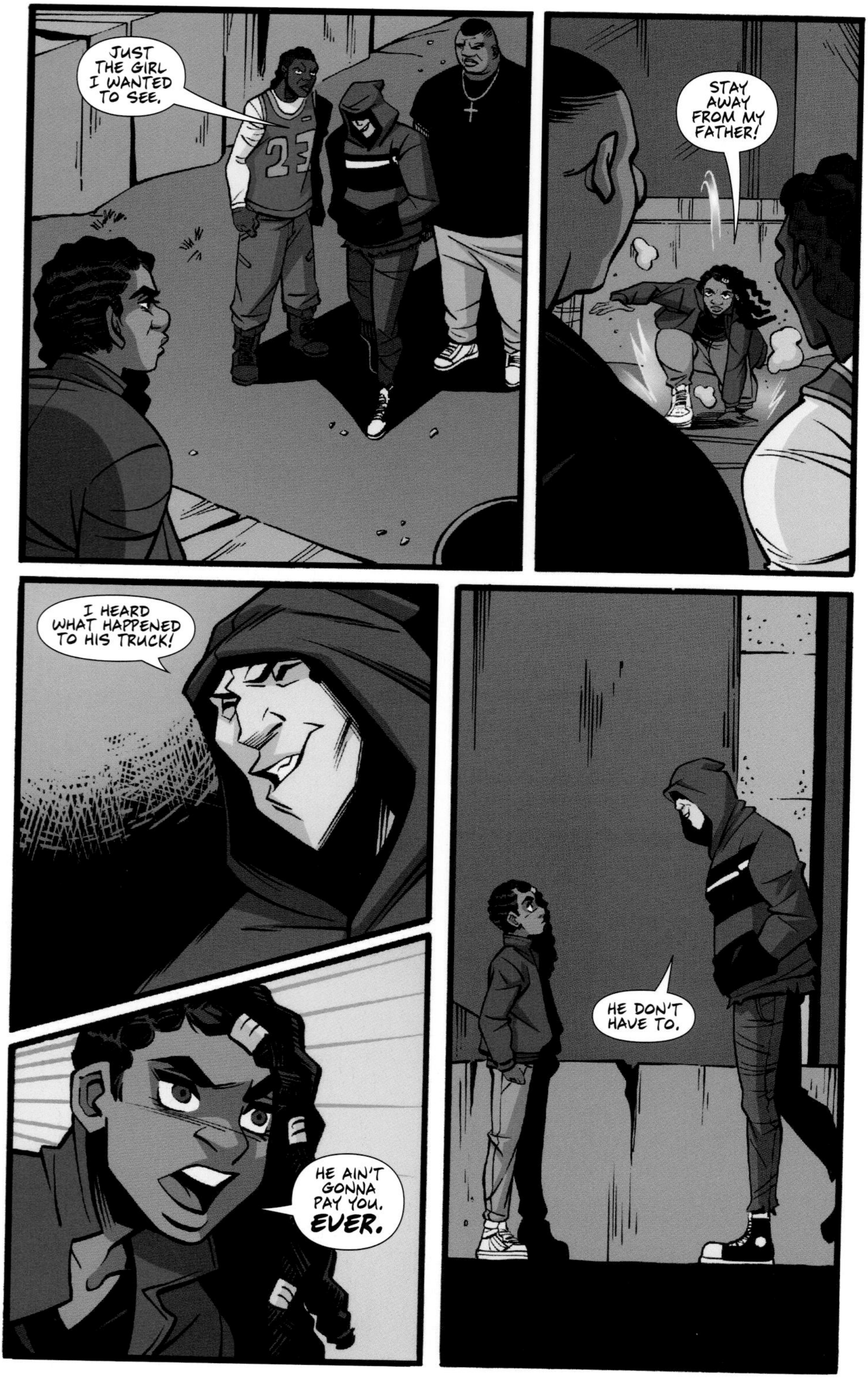
JUST THE GIRL I WANTED TO SEE.
STAY AWAY FROM MY FATHER!
I HEARD WHAT HAPPENED TO HIS TRUCK!
HE AIN'T GONNA PAY YOU. **EVER.**
HE DON'T HAVE TO.

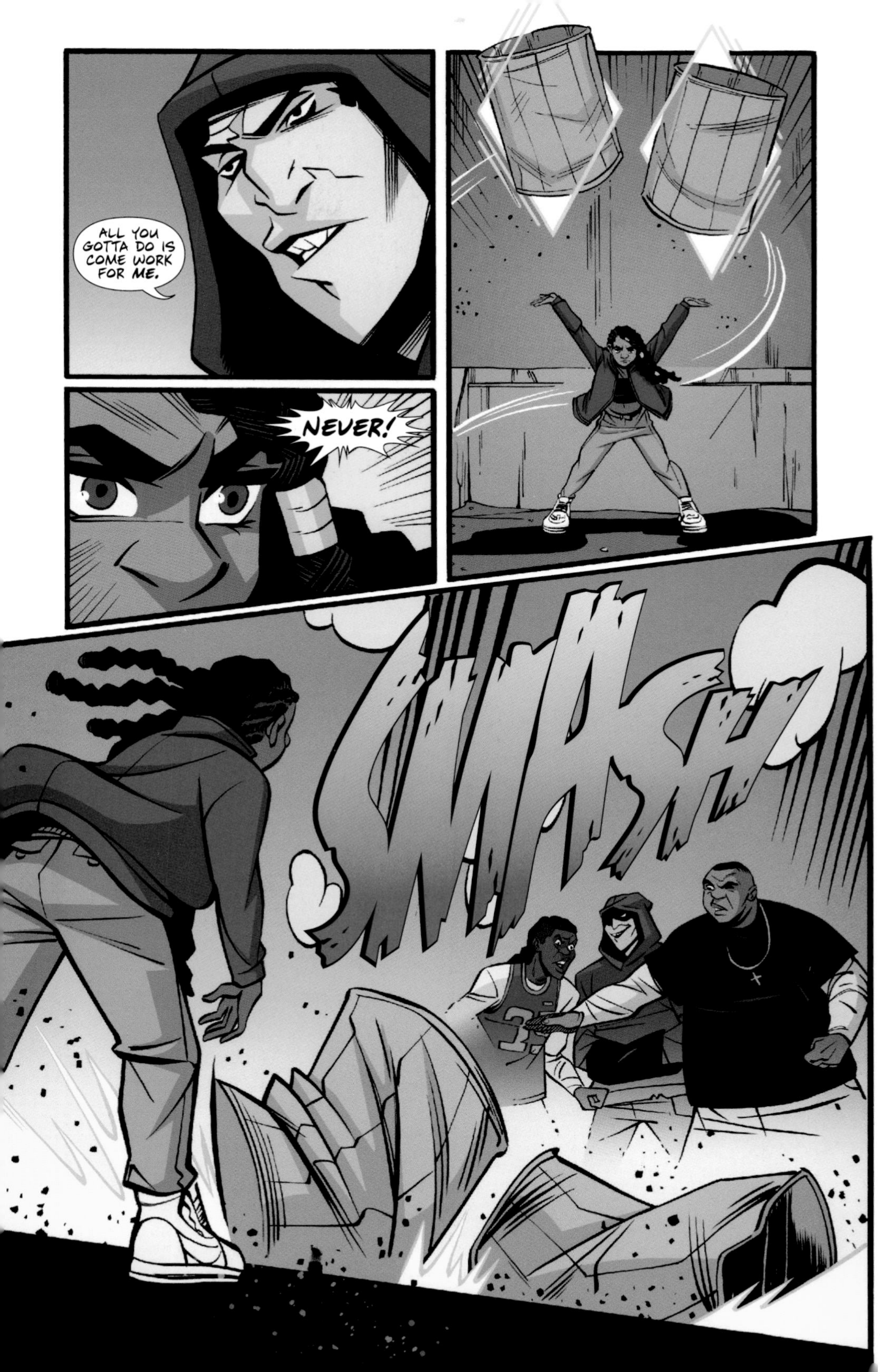
ALL YOU GOTTA DO IS COME WORK FOR ME.
NEVER!

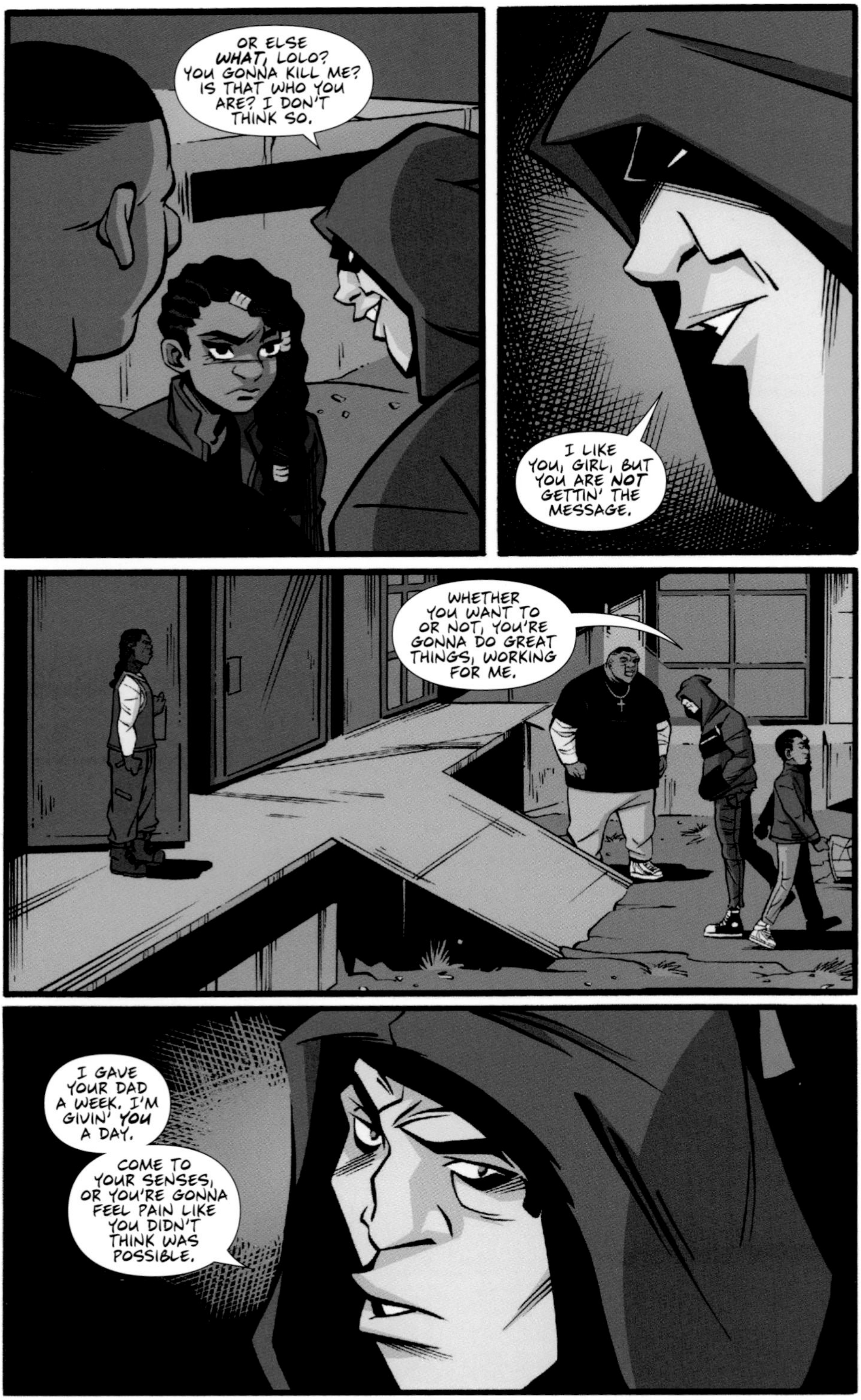
OR ELSE WHAT, LOLO? YOU GONNA KILL ME? IS THAT WHO YOU ARE? I DON'T THINK SO.
I LIKE YOU, GIRL, BUT YOU ARE NOT GETTIN' THE MESSAGE.
WHETHER YOU WANT TO OR NOT, YOU'RE GONNA DO GREAT THINGS, WORKING FOR ME.
I GAVE YOUR DAD A WEEK. I'M GIVIN' YOU A DAY.
COME TO YOUR SENSES, OR YOU'RE GONNA FEEL PAIN LIKE YOU DIDN'T THINK WAS POSSIBLE.

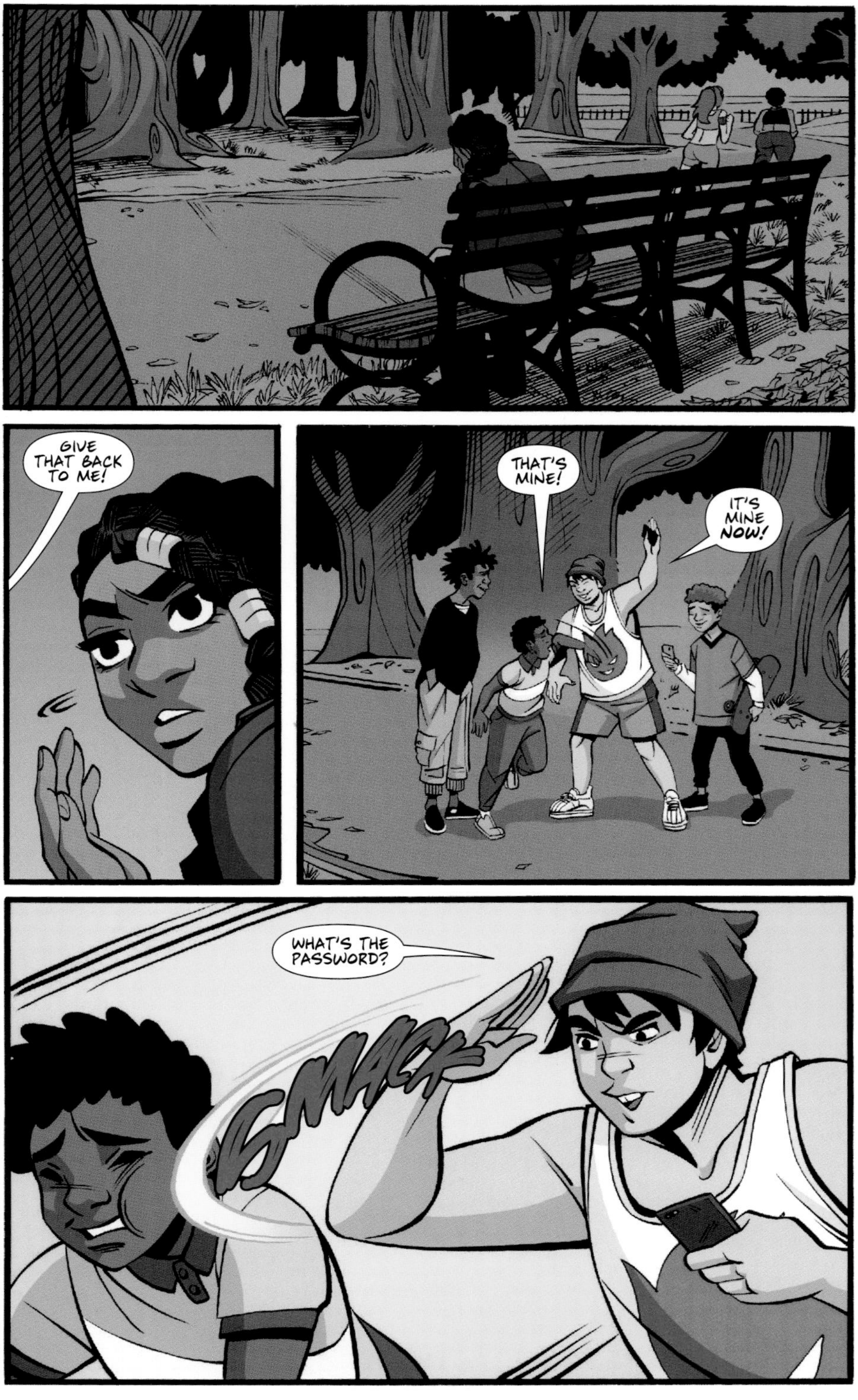
GIVE THAT BACK TO ME!
THAT'S MINE!
IT'S MINE NOW!
WHAT'S THE PASSWORD?
SMACK

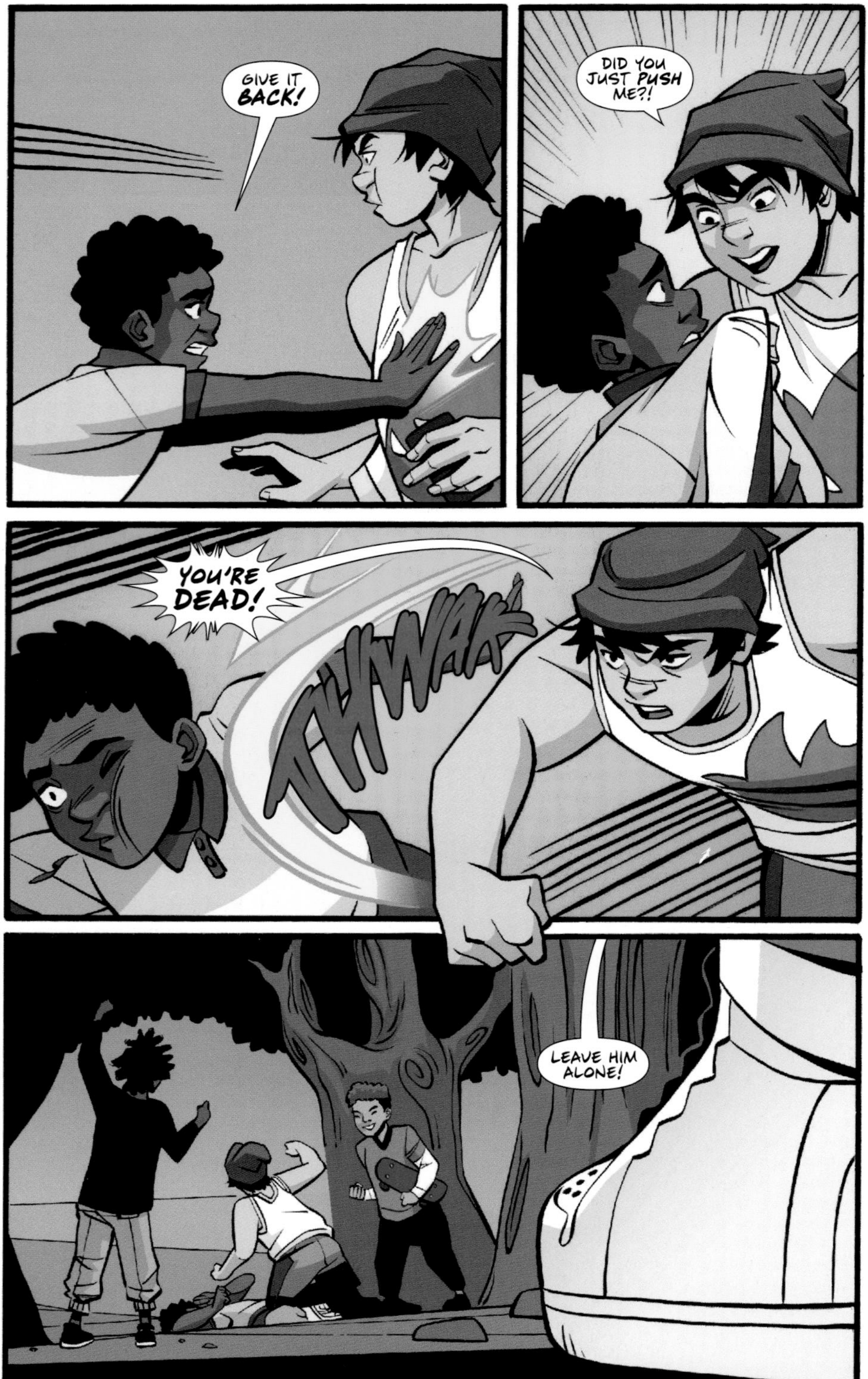
GIVE IT BACK!
DID YOU JUST PUSH ME?!
YOU'RE DEAD!
THWAK
LEAVE HIM ALONE!

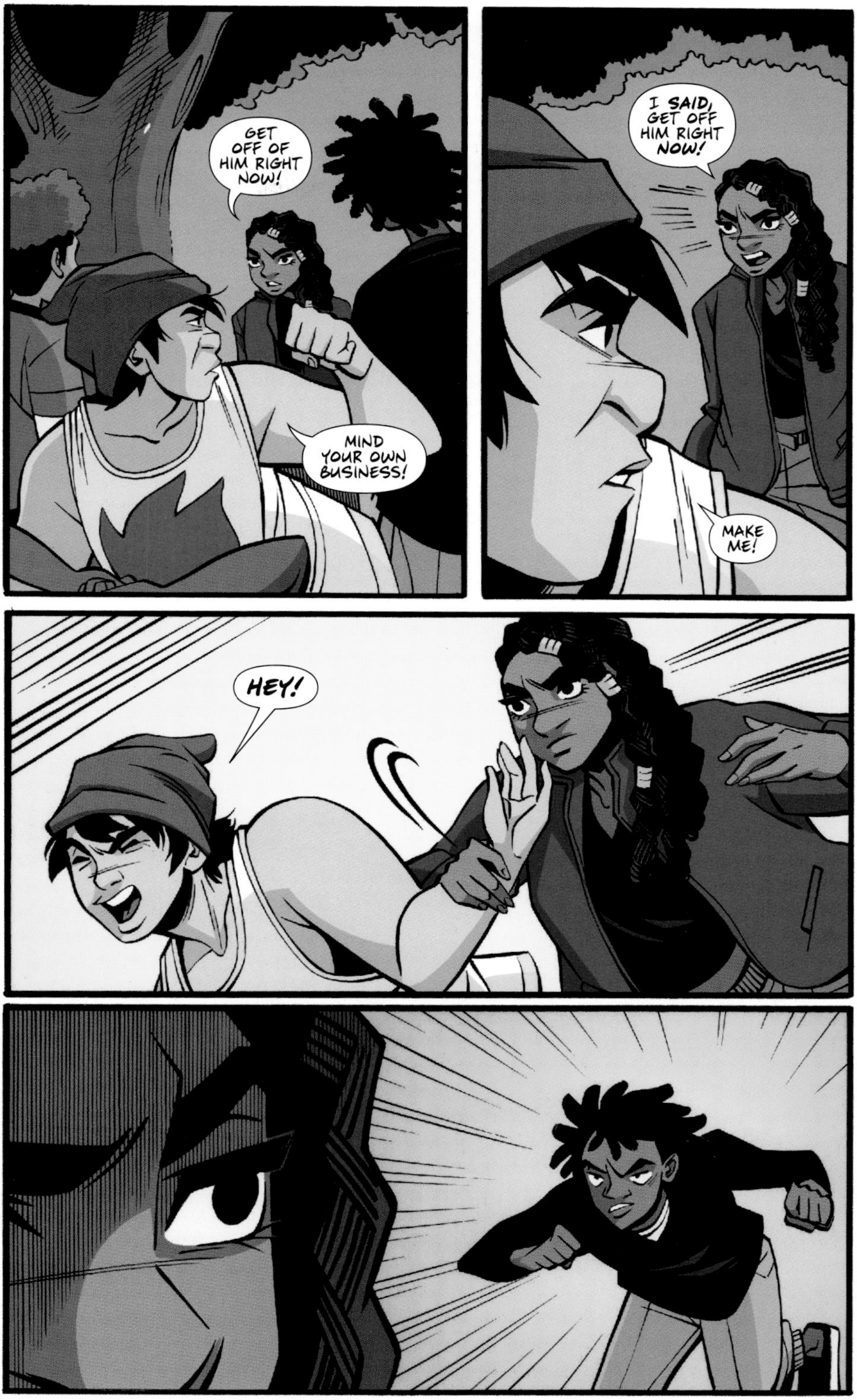
GET OFF OF HIM RIGHT NOW!
MIND YOUR OWN BUSINESS!
I SAID, GET OFF HIM RIGHT NOW!
MAKE ME!
HEY!

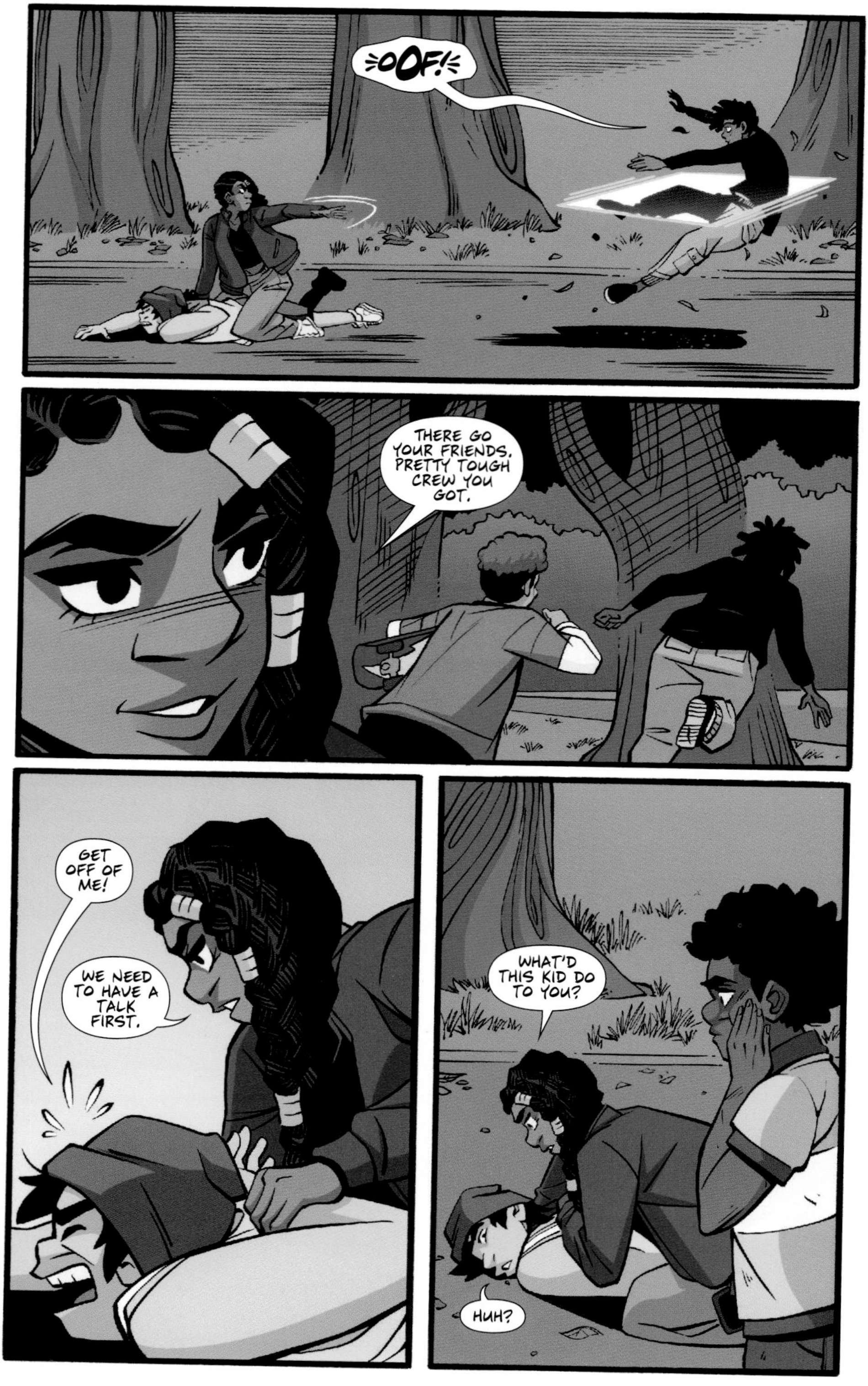
OOF!
THERE GO YOUR FRIENDS. PRETTY TOUGH CREW YOU GOT.
GET OFF OF ME!
WE NEED TO HAVE A TALK FIRST.
WHAT'D THIS KID DO TO YOU?
HUH?

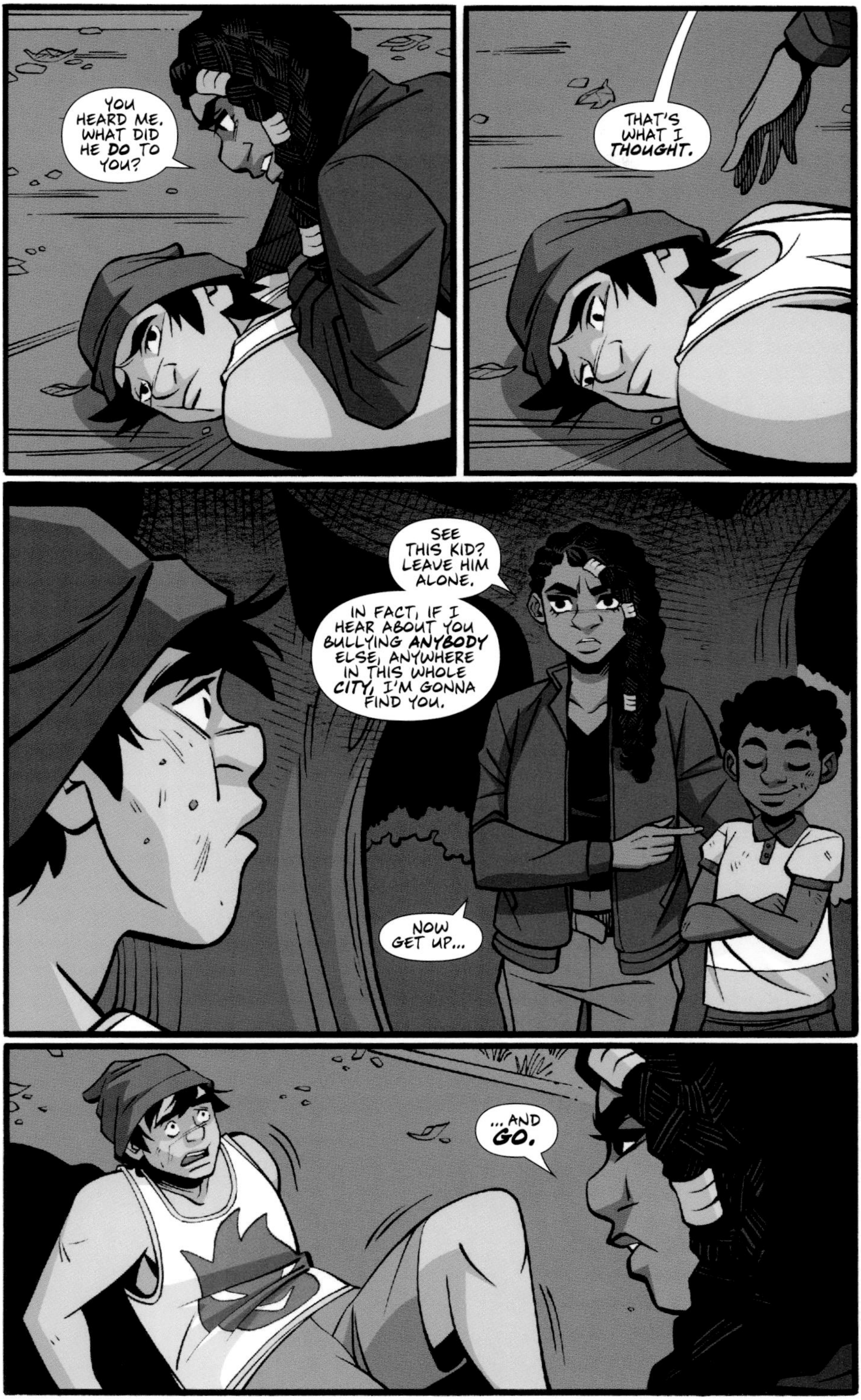
YOU HEARD ME. WHAT DID HE DO TO YOU?
THAT'S WHAT I THOUGHT.
SEE THIS KID? LEAVE HIM ALONE.
IN FACT, IF I HEAR ABOUT YOU BULLYING ANYBODY ELSE, ANYWHERE IN THIS WHOLE CITY, I'M GONNA FIND YOU.
NOW GET UP...
...AND GO.

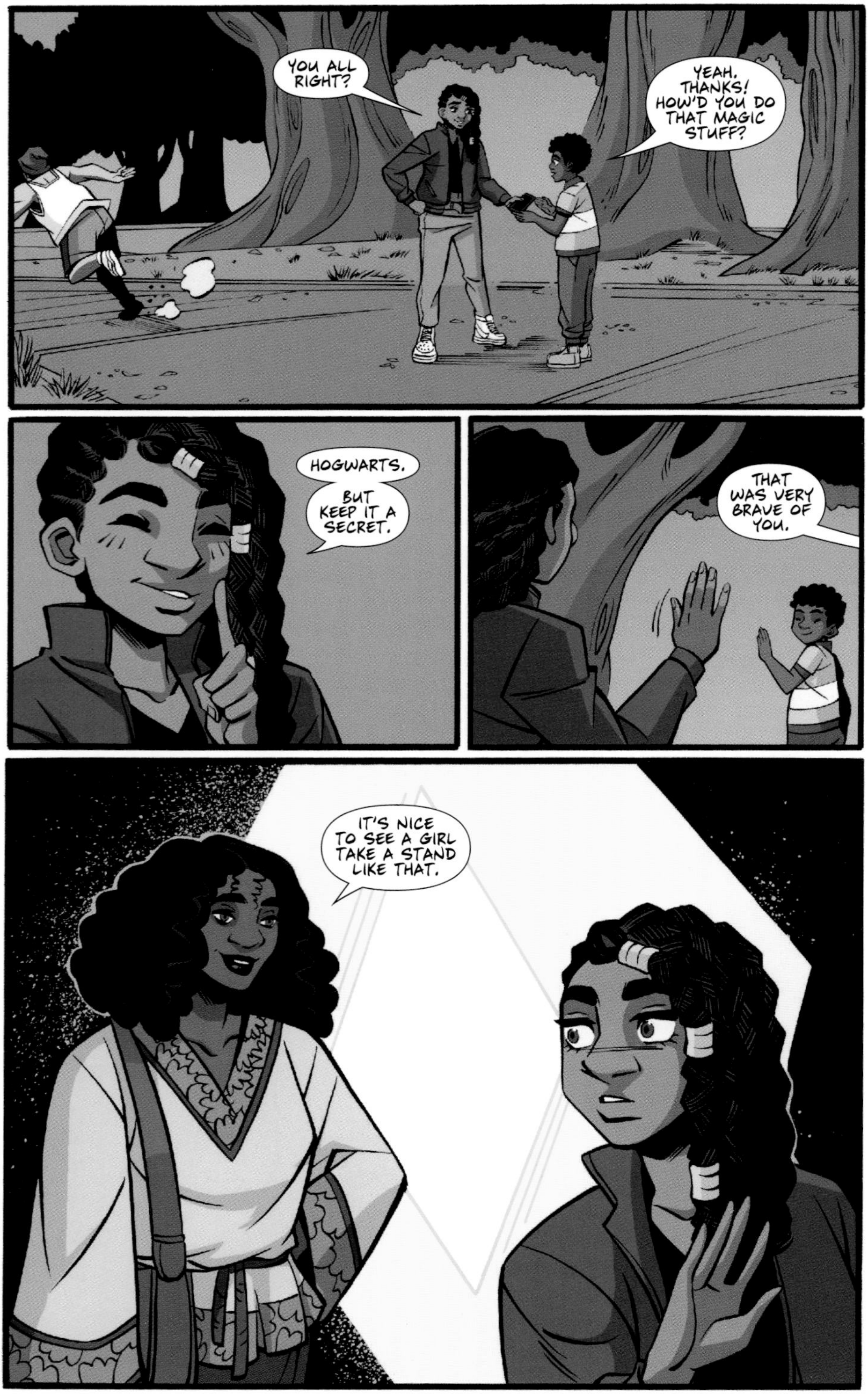
YOU ALL RIGHT?
YEAH, THANKS! HOW'D YOU DO THAT MAGIC STUFF?
HOGWARTS.
BUT KEEP IT A SECRET.
THAT WAS VERY BRAVE OF YOU.
IT'S NICE TO SEE A GIRL TAKE A STAND LIKE THAT.

CHAPTER 8

FALLIN'

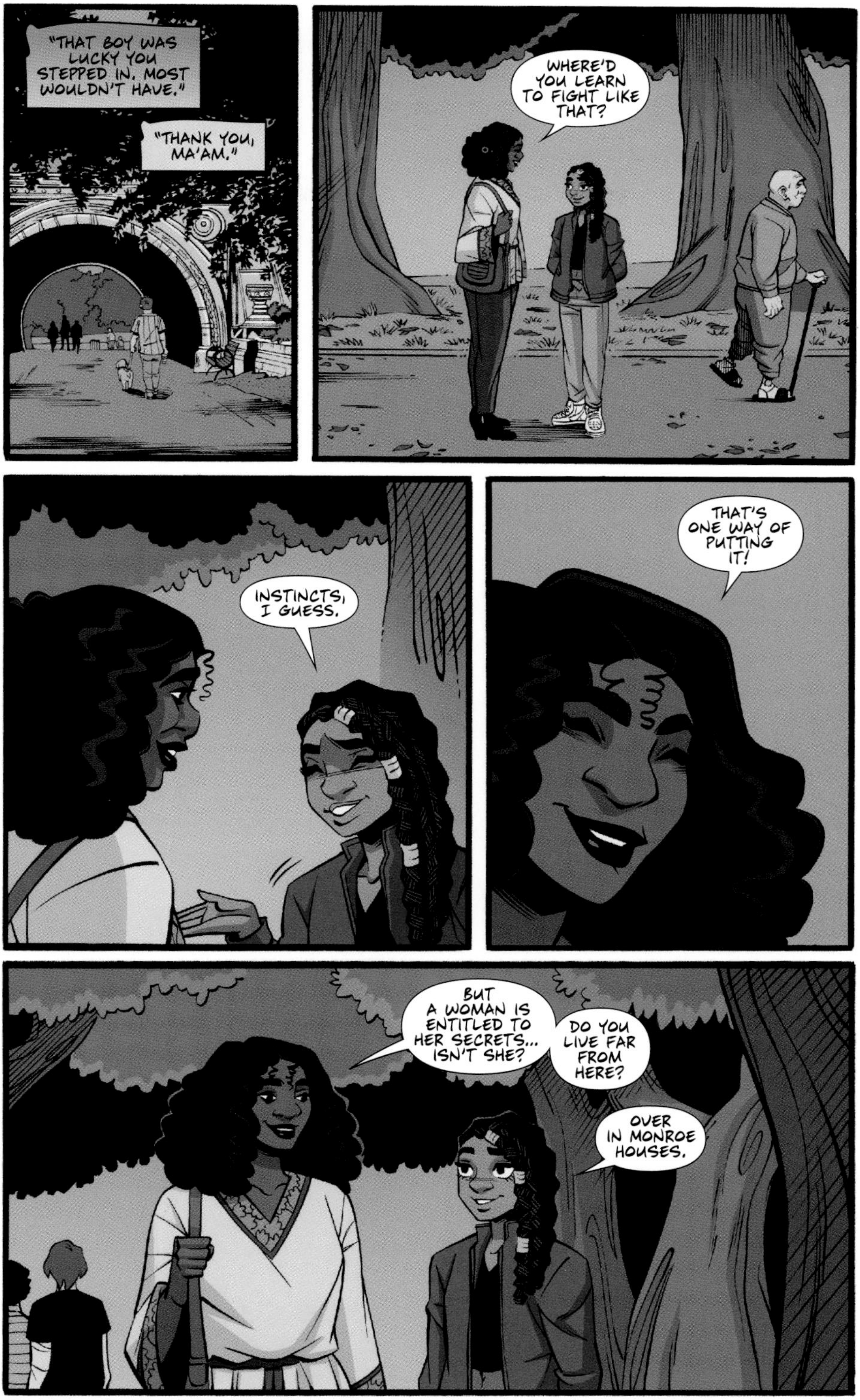
"THAT BOY WAS LUCKY YOU STEPPED IN. MOST WOULDN'T HAVE."
"THANK YOU, MA'AM."
WHERE'D YOU LEARN TO FIGHT LIKE THAT?
INSTINCTS, I GUESS.
THAT'S ONE WAY OF PUTTING IT!
BUT A WOMAN IS ENTITLED TO HER SECRETS... ISN'T SHE?
DO YOU LIVE FAR FROM HERE?
OVER IN MONROE HOUSES.

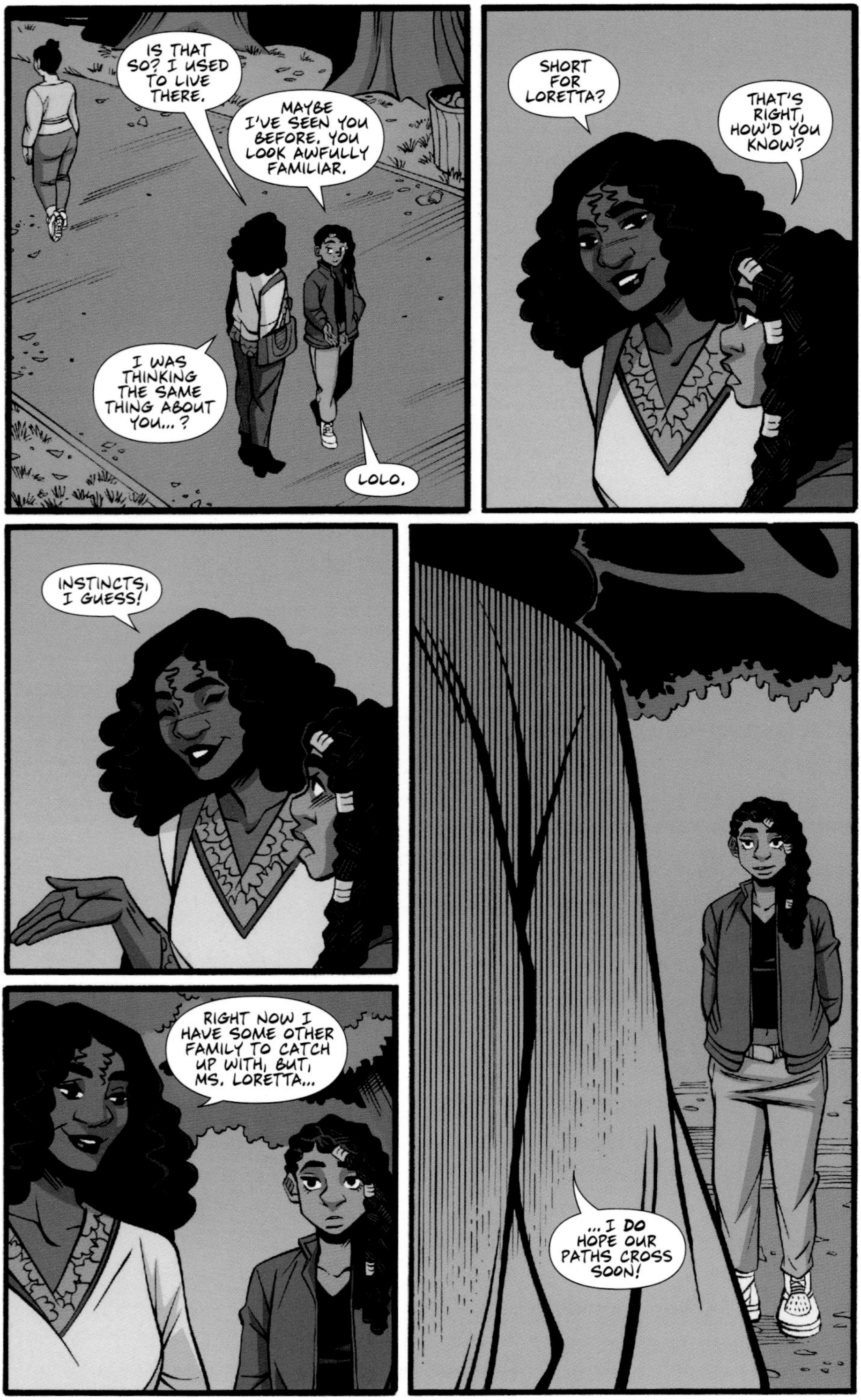
IS THAT SO? I USED TO LIVE THERE.
MAYBE I'VE SEEN YOU BEFORE. YOU LOOK AWFULLY FAMILIAR.
I WAS THINKING THE SAME THING ABOUT YOU...?
LOLO.
SHORT FOR LORETTA?
THAT'S RIGHT, HOW'D YOU KNOW?
INSTINCTS, I GUESS!
RIGHT NOW I HAVE SOME OTHER FAMILY TO CATCH UP WITH, BUT, MS. LORETTA...
...I DO HOPE OUR PATHS CROSS SOON!

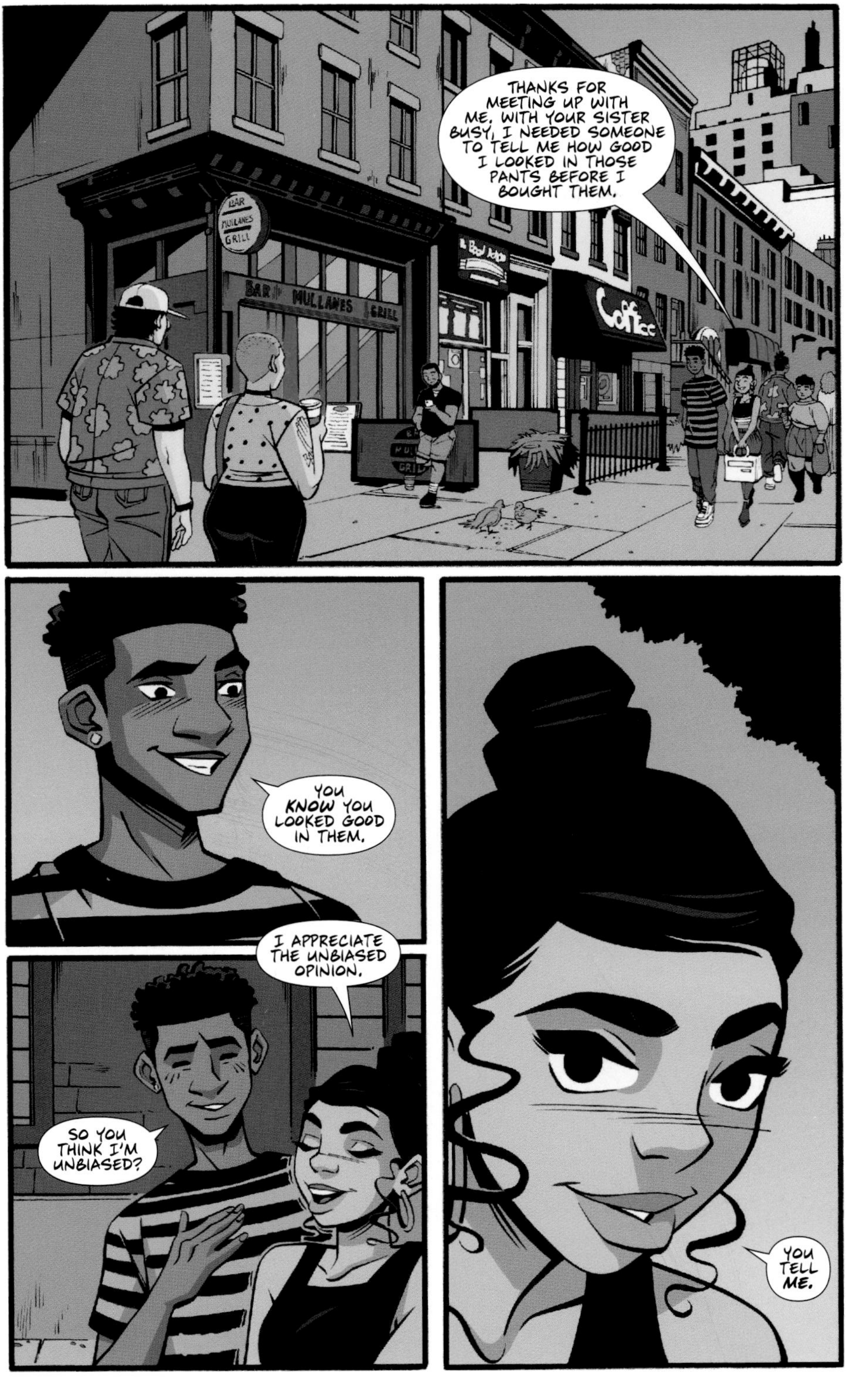

THANKS FOR MEETING UP WITH ME. WITH YOUR SISTER BUSY, I NEEDED SOMEONE TO TELL ME HOW GOOD I LOOKED IN THOSE PANTS BEFORE I BOUGHT THEM.
BAR MULLANES GRILL
BAR MULLANES GRILL
Coffee
YOU KNOW YOU LOOKED GOOD IN THEM.
I APPRECIATE THE UNBIASED OPINION.
SO YOU THINK I'M UNBIASED?
YOU TELL ME.

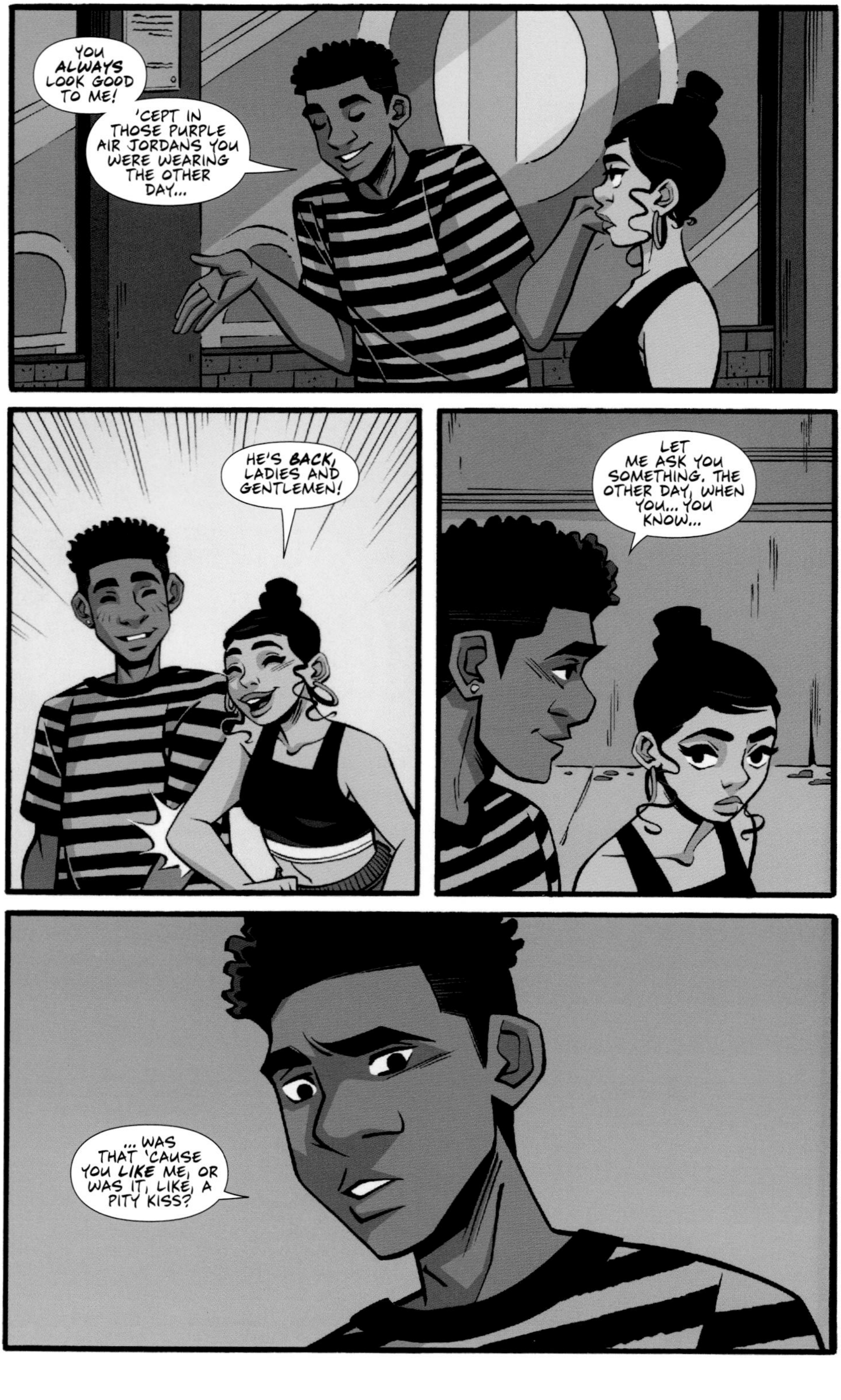
YOU ALWAYS LOOK GOOD TO ME!
'CEPT IN THOSE PURPLE AIR JORDANS YOU WERE WEARING THE OTHER DAY...
HE'S BACK, LADIES AND GENTLEMEN!
LET ME ASK YOU SOMETHING. THE OTHER DAY, WHEN YOU... YOU KNOW...
... WAS THAT 'CAUSE YOU LIKE ME, OR WAS IT, LIKE, A PITY KISS?

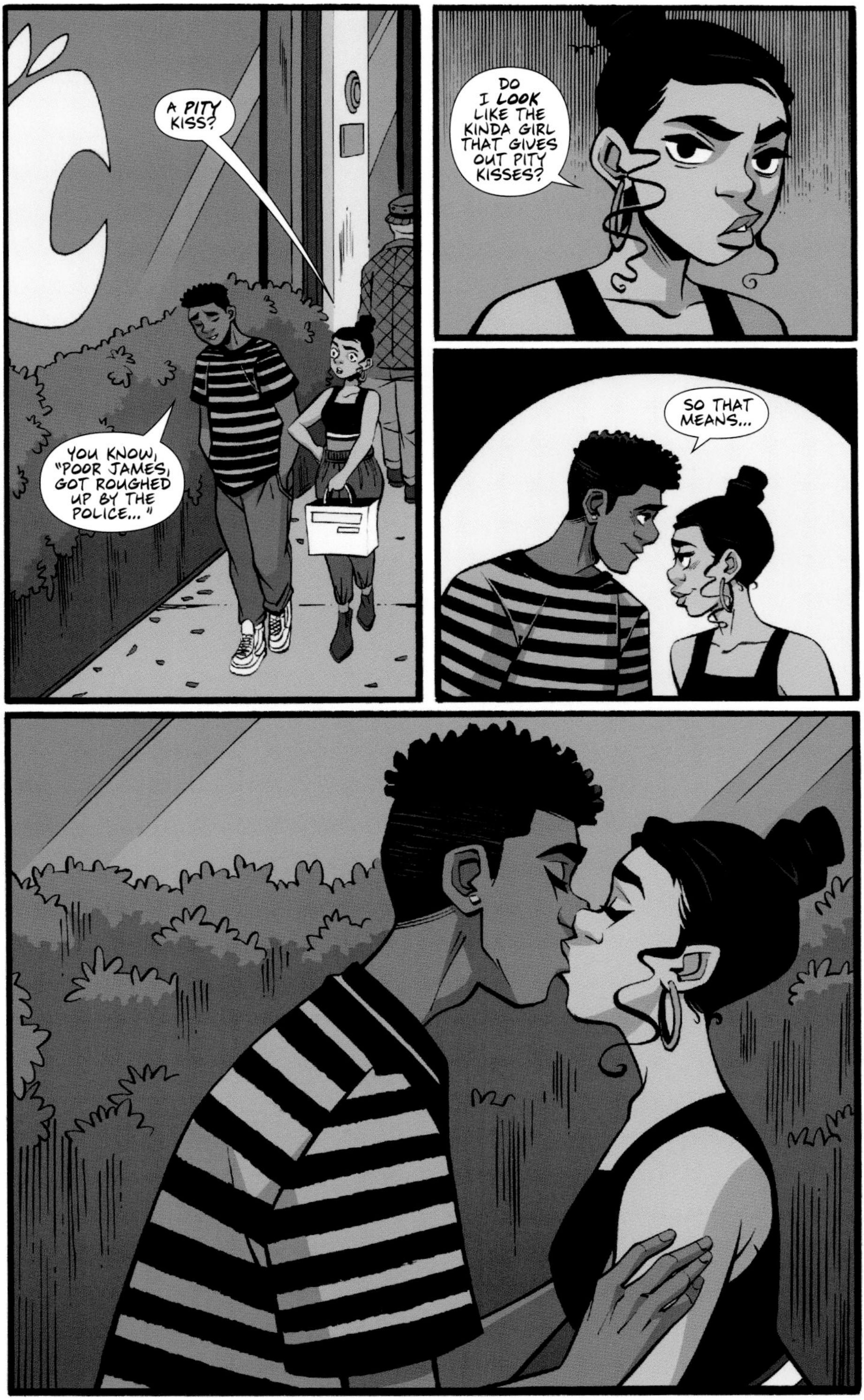
A PITY KISS?
YOU KNOW, "POOR JAMES, GOT ROUGHED UP BY THE POLICE..."
DO I LOOK LIKE THE KINDA GIRL THAT GIVES OUT PITY KISSES?
SO THAT MEANS...

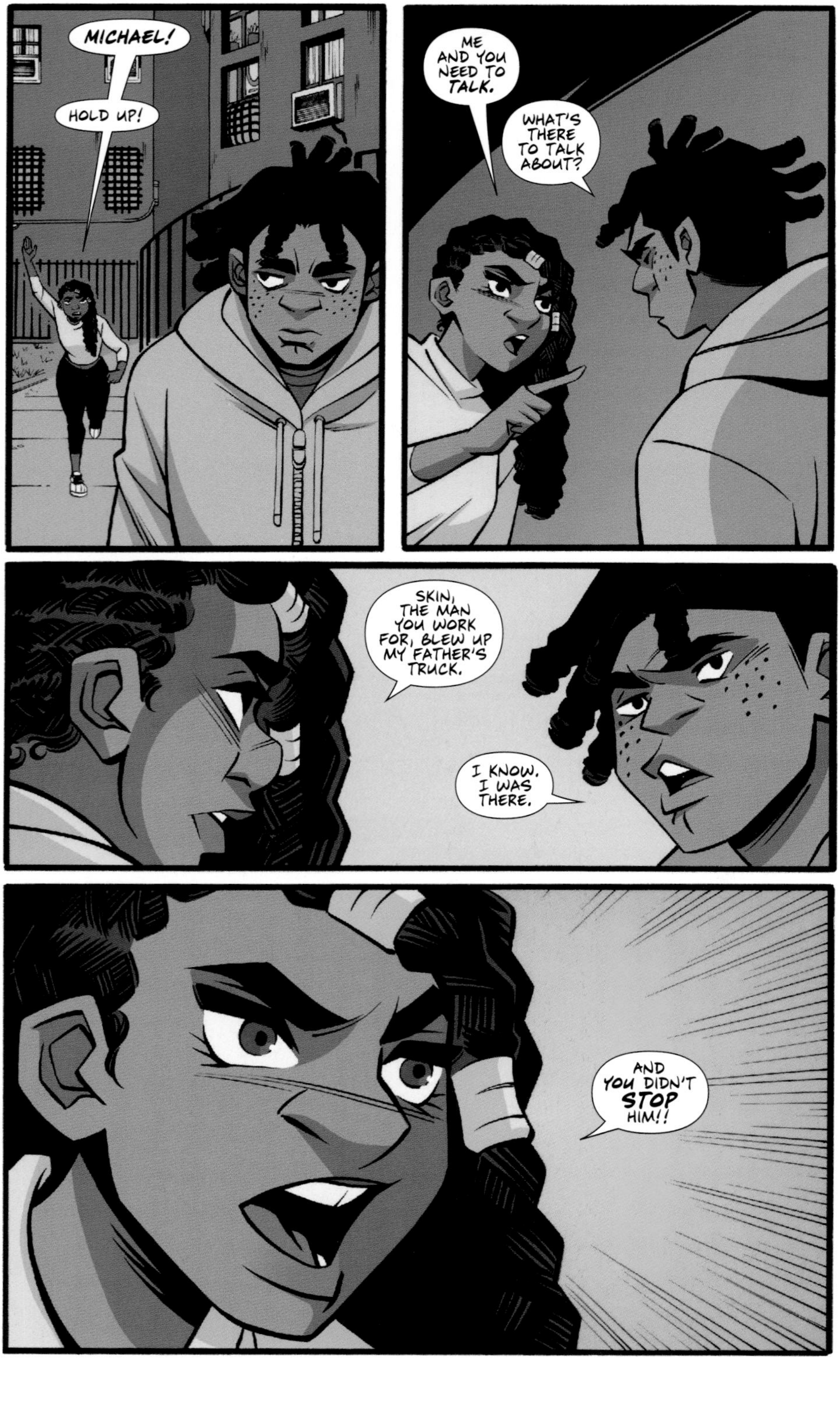
MICHAEL!
HOLD UP!
ME AND YOU NEED TO TALK.
WHAT'S THERE TO TALK ABOUT?
SKIN, THE MAN YOU WORK FOR, BLEW UP MY FATHER'S TRUCK.
I KNOW. I WAS THERE.
AND YOU DIDN'T STOP HIM!!

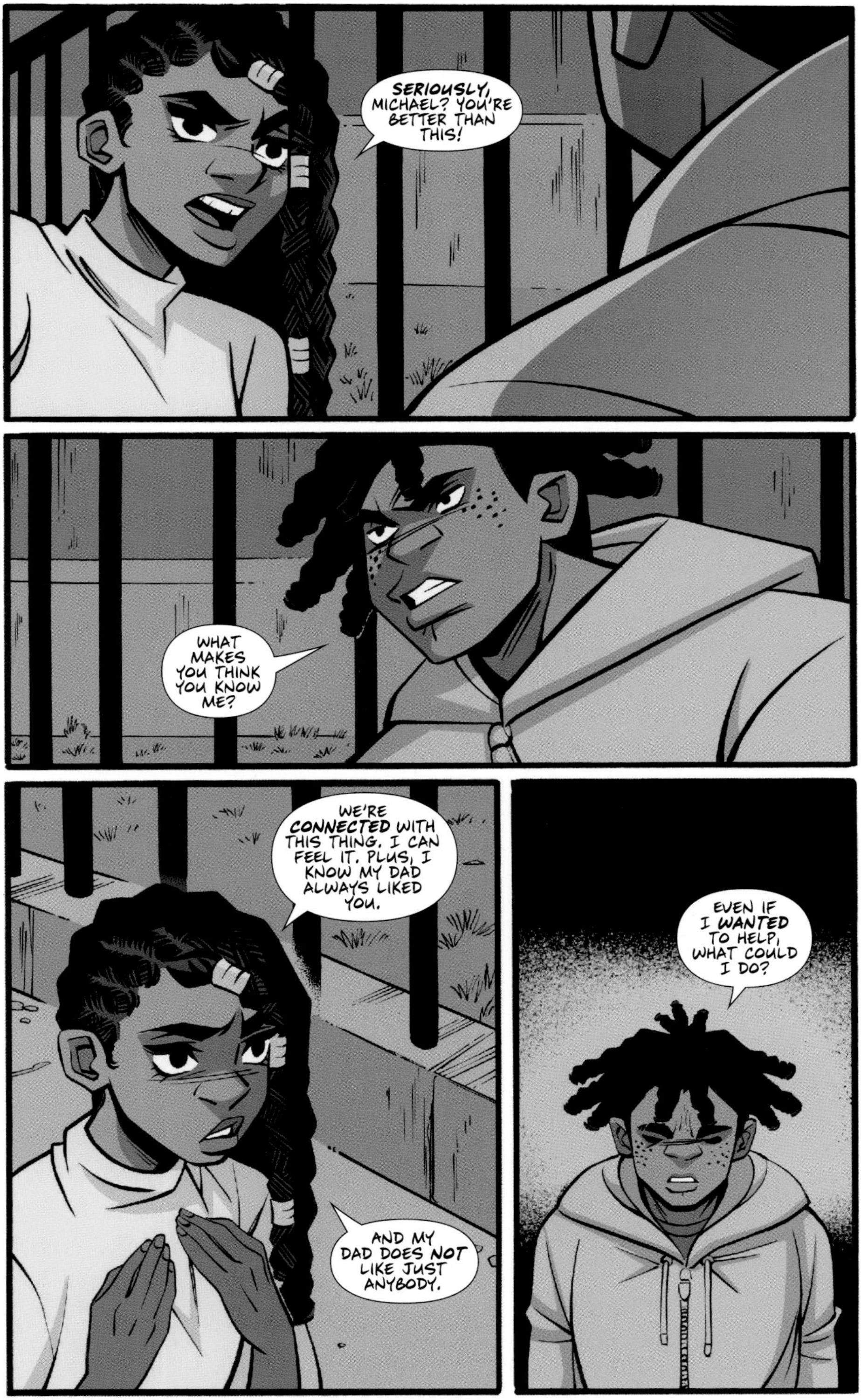
SERIOUSLY, MICHAEL? YOU'RE BETTER THAN THIS!
WHAT MAKES YOU THINK YOU KNOW ME?
WE'RE CONNECTED WITH THIS THING. I CAN FEEL IT. PLUS, I KNOW MY DAD ALWAYS LIKED YOU.
AND MY DAD DOES NOT LIKE JUST ANYBODY.
EVEN IF I WANTED TO HELP, WHAT COULD I DO?

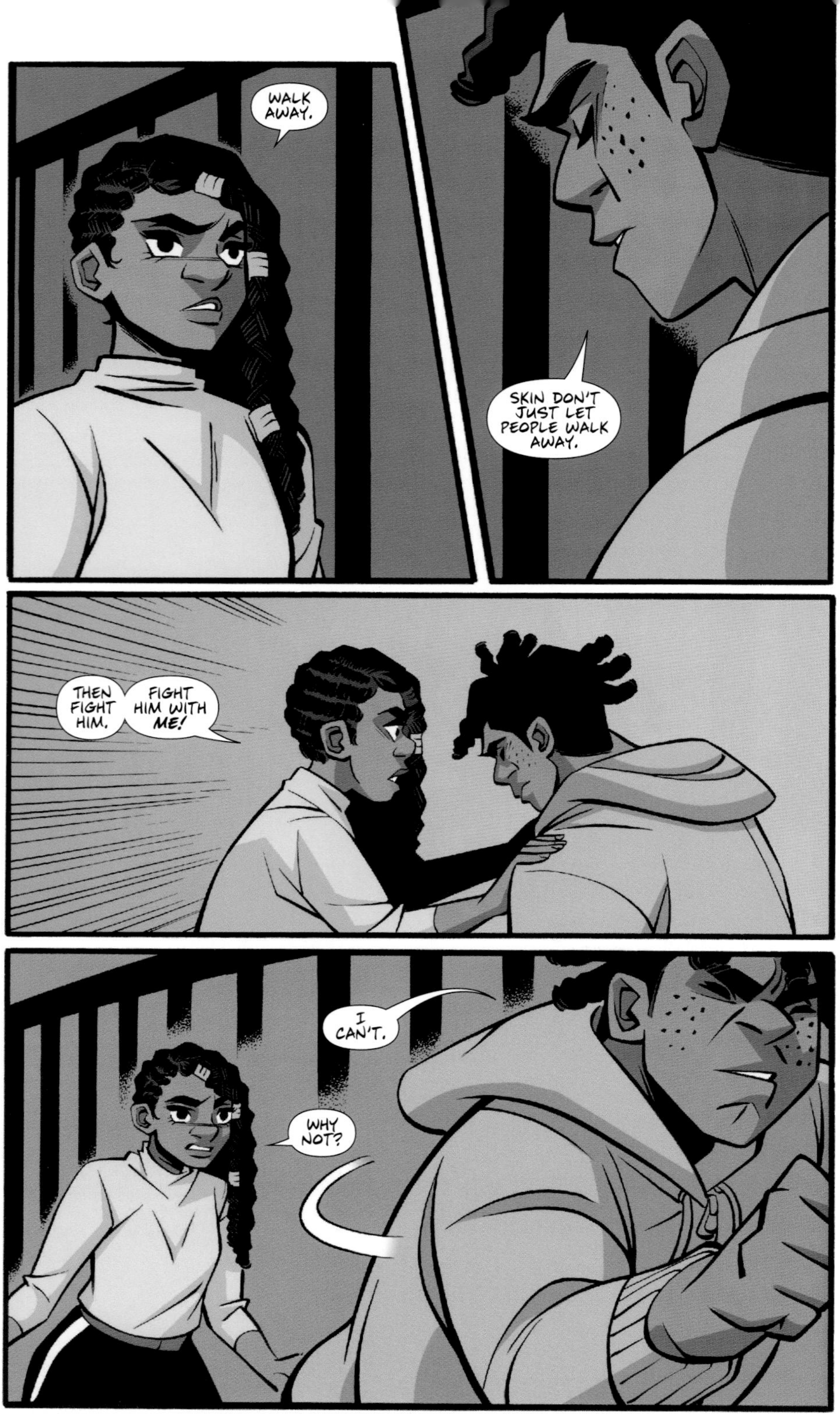
WALK AWAY.
SKIN DON'T JUST LET PEOPLE WALK AWAY.
THEN FIGHT HIM.
FIGHT HIM WITH ME!
I CAN'T.
WHY NOT?

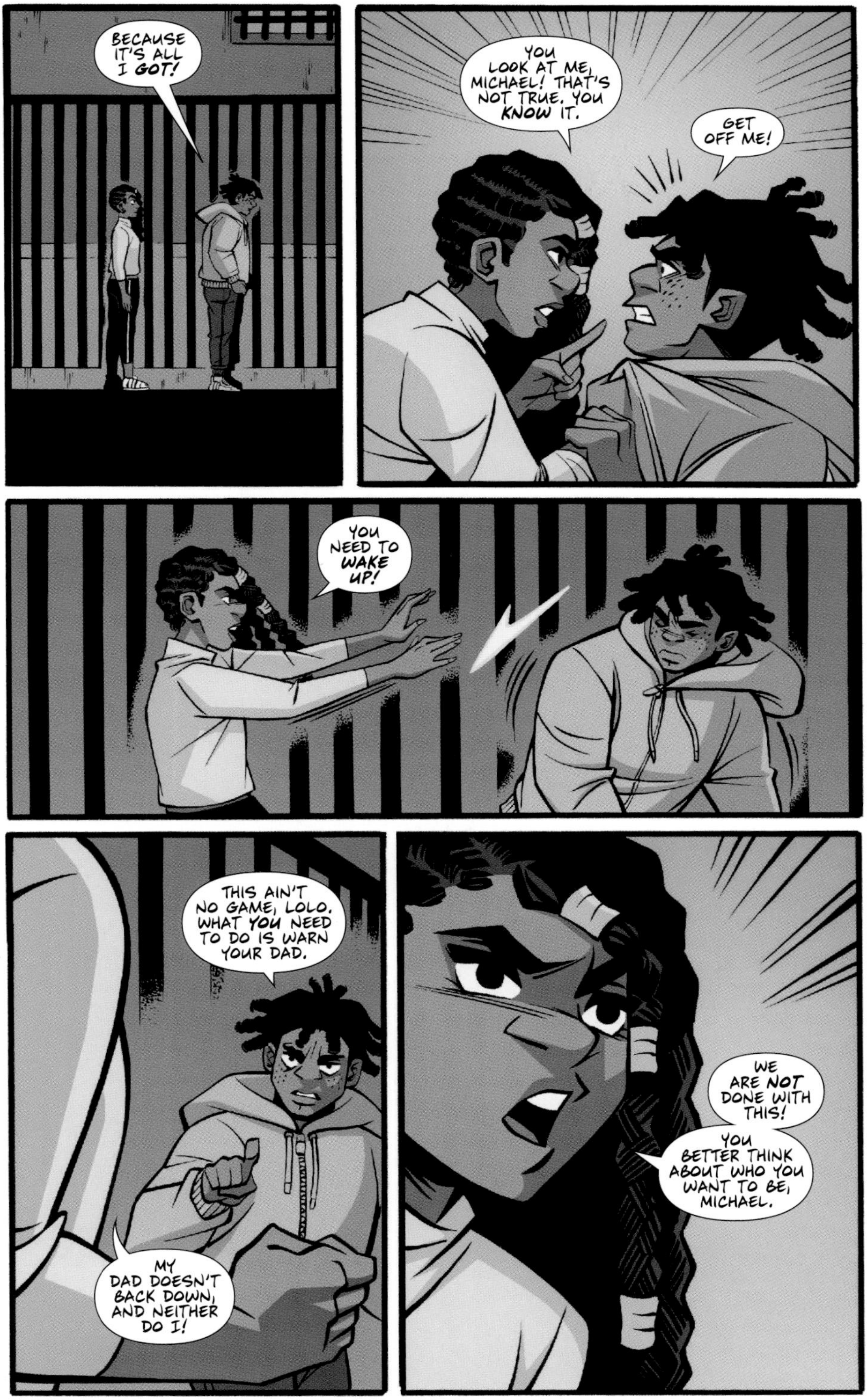
BECAUSE IT'S ALL I GOT!
YOU LOOK AT ME, MICHAEL! THAT'S NOT TRUE. YOU KNOW IT.
GET OFF ME!
YOU NEED TO WAKE UP!
THIS AIN'T NO GAME, LOLO. WHAT YOU NEED TO DO IS WARN YOUR DAD.
MY DAD DOESN'T BACK DOWN, AND NEITHER DO I!
WE ARE NOT DONE WITH THIS!
YOU BETTER THINK ABOUT WHO YOU WANT TO BE, MICHAEL.

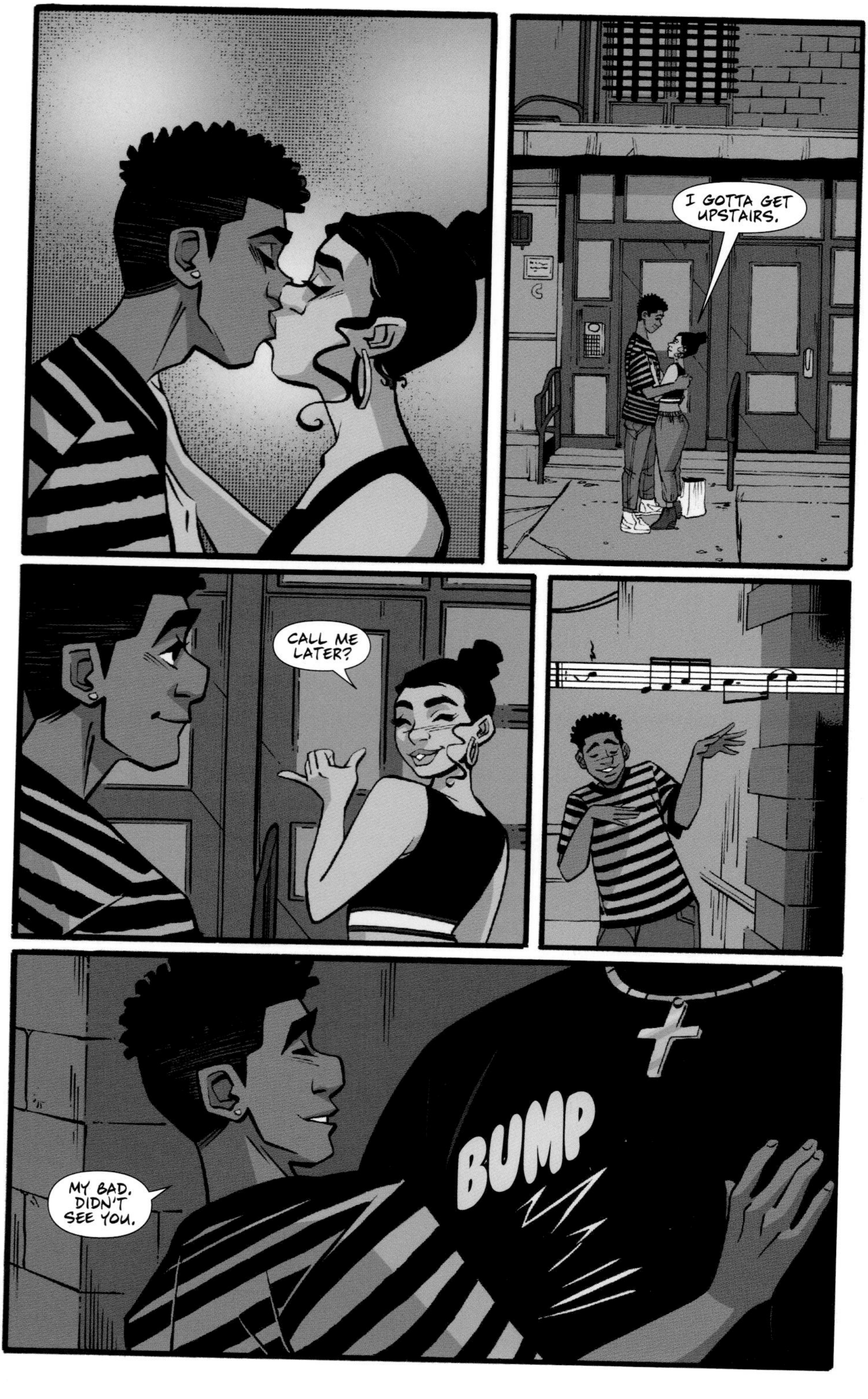
I GOTTA GET UPSTAIRS.
CALL ME LATER?
BUMP
MY BAD. DIDN'T SEE YOU.

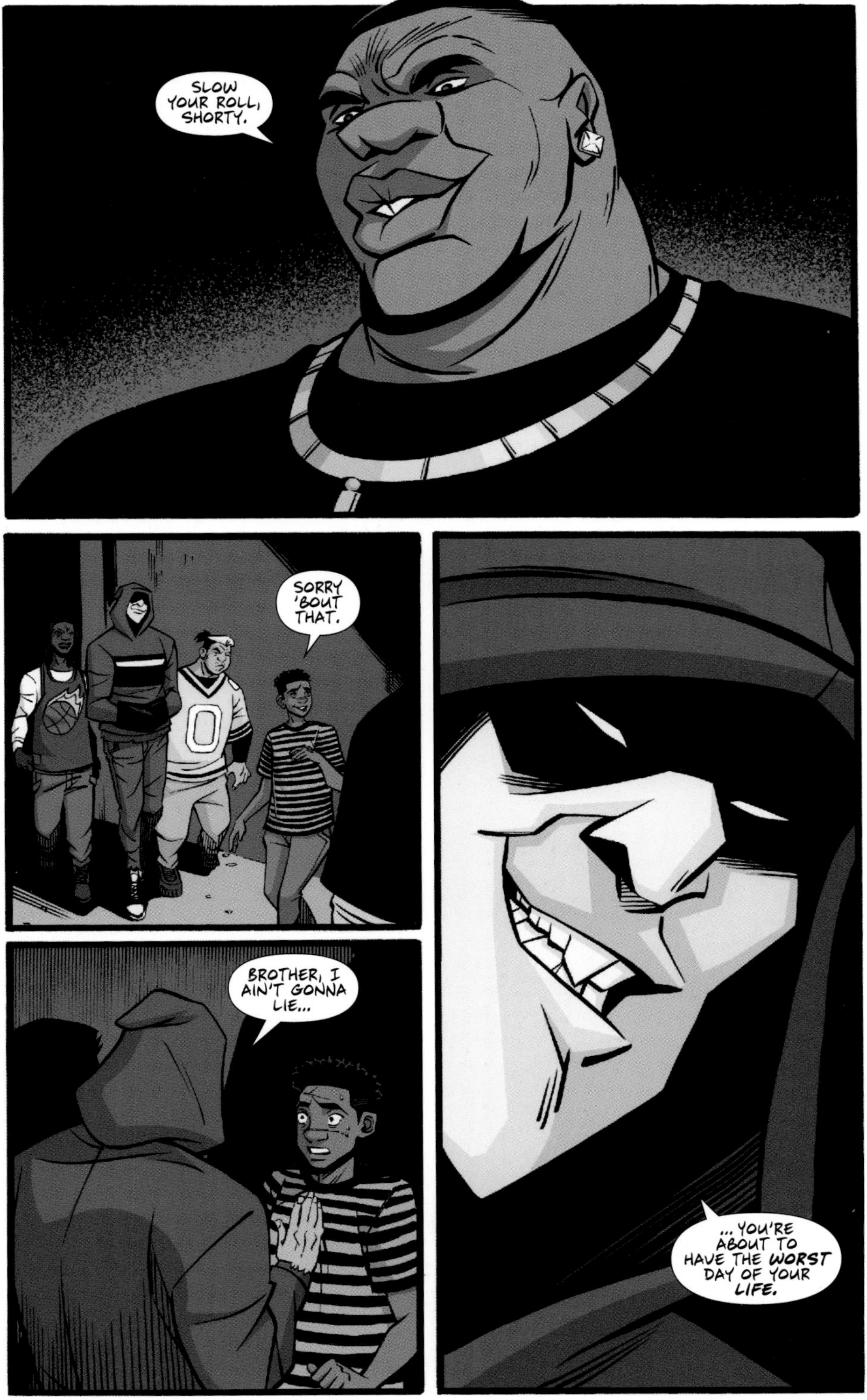
SLOW YOUR ROLL, SHORTY.
SORRY 'BOUT THAT.
BROTHER, I AIN'T GONNA LIE...
...YOU'RE ABOUT TO HAVE THE WORST DAY OF YOUR LIFE.

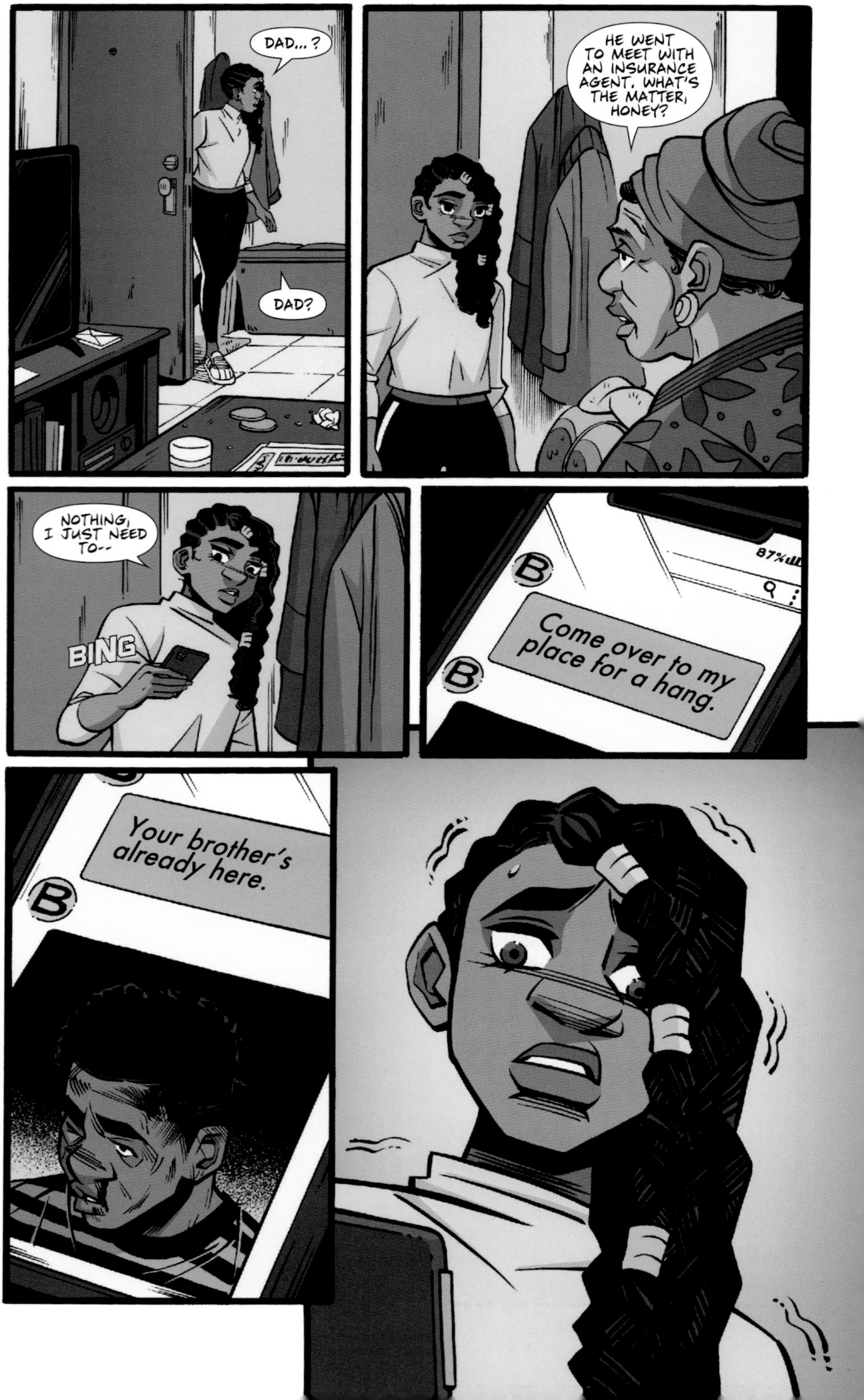
DAD...?
DAD?
HE WENT TO MEET WITH AN INSURANCE AGENT. WHAT'S THE MATTER, HONEY?
NOTHING, I JUST NEED TO--
BING
87%
Come over to my place for a hang.
Your brother's already here.

CHAPTER 9

GIRL ON FIRE

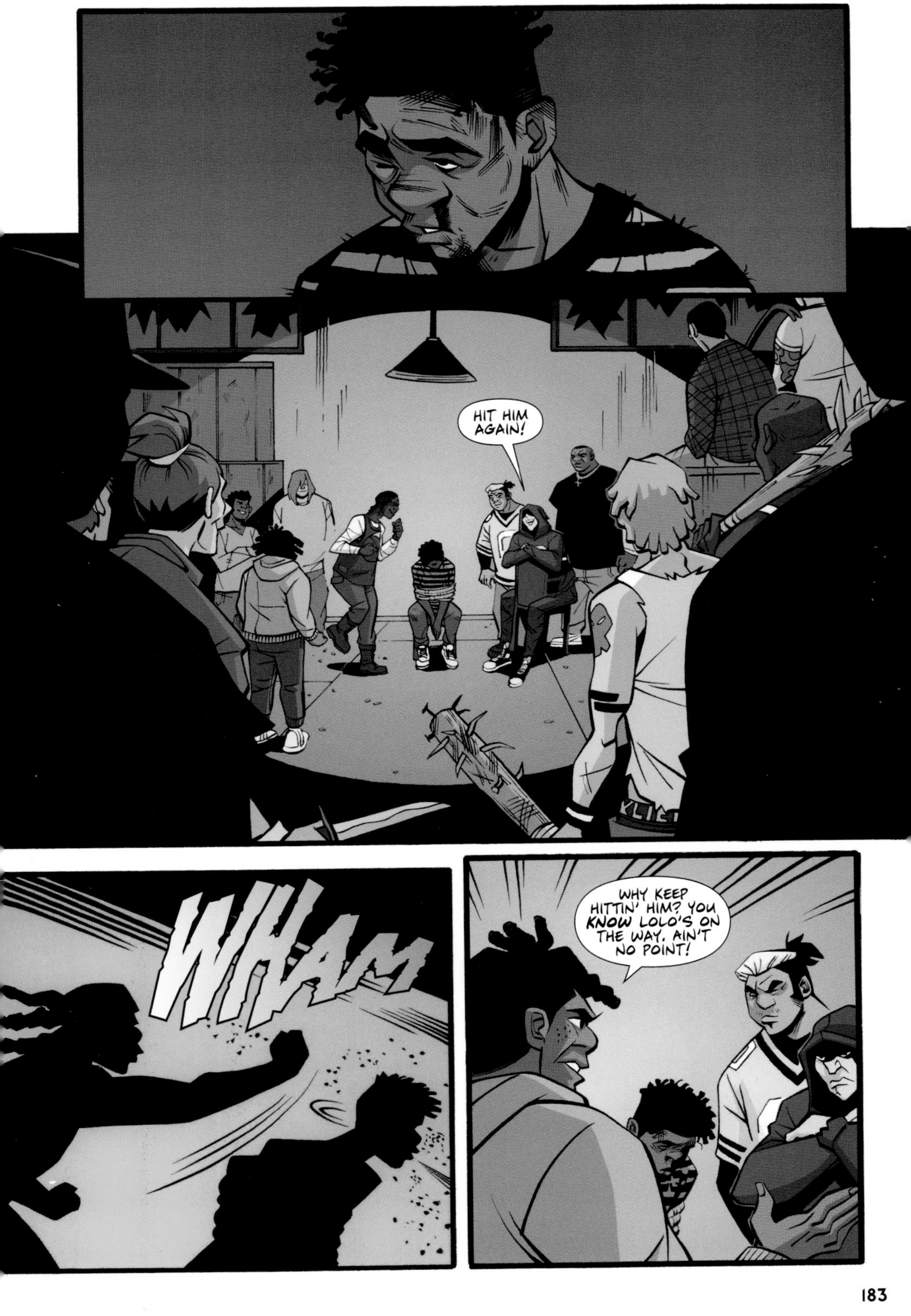
HIT HIM AGAIN!
WHAM
WHY KEEP HITTIN' HIM? YOU KNOW LOLO'S ON THE WAY. AIN'T NO POINT!

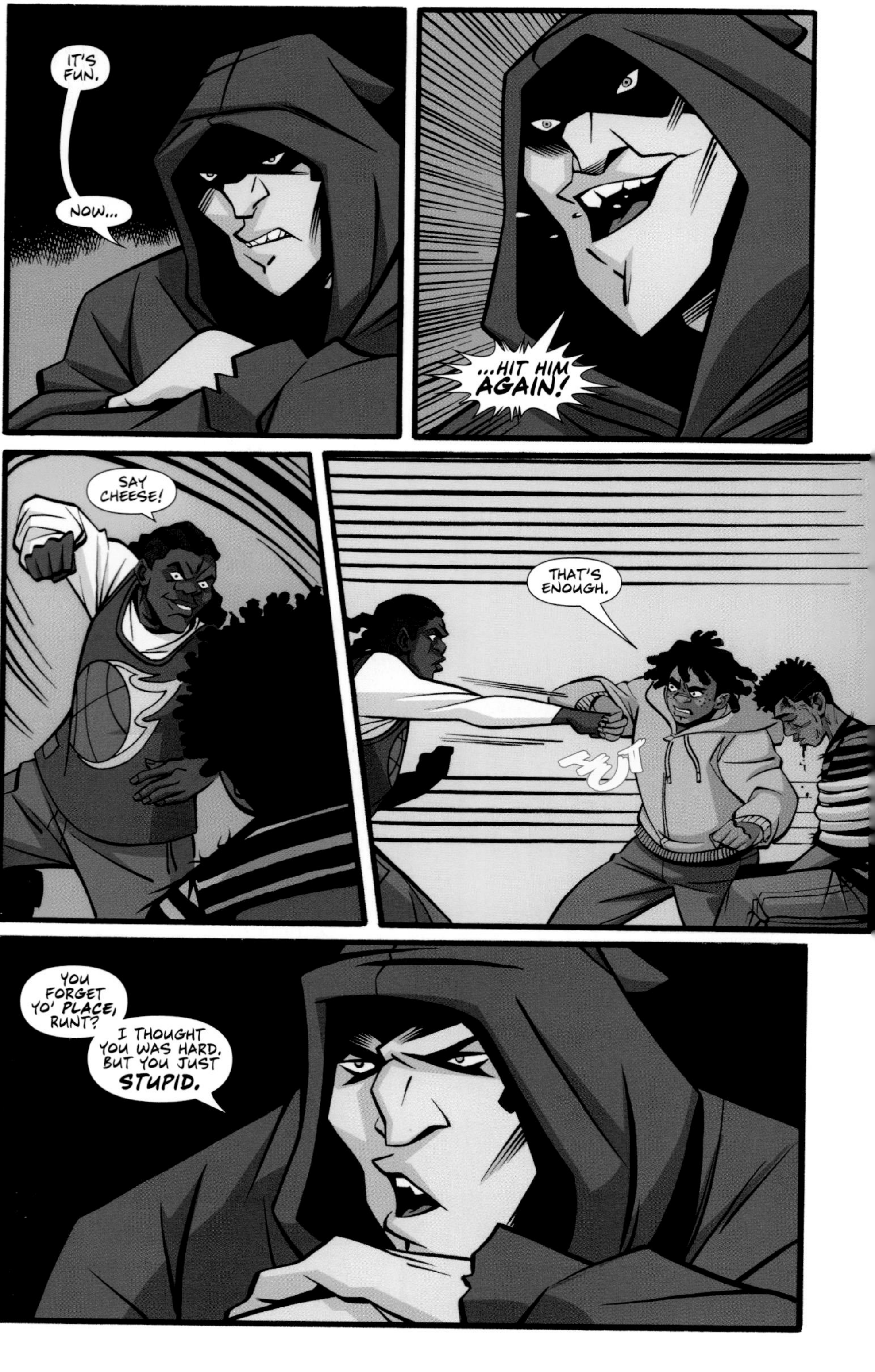
IT'S FUN.
NOW...
...HIT HIM AGAIN!
SAY CHEESE!
THAT'S ENOUGH.
YOU FORGET YO' PLACE, RUNT?
I THOUGHT YOU WAS HARD. BUT YOU JUST STUPID.

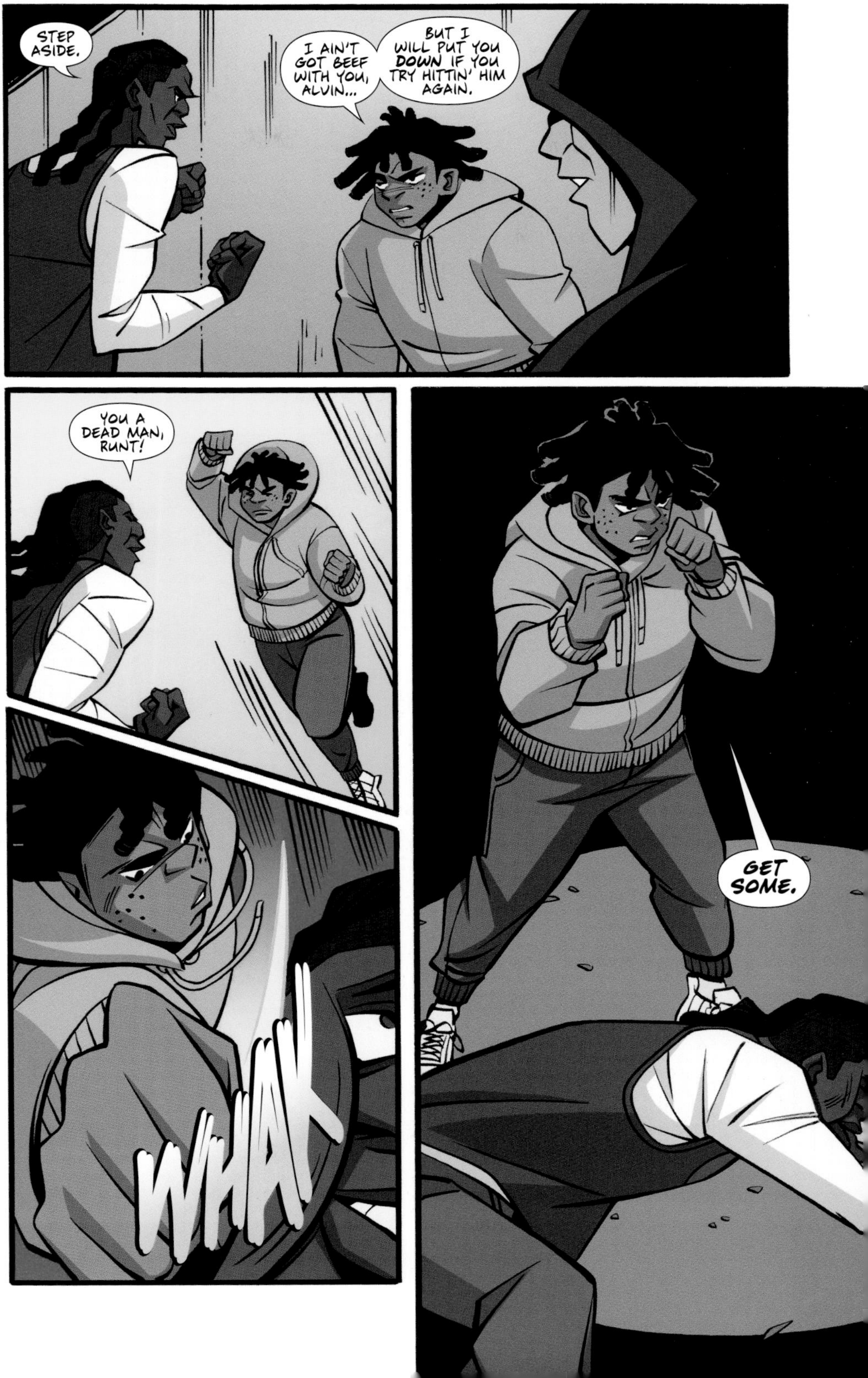
STEP ASIDE.
I AIN'T GOT BEEF WITH YOU, ALVIN...
BUT I WILL PUT YOU DOWN IF YOU TRY HITTIN' HIM AGAIN.
YOU A DEAD MAN, RUNT!
WHAK
GET SOME.

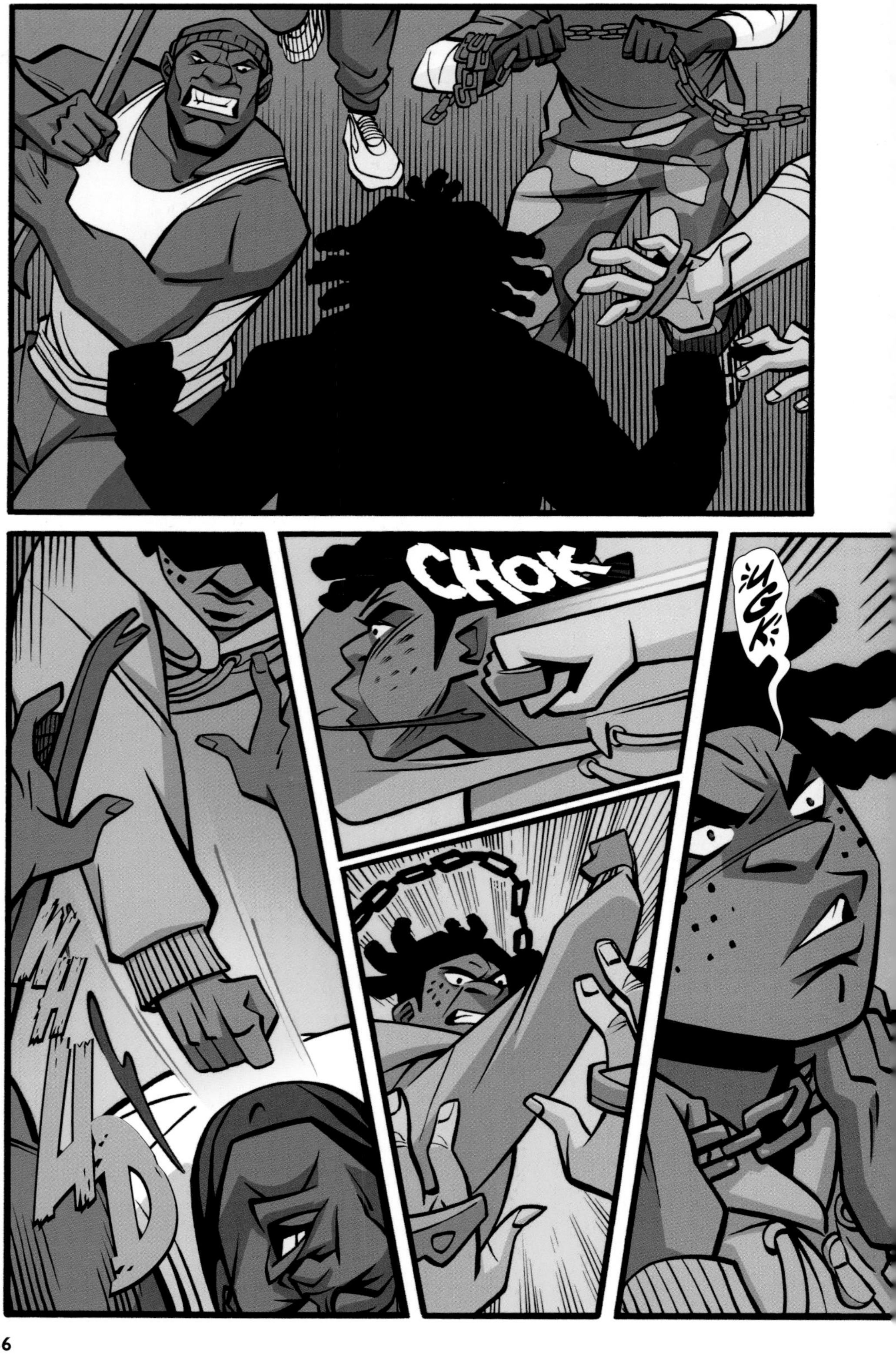
WHUD
CHOK
UGK

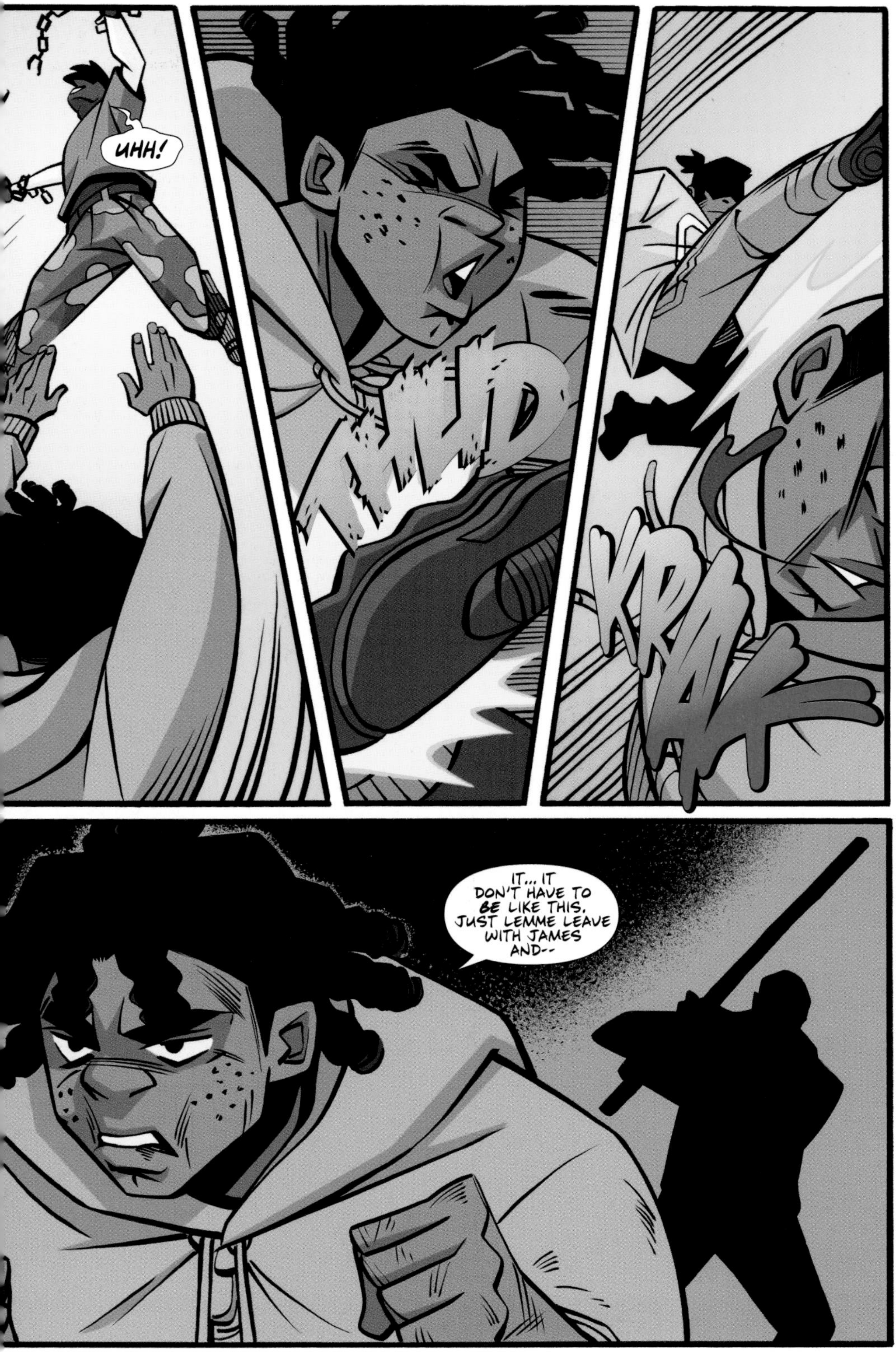
UHH!
THUD
KRAK
IT... IT DON'T HAVE TO BE LIKE THIS. JUST LEMME LEAVE WITH JAMES AND--

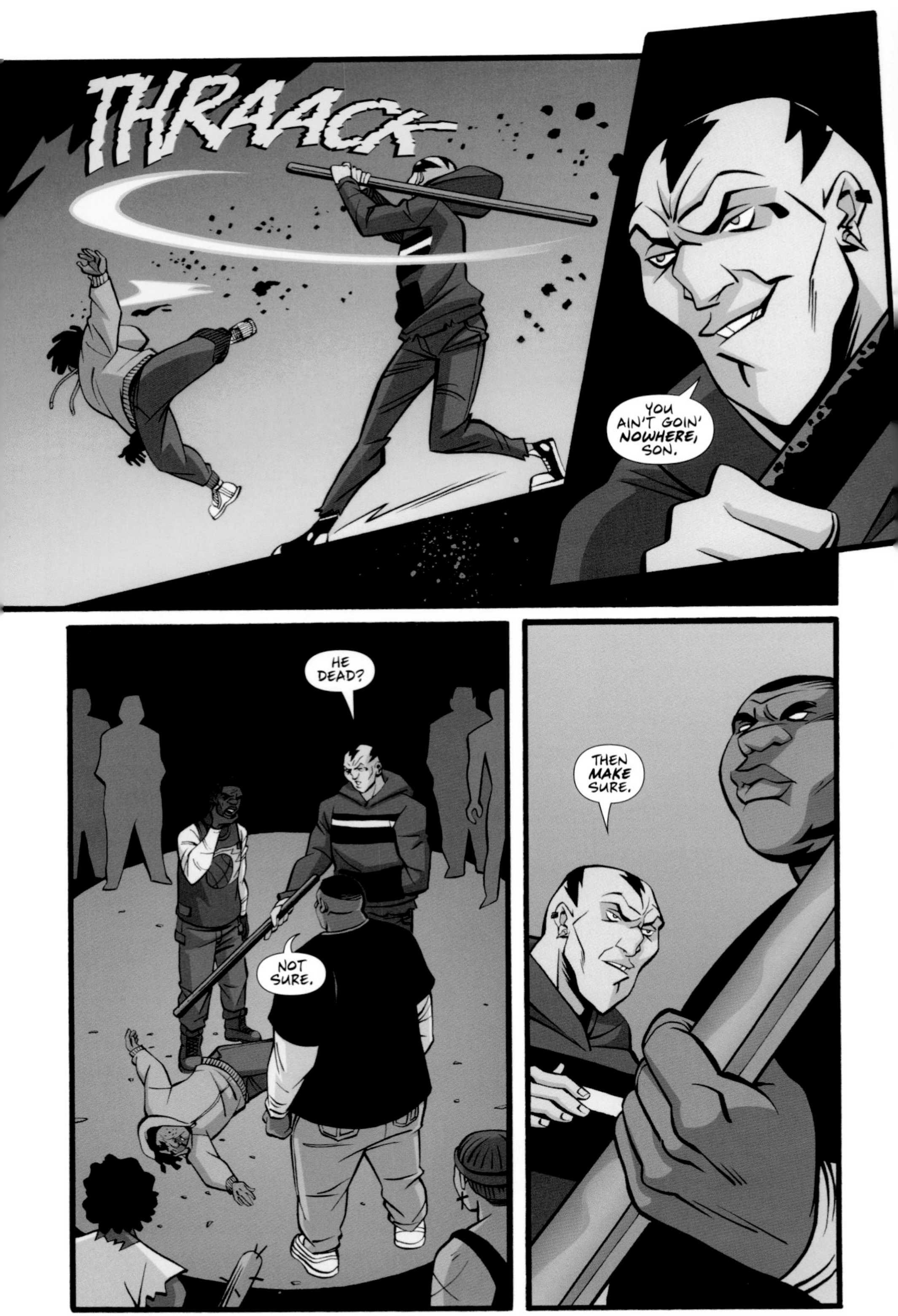
THRAACK
YOU AIN'T GOIN' NOWHERE, SON.
HE DEAD?
NOT SURE.
THEN MAKE SURE.

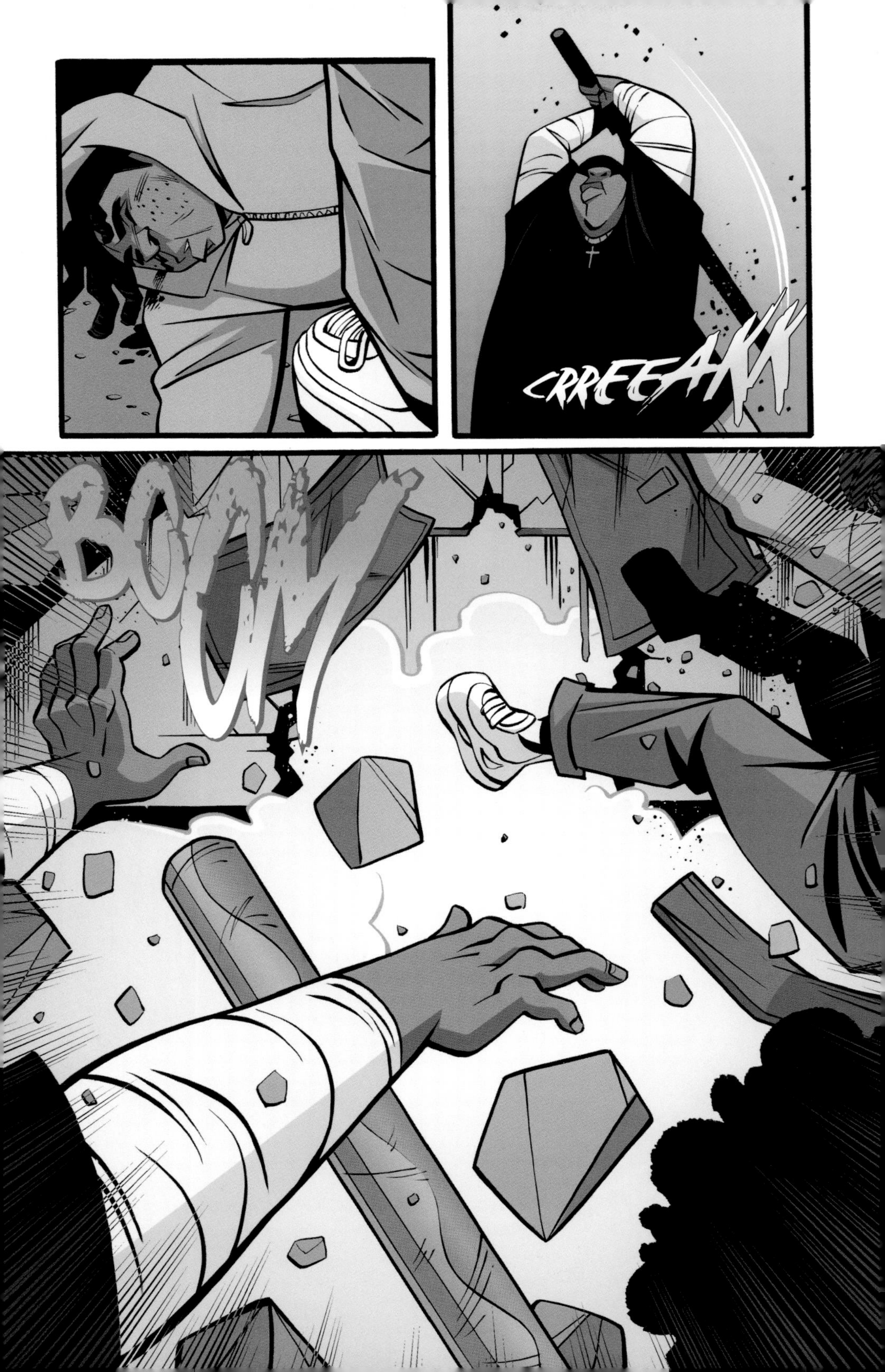
CRREEAKK
BOOM

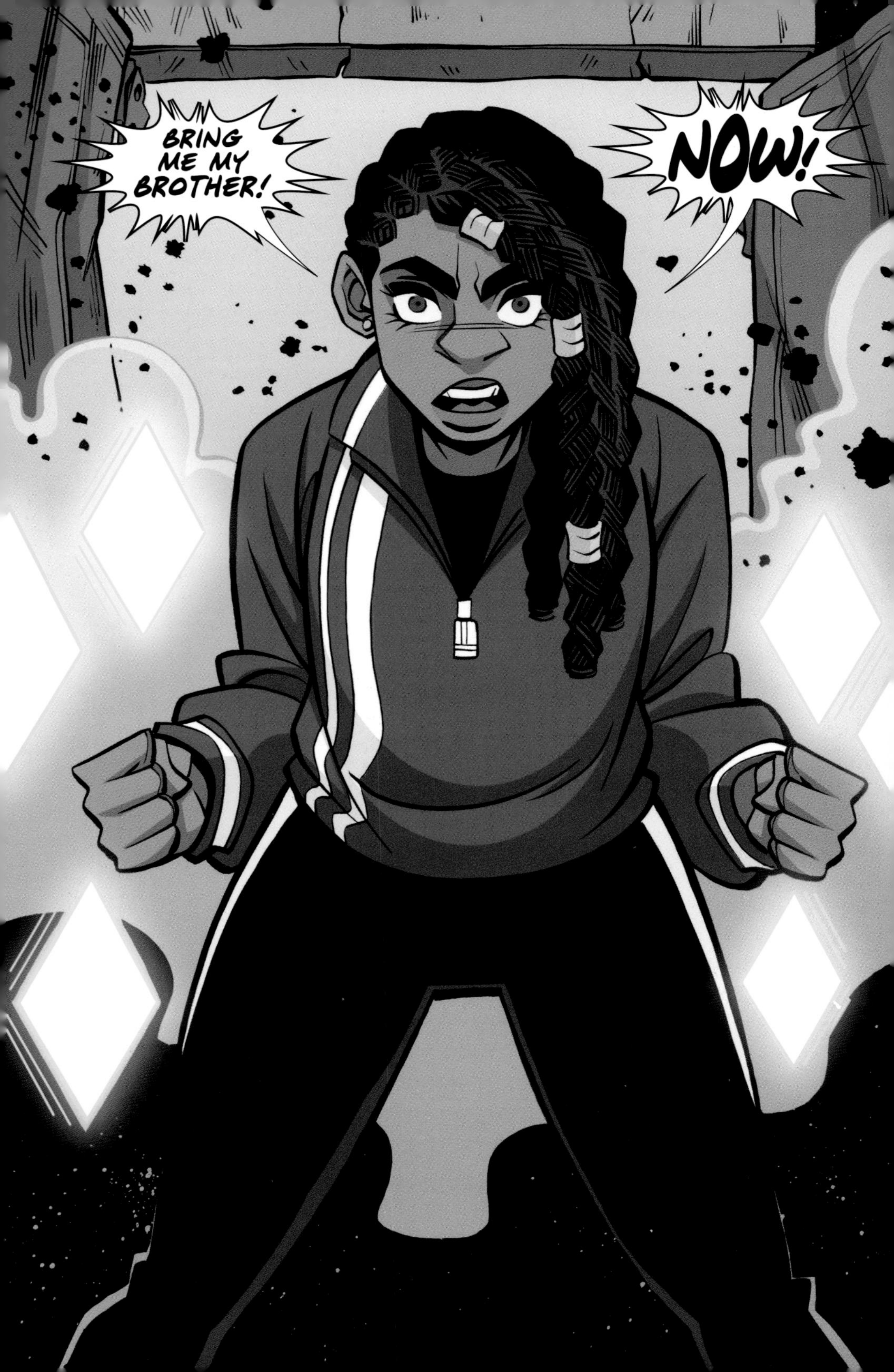
BRING ME MY BROTHER!
NOW!

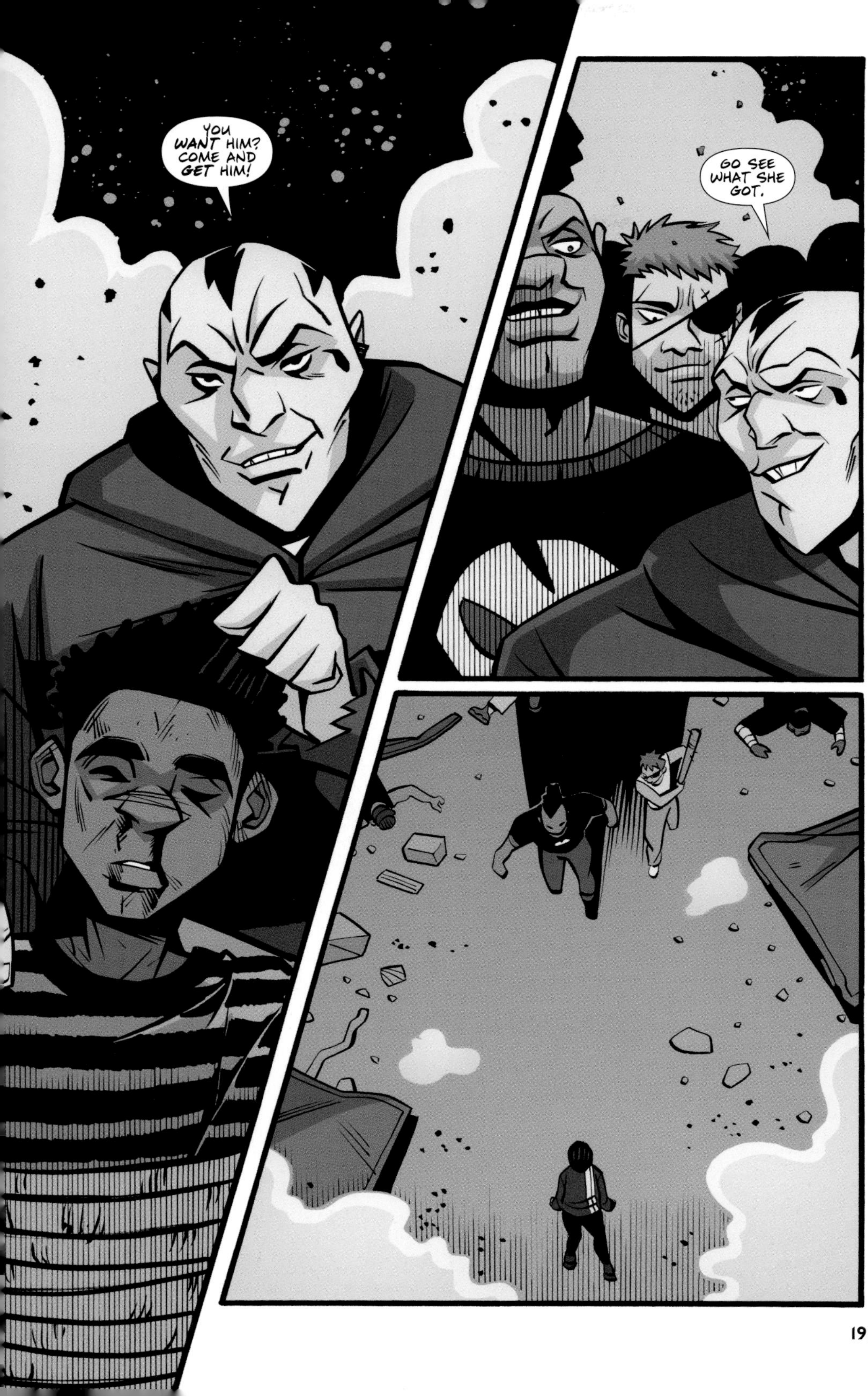
YOU WANT HIM? COME AND GET HIM!
GO SEE WHAT SHE GOT.

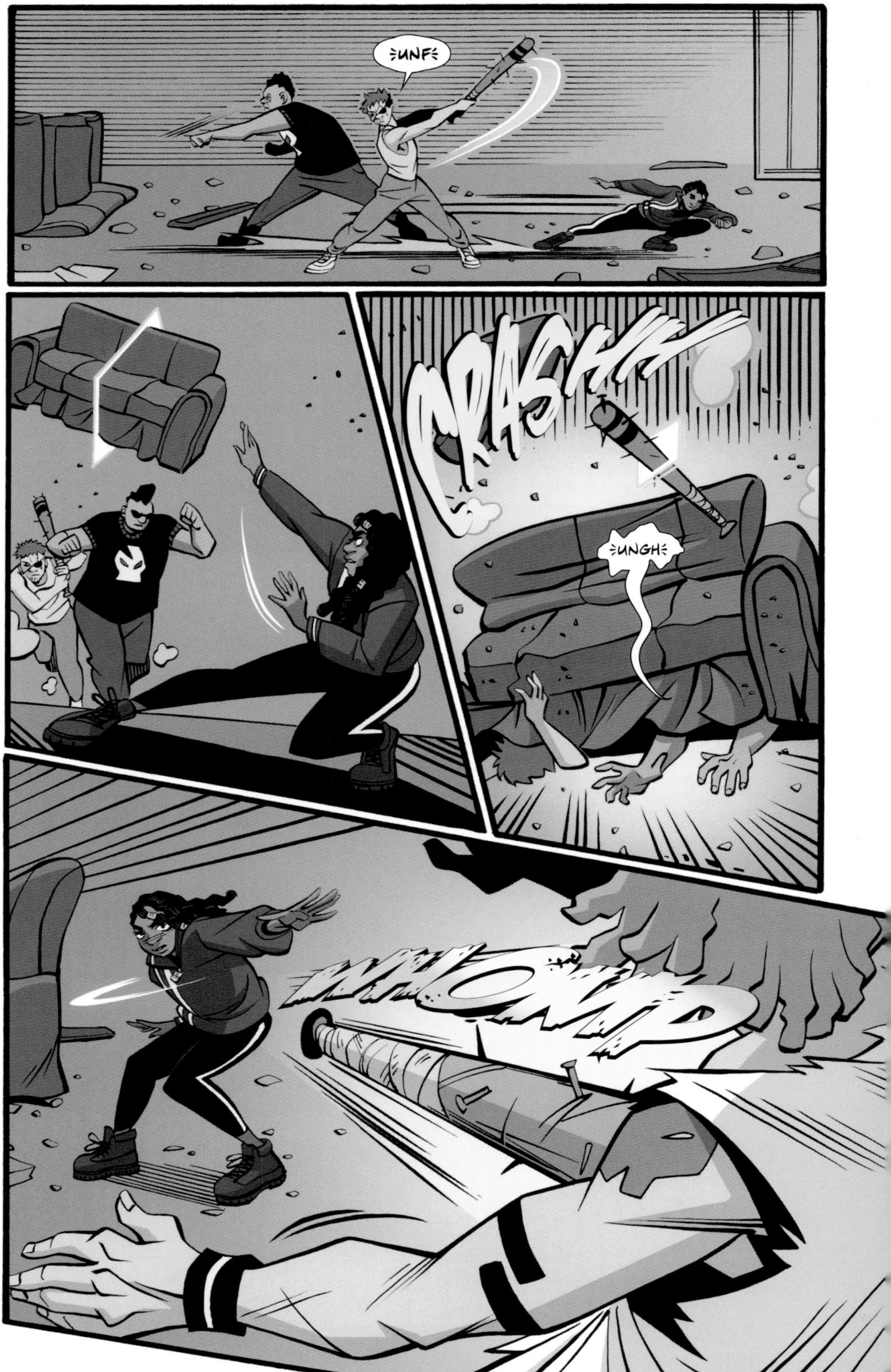
UNF
CRASH
UNGH
WHOMP

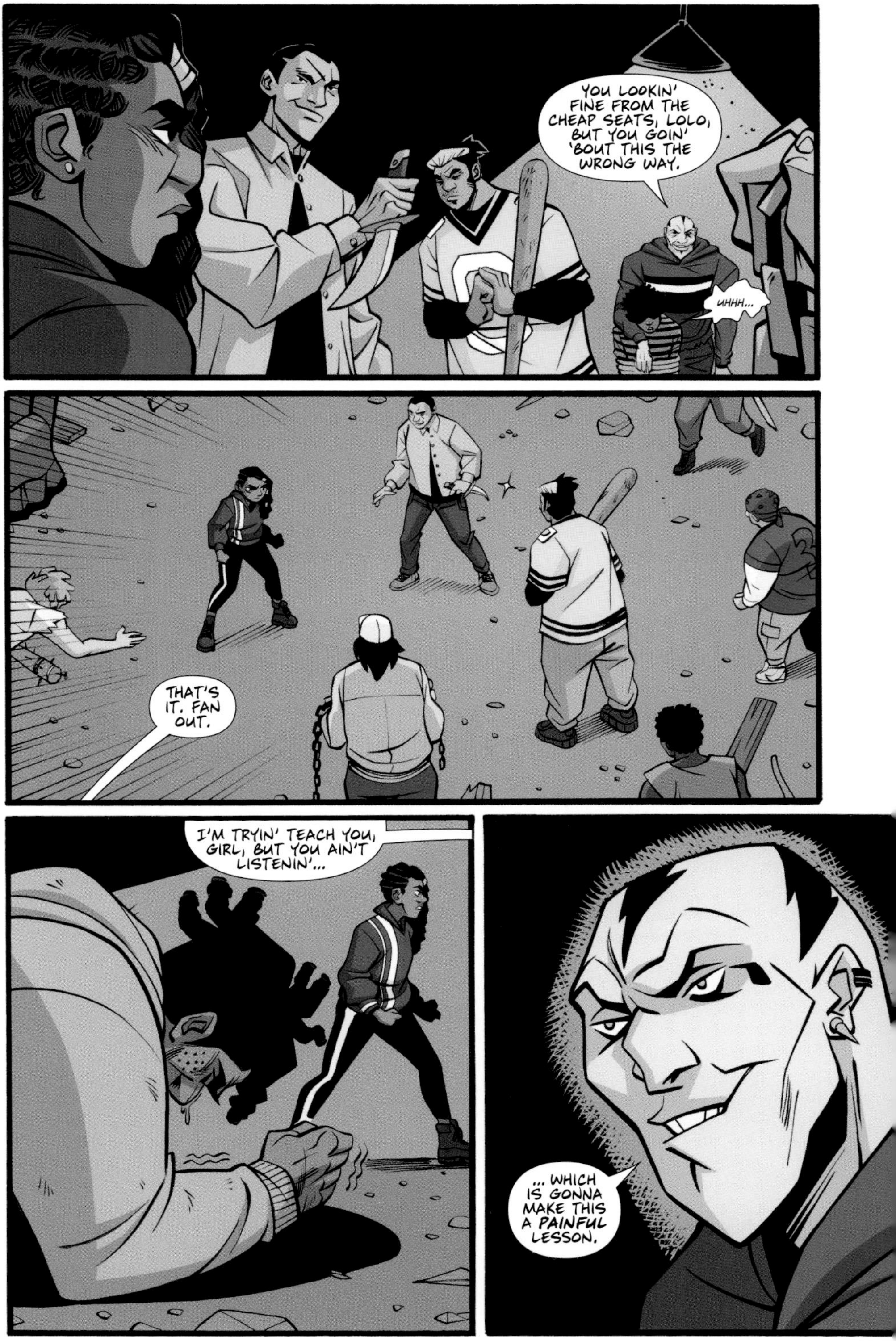
YOU LOOKIN' FINE FROM THE CHEAP SEATS, LOLO, BUT YOU GOIN' 'BOUT THIS THE WRONG WAY.
UHHH...
THAT'S IT. FAN OUT.
I'M TRYIN' TEACH YOU, GIRL, BUT YOU AIN'T LISTENIN'...
... WHICH IS GONNA MAKE THIS A PAINFUL LESSON.

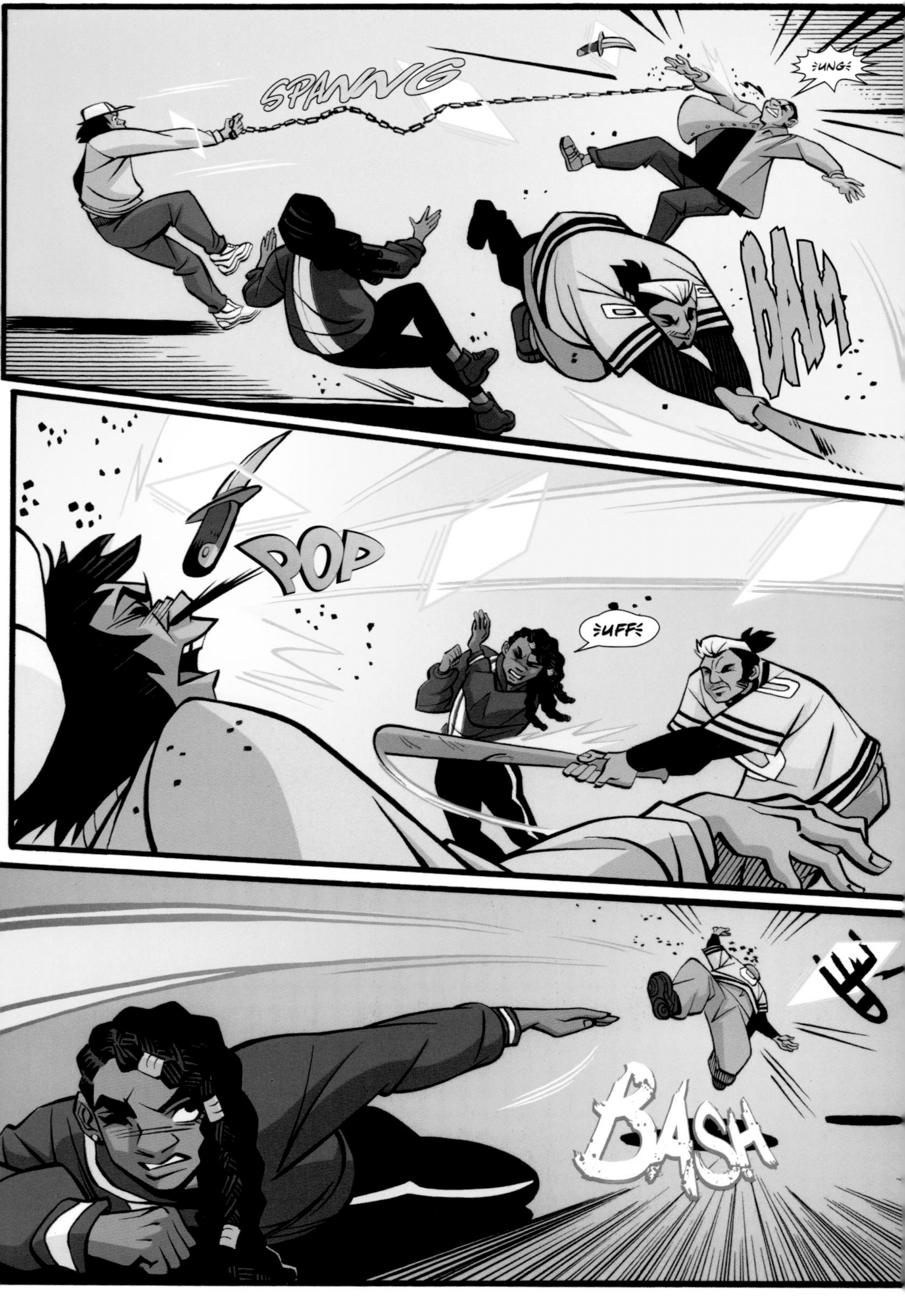
SPANNG
UNG
BAM
POP
UFF
BASH

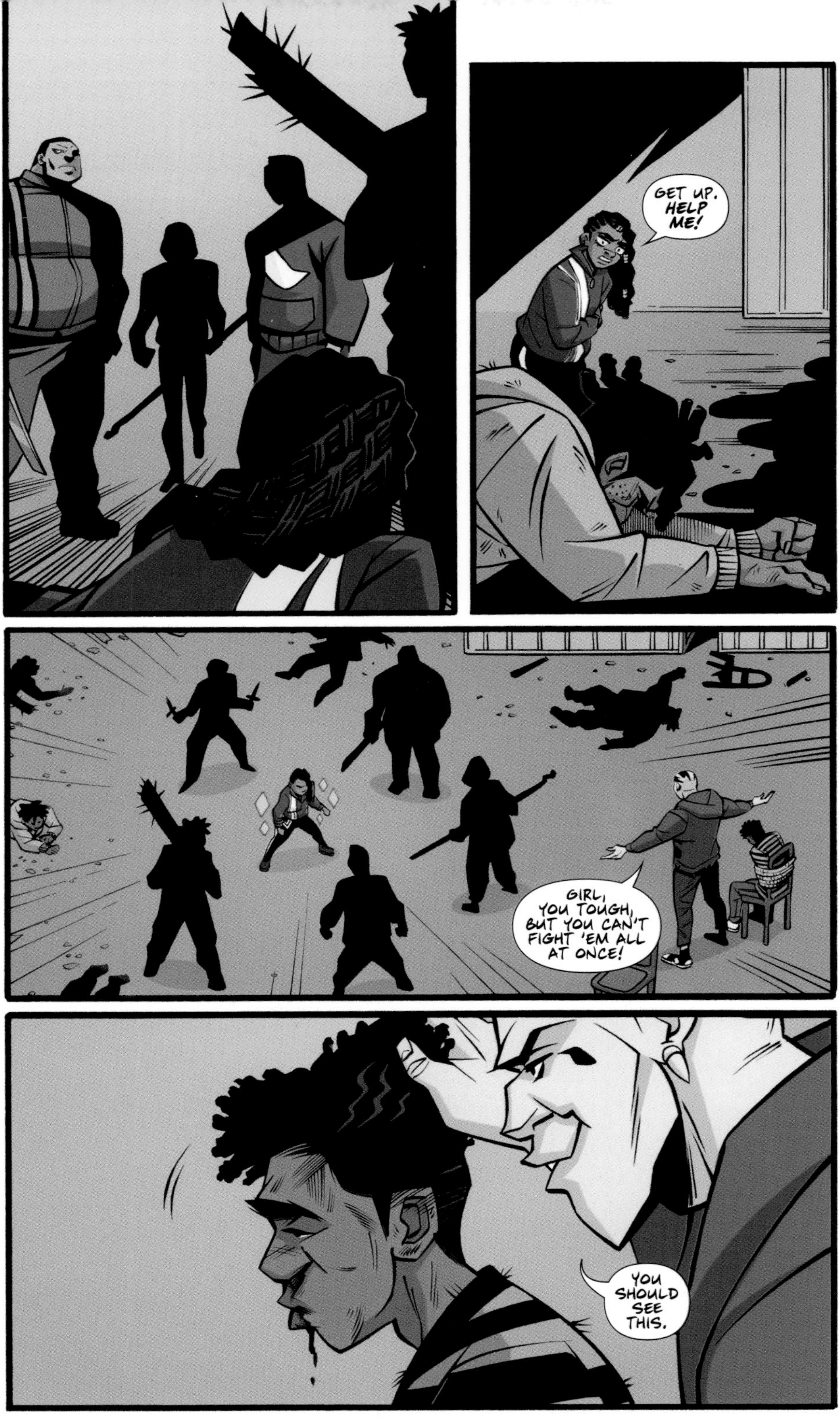
GET UP. HELP ME!
GIRL, YOU TOUGH, BUT YOU CAN'T FIGHT 'EM ALL AT ONCE!
YOU SHOULD SEE THIS.

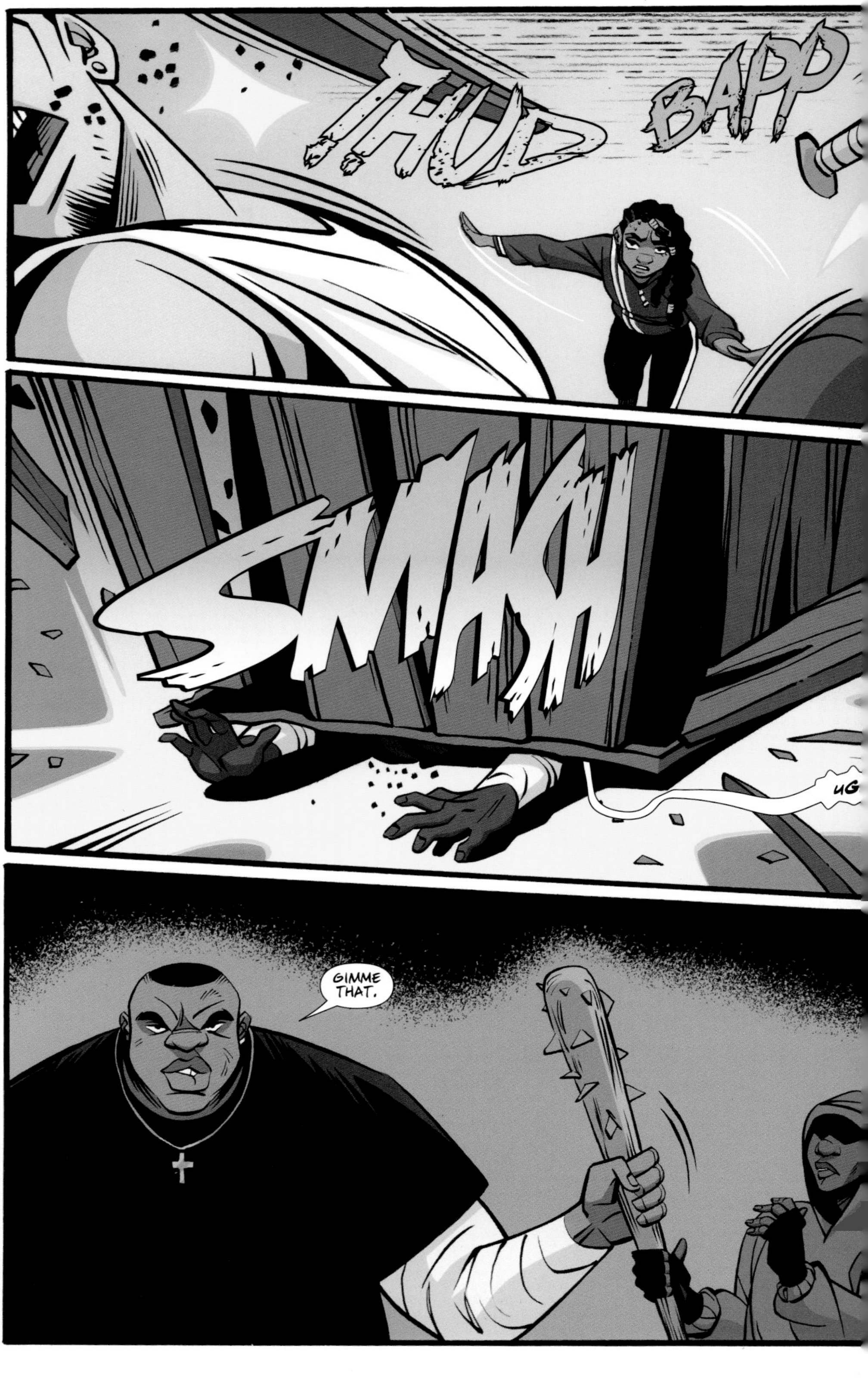
THUD
BAPP
SMASH
UG
GIMME THAT.

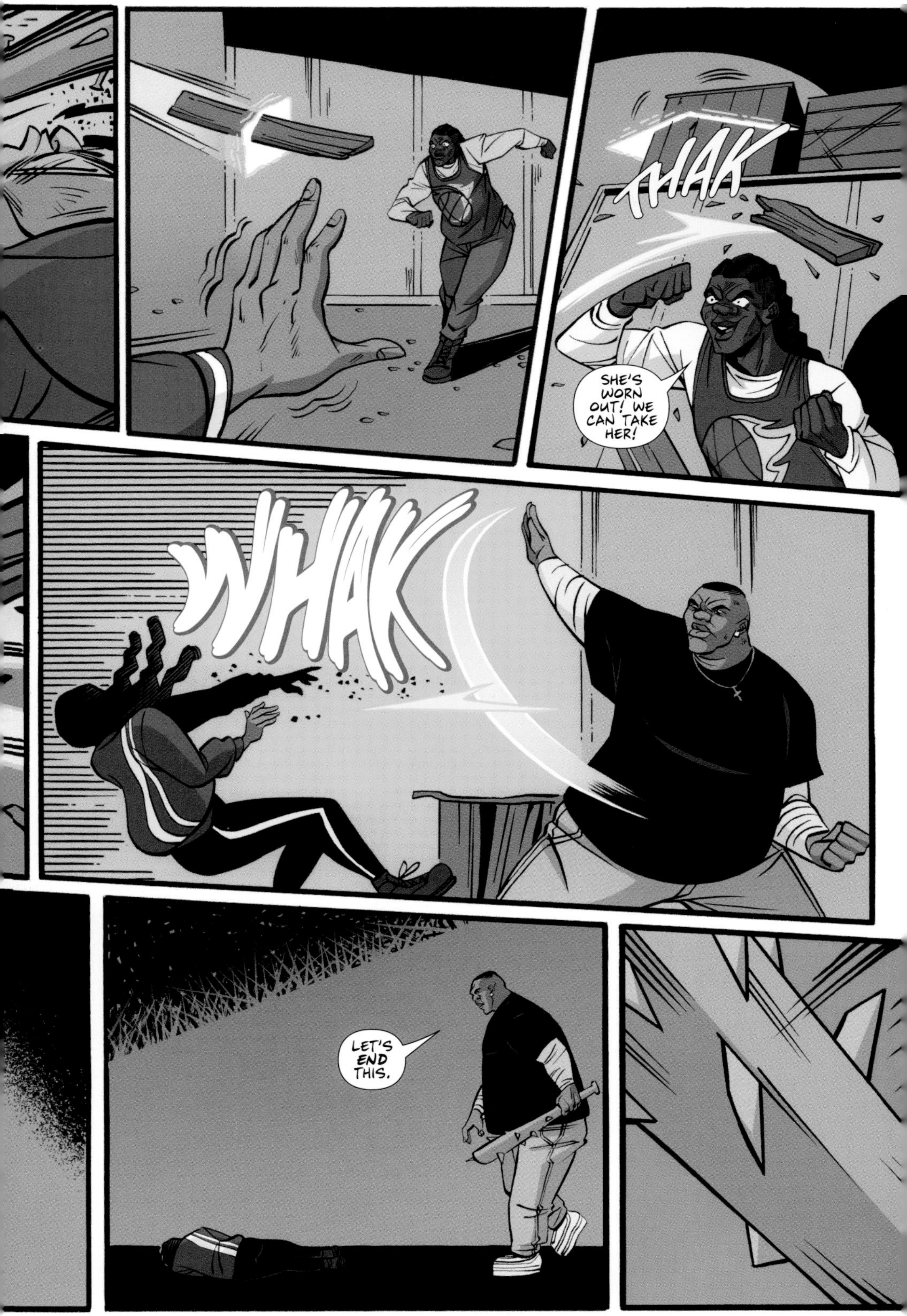
THAK
SHE'S WORN OUT! WE CAN TAKE HER!
WHAK
LET'S END THIS.

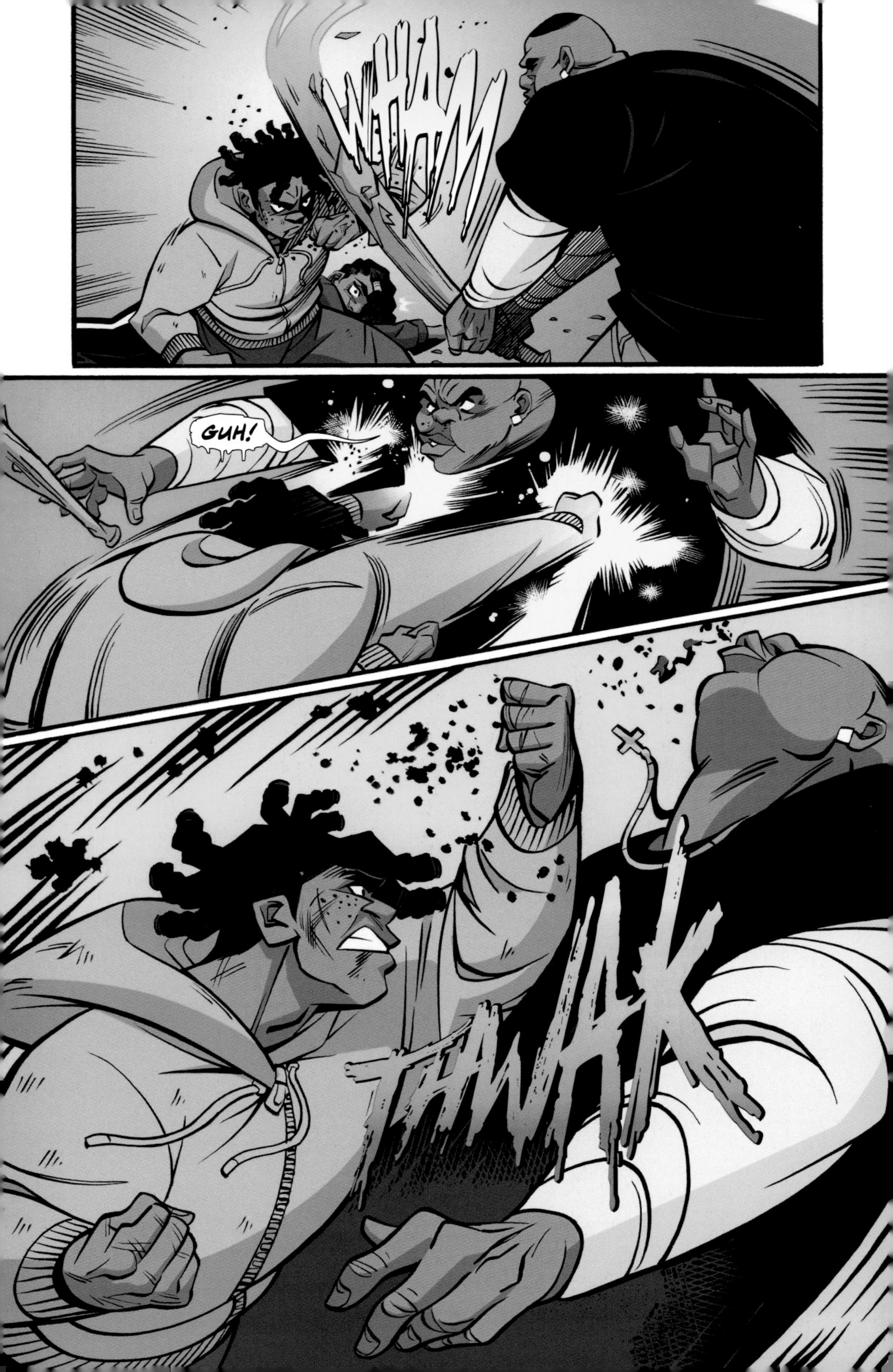
WHAM
GUH!
THWAK

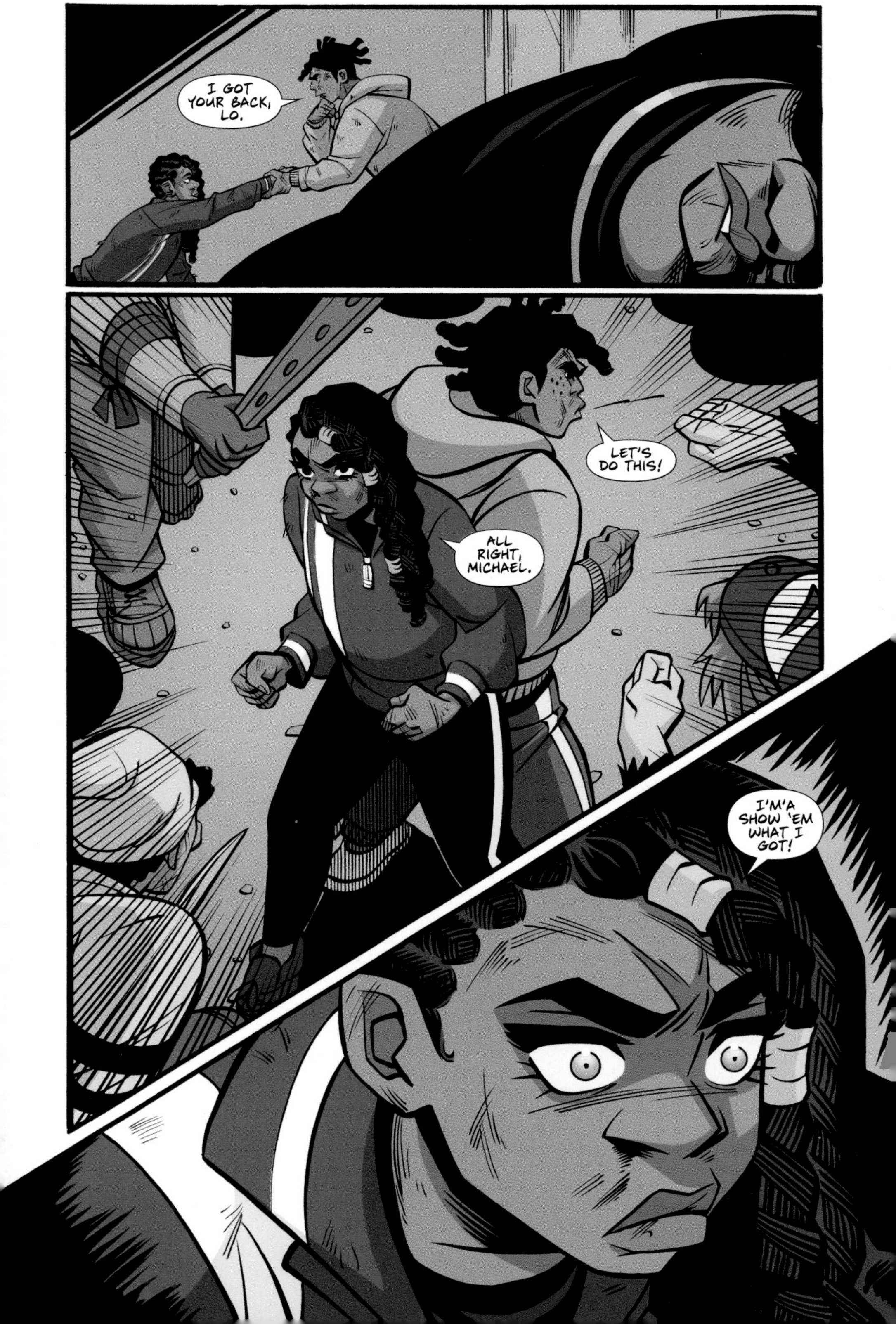
I GOT YOUR BACK, LO.
LET'S DO THIS!
ALL RIGHT, MICHAEL.
I'M'A SHOW 'EM WHAT I GOT!

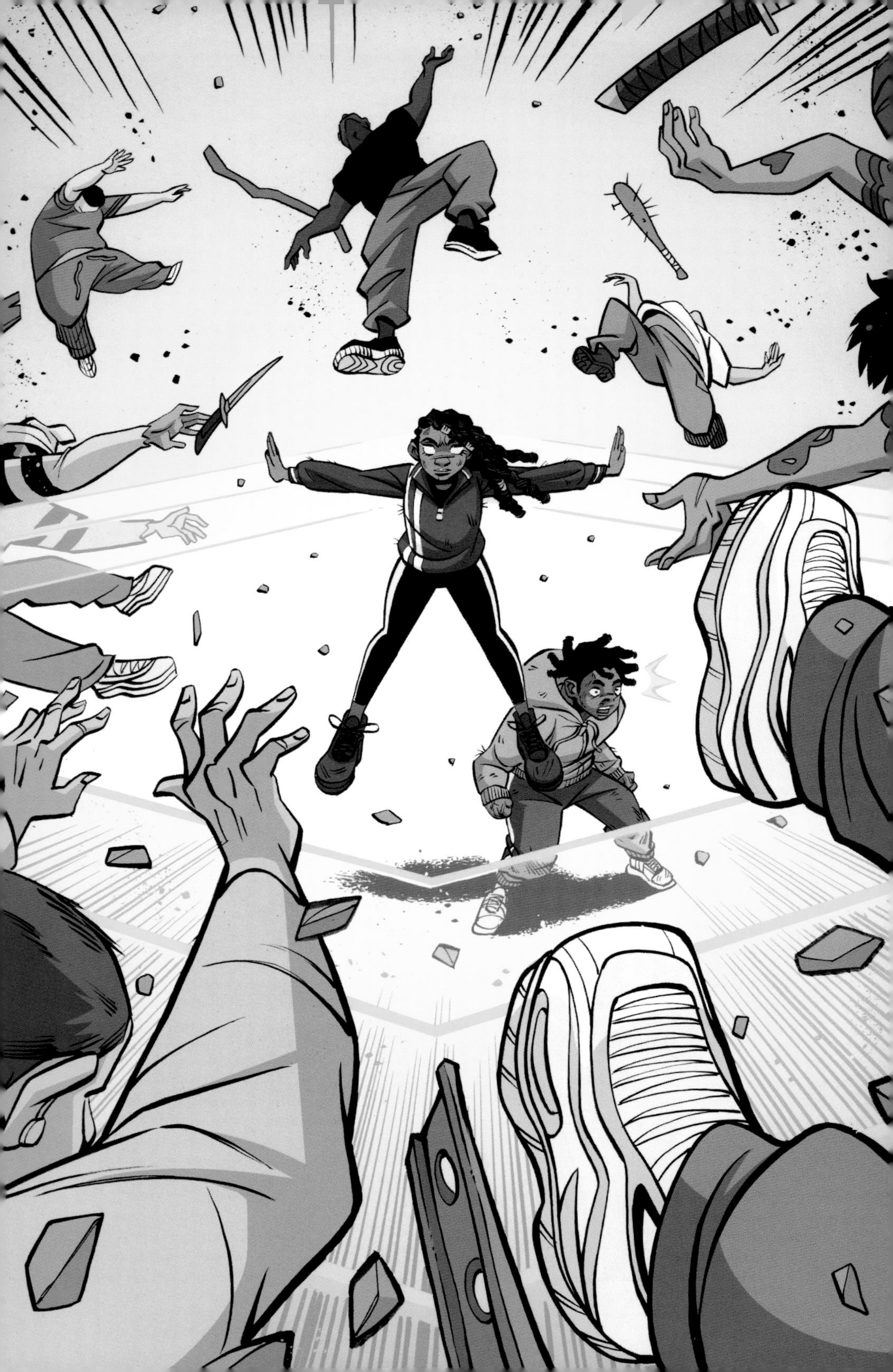

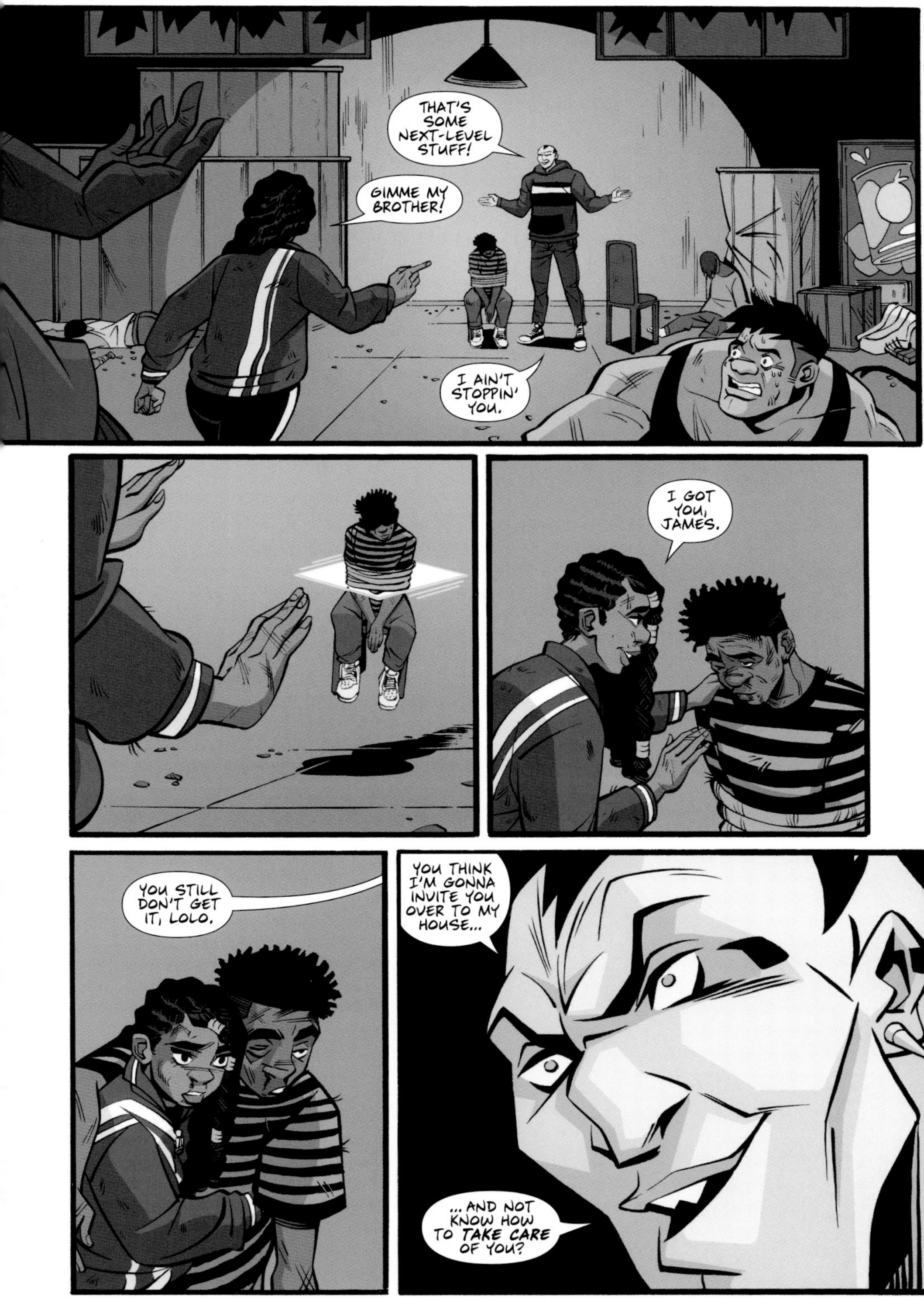
THAT'S SOME NEXT-LEVEL STUFF!
GIMME MY BROTHER!
I AIN'T STOPPIN' YOU.
I GOT YOU, JAMES.
YOU STILL DON'T GET IT, LOLO.
YOU THINK I'M GONNA INVITE YOU OVER TO MY HOUSE...
...AND NOT KNOW HOW TO *TAKE CARE* OF YOU?

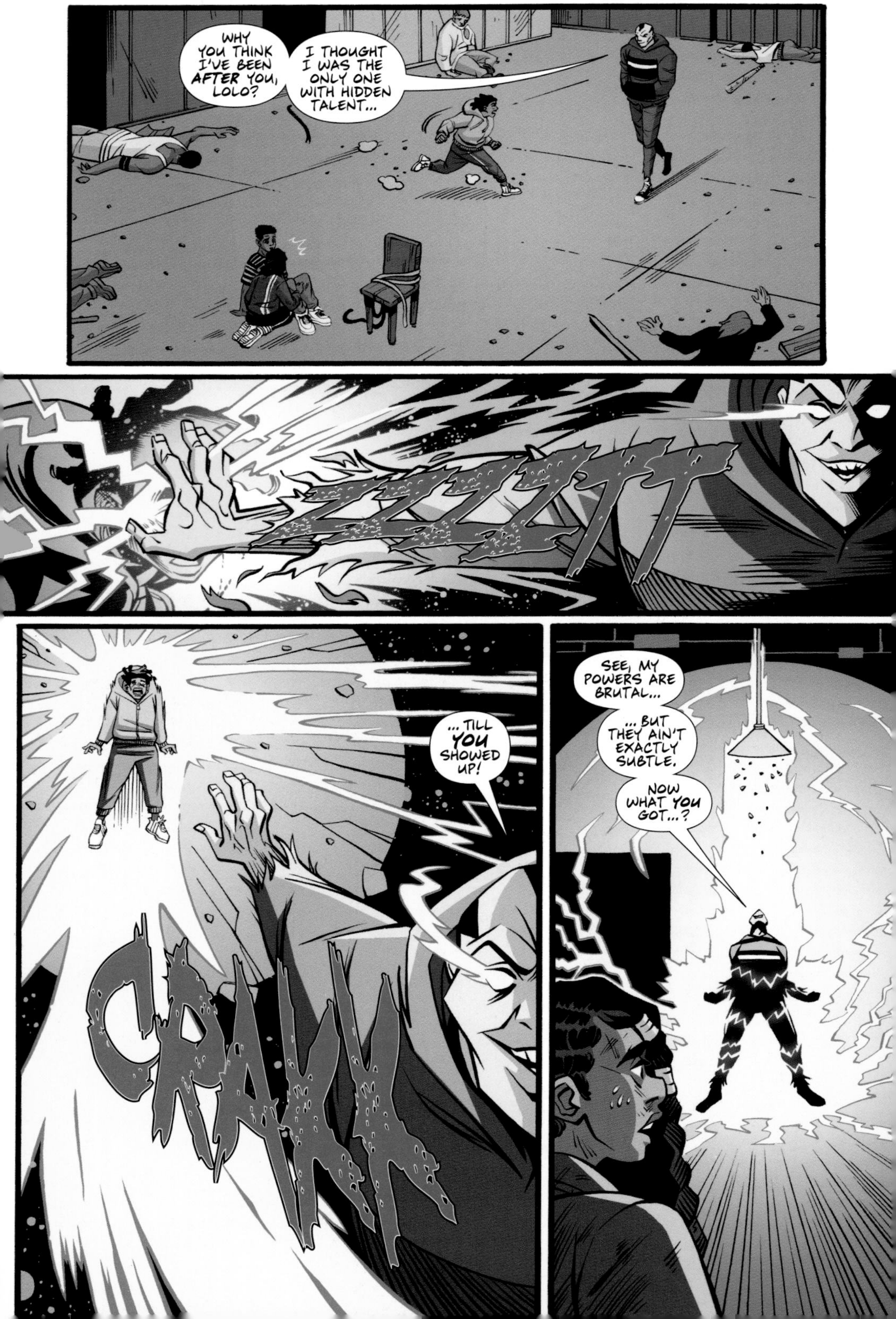
WHY YOU THINK I'VE BEEN AFTER YOU, LOLO?
I THOUGHT I WAS THE ONLY ONE WITH HIDDEN TALENT...
ZZZZTT
...TILL YOU SHOWED UP!
CRAKK
SEE, MY POWERS ARE BRUTAL...
...BUT THEY AIN'T EXACTLY SUBTLE.
NOW WHAT YOU GOT...?

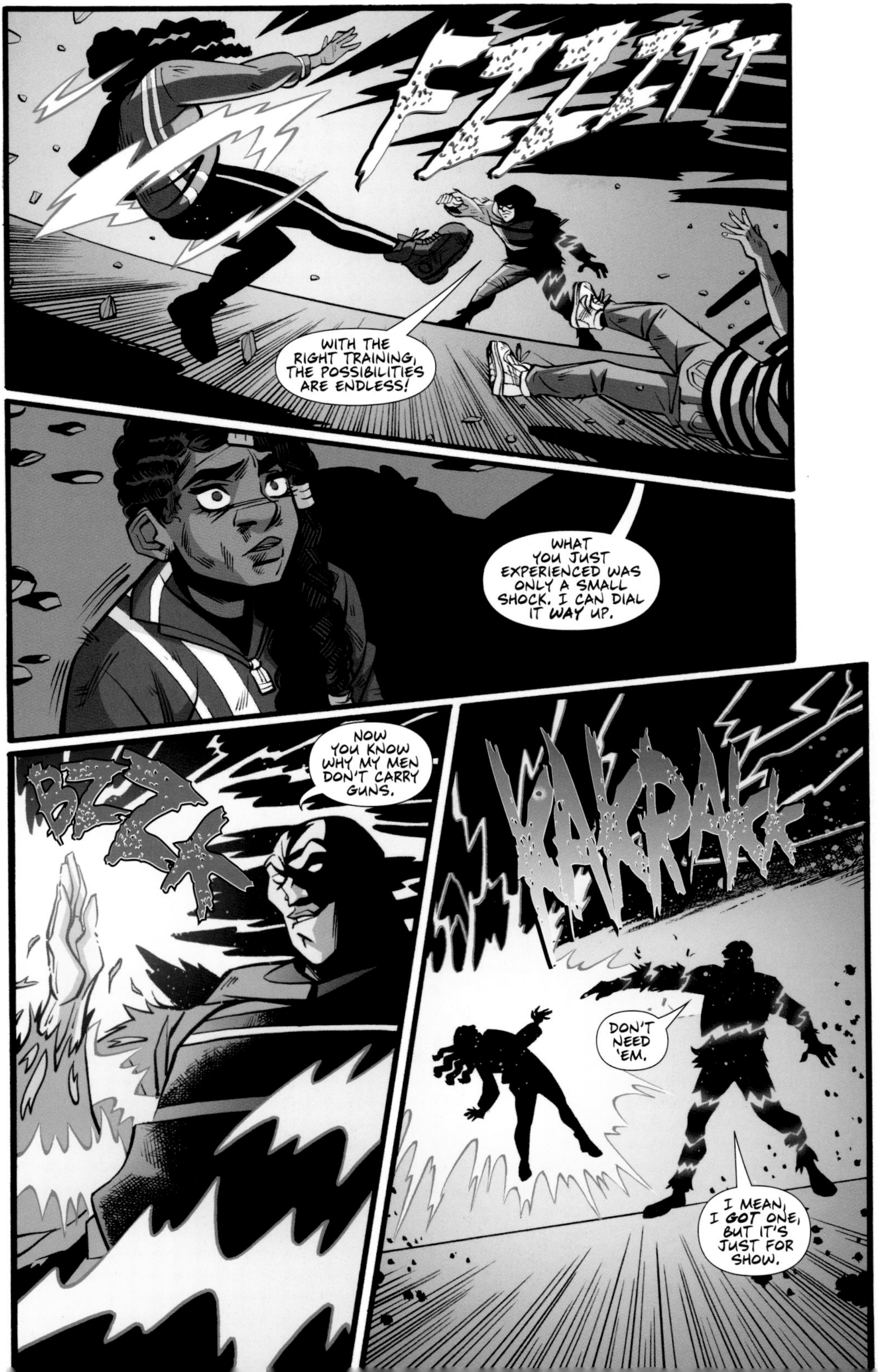
FZZZTT
WITH THE RIGHT TRAINING, THE POSSIBILITIES ARE ENDLESS!
WHAT YOU JUST EXPERIENCED WAS ONLY A SMALL SHOCK. I CAN DIAL IT WAY UP.
BZZK
NOW YOU KNOW WHY MY MEN DON'T CARRY GUNS.
KAKRAKK
DON'T NEED 'EM.
I MEAN, I GOT ONE, BUT IT'S JUST FOR SHOW.

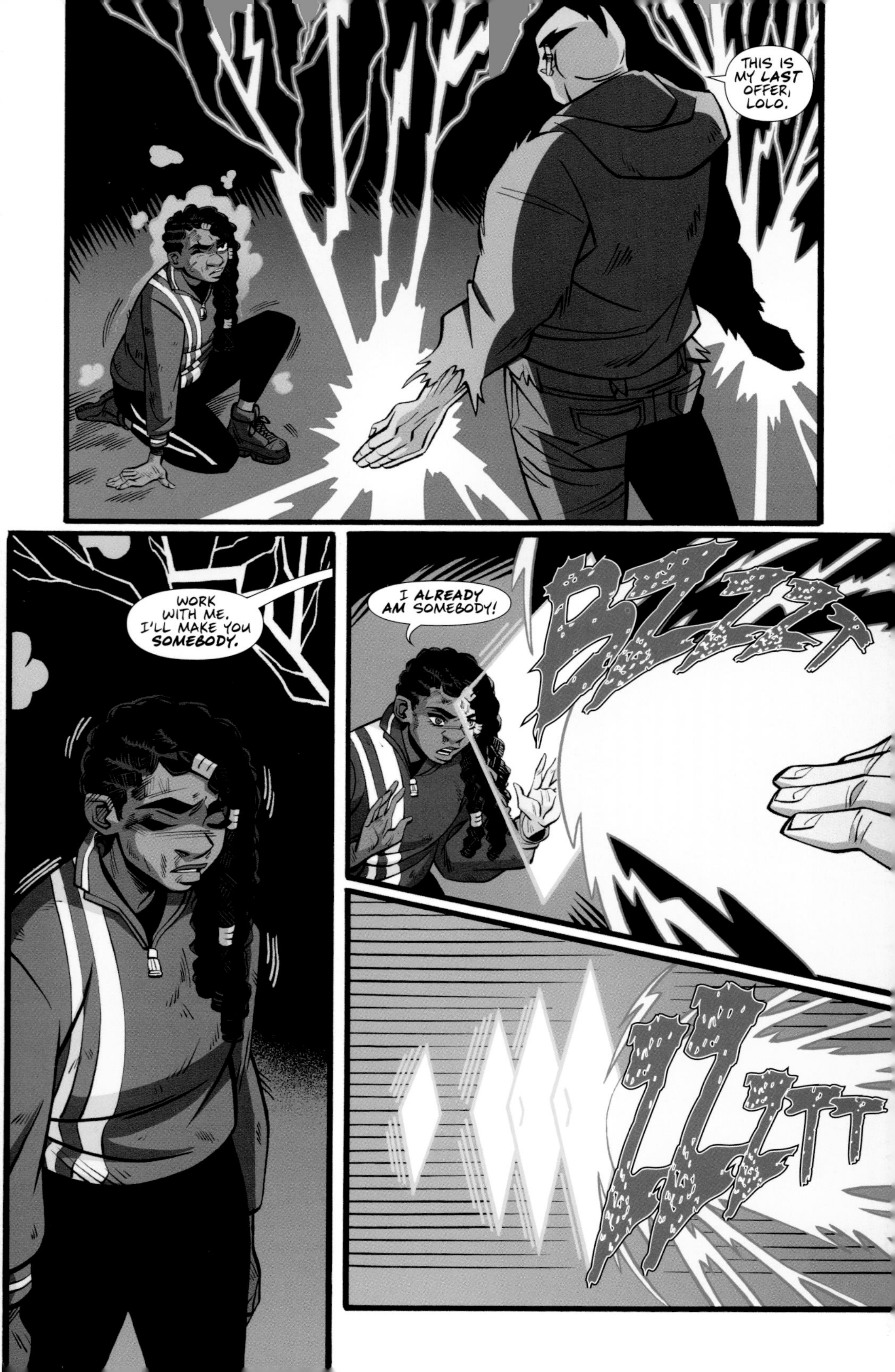
THIS IS MY LAST OFFER, LOLO.
WORK WITH ME. I'LL MAKE YOU SOMEBODY.
I ALREADY AM SOMEBODY!
BZZZT
ZZZTTT

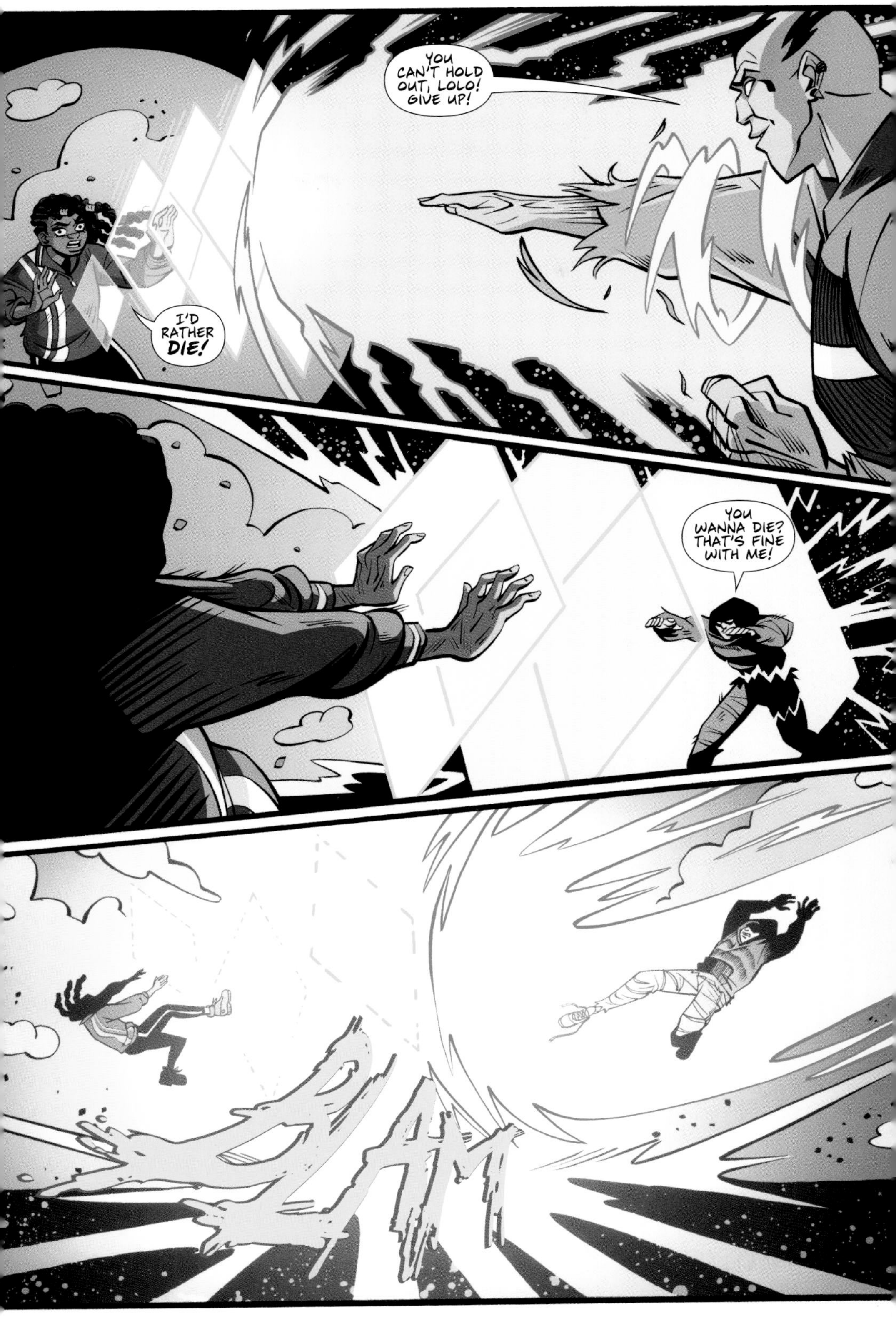
YOU CAN'T HOLD OUT, LOLO! GIVE UP!
I'D RATHER DIE!
YOU WANNA DIE? THAT'S FINE WITH ME!
BAM!

YOU'RE MORE TROUBLE THAN YOU'RE WORTH, LOLO.

I'M 'BOUT TO GIVE YOU EVERYTHING I GOT.

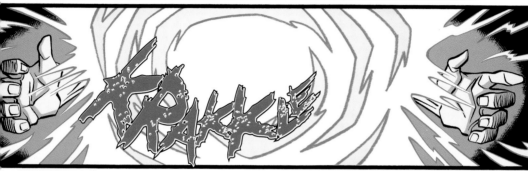

KRAKKLE

BBRAKXXXX

FSHHHH

TSS TSS TSS

TSS TSS

WHAT DID YOU DO?

YOU GAVE ME EVERYTHING YOU GOT. NOW YOU GOT NOTHING LEFT.

I'M'A KILL YOU!

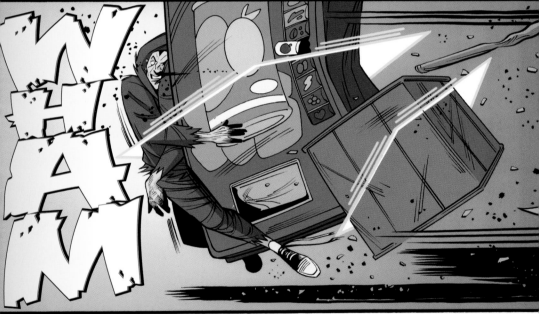
WHAM

UNGH...

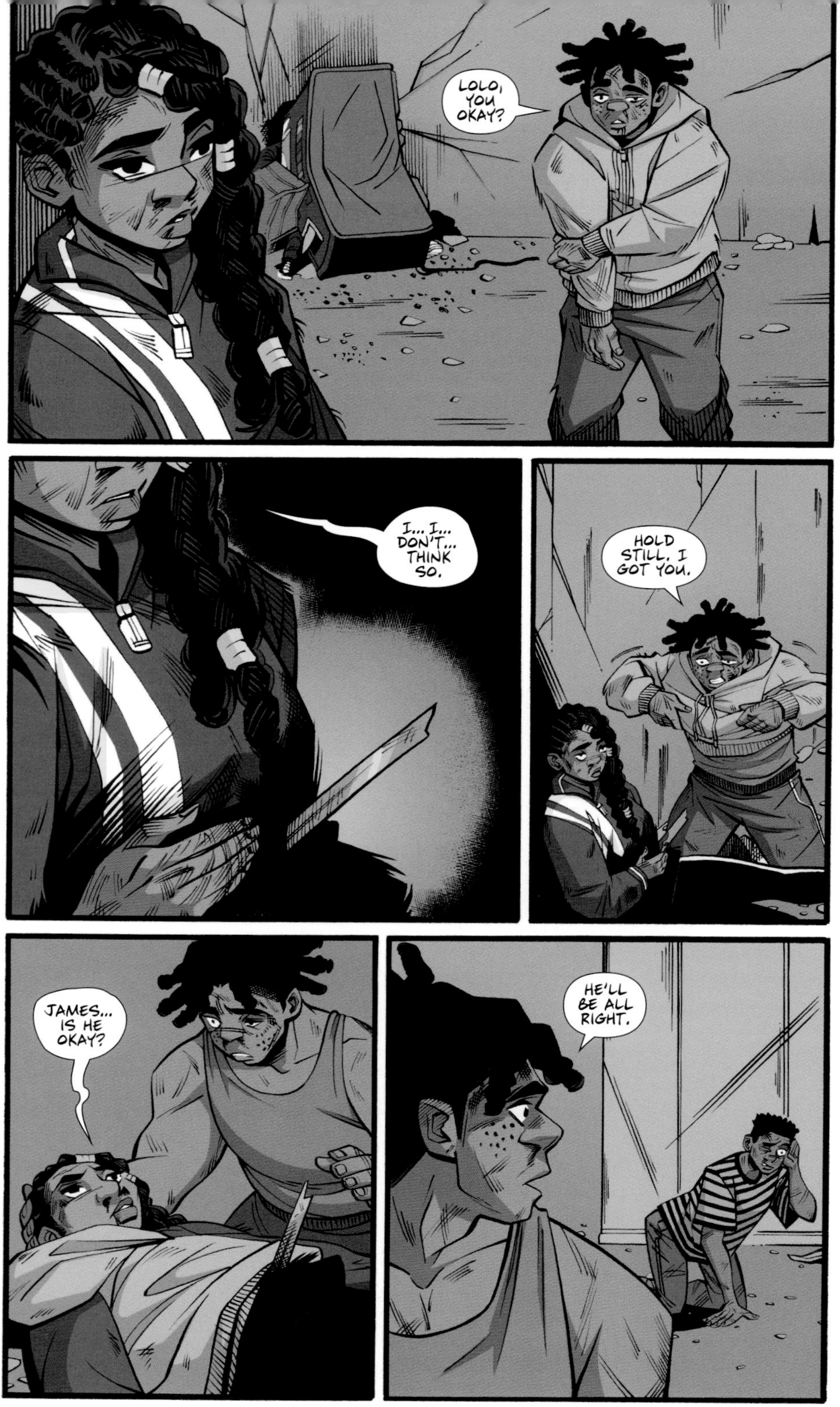
LOLO, YOU OKAY?
I... I... DON'T... THINK SO.
HOLD STILL. I GOT YOU.
JAMES... IS HE OKAY?
HE'LL BE ALL RIGHT.

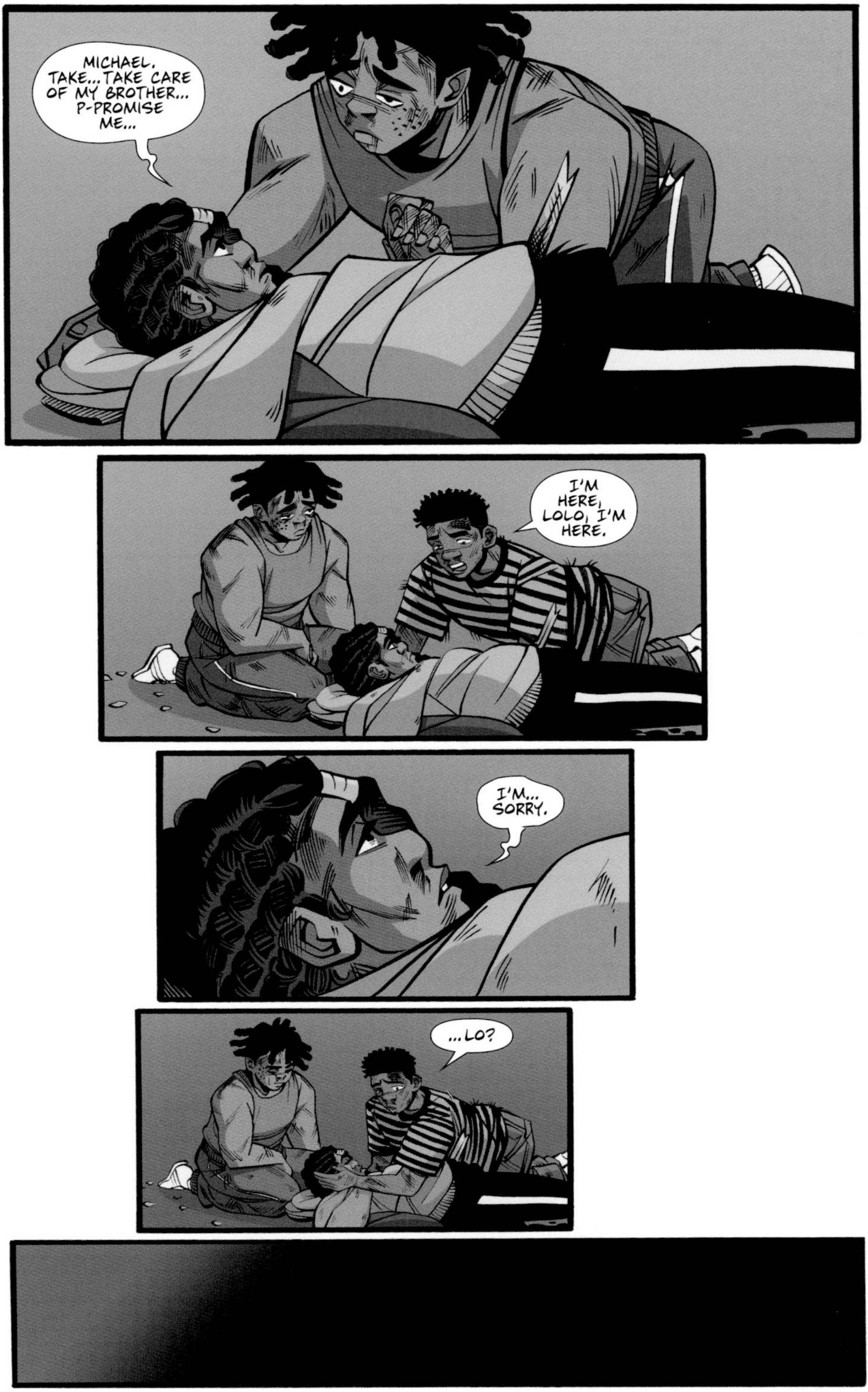
MICHAEL. TAKE... TAKE CARE OF MY BROTHER... P-PROMISE ME...
I'M HERE, LOLO, I'M HERE.
I'M... SORRY.
...LO?

EPILOGUE

WHAT YOU DO FOR LOVE

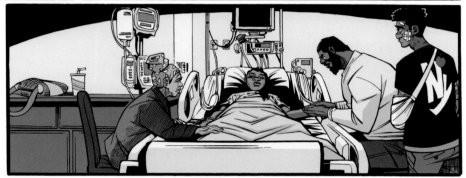

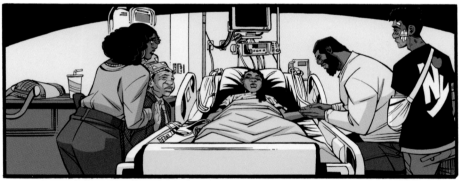

IT WAS TWO WEEKS BEFORE A VOICE CUT THROUGH THE DARKNESS.

LET MY HEALING TOUCH FLOW THROUGH YOU.

EVEN BEFORE I OPENED MY EYES, I KNEW THAT IT WAS MY MOTHER.

THAT'S IT, DARLING.

MOM?!

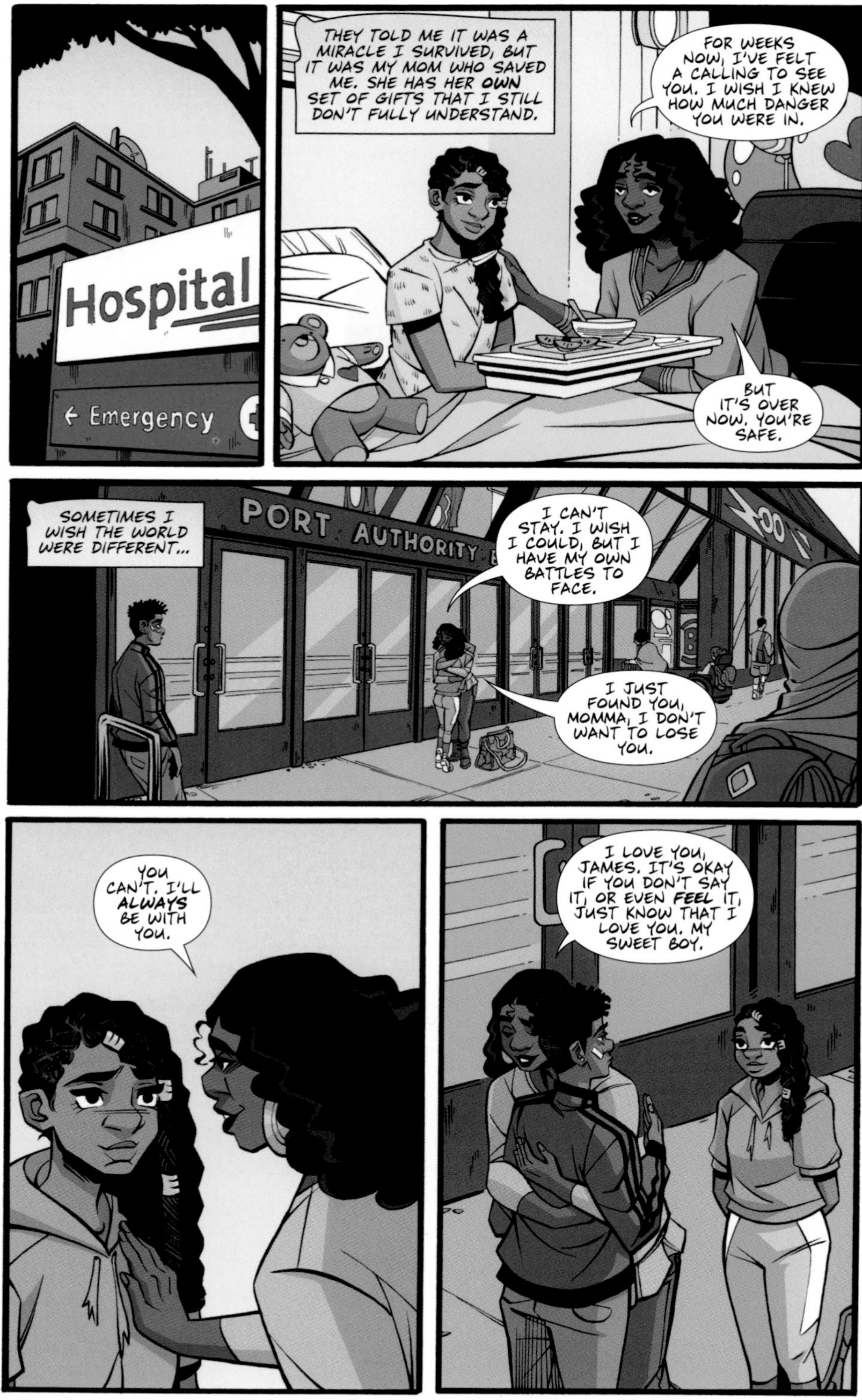
Hospital
← Emergency
THEY TOLD ME IT WAS A MIRACLE I SURVIVED, BUT IT WAS MY MOM WHO SAVED ME. SHE HAS HER OWN SET OF GIFTS THAT I STILL DON'T FULLY UNDERSTAND.
FOR WEEKS NOW, I'VE FELT A CALLING TO SEE YOU. I WISH I KNEW HOW MUCH DANGER YOU WERE IN.
BUT IT'S OVER NOW. YOU'RE SAFE.
SOMETIMES I WISH THE WORLD WERE DIFFERENT...
PORT AUTHORITY
I CAN'T STAY. I WISH I COULD, BUT I HAVE MY OWN BATTLES TO FACE.
I JUST FOUND YOU, MOMMA. I DON'T WANT TO LOSE YOU.
YOU CAN'T. I'LL ALWAYS BE WITH YOU.
I LOVE YOU, JAMES. IT'S OKAY IF YOU DON'T SAY IT, OR EVEN FEEL IT, JUST KNOW THAT I LOVE YOU. MY SWEET BOY.

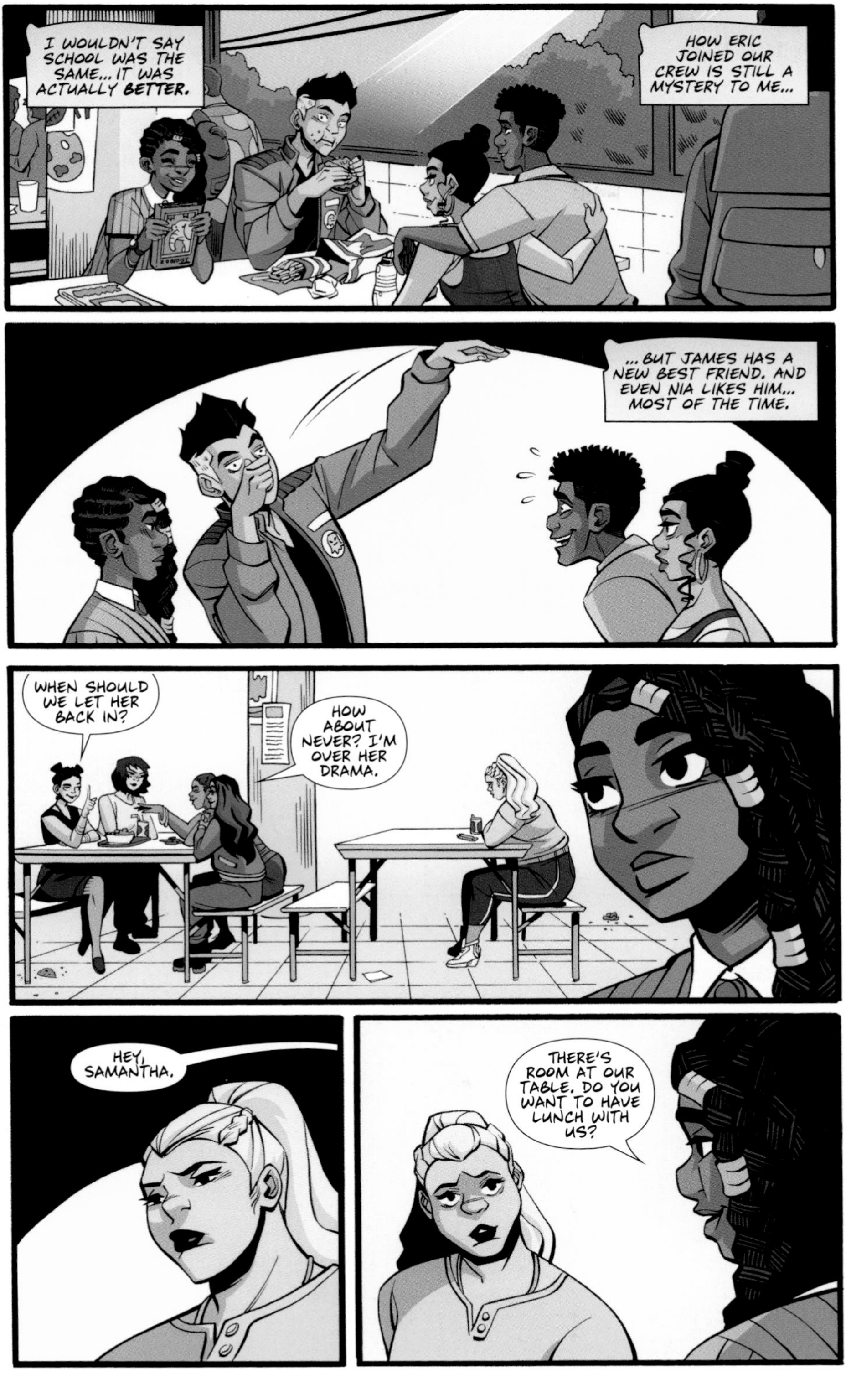

I WOULDN'T SAY SCHOOL WAS THE SAME... IT WAS ACTUALLY **BETTER.**
HOW ERIC JOINED OUR CREW IS STILL A MYSTERY TO ME...
...BUT JAMES HAS A NEW BEST FRIEND. AND EVEN NIA LIKES HIM... MOST OF THE TIME.
WHEN SHOULD WE LET HER BACK IN?
HOW ABOUT NEVER? I'M OVER HER DRAMA.
HEY, SAMANTHA.
THERE'S ROOM AT OUR TABLE. DO YOU WANT TO HAVE LUNCH WITH US?

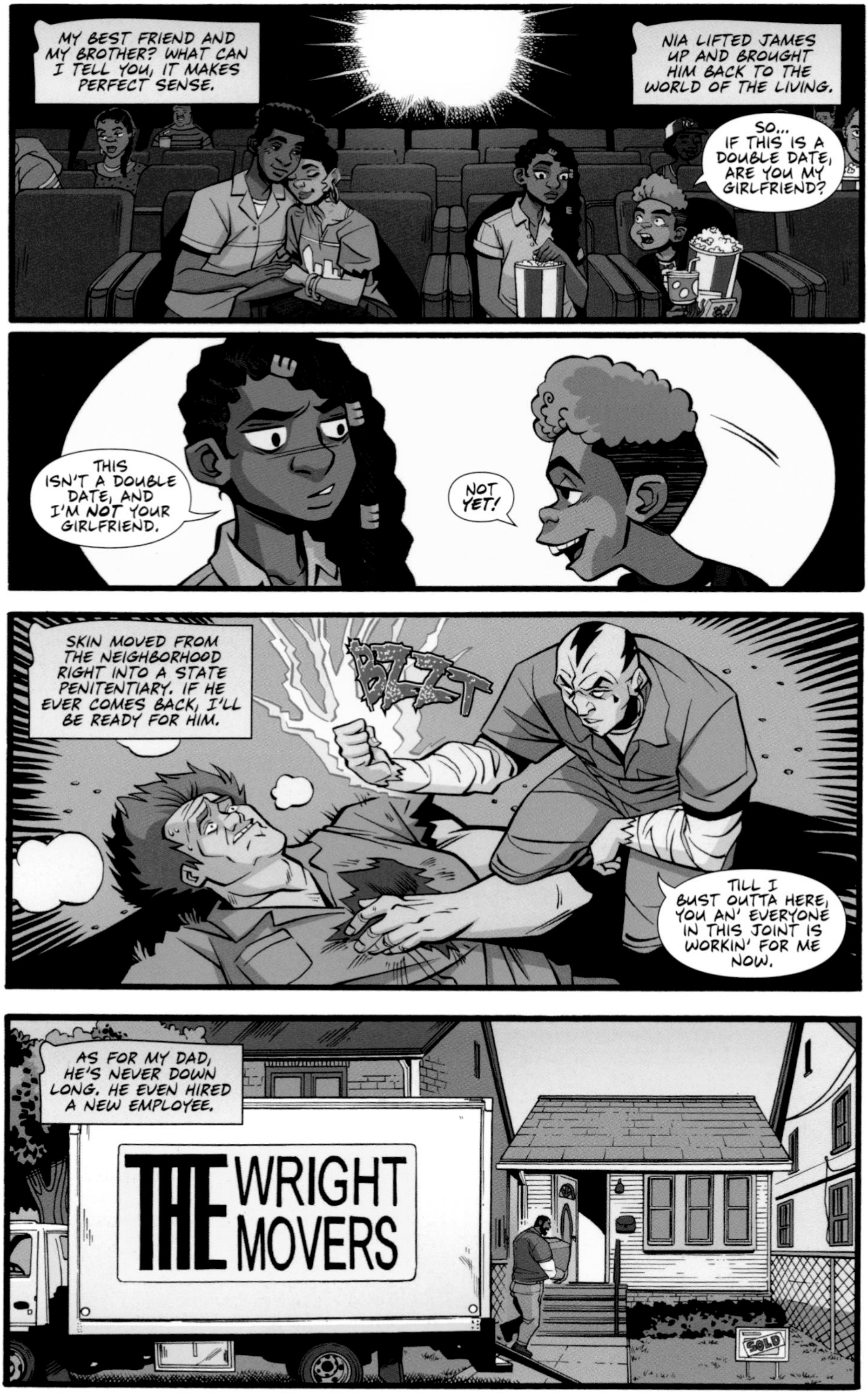
MY BEST FRIEND AND MY BROTHER? WHAT CAN I TELL YOU, IT MAKES PERFECT SENSE.
NIA LIFTED JAMES UP AND BROUGHT HIM BACK TO THE WORLD OF THE LIVING.
SO... IF THIS IS A DOUBLE DATE, ARE YOU MY GIRLFRIEND?
THIS ISN'T A DOUBLE DATE, AND I'M **NOT** YOUR GIRLFRIEND.
NOT YET!
SKIN MOVED FROM THE NEIGHBORHOOD RIGHT INTO A STATE PENITENTIARY. IF HE EVER COMES BACK, I'LL BE READY FOR HIM.
BZZT
TILL I BUST OUTTA HERE, YOU AN' EVERYONE IN THIS JOINT IS WORKIN' FOR ME NOW.
AS FOR MY DAD, HE'S NEVER DOWN LONG. HE EVEN HIRED A NEW EMPLOYEE.
THE WRIGHT MOVERS
SOLD

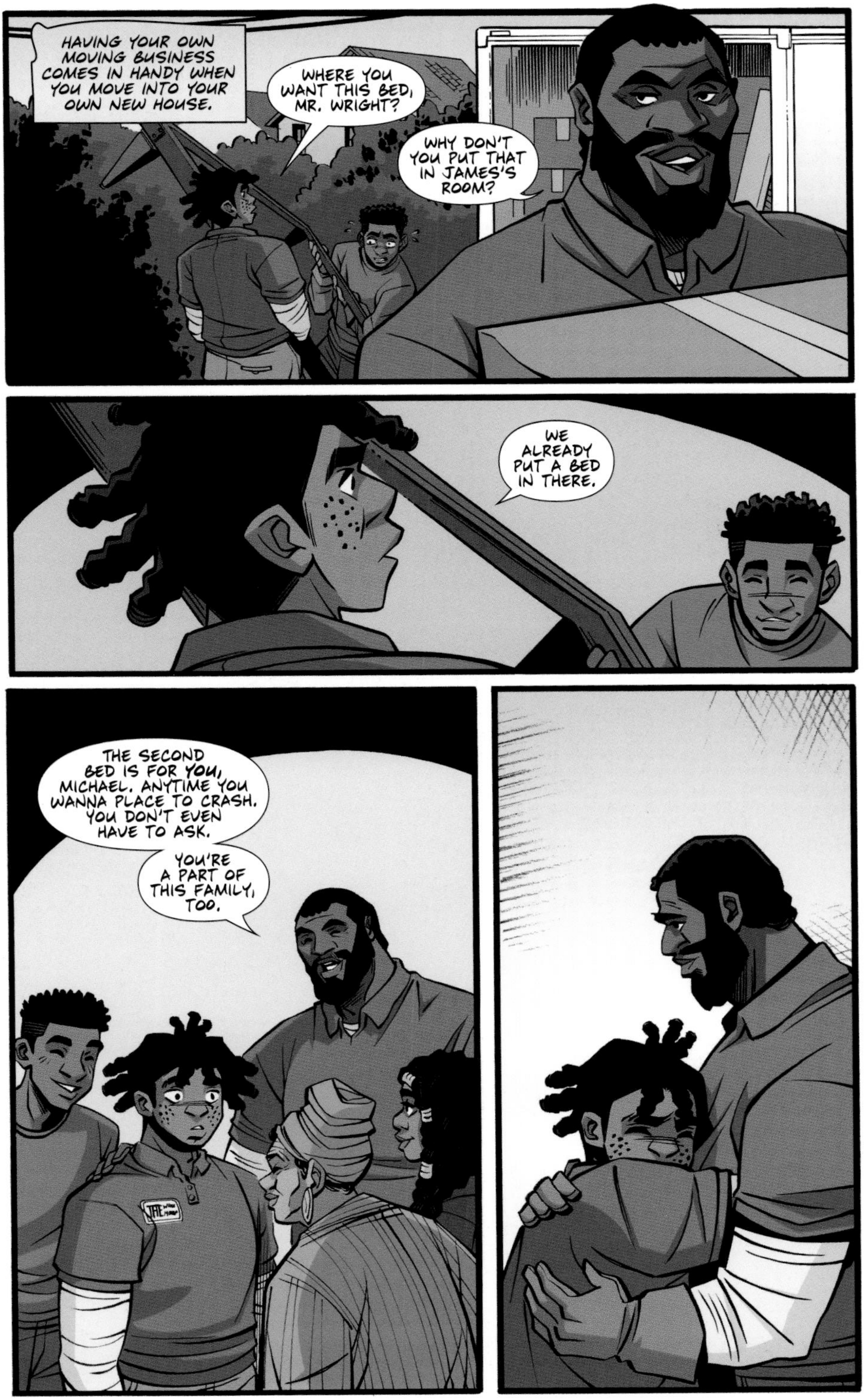
HAVING YOUR OWN MOVING BUSINESS COMES IN HANDY WHEN YOU MOVE INTO YOUR OWN NEW HOUSE.
WHERE YOU WANT THIS BED, MR. WRIGHT?
WHY DON'T YOU PUT THAT IN JAMES'S ROOM?
WE ALREADY PUT A BED IN THERE.
THE SECOND BED IS FOR YOU, MICHAEL. ANYTIME YOU WANNA PLACE TO CRASH. YOU DON'T EVEN HAVE TO ASK.
YOU'RE A PART OF THIS FAMILY, TOO.

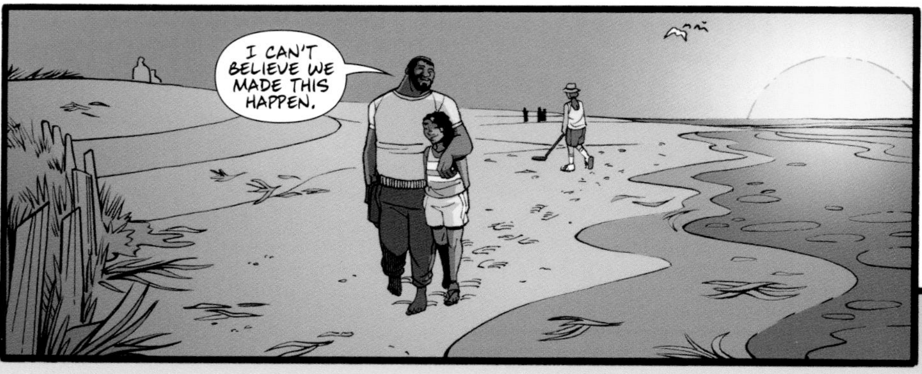

I CAN'T BELIEVE WE MADE THIS HAPPEN.

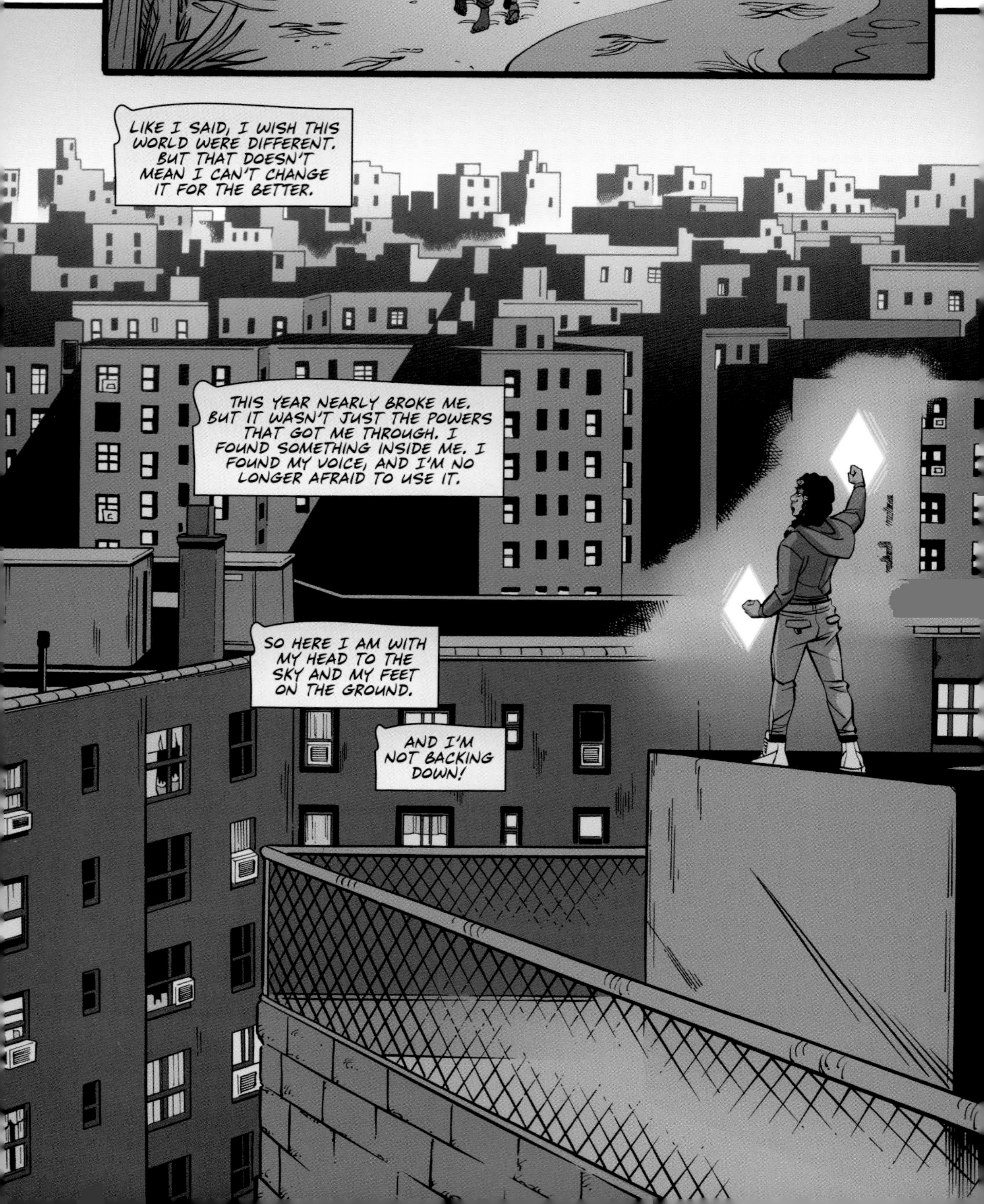

LIKE I SAID, I WISH THIS WORLD WERE DIFFERENT. BUT THAT DOESN'T MEAN I CAN'T CHANGE IT FOR THE BETTER.
THIS YEAR NEARLY BROKE ME. BUT IT WASN'T JUST THE POWERS THAT GOT ME THROUGH. I FOUND SOMETHING INSIDE ME. I FOUND MY VOICE, AND I'M NO LONGER AFRAID TO USE IT.
SO HERE I AM WITH MY HEAD TO THE SKY AND MY FEET ON THE GROUND.
AND I'M NOT BACKING DOWN!

Looks like a girl but she's a flame
So bright she can burn your eyes
Better look the other way
You can try but you'll never forget her name

—"Girl on Fire,"
Alicia Keys

ACKNOWLEDGMENTS

We've had an amazing family working arm in arm with us on this journey. First, this book exists thanks to Susan Lewis, who introduced us to each other and suggested we might write something special together. Thank you, Susan. It's a blessing to work with a great editor; on this book we had two. Frank Pittarese, who was with us when we first started to kick the tires and guided us all the way through; and David Linker, at HarperCollins, who despite insisting he's a "behind-the-scenes guy" is a prime-time editor. Thank you both for your unwavering attention to detail and devotion to excellence. Thanks to the sublime Charlie Olsen and his team at InkWell Management, who had the good sense to sell this book to Harper. And to our team at HarperCollins, thanks for believing in our vision and understanding the importance of this story. This was a labor of love for everyone at AK Worldwide. In particular, a special thanks to two real-life superheroes, DJ Walton and Ana Lara. At LBI, my powerhouse partner, Julie Yorn; Patrick Walmsley (who is the best follow-upper in the game!); and the rest of the team were available for countless Zooms and conference calls to provide guidance as they helped carry the torch through the pandemic. A big thanks to Chris Knight, Roc Nation, and Lede and to the Inner Station team, in particular, Mike Klein, Caleb Kramer, and Jon Nathan. A special thanks to Adriana Pezzulli for generously sharing her expertise. A tremendous thank-you to Brittney Williams for her visual talents, for embodying, illustrating, and bringing Lolo's world to life; we are grateful! And to the rest of the extraordinary art team, Ronda, D. Forrest, and Saida, thanks for the beautiful work. Finally, *Girl on Fire* is anchored by our heroine, Lolo Wright. To everyone who's embarking on an incredible adventure uncovering your superpower: this is for you! Keep the flames burning!!

With love and gratitude,
Alicia & Andrew